The White Shadow

Also by Andrea Eames

The Cry of the Go-Away Bird

ANDREA EAMES

The White Shadow

Harvill *Secker*

LONDON

Published by Harvill Secker 2012

2 4 6 8 10 9 7 5 3 1

Copyright © Andrea Eames 2012

Andrea Eames has asserted her right under the Copyright, Designs and Patents Act 1988
to be identified as the author of this work

First published in Great Britain in 2012 by
HARVILL SECKER
Random House
20 Vauxhall Bridge Road
London SW1V 2SA

www.randomhouse.co.uk

Addresses for companies within The Random House Group Limited can be found at:
www.randomhouse.co.uk/offices.htm

The Random House Group Limited Reg. No. 954009

A CIP catalogue record for this book is available from the British Library

ISBN 9781846555695

The Random House Group Limited supports The Forest Stewardship Council
(FSC®), the leading international forest certification organisation. Our books
carrying the FSC label are printed on FSC® certified paper. FSC is the only forest
certification scheme endorsed by the leading environmental organisations, including
Greenpeace. Our paper procurement policy can be found at
www.randomhouse.co.uk/environment

Typeset in Perpetua by Palimpsest Book Production Limited,
Falkirk, Stirlingshire
Printed and bound in Great Britain by
Clays Ltd, St Ives PLC

Chapter One

It ends here, inside an elephant: in its cavernous ribcage, wet with sluggish blood, where a thin man sits folded, hugging rock-grazed knees. It ends here, and I am alone.

I have to think of something, here, to keep from going mad, as I wait for morning. I need to know where this began – not to blame nor to mend, but simply to know.

Dzepfunde, we say, when the storyteller pauses. *Go on.*

It began when my father told me that every person has two shadows: a black one and a white. The white shadow, *mweya*, is the soul and the black shadow, *nyama* – a word which also means 'meat' – is the flesh.

'The *mweya* climbs out of the body after you die, in the form of a worm.'

'A worm?'

My father smiles across the years. 'That is why we make a hole from the grave to the outside with a hollow reed, leaving a tunnel. The worm will crawl out and into an animal, and that animal becomes an ancestral spirit.'

I remember the strength of his heartbeat as I rested my ear against his chest; the strength of his hands.

'The spirits of chiefs become clan spirits – *mhondoro* – powerful lions and protectors of our people.'

'That is us,' I say. 'Our totem is *shumba*, the lion.'

'That is true, but a totem animal is a different thing from a *mhondoro*,' said Baba. 'A totem animal protects just the family.

The *mhondoro* works for everyone. And they come only from the spirits of chiefs and of their sisters.'

That is how I learned from my father that sisterhood is a powerful thing; family more powerful still. Carrying on the family line is everything. If you do not have children you cannot become an ancestor yourself, watching over the family and accepting their offerings.

I shift my weight and sit cross-legged now in the congealed blood. Cross-legged because I am a man, taught to be a man as my father was taught: if you have the misfortune to be a woman, you must hold your legs straight in front of you so that no menstrual blood can escape to redden the already red ground. I do not know why we think that the rich blood of women, which comes from preparing the womb for more children – future ancestors – will stain and pollute our earth; it is already polluted, with the blood of men and boys, women and girls, killed in battles and in other, less noble ways. Nevertheless, this is what we believe. It is difficult to be a woman, and I am only now realising quite how difficult it is.

Women are dangerous, I was taught. Women have a natural tendency to become witches. Everyone knows this; and witches are the only thing that can break the unbreakable line of family, as live children become adults become animals become ghosts.

Children become adults become animals become ghosts.

I can feel that I am almost there. I am coming to some understanding. I clutch my knees tighter. I lower my head onto the cool, damp skin of my arm; and I wait.

Chapter Two

It began when the second child was born to our family, and my father fell in love.

I can tell you that Baba was not a man who fell in love easily. He was not a man who did anything softly or easily, with his big voice and his big hands and his chest like a drum – a man known in the village for his kindness and generosity but also for his strength. He told me that he did not sleep at night as I did, and I believed him. He told me that, when Amai and I slept, he left our small house on the *kopje* to wrestle leopards that would otherwise eat us in the night.

'Who do you think looks after you and your mother when you are being lazy in bed?' he said. 'That is why I am so strong. Because I have eaten the hearts of many leopards.'

When I was very young, I tried every night to stay awake so that I could go hunting with my father. I held my eyelids open until the eyeballs felt dusty and sticky in their sockets, like sweets that had been sucked and then dropped in the dirt. I pinched my arm over and over until it went numb, and I kicked my legs against the mattress.

My father watched me from his chair in the corner, smiling. 'You are doing well, Tinashe. Maybe tonight you will hunt the leopard with me.'

I saw the leopard in my mind: as big as a house, a creature of fur and claws and flames and oil, with sun-blackened eyes. I imagined killing it with a spear and watching its bright red blood bloom like a flower on its pelt. I imagined my father cracking open the ribs of the leopard like the shell of a pecan nut and pulling out the red heart, still beating and fluttering in his hands as it tried to break free. I would bite into the heart as I bit into the red skin of an apple. I would taste fire, and meat.

When I woke in the morning, I could not believe I had fallen asleep. 'Why didn't you wake me?' I asked Baba every time.

'I was too busy fighting the leopards,' he would always say.

I felt safe knowing that my father was looking after us. When I was curled into a fat ball in bed – a little black tick clinging to my mother's hide – my strong father was out in the darkness, keeping the bad things away. Baba was not one to show affection with kisses or embraces but, sometimes, when he had just eaten and he was feeling full and content, he would let me rest my head on his chest and hear that his heartbeat was strong and full of blood, the way a man's heartbeat should be.

'What are you laughing at, hey?' My father got his hand under my arm and groped for the ticklish spot. 'What are you laughing at?'

I burrowed my head deeper into his lap, smelling sweat and the hot-meal smell of body odour and, beneath that, the sweet and mysterious smell of his *mboro*. I was not afraid of it. I had seen it many times, when he was pissing in the yard. He made fun of my small one when Amai washed me in the tin tub. Mine would be like his one day, when I was a man.

'It is good to be a man,' Baba said. 'We make children, and children are the greatest wealth.'

These were the days when the *kopje* was a peaceful place, perched on its lion-brown hill and overlooking the dry sweep of the tribal lands. We had wealth, in this village: brick houses, good crops of maize, strong herds, a shop that never ran out of sugar and Coca-Cola, and a market for the people who passed through on their way to the town. The scrubbed-bare hillside gave way to trees – acacia, mopane, msasa – and then the tea-brown river. Policemen – a few black, but mostly white – looked after our village and the others in the area, but I did not see them very often. Trouble was rare, and when it occurred we could manage it ourselves, with the help of the witch doctor and the older men in the village. I played with the other kids in the red dirt and ate sour fruit from the bush and thought the *kopje* would stay that way for always – but a change was coming. Because children are the greatest wealth, we prayed in church every Sunday for Amai to give the family another boy.

'A boy makes the family stronger,' said Baba. 'A girl is with the family only until she marries. She is a little stranger in the house.'

I drew myself up to my full, male, three-year-old height. Baba and I were the men of the house, and we made the family strong.

On Sundays, in preparation for our prayers, Amai washed me in the yard with Sunlight soap, and then rubbed me all over with Vaseline until my skin was soft. I wore my best suit to church and knelt on the little cushions with my mother and father, praying for a boy. Amai told me to sing as loudly as I could so that *Mwari* would know we were grateful to him for hearing our prayers.

After church, the women pulled Amai aside and chattered to her. I held her hand and swung on it, impatient to get home and away from these fat women, but it was difficult to get Amai to come away. The women asked her questions in low voices, about milk and blood and what she was eating, and she answered almost in a whisper.

'Mai! I want to go home.'

'*Nyarara*, Tinashe.'

There were mysterious recommendations – put this herb on your *sadza*, sleep with a pillow under your feet, make sure you do not wash yourself too soon after – but this one was hushed before I could hear it all.

'Good luck!' said the women as we moved away.

Baba was working to make the baby too. His friends shouted at him as we passed: 'Have you planted your seed yet?'

Baba pretended to be angry, but I could tell that he was pleased.

When Amai fell pregnant, we gave thanks. It was a miracle, Amai said. I was three years old. The fact that my mother was growing a person inside her stomach like a *mielie* seed growing into corn did not seem any more miraculous to me than the sun rising every morning, or water falling from the sky when it rained.

'Now, Tinashe, you will be a good boy for your mother, yes?' said Baba. He laid his palm on my head. 'You are going to be an older brother.'

I felt my chest swelling, my voice deepening. I was Baba's second-in-command, and my little brother would have to listen to me. I imagined him following me as I ran with the *kopje* gang; watching me as I dived into the deepest part of the river and climbed the highest trees.

Pregnant, Amai changed. She moved slowly and gracefully, as she did when carrying a basket on her head. She made strange noises – groans, little sighs. Her skin became taut and purple. When I tried to lift her belly in my two hands, it felt like the bucket Baba carried from the well; even if I braced myself and spread my legs as far apart as they would go, I could not lift it.

Amai swelled up like a big hippo, Baba said. He only said this to me, though. To my mother, he said that she was the most beautiful woman in the world. 'You are glowing,' he said, or 'You look like a queen.'

She did look like a hippo, I thought. She yawned like a hippo. She fell asleep whenever she sat down. Her bottom was so big and round that she had only to bend her knees for it to touch the seat of her chair. When she lowered her weight to the seat, she puffed her cheeks up and blew — '*Pfooo*'— out of her lips. I found it hard not to laugh, watching her.

'Tinashe,' she shook her finger, 'one day you will have a wife and a baby, and you will have to tell your wife big lies as well, and watch her getting fatter and fatter. So don't you laugh at me.'

I could tell that she was not really angry. I buried my head in the crook of her elbow, inhaled her warm-bread smell and took a sliver of her skin between my lips as if I were going to eat her. When I did this she pretended to be very afraid and said, 'Don't eat me, Tinashe, or who will cook dinner for you and your father tonight?'

I laughed. When I rested my ear against her stomach I heard sloshing and splashing.

'It is your brother swimming,' Amai said.

I pictured him paddling after a bit of *sadza* that Amai had swallowed and stuffing it into his mouth with webbed fingers. I loved to swim, and I was glad my brother loved to swim, too.

As the months passed and the birth of my brother approached, Baba whistled and sang, and grabbed Amai's bottom as she walked around the house. 'You are my delicious eggplant,' he said to her, and other silly things like, 'You are a gourd, round and ready to burst.'

We received a letter from Babamukuru, my uncle. He was Baba's oldest brother — the head of the family, and the most successful man to come from the *kopje*. Not only had he finished high school, but he had also attended university on a scholarship and now worked at an important job at an office in town.

He had a silver car and a big house, and everyone in the village knew that when Babamukuru spoke, he spoke wisely. In this letter, he told us it was good that the baby danced in the womb as it showed he would grow to be strong and active.

'Remember how still Tinashe was,' he wrote. 'We were not even sure if he would come out alive.'

Baba laughed at this, but I did not want Babamukuru to think that I was small and weak.

My parents discussed suitable names for my brother that day. It was an important discussion that took a long time, as names are important and shape your destiny. Tinashe means 'God is with us'.

'We must call him Mambo,' said my father, 'the King.'

'Shush.' My mother did not like this. It would be tempting fate to give a child a name like that, particularly a second child. 'We shall call him Simbarashe.'

The power of God. It was a powerful name, like mine, fitting for a younger son and brother.

When Amai was due to give birth, her mother and aunties and sisters came to stay with us. The house filled with women, smelling of perfumes and cooking fires. They shooed me off with flapping aprons and flapping hands.

'*Nyarara!* Give your mother some peace!'

'Go and do something useful.'

I have never in my life done as many chores as I did that week. If I sat still for five seconds, the aunties thought I was being lazy.

'Look at that one sitting there as if he is a king!' they would say, and give me something to do.

I fetched water in the small bucket, the only one I could lift, which meant I had to go back and forth from the well five or six times, with the metal hitting my shins and giving me bruises. I ground up the *mielie* meal and went with coins to get milk and bread from the store. I did nothing right. I left the *mielie* meal too lumpy for *sadza*. I bought the wrong bread and too little milk.

'He is useless, this one,' said the aunties and clicked their tongues. It was not a good week for me. Baba was out at work during the day and then out with his friends in the evenings.

'I need to get away from all these women,' he whispered to me loudly. He knew the aunties could hear him.

'Eh-eh!' they said. 'Typical man.'

They loved my father. He was big and good-looking and they liked to fuss around him, getting his dinner and his beer. I wanted to go with him to the shebeen, but I was too young. Instead, I stayed outside in the evenings, pretending to chop firewood, listening to the screeching and giggling from indoors and peering in through the windows when I could.

'*Maiwe*, these men do not know what they do to us,' said one of the aunties, shaking her head. 'They do not know the pain we go through.'

'All from one little thing!' said another auntie, and mimed something with her fingers, as if she were measuring the length of a tiny fish. The aunties laughed.

'What little thing?' I asked through the window, and this made them laugh even more.

'You will find out one day,' they said.

On the night that my mother gave birth I heard her screaming terrible screams. With each scream a cry went up from the other women.

'*Aii*!'

'*Maiwe*!'

And then a short silence before the next one. I wanted to go to Amai, but when I knocked on the door, one of the aunties shooed me away.

'This is women's business!' they all said.

9

There was a woman's world and a man's world. The woman's world was cosy, full of chatter and talk and warmth and food. The man's world was a lonely place, outside a closed door, in the noise-filled night.

'Tinashe.' My father was home. I wanted to ask what was happening – why Amai had to be in so much pain. Why it was so important. But you did not ask questions like these. If I sat down with Baba and tried to talk to him about how I felt and what I thought, he would have given me a smacked bottom or pinched my ear and told me to be quiet. A man is supposed to be able to sort out his own problems without all the jibber-jabber that women are allowed to make. 'It has started, Baba,' was all I said.

'Good boy.'

The moon was full and red; the stars angry. No one remembered that I had not eaten, and I did not remind them. I found pride in that. I was a man, after all, sitting out on the *stoep* with my father, while inside the women attended to mysterious women's business.

Baba pulled a packet of cigarettes out of his pocket.

'Can I have one?' I asked.

Baba laughed, but slid one of the slim sticks out of the packet and lit it for me. 'That's right.' He tilted the end of the cigarette up. 'Do not chew it.'

The cigarette tasted like fire, and my tongue curled up to the roof of my mouth in protest. I held my cough inside, and blew a plume of smoke. My father and I did not speak. We sat in silence, looking at the stars in the sky and the stars of street lamps spread out below us on the road from the *kopje* to the town.

'How much longer, Baba?'

'Not long, I hope,' he said. 'I want my dinner.'

I heard a far-off wail that made my heart jump and raised the hairs on my arms. 'Baba!'

'It is done,' he said, and stood up.

I scrambled to my feet and followed him, my heart still beating hard. 'That was the baby?'

'Of course. Have you not heard a baby crying before, Tinashe?'

I had. But that cry had not sounded like a baby to me.

An auntie opened the door for us. '*Namachena!*' she said to Baba, as if it were he who had come safely through a dangerous time. 'You can come inside now.'

Amai sat up in bed. She was shining with sweat, and looked like she had seen horrors. 'Here.' She held the baby out to my father – an offering. It had long arms and legs, and was stretched to its full length.

'It looks like someone has sneezed on it,' I whispered to one of the aunties, seeing the pale film of mucus on its skin.

'Shush!'

The baby lengthened its wrinkly neck to peer at us with bold eyes. It did not cry. My father took it and held it at arms' length, letting its legs dangle.

'A girl,' said Baba. He looked at the pale pink cleft between her legs. My hand went to my *mboro*, feeling its comforting bulge in my shorts, confirming that I was a son of the house and a hunter who would one day eat the heart of a leopard.

'A girl,' chorused the aunties, shaking their heads.

'It is a girl,' said my mother. Seeing the worn edges of her mouth pull up into a smile made me feel suddenly and fiercely protective.

'Amai,' I said, and climbed up on the bed. I gave her a hug, but I could feel her straining past me to the new baby. I touched a bead of sweat on her forehead.

'Tinashe! Stop bothering your mother,' said an auntie, and pulled me off.

My father said nothing more. He held the baby apart from his body, as if she did not belong to him.

'I am sorry, Garikai,' said Amai.

The baby coughed with her little cat-mouth, then closed it and stared at Baba.

'*Hazvinei*,' said my father after a pause. A word meaning 'It does not matter.' He held her bloody body close, cradled her in his big arms and cupped her small skull in his palm.

'Now life has been divided, and each will die alone,' said one of the aunties. This is what was said when a girl, a little stranger, was born. If it had been a boy, my auntie would have said congratulations, the home has grown.

Secretly, I was not sorry. Now I was the only son of the house. There would be no competition for my position; no younger brother to tag along when Baba took me hunting or bought me my first beer at the shebeen. But I felt sad for that lost brother, too. The ghost of Simba hovered like a moth above the bed, above the smells of sweat and toilet odours. I looked up into his insect eyes and said that I was sorry, and I watched him float to the window and disappear.

It is all right, I thought. I will not mind having a sister. I will be in charge.

Chapter Three

I did not understand Hazvinei's power – not then.

As soon as my sister arrived, I forgot what life had been like without her. I sat with Amai all day, waiting to be allowed to take Hazvinei in my arms and smell her sharp, herbal scent. I held my hand against hers and marvelled at the honey of her skin.

Hazvinei was an unnatural baby from the start, and did not behave or look as babies were meant to. She had a neat row of little, pointed teeth, and liked to bite. Amai bought her cheap plastic teething rings, and Hazvinei chewed right through them in two weeks. She liked to bite people too, and was not an affectionate baby with anyone but Baba. Those scars on my arms from the first year of her life still shine pale on my skin; little threads of light. Amai was not spared either. When feeding, she yelped and drew her breast away from Hazvinei's mouth.

'*Aiii*, this one!'

A ring of toothmarks around the nipple, joining all the other scrapes and nips.

'She is too much,' said Amai, shaking her head. 'You were not as naughty as this one, Tinashe.'

Hazvinei was not interested in the usual baby games. When I tried to play peek-a-boo with her, she stared at me as if wondering why I found this silly game so amusing. Sometimes, though, she smiled and reached her hand to touch me, fanning out her little fingers. Enchanted, I clutched them; and then her face turned stormy, and she howled.

I could not win.

'Tinashe, stop bothering your sister!' Or, 'Tinashe, play with your sister!'

Baba was besotted with her from the first moment he held her bloody body. When he came home he went straight to Hazvinei, to pick her up and talk to her. My little lioness, he called her, as he ordered me to look at her little curled nails and the fine whorls of black hair that grew on her head. 'Isn't she beautiful, Tinashe?' he said.

I always agreed. Yes, she was beautiful. Yes, she was a little lioness. She never bit Baba. She crooned and flirted with him, waving her hands in his face – smiling, giggling. I watched Baba as he played with Hazvinei. He was in love with her, I knew, but I was his son and would bring strength to the family one day. That was something that even Hazvinei could not take away from me.

'You must look after your sister,' Baba told me.

I joined in for a while to see if that would help, and if Baba would then be proud of me as well. As Hazvinei grew from a beautiful baby into a beautiful toddler, I took careful note of all her achievements.

'Baba, she is walking, come and see.'

'Baba, she has eaten her first carrot.'

I brought these things to my father and dropped them at his feet.

'Good boy, Tinashe,' he said. And that was all.

Even the strange whites that came into the *kopje* from time to time remarked on Hazvinei during those first two years. They were skinny men – boys, really – with brown canvas uniforms and too-short hair.

'Pretty baby,' they said to Amai when she passed. Hazvinei glared at them from her cloth sling on Amai's back. Amai gave the white men a slow, loose-lipped smile, pretending not to understand, and I clasped her hand tightly. I felt her bones beneath my fingers, brittle as a bundle of sticks.

'Watch that one, hey,' said the whites. 'She will break hearts.'

Hazvinei bared her teeth, and they laughed. We moved out of earshot.

'More and more of them come,' said Amai. 'Like white ants on jam.'

'Why, Amai?'

'No reason, Tinashe.' And she patted my head. 'Do not worry yourself about it.'

I knew that something called UDI had been declared just after Hazvinei's second birthday, and that it was a very important thing that made the men of the *kopje* worried when they listened to the news on the radio, but I did not know what it meant. Baba had tried to explain it to me, but I was left with the confused idea that we had killed the Queen of England. Nothing seemed to change; we still lived in Rhodesia, Ian Smith was still the Prime Minister and, apart from the new whites who appeared more and more frequently, the *kopje* seemed as sleepy and content as ever. The men in the *dare* grumbled as they sipped their beer, and eyed the white men with flat, suspicious stares, but the older men were always stern and mysterious. I did not see anything strange about this. I was more concerned with my sister's biting, and I told my friends about it as we played together in the shallow part of the river. Our mothers washed our clothes nearby, keeping an eye on us.

'Perhaps she is not a human at all,' said Little Tendai. He was not one to talk. He had one deformed foot that scraped along the ground when he walked, and he looked like a little rat with his pointed nose and teeth that stuck out. People in the *kopje* whispered that his father had tried to leave him outside for the animals when he was born, but that his mother had stormed and cried and persuaded him to let the baby live.

'Perhaps she is a *tsoko*.' Little Tendai grinned.

'*Nyarara*, Tendai.'

'Monkeys like to bite.'

'My sister is not a monkey.'

'How do I know you are telling the truth? I have not seen her.'

'You have seen her.'

'Only on your Amai's back. She is in a blanket. How do I know she does not have fur under that blanket?'

'Tendai, you are crazy,' said Chipo, my other good friend. She smoothed her blue dress with both hands. Chipo was always neat and tidy, no matter what games we played, and she had a pleasant voice that reminded me of the Cape turtledoves that woke me in the mornings.

'I will show her to you,' I said to Tendai.

'All of her? Even the fur?'

I moved to pinch him, but he darted out of reach. 'You will see that she has no fur.'

'When?'

'Tomorrow. When my Babamukuru is here.'

'Your Babamukuru is coming?' Little Tendai was impressed, despite himself. My Babamukuru was a mighty figure on the *kopje*; a man who owned a big white house and had an important job, to which he wore trousers and polished shoes with proper laces. Few of us *kopje* kids had been to the town, but we knew that it was a place full of wonders. Having a relative there made me special. Tendai was jealous, I knew.

Babamukuru did not come home often, but when he did, he brought enough food for everyone, and the family came together for a big party. Tomorrow night he was to bring my cousin Abel, whom I had not seen since Hazvinei's birth.

'Yes. And he will bring a whole *mombe* with him for us to eat.'

16

Little Tendai scoffed. 'You lie.'

'No. You wait and see.'

'Fine. And I will wait to see this monkey sister of yours, as well.' He put two fingers in the corners of his mouth and drew them back to make a gaping, ugly face.

Babamukuru telephoned that afternoon to tell us that he and Abel were still coming to the *kopje*, but that Tete Nyasha could not, because she was caring for a sick auntie.

'That is just what I expected,' said Amai, who did not like Tete Nyasha. Tete and Babamukuru had been married for a long time before she had given birth to Abel, and Amai thought that she had waited too long. Amai and the aunties talked about this often: not just Tete Nyasha (although she was a favourite source of gossip), but any woman who had not borne children, or who was married for many years before having a child.

'The wife of VaMakoni still is not pregnant.'

'But she smiled at me when I asked her at church!'

'Well, her mother has told me that she is not.'

'Eh-eh. Four years now, and no child.'

'And she looks healthy.'

'Perhaps she is . . .' and here the conversation dropped to a whisper, and I could not hear it.

'She would not dare to do such a thing.'

'But these young girls, they do not want to lose their figures. They are more interested in shaving their legs and buying dresses like the ones the white women wear.'

'*Mukadzi wako haana mbereko wana mumwe.*'

'But where would he find another one in this village?' An auntie shook with fat chuckles. 'All the women here are skinny like my broom. If you want children, you need a woman who is ripe.' She cupped one breast in each hand, and the other aunties cackled and clucked like our chickens.

'*Iwe!*' Amai held her hands over my ears as if I should be

offended, but I could feel the rumble of her laugh through her bones.

On the morning of Babamukuru's visit, there were many chores to be done. First, we cleaned ourselves, heating water in the pot until there was enough for washing. Amai combed my hair, dragging at the curls until I yelped like a whipped dog, and rubbed Vaseline all over my skin before applying it to her own and Hazvinei's as well. I did not like the soft, greasy feeling of the Vaseline but, when it had soaked into my skin, I shone brown and bright as a nut. Next, Amai cleaned the house. She rubbed red polish into the floors and swept the dust in the yard until it was a smooth swathe of burned powder. The house and yard gleamed red, and the chickens pecked at the new grubs turned up by the sweeping. The house was always clean, but when Babamukuru came to stay it was the smartest and shiniest house on the *kopje*.

'Why does Babamukuru only come to see us once a year?' I asked Baba that morning. 'Why have we never been to visit him?'

'Because he is a very busy and important man.'

'You are very busy and important too, Baba.'

Baba smiled. 'Ah, but I do not have to wear my church clothes every day. When you grow up and get a job, Tinashe, make sure it is one where you have to wear your very best clothes. If it is a job where you do not get dirty, then it is a good job.'

I liked the dirt, and could think of nothing worse than wearing my hot, scratchy church suit every day. 'I want to be like you, Baba.'

He laid a hand on my head. I could feel the hard patches on his palm from where he held his *badza* and his spade. 'You will change your mind when you are older, Tinashe.'

Amai set me to work as well. I washed down our outside latrine with water and Lifebuoy soap.

'Is it true that Babamukuru has a toilet indoors?' I asked her as I scrubbed.

'Yes, Tinashe. It is true.'

I knew that a toilet indoors was considered to be the height of wealth, but I did not see why. Our latrine smelled, even when it had just been cleaned, and there was always a fly buzzing around it. I did not know why you would want that smell and that fly to be indoors, where you slept and ate. Babamukuru had grown up with a latrine just like ours, I knew, and he must have dropped his trousers in the bush now and then, as I did. To go from that to a big white house where water came out of a tap when you turned it! It was like a mosquito flying to the moon.

Hazvinei watched me with slanted, curious eyes as I worked. She was two years old now, but had not started to speak as normal children did, in babbling sounds and sudden words. Instead, she was silent well beyond the point at which she should talk, and women in the village had started to mutter about her. She was strange, they said. Perhaps something was wrong with her. Superstitious nonsense, Baba said, but Amai kept Hazvinei close to her side when they walked. Hazvinei stayed beside her obediently enough – her thumb firmly wedged in her mouth, and her eyes bright and knowing.

After Little Tendai called her stupid, though, no one muttered about Hazvinei in front of me.

'Your sister is not right in the head,' he had said one day. 'Amai says so. She says that Hazvinei must have been cursed.'

Little Tendai's mother and her curses! Amai told me that she only believed in them so strongly because of Tendai's foot, and that she should pay more attention to her drunken husband than to her magic and talismans.

'That is not true,' I said. 'She will speak. She is just slower than some babies.'

'She is not a baby any longer,' said Little Tendai. 'She is a monkey. Just like I said. She is going to grow a tail and run away into the trees.'

'*Nyarara*, Tendai.'

Tendai danced around me on his twisted foot. 'Your sister is a *tsoko!*' He made monkey noises and scratched under his arms. He was so busy being a monkey that he did not notice I had punched him until two lines of snot and blood ran from his nose. He did not cry, because men did not cry, but his eyes became wet.

'Do not ever say such things about my sister again,' I had said, and left him sitting in the dust.

Perhaps remembering my recent bad behaviour, Amai said, 'You will be very polite to your Babamukuru, Tinashe.'

'Yes, Amai.'

'He is the head of the family and we must be very grateful to him for his kindness to us.'

I watched sweat collect in the crook of her elbow and slide onto the floor, where it quickly evaporated.

'Yes, Amai.'

'Good boy.'

I went with Amai and Hazvinei to fetch water from the river for cooking. On the way, we stopped to tell our neighbours about Babamukuru's visit. They knew already, because of the gossip, but when we told them they clicked their tongues and exclaimed. I felt very proud to be part of such an important family. Even the murmurings about trouble on the borders were overtaken by shouts of excitement about the coming party.

Something pale at the corner of my eye caught my attention and distracted me from Amai and the relatives. A flicker of white, like a ghost. Two white men in brown uniforms stood outside the tiny clinic where I got my injections and cough syrup; two pairs of tanned legs rose from shoes made of hide. They were rough-voiced, loud-laughing, with God-like beards and patchwork skin – red, brown, orange, pink, white – with empty eyes like clean water. They stared at my mother.

'Where are you off to, *Mai*?' one of them called.

Amai made her face flat and stupid-looking, so that she did not look like Amai anymore, and ignored them. We did not speak to the white men in the *kopje*, even when they bought us cans of Coke and bars of chocolate. We could clap our hands and say '*Mazvita tatenda*' and smile and smile, but that was all.

'What are they doing here, Amai?'

'They are asking questions, Tinashe. Now be quiet.'

'About what?'

'About who we have seen.'

'What do they want to find out?'

'It does not matter, Tinashe. Because we will not tell them. Be a good boy and stay quiet, OK?'

'Yes, Amai.'

'*Iwe!*' One of the white men called to us again.

'Keep walking,' said Amai.

'*Iwe!* You!'

Amai stopped.

'Where are you going?'

'We are going to the river, sir.'

'So you are not going to the rebels, then?' said the white man. He stood a little too close. I could smell his breath even from where I stood, and I wondered what Amai thought of it.

'The rebels, sir?'

'Don't play stupid with me.' The colour of the air changed. 'Are you going to the rebels?'

'No, sir. I do not know where they are.'

'You are not taking them supplies? Medicine?'

'We are going to the river, sir. For water.'

I felt the white man's eyes flick to Hazvinei. She was squinting her eyes against the brightness. He fingered his belt, letting his yellow nails stray towards his gun, and stroked it with one finger. It seemed to comfort him. 'Well,' he said, 'we'll be keeping an eye on you. Understand?'

'Yes, sir.'

'This your boy?'

'Yes, sir.'

The white man moved to touch my head. I shrank back, and he patted empty air. The white men laughed, a harsh sound.

'He is scared of you, Henrik,' said one of the other men.

I could retreat no further, and did not escape the pat on the head this time.

'Good to learn the lesson early, eh? Eh?'

They laughed again.

'Hokay,' said the man called Henrik. '*Voertsek.*'

Amai took my hand. I could feel anger in the curve of her fingernails and the heat of her palm. We walked together, away from the white men, until we could no longer hear their laughter.

They were ghosts, these white people who passed through our town – thin and bitter as woodsmoke; pale like the palms of our hands or the soles of our feet; half-people; not-people. I turned to wave at the ghosts, and one of them lifted his hand without thinking. I could see right through it. I turned away from them to dip my bucket into the river – flat and sleeping in the sun today, like a snake with a full belly. It butted and nuzzled my hand. Friendly and harmless – until it was not. I would teach Hazvinei to swim in our river, when she was older. For now, I helped Amai to carry her buckets up the hill, skipping beside her because I was too excited to walk slowly.

'Careful, Tinashe. Do not spill any.'

At home, the relatives began to arrive. Aunties like fat,

cackling hens; uncles with beards and deep voices; cousins like brown ants, scurrying everywhere and getting in the way. The women began the cooking while the men sat around the fire, talking and stroking their chins. I did not have to help with the cooking, because I would be a man and a hunter of leopards one day, but I knew that Amai would kill a chicken for the occasion and I wanted to watch. She did it with such speed: clever fingers catching the bird under one arm; firm hands bringing the *badza* down upon its neck. The blood ran sweet and red, and my saliva ran freely too as I thought of the meal to come. We did not have meat very often; not meat with rice and gravy as we would have tonight. Amai dunked the chicken in boiling water to loosen its feathers and then sat with her sisters and sisters-in-law, laughing and plucking.

I had to get dressed. 'Must I wear a shirt, Amai?' My white church shirt, with the stiff collar.

'Yes, Tinashe.'

I pulled on my grey trousers and felt the sweat start on my legs as soon as the wool touched my skin. I pulled on my thick socks and my smart black shoes that I had polished all by myself to a fine mirror-like shine, and I presented myself to Amai for inspection.

'Very good, Tinashe,' she said. 'Now keep yourself clean, yes? Otherwise you will get a clap. Wait for Babamukuru and tell us when he is coming.'

I waited outside on a rock, sitting very carefully so that my trousers and shirt stayed clean. When I saw the dusty silver car winding up the *kopje*, I ran inside. 'Amai! Babamukuru is here!'

'I hope you have not been running in the dust.'

'No, Amai! Babamukuru is here!'

'I heard you. Settle down.'

Babamukuru's big silver car was red along the bottom from

the dust and mud. When he had bought it, many years ago now, he had driven it up the *kopje* to show Baba. This had become a famous story on the *kopje,* told many times around the fire with laughter and shaking of heads, because the car had stalled halfway up the hill. When it had finally reached our house, it was pushed by twenty of the *kopje* boys and followed by a trail of small children, dogs and chickens. Handprints and dust had spoiled its sheen by then, but Babamukuru was still fat with pride.

'Hey?' he had said. 'Pretty good, hey?'

Baba and Amai had exchanged glances. 'Very nice,' Baba had said.

The car was still big, but no longer shiny. The relatives went out onto the road to watch it arrive, and when it stopped, and the door opened, the ululating began. The women clapped their cupped hands together and sang the praises of this big, wealthy man from town who had made our family the most successful family on the *kopje.* The men looked stern and impor-tant. The children scuffled together in the dust, releasing their excitement by pushing and slapping one another, until their mothers told them to calm down and be silent for Babamukuru's arrival.

Babamukuru filled the whole doorway of the car. He unfolded himself, and we saw the full magnificence of his grey suit and smart, striped tie.

'It is his school tie,' whispered someone, and a murmur of approval went around the group.

'*Masikati*,' said Babamukuru. He greeted each member of the family in order. There was a complicated hierarchy, and it would have been easy to offend someone, but any mistakes he might have made were forgiven at once because he was Babamukuru and the head of the family.

'Little Tinashe,' he said when he came to me, and lifted me

up. His sweat smelled different from any other sweat: onions and cigarette smoke and eucalyptus from the throat lozenges he liked to suck. When he bent down to kiss me his breath was hot and minty in my nose, with just a memory of stale beer, and his cheek scratched mine. He released me and I stood, dazed and overpowered by my magnificent uncle.

Baba shook Babamukuru's hand. I had thought Baba was the biggest man in the world, but Babamukuru's hand swallowed up Baba's as a crocodile swallows a buck. They stood with clasped hands for a moment, as if they were about to start a tug-of-war. They did not smile.

'It is good to see you,' said Baba.

'It is good to be back,' said Babamukuru.

Behind him, aunties, uncles and cousins emptied the car boot of its heavy load of food. My stomach made a rude noise. I could taste the gravy already.

'Tinashe.'

'Abel!' In the excitement, I had not seen him get out of the car.

'Standing there, dreaming like an old elephant.'

My older cousin was taller and bigger than me, with straight white teeth and a dark, handsome face. He wore smart town clothes: blue canvas trousers with buttons and stitching on the pockets, and a shirt with a collar. My smartest church clothes looked drab and grey next to his. He even had lace-up *takkies* with a stripe on the side, like a real football player's. When he rubbed my head with his fist, however, I forgot to be in awe of him, and we pushed and pulled each other happily in the dust.

'Boys! Do not get dirty.'

Too late. We joined the other children to run in the red dirt, holding our hands out to catch sparks from the cooking fire.

The party was long, full of eating and dancing and singing. There was no meat left once the adults had eaten, but I did not mind; the dark, sweet gravy was luxury enough. Abel, however, was annoyed that there was no chicken left for him.

'We have chicken every night at home,' he said.

'You lie.'

'It is true. And we have potatoes and vegetables and gravy, as much as we want.'

How I wanted to visit Babamukuru's smart house in town! We had never been there, and it would be rude to ask for an invitation. I looked into the orange and black of the cooking fire and wished for Babamukuru to ask us to come. Perhaps the spirits in the fire would hear me. Perhaps he would ask tonight.

'The gravy is good,' I said.

Abel shrugged. 'It is all right.' Clearly he had better gravy in town. To punish him, I bumped his elbow so that some of the food on his plate slopped onto the ground.

When Babamukuru had eaten, his stomach strained through the gaps between his shirt buttons.

'Tinashe, let me have a look at you.' He lifted me onto his lap. This close, his glasses winked and shone and hid his eyes. He laughed a hot, chicken-flavoured laugh. 'He is skinny, this one. With big ears.'

It was true that my ears stuck out.

'He will grow into them,' said Amai.

'Of course he will,' said Babamukuru. 'He is a handsome boy.'

I heard Abel snigger. I ignored him. Babamukuru's face, shining with sweat and good food, beamed on me like the sun.

'What do you want to do when you grow up, Tinashe?'

I might have answered differently before dinner, but now,

fat and hot with good food and a warm fire and snugly installed on Babamukuru's knee, I knew what I wanted.

'I want to be like you, Babamukuru,' I said. This pleased the adults; the aunties clapped their hands and laughed, and the men stroked their chins and smiled.

'You want to go to high school? You want to go to university?'

'Yes, Babamukuru.' I had not thought about this before, but yes, I did want to go to high school and to university if it meant I would have a nice car and a striped tie like my uncle's.

'Good boy.' He smiled. His smile smelled like beer, and I could see a piece of gristle between his front teeth. 'I will make sure that you do.'

'Thank you, Babamukuru.'

This announcement was more important than I had thought. I heard a ripple of approving sound among the adults, and then a chorus of praise.

Amai knelt and clapped her cupped hands together. 'Thank you, Babamukuru. You are too good to us,' she said.

I heard Baba's voice among the chorus of thanks, but he was quiet and sounded strange – not like Baba at all.

Babamukuru waved a generous hand. The heavy gold ring on one finger winked in the light. 'You are a clever boy, Tinashe. You will do well. Here.' He reached into a pocket and pulled out a sweet wrapped in plastic. It was furry with pocket lint, and smelled like medicine. It felt so good to be praised! I took the sweet, and Babamukuru patted my back and pushed me off his lap.

'Let us see this girl, then,' he said, without much enthusiasm.

Amai held Hazvinei where he could see her. He did not touch her, but examined her through his little glasses as if she were a new and interesting type of animal. 'She is beautiful,' he said. '*Makorokoto.*'

'*Mazvita tatenda*. Thank you,' said Amai and Baba. I thanked him too. Everyone relaxed. Now that Babamukuru had seen Hazvinei and approved, we could all sit back in our chairs and laugh and talk. Hazvinei clenched her fists and gurgled as Amai put her down. Little Tendai was right; she did look like a little brown monkey.

'Can I have some of your chicken, Baba?' said Abel, reaching for his father's plate.

Babamukuru slapped his hand away. 'Do not be rude, Abel. Eat your dinner that your auntie has made for you.' He turned to Baba. 'This one, he thinks he is a king.'

'It is living in town that does it,' said Baba. 'Where there are no chores to do. His life is too easy.' He smiled at Abel to show that he was joking.

'You are right,' said Babamukuru. 'He needs to learn that not everyone is as lucky as he is. Hey?'

Abel scowled.

I waited until after our meal; until the time when Baba leaned back in his chair and blurred at the edges, and became more inclined to grant requests and play games.

'Baba, can I take Hazvinei to show to my friends?'

'You will have to be very careful, Tinashe.'

'I will be very careful, Baba. I promise.'

Baba lifted Hazvinei from the floor. She had slept an angry, red-faced sleep on the mat, her tiny fists clenched and her teeth bared. Now she woke, and stared with bright eyes.

'Do not go further than the *stoep*,' said Baba, and gave her to me. I felt her familiar weight, the pudge of her bare feet against my skin. She was hot and restless.

'*Mazvita tatenda*, Baba.'

I took Hazvinei outside, walking as carefully as if I were

carrying an egg. Abel followed, bored by the firelight and the games of our cousins. Little Tendai and Chipo were waiting outside for the promised sighting, freed from their after-dinner chores for this special occasion.

'Is that your Babamukuru's?' asked Little Tendai, staring wide-eyed at the silver car.

'Yes.' I knew that Little Tendai had never seen such a nice car, and I felt proud of my uncle.

'I will drive it one day,' said Abel.

'I like red cars better,' said Little Tendai.

'Red cars show the dust,' said Abel with authority. Little Tendai was silenced. Chipo reached her fingers towards my sister's face.

'Careful. She bites.'

'She is very pale,' said Little Tendai. 'She is like a white. Has your mother given her too much milk?'

It was rude to talk about my mother, but I did not say anything. Little Tendai had a way of pinching and twisting the skin of my underarm that was very painful, and I did not want to yelp in front of my city cousin.

'Can I hold her?' asked Chipo.

'I am not sure if Baba would like that.'

'Your Baba would not mind.' She held out her arms.

Hazvinei put out her hand, fingers splayed and reaching, and touched Chipo's face. She made a sound like a laugh.

'She likes you,' I said.

Chipo held her for a moment before giving her back to me. '*Makorokoto*,' she said. 'Your sister is growing big. She is beautiful.'

Abel waved his hand in front of Hazvinei's face, then yelped and jumped back. '*Maiwe!*' He sucked his finger.

'What?'

'She bit me!'

Chipo laughed.

'I am serious!' said Abel. 'Look, there is blood!'

'I need to take her back inside.' The *stoep* was dew-wet with evening.

'She is a little demon.' Abel waved his hand in front of her face, watching her dark, sharp eyes move back and forth. How tall and authoritative Abel looked to me then! He had an air of always knowing adult secrets. I held Hazvinei with her face to my chest, and moved away from him.

'*Iwe!*' Little Tendai called after me. 'Make sure to watch her tonight. The *tokoloshes* might want to steal her back.'

'*Nyarara!*'

'Maybe she is a *chipunha*,' said Abel. 'Maybe she is a ghost.'

'Ghosts do not bite.'

'Well, there is something wrong with her.' He shook out his injured hand. 'Take her back inside, and let's go and feed the chicken bones to the dogs.'

Abel always had good ideas. We climbed the steps to the *stoep*, towards the laughter and the smell of good gravy, while Chipo and Tendai melted into the soupy night air.

Chapter Four

Babamukuru and Abel stayed with us that night. As an honoured guest, Babamukuru was given a room of his own; Abel, however, had to sleep with me and the male cousins, listening to the chorus of sleepy farts and breathing in the grubby-toothed breaths of a dozen exhausted boys.

'I have my own room at home,' said Abel when we sluiced our skin with water in the morning. Naked, he was softer and paler than I had expected, with no hard pads to his feet and hands. I sneaked a glance at his *mboro* and saw that it was bigger than mine.

'I sleep on my own here,' I said, 'when no one is visiting.'

This was another sign of our high standing in the *kopje*, thanks to Babamukuru – a house where both Hazvinei and I would have our own bedrooms as we grew.

Abel shrugged, unimpressed.

The adults gathered around the radio as usual to listen to the previous day's events, and the kids played football in the dusty yard. I was aware of Babamukuru's gaze on us and played better than I had ever played, scoring two goals between the sticks stuck upright in the dirt. I saw many of the other cousins glancing towards him as well. Everyone admired Babamukuru. When our football, a plastic bag stuffed with newspaper, exploded into shreds, we played with stones instead, kicking them through the dirt and bruising our toes. Before long, Abel became tired from the night's festivities and left us to lie in the shade and eat figs from the tree.

'*Vana!*' Amai appeared in the doorway. The cousins scattered like chickens. 'Breakfast.'

We sat down together to eat. Amai poured us tea in enamel cups and stirred in spoonfuls of sugar. When we had finished, Babamukuru clasped his hands on the table and leaned forward. An announcement was coming.

'Abel will stay here until school starts.'

'*Pamusoroi?*' said Baba, spoon halfway to his mouth. 'I beg your pardon?'

'Baba?' Abel looked up from his breakfast.

'I have decided that you need to learn to be more like Tinashe,' said Babamukuru. 'Do some chores. Learn to take care of yourself. Learn to be a man.'

Abel swallowed. I sat up straighter in my chair, as a man would.

'If that is all right with you, brother,' Babamukuru said to Baba. 'I do not want to inconvenience you.'

Mere politeness; of course we would do as Babamukuru asked.

'If I remember, brother,' said Baba, 'When we were younger you believed that the only place for a man was in the city – in school.'

'I want Abel to have the best of both, as I did,' said Babamukuru.

A short silence.

'That is fine.' Baba smiled at Abel, who did not smile back. 'We will enjoy having Abel here.'

'But Baba . . .' Abel began.

'*Nyarara*, Abel.' Babamukuru wiped his mouth. 'I have decided.'

'Baba, my friends . . .'

'You will make new friends,' said Babamukuru with finality. 'Tinashe, keep him out of trouble. Do not let him misbehave.'

Abel banged his spoon against his bowl as he ate, but said nothing more. We finished our breakfast in silence.

'Tete Nyasha will not be happy,' Amai whispered to me afterwards. 'She will miss her baby, her one son. She will not be able to coddle him.' Amai hummed to herself and did her morning chores with more enjoyment than usual, thinking of Tete's discomfort.

When the silver car coughed into life and ploughed its path down the dirt road from the *kopje*, Abel was not sitting in the front seat. Instead, he cried angry tears behind the chicken run. I waited for him to emerge, but the sun moved in the sky and there was still no Abel to be seen.

'Baba, Abel won't come out.'

'Give him some time, Tinashe.'

'Why does he not want to stay with us?'

'He just does not know what to expect,' said Baba. 'That is all.'

I did not understand this. I was excited to have my town cousin visit. I wanted to take him swimming in the waterhole, to teach him the best way to poke an ants' nest and to catch *mopane* worms for him to eat. I was even willing to show him where to find the discarded Coke bottles that we could exchange for coins at the bottle store. 'He is stupid,' I said.

'Tinashe!' Baba cuffed me around the ear. 'Do not be rude.'

I rubbed at the side of my head. It stung. 'I am sorry, Baba.'

'You do not know what it is like for him,' said Baba. He stared in the direction of the chicken run, and I could see sadness on his face. 'His life might not be as easy as you imagine.'

With running water and gravy every night? I doubted it, but I said nothing.

'Go and find your cousin and talk to him.'

Hazvinei lay on her stomach on the cool tiles while Amai shelled peanuts. She bared her teeth at me in a smile.

'Yes, Baba.'

I left the three of them on the *stoep* and went to find Abel. The chickens smelled like dirty clothes, craning scaly necks and making frantic, muttered noises as I came towards them, forgetting that it was I who fed them their millet every day. Perhaps they were still nervous after the disappearance of one of their sisters the night before.

'Abel?' Silence – but that special silence when you know that someone is listening and holding their breath. 'Abel, I know you are here.'

A rustle, and a sniff. Distress among the chickens. I climbed over the mess of green-white droppings and discarded feathers to find Abel hunched and hidden. 'What are you doing?'

'Leave me alone.'

'Why are you sitting over here?' I tried to make myself comfortable next to him.

'Go away.'

'Baba told me to come and find you.'

'Well, you have found me.' He wiped the back of his hand across his face. When he drew it away it glistened with a pale, slick line of tears and snot.

'Don't be stupid.' I picked up a twig and started to trace patterns in the dirt.

'You are stupid.'

'Why don't you want to stay here?'

'You don't even have an indoor toilet,' said Abel. 'I do not like the food. I do not like sleeping on the floor. I do not like drinking your water that tastes like dirt. I do not like your sister who bites me.'

I pushed him over. He stared at me with wide, startled eyes, and then pushed me back. We rolled in the mess of mud and chicken droppings, our clothes becoming streaked with red and sloppy grey in equal amounts. Abel's sweat stung my eyes.

He dug his sharp nails into my arm, leaving little bloody half-moons, and I twisted at his ear until he yelped. When we tired, we fell apart and lay panting in the dirt. I felt pleasantly disposed towards Abel now, because this I could understand, this sort of fighting and pinching, 'I'm going to the river,' I said, and got to my feet.

'I'm coming,' said Abel.

We raced each other down the hill to the water, skidding on the loose stones and shouting. When we reached the bottom, it was Abel who jumped into the river first, shoes and all. His dark head dipped under the brown water, then emerged, coughing. I followed. We swam, splashing each other and ducking our heads under, shaking off the flies that landed on our slick wet faces when we emerged. Abel was good at swimming. When I climbed out of the water, my clothes dried stiff with grit against my skin, and the sun dissolved the droplets as quickly as they ran off me.

The river ran red and swollen in the rains and trickled slow and sticky in the summer. It began in the Eastern Highlands, where it was sharp with pine and salty with mountain soil, and it ran down through the flat yellow grasslands, muddy metal shanty towns and even the big city, until it came to the brown, bald sweep of earth where we lived.

You should not open your mouth in the river, but we did. It tasted of silt, of ammonia, of soap, of blood – tastes from upriver, borne to us from other villages and towns. We gave it our own flavours, on the *kopje*, before releasing it. It carried bugs apt to swim into a carelessly opened mouth; leaves and flowers from plants we had never seen. Sometimes an old shoe floated past, or a lost toy, bloated and swollen with river water. Sometimes the bloated, swollen thing was not a thing at all but an animal, tempted too close to the current.

We used the river for washing – ourselves and our clothing.

There was a special place where the women bathed, and a special place where the men bathed – far apart. We children could swim wherever we wanted – until that mysterious point, dreaded and ill-understood, when it would suddenly be unsuitable for us to see one another naked. The river would watch us as we grew. It would see the feet that paddled at its edges broaden and lengthen. It would see Abel urinate in the water – he and the other boys who thought it was funny to see the yellow merge with the brown and laugh at the girls who screamed and swam away from the warm patches. It would watch me teach Hazvinei how to swim, and then it would watch as she became a better swimmer than me and did somersaults and handstands, rooting her long, brown fingers into the silky powder of the riverbed and collecting a halo of bright bubbles on her pale skin.

Now Abel surfaced, laughing. 'This is the same river that runs through town,' he said. 'It is different there.'

'How is it different?'

'There is rubbish floating in it. And I am not allowed to swim there.'

I knew then that I had won him over. No one could resist my river.

That night at dinner, Amai served Abel the biggest portion of *sadza* and relish, and the biggest cup of tea with six sugars stirred in.

'How are you enjoying your time with your family, Abel?' said Baba.

'It is good, Babamudiki,' said Abel without looking up. He pushed his *sadza* around the plate.

'It will get cold,' said Amai.

'Do you have any potatoes, Amainini?' said Abel.

'No, Abel.'

We ate in silence.

'Babamudiki?'

'Yes, Abel?'

'I need the bathroom.'

'Then go to the bathroom.'

Abel sucked in his lips and looked out of the window at the blackness. Baba followed his gaze. 'Tinashe, go with your cousin.'

'But Baba, I am still eating.'

'Tinashe.'

I knew that tone. I slid down from my seat and led Abel outside. The crickets clicked and trilled in the long grass, and I heard a deep-throated whoop in the distance.

'What is that?' Abel, wide-eyed.

'A hyena,' I said. I made my voice low and growling. 'He is probably looking for children for the *muroyi's* supper.'

'Shut up.'

'You shut up.'

We stood for a moment.

'Why do I have to go with you?' I said. 'Why can't you go to the bathroom on your own?'

'I can.'

'Fine, then go.'

Abel hovered, looking at the black shape of the toilet. 'What about the *tsotsis*?'

'The *tsotsis*?' I was confused. 'There are no thieves here. It is a safe place.'

'I don't mean thieves,' said Abel. 'I mean the rebels. The ones Baba hears about on the radio.'

'I don't know what you are talking about,' I said. 'There are no rebels here. The policemen look for them, but they do not find anybody.'

Something rustled by Abel's feet, and he jumped. I gave in. 'Come on, then. And hurry up.'

The latrine had a single bare light bulb at its entrance, a luxury in the *kopje*, where most toilets were darker than night and you had to find your way by feel. I switched on the light. Moths winked into life, circling the light bulb and dying tiny moth deaths when they flew too close.

Abel shuffled inside. I heard him unzip his trousers. 'Do not listen.'

'I won't listen.'

A short pause.

'I can tell you are listening.'

'I am not listening!'

A trickle. I stood with my back against the concrete and watched the moths swoop drunkenly. I heard a muffled fart, and giggled.

'I knew you were listening!'

'I am not listening.'

The door creaked. Abel's eyes shone white in the darkness.

'Ready to go back inside?'

'You said you wouldn't listen,' he said and walked ahead of me into the house, head high, alone. I followed, hearing the hyena laugh behind us.

Abel shared my room. We slept on a mattress on the floor, under a rough brown blanket. Hazvinei still slept with Baba and Amai in the next room, and I heard her muffled grumblings and sudden chuckles under the low murmur of their voices. I lay still, listening to Abel's shallow bubble of breath and smelling the greasy scent of his skin. It took me a while to realise that he was crying.

'Abel? Abel!'

'What?'

'What is wrong?'

'Nothing.' He rolled over, away from me.

'You are crying.'

'No, I'm not.'

'It's all right,' I said. 'You will like it here. And it is only for a few weeks.'

Abel pulled the blanket over his head. I rolled closer to him and felt his fresh sweat and tears on my cheek. 'Babamukuru will come and get you if you write to him.' I said. 'You know he will.'

'Shut up,' said Abel, so quietly that I almost didn't hear him. 'You don't know anything.' He made his breathing slow and even, so that I would think he was asleep. I lay in the dark for a long time, listening to the voices from the next room.

It took a few days for Chipo and Little Tendai to come and visit again. They saw that my wealthy cousin had moved in with us and they were afraid to approach him. Instead, they circled the house as the mangy village dogs circled the cooking fires, looking for scraps.

'Your friends are stupid,' said Abel.

'They are shy.'

'Why?'

'They do not know you.'

After days of complaints, misery and tears, Abel had woken that morning with a smooth, untroubled face. No tears today. He had spoken to Amai and Baba politely that morning, played with Hazvinei and helped me feed the chickens. Amai and Baba were very happy, but I was a little afraid of this new, composed Abel.

'Are you glad to be here now?' I said. 'Are you happy that Babamukuru asked you to stay?'

'I have to do what Baba says.'

'I know that.'

'We all have to do what Baba says.'

'I know that. But still?'

He did not answer me. Instead, he vaulted over the fence and ran to Chipo and Little Tendai.

'Abel, wait!'

But it was too late. Between Abel's jump over the fence and my catching up to him, he had already become the new leader of our gang.

'Chipo, you are in goal. Tendai, you are defending. Tinashe, you are at the front with me.'

There were some advantages to being Abel's cousin. He had first kick of the ball, but I had the second. We all grew very good at football that week – even Chipo – and we were the envy of the other *kopje* kids.

Our house was among many other houses exactly the same. We kids from the *kopje* looked down on the kids who lived in the village in the valley below, and we fought with them every day. We all had our jobs. I was in charge of finding good clumps of red earth to throw at the kids from the bottom of the hill and rhino beetles to put in their clothes when they went swimming in the waterhole. The oldest kids in the gang were twelve years old, and they looked like giants to me.

'Your cousin is a cool *mukomana*,' said the older boys, and patted me on the head. A cool boy. They had never called me a cool boy.

The girls of the *kopje* did not run with our gang because they had too many chores to do, and they shook their fists at us as we ran free down the hill or played football in the dust.

'You don't know how lucky you are,' said Chipo, who could only occasionally sneak away from her grandmother to join us in our games. 'Boys have an easy life.'

'That is how it should be,' said Abel, and laughed.

Having Abel in the *kopje* gang elevated our status. We now

had a town boy who not only owned his own pair of white *takkies* but also a proper football, a shirt with a stiff collar and a collection of multicoloured marbles that he carried in a string bag. His father had a job in town and a big silver car. Abel was our prize, and we taunted the bottom-of-the-hill boys with him. We won all the football games now, and we had the waterhole to ourselves whenever we wanted it. And Abel took to his new role as leader very easily, bossing around even the older boys. On the rare occasion that one of them challenged him, he had an answer for everything.

'What do you know about it? You have never even seen a road with tarmac. You have never even been to the cinema.'

Unanswerable. We all deferred to Abel's superior knowledge. This applied to the wider world, as well. Abel told us about the *tsotsis*, rebels who had started to cause trouble around the country. It was all very confusing. Rhodesia did not want to be ruled by Britain and the rebels did not want to be ruled by Rhodesia. I had questions, but I saw the older boys nodding and stroking their chins as the men did in the *dare*, and I kept quiet. I must be ignorant, I thought.

'You do not know what is going on, here in this small village,' said Abel. 'In town we know about these things.'

When Babamukuru came to collect Abel the next week, he was happy with what he saw. Tete Nyasha would not be so happy with the state of Abel's nice clothes, I thought. *Kopje* dust was notoriously difficult to remove. Abel showed off for his father as we brought the village cattle back into the *kraal*, flicking a switch at their flanks and shouting as if he knew what he was doing, rather than just getting them excited and making my job more difficult.

'The boy is learning,' said Babamukuru when we came inside. 'Tinashe is a good influence on him. Eh, Tinashe?' He patted my head. Abel grinned at me from behind his father's back.

'We will do this again,' said Babamukuru. As an after-thought, he turned to my father. 'If that is all right with you, Garikai.'

'Of course, brother,' said Baba. 'You know that I will always do as you ask.' He spoke gently, but there was something in his voice that made Babamukuru give him a sharp look before pressing his hand in farewell. 'Take care, brother.'

When the silver car pulled out of the yard and started its journey down the hill, I felt a small hand pull at the hem of my trousers – Hazvinei. She looked up at me with wicked eyes.

'He will come back, Hazvinei,' I said, and I did not know whether I was glad or sorry.

Our family hardly ever received letters and so, when the packages arrived a few days after Abel's departure, I did not know what they were.

'Baba!' I ran to him. 'Look.'

Two big brown boxes, wrapped in paper and string. He picked them up and cradled them in his arms – the way Amai held the chickens before snapping their necks.

'What are they, Baba?'

'Nothing for you to worry about, Tinashe.'

'But one of them has my name on it,' I said. I had seen the strong, decisive 'T' on one of the labels.

Baba was stern. 'You do not read my letters, Tinashe. You know that.'

'Sorry, Baba.' I retreated.

Baba and Amai discussed something special that night, I knew. I heard their voices humming like the crickets outside. In the morning, they called me to the table.

'*Mangwanani,* Tinashe,' said Baba. He was very grand and ceremonial. The two brown-paper and brown-string packages sat on the brown table, thrillingly anonymous.

'These packages have arrived for you and Hazvinei from town,' he said, 'from Babamukuru.'

'For us?'

'Yes.' Baba's hands hovered over the packages, as if he were reluctant to give them to us. His fingers closed, then released, and he stepped back and let us tear off the paper and reveal our treasures. At least, I could have torn off the paper, but instead I took it off carefully and folded it. I wanted to keep that label with its strange, square writing in black ink: that triumphant T.

Toys. A doll for Hazvinei, with yellow hair and eyes that opened and shut like real ones. Its skin had a milky, underwater look, like a water spirit's. For me, a toy truck. I had never before seen anything so shiny and new. It had little silver wheels and a red, red body, redder and shinier than anything on the *kopje*. We had no new things in that place where even the sheets of corrugated iron on our roof were second-hand; everything came to us scuffed, stained and warm, smelling faintly of other people's fingers or armpits or feet. I was overwhelmed by the hot-plastic smell of newness. To have a toy made in a factory, put in a beautiful box with a window in it and sent to me and to me only – this was wealth beyond anything I had imagined.

I learned a lesson that day. The new, shiny truck made our house smaller and shabbier, the road dustier, the holes in my shoes even bigger than before. I think that this is what Baba had feared when the packages arrived.

I wrote a thank-you letter to Babamukuru. Baba – who kept his school-learning carefully folded and stored in his head, like the linen Amai kept between waxed papers in the kitchen drawer – would have written them for us, but Amai persuaded him to let me try, as Baba had been teaching me my letters to prepare me for school.

'Tinashe can write well now,' she said. 'He learned very quickly.'

I ducked my head down so that Baba would not see how pleased and embarrassed I was.

'He will do a good job.'

Baba put the fear of God into me, or rather the fear of Babamukuru, which was the same thing. Write neatly and do not make any mistakes, because we do not have many pieces of paper to use. Make sure to spell 'thank you' correctly, or Babamukuru will think you are stupid. Do not lean your hand on the paper, you will smudge it. And write in English!

Baba's eyes did not move from side to side when he looked over my letter. He glanced at it once, and gave it to me. 'Very good, Tinashe.'

What a man my Baba was, that he could read an entire letter in just one glance! Flushed with my success and my new toy, I said, 'Babamukuru is a wonderful man, isn't he, Baba? To give us these beautiful things? He must be very rich.'

'Yes, Tinashe.'

'One day I will be rich like Babamukuru and everything in my house will be new,' I said.

Baba looked around at the vinyl kitchen table and the sagging green sofa. He touched my head, gently. 'I am sure you will be just like Babamukuru one day, Tinashe.'

We posted the letter, and I played with my new red truck until the bottom-of-the-hill gang stole it from my windowsill and dropped it in the waterhole. When I fished it out it was scratched and soiled and smelled of old water-weed, and it did not give me the same shiny-new feeling as before.

Chapter Five

After that, Abel came to stay with us during every one of his school holidays. As soon as term ended, Babamukuru drove him to the *kopje* in his silver car.

'It is good for him to spend time with Tinashe. He is a good influence,' said Babamukuru.

The idea that I could be any sort of influence over Abel! But I liked Babamukuru to think well of me, and so I did not contradict him.

Babamukuru and Baba had grown up in the *kopje* just as Hazvinei and I did – not in a house with a polished red *stoep* and white-washed walls, but in the poorest of poor huts. It was a testament to Babamukuru's success that the family now had the best houses on the *kopje*. The village knew my uncle and father as Mutungamiri – or Tunga – and Garikai. Brothers. Mutungamiri means 'leader', a fitting name for an older son, and Garikai means 'live in peace and comfort'. Babamukuru was destined to go out into the world. Baba was destined to stay home.

'I have a good life,' Baba said often. 'I have a beautiful wife, a comfortable home and two strong children. What more would I need?'

A big silver car, a striped school tie and an indoor toilet, I thought but did not say. Baba seemed so content with village life that I imagined he had chosen not to go to high school, but when I asked him, I found out that this was not true.

'I was put forward for the same scholarship as your Babamukuru,' he said.

'But you did not win it?'

'I did not go to the examination,' said Baba. 'Our father was sick, and I did not want to make the journey to town and leave him alone. Our mother had died the year before. So I stayed with him and your Babamukuru went to the exam.'

'Did you go back to school?'

'There was not money for both of us,' said Baba, and I knew that I was not to ask him anything more.

'Your Babamukuru has done well for us,' people on the *kopje* told me often. 'He is a great man.' They also said, 'Your father is a good man. He is generous.' I knew, however, that they admired Babamukuru more, and that Baba had a reputation for being too generous – lending money unwisely; turning a blind eye to people's faults. That is why he took in the three-legged dog that we called *twiza*, giraffe, for its skinny neck and protruding spine. The dog did not live, and it became a familiar joke on the *kopje*. 'Is it going to be a chicken with no head next, Garikai? Or a goat with no udders?'

Abel grew used to life in the village. He did sometimes roll his eyes and sigh when I failed to understand something that seemed obvious to him, but Abel enjoyed rolling his eyes and sighing. 'You have such big ears, Tinashe, and yet you hear nothing that I tell you,' he liked to say.

We woke up together on the mattress, ate breakfast together and performed our chores together. This was my chance to outshine Abel, for I knew very well how to herd the goats and take care of the *mielie* plants. I watched my cousin chase the retreating rumps of the animals, waving his arms and shouting, and I laughed until I had a pain in my side.

'You have trained them wrong, Tinashe,' said Abel when he returned, out of breath. 'They do not listen to me.'

We walked the goats to pasture down the long, red-dirt road, flicking at them with long switches I cut fresh from the trees every day. Sometimes we became bored with watching the goats, and fought with our switches instead. Abel became adept at flicking his stick across the backs of my knees, leaving a skinny red welt that stung when my sweat trickled over it. We threw stones at birds in the trees, and caught flies between our two hands.

'One day I will have a gun,' said Abel, 'and I will be able to shoot as many birds as I want.'

'And where are you going to get this gun? Is Babamukuru going to give it to you?'

'I will buy it for myself. With my own money.'

'Then you will have to wait until you have finished university and you have a good job.' I flicked the tender end of my switch against his back, tickling him.

'I am not going to university. I am going to work like a real man.'

We scuffled and pinched each other in the dust. I did not pay attention to Abel's words. He was showing off, I knew. Why would anyone want to work like Baba did when they could instead wear a smart suit and drive a car like Babamukuru's?

As Hazvinei grew and started to walk, Amai sent her to herd the goats with us. 'Give me some peace and quiet,' she said. 'This one causes too much trouble.'

Hazvinei walked slowly, and we had often to stop and carry her. Abel became impatient. 'Why does she have to come with us? She is useless. She should sit at home on the *stoep* and play with bugs.'

'Amai is busy.' I did not mind looking after Hazvinei. I liked her pudgy hand in mine; the way she trusted me to lead her safely.

'She is a little demon,' said Abel, who had never forgiven Hazvinei for biting him. 'She cannot even talk. There is something wrong with her.'

It was true that Hazvinei did not talk. She could understand us very well – we saw it in her sharp, clever face – but she made only wordless sounds. Amai pretended that this was nothing to worry about, but I saw her coaching Hazvinei, her hands splayed around her mouth as she exaggerated its movements.

'A-ma-i. A-ma-i. Say it, Hazvinei. You can say A-ma-i.'

Hazvinei stared at her, unblinking.

'Ba-ba. Say Ba-ba.'

Nothing. Amai would straighten and brush off her apron. 'It will come in time,' she said. 'You cannot rush these things.'

Hazvinei adored Abel. She followed him on pudgy legs, keeping up with him even when he walked as quickly as he could. He ordered her about, and she loved to obey. I trailed behind them both. He called her little lioness, as Baba did, but he called me *Nzou*, elephant, because I was always slow and dusty and lagging behind and I could not keep up with them.

'You have a long memory like an elephant,' said Abel, 'but you cannot run. You are as bad as Little Tendai.'

There were many things that we children were not allowed to do and only rarely was there a simple explanation. Abel and I were told never to urinate on the same spot at the same time. If we did, Baba told us that Amai would get backache. I loved to blow into Coke bottles and make a whistling sound. The aunties told me that, if I continued to do this, Amai would chase my whistle into the bottle and become trapped inside. Why did they not just tell me that the noise was irritating? Why create such an elaborate punishment?

Many rules surrounded the use of the fire as well. You could not sit too close to it, jump over it, warm your feet at it or put your hands too close to it, because each of these taboos carried its own mysterious punishment – illness, infertility, bad fortune. Girls were not allowed to sit in forbidden parts of the kitchen ('you will damage your insides and not be able to conceive'), nor make themselves garlands of leaves and grass for their hair ('you will give birth to crippled children').

Our future wives and husbands were often mentioned.

'Do not put your dirty fingers in the pot, Tinashe, or your wife will get sick and die!'

Our spouses would be fragile creatures, if my dirty fingers could kill them off. I did not put my hand in the pot again, though.

When the moon was bright and fat in the sky, curled in on itself like a *chongololo*, we boys and girls of the *kopje* gathered outside to play *Sarura Wako*, a game where we chose husbands and wives from among our friends. The adults did not mind us playing this game, as they had also played it as children, and their parents before them, all the way back to the place where stories start. Each of us knew that we were one in a long line of ancestors, like beads on a string, and it was our duty to keep that string intact and to add as many beads as we could. We also played *Mahumbwe*, where we paired up and pretended to keep house together as man and wife. I paired with Chipo, who had a way of putting one hand on her hip and wagging one finger that was truly awe-inspiring, just like a real Amai.

'You were out at the shebeen all night!' she shouted at me. 'Why are you not home with your children?'

We all knew that Chipo's father drank too much, and that he was often to be found snoring on the steps of the shebeen in the morning. It added a depth to her performance that was very impressive.

Little Tendai could not keep up with our games, but he liked to tell us stories about how his twisted foot came to be deformed. He insisted that it was because a *muroyi* had put a curse on him. 'Sometimes witches do not know they are witches,' he said. 'They wake up in the morning covered in blood and they do not know how it got there.'

'*Nyarara*, Tendai.' I rubbed at the goosepimples on my arms.

'They walk in the night,' he said. 'And they eat children, my father said. What do you think happened to my foot?'

We all looked at his twisted ankle, even though we had heard this story before. His toes grew strangely, some of them very fat and some of them thin and wiggling like *mopane* worms. He left dragging, uneven footprints in the dust.

'A *muroyi* cursed me,' said Little Tendai.

Abel said something rude.

'Because she wanted to marry my father,' Little Tendai continued unperturbed, 'she put a curse on my mother when she was pregnant. It would have been worse, but my father found out about the curse and he told the N'anga.'

We listened despite ourselves.

'What happened?' said Chipo.

'They called a witch-smeller,' said Little Tendai. 'And he found the witch. If they had not found her, I would have been born dead. Instead I just have this.' He wriggled his toes.

'She should have taken your big flapping mouth,' said Abel.

We all knew of the N'anga and the witch-smellers. We children were told to keep as far away from them as possible and to never bother them in case they turned us into frogs or monkeys. I only ever saw the N'anga from a distance: a hunched, skinny figure under a mangy cloak, striding through the *kopje* and leaning on his tall staff, stopping only to point a skinny finger at some naughty child or to spit a fat, brown wad of chewing tobacco into the red dust. The witch-smellers I did not see, because they did not emerge until they were needed.

In the year that I turned seven, I started going to the little village school, run by the one man on the *kopje* with a high school education. Little Tendai and I were released temporarily from our chores for our lessons. Sometimes the schoolhouse would be full, but often there would be only two or three children inside. It all depended on how the crops were doing and whether a boy was needed to tend the herds.

Baba let me go to school for a few hours most days. 'Because you have to grow up to be an educated man like your Babamukuru. Isn't that right, Tinashe?'

Little Tendai was at school most days as well, because his deformed foot made him slow at performing a son's tasks. Our first lessons consisted of chanting the alphabet in English. 'A – apple,' is how we always began. 'Apple' was the first word in all our cardboard-covered picture books, as well. B could be 'ball' or 'boat' or 'bear', but A was always Apple. I wondered at the English fascination with this fruit, even more when we started to learn the Bible stories and heard about Adam and Eve and the Snake and the Apple.

Abel's teachers gave him work to do during the school holidays, sending him to us with a parcel of shiny textbooks, each containing a satisfying wedge of slick white pages. At the *kopje* school, we shared one or two books between all of us. I could never have imagined such wealth. Abel was also given a different brown-covered exercise book for each subject. They smelled of something that thrilled me, and I realised finally that this smell was newness – the smell of something crisp and untouched, like ink fresh from a pen, the sheen of newly polished shoes, the smell of my shiny red truck that was no longer shiny and red. To own a book covered with a coloured dust-jacket – this was wealth beyond the magnificence of Babamukuru's indoor toilet.

'You can have them,' said Abel, pushing a pile of books to me.

'Really? You don't want them?'

He shrugged. 'The teachers will give me more.'

'They will?'

'They have cupboards full.' He stretched his hands wide apart to show me how expansive these magical cupboards were.

I took great pleasure in writing my name in these books – an upright, confident 'T' for Tinashe, followed by my last name, in my best handwriting and with my blackest pencil. I craved more.

'I don't know why you bother,' said Abel.

We sat on the banks of the river, letting our feet dangle in the water. I had a book open on my lap, and was tracing the lines of words with my finger. Four-year-old Hazvinei lay on the grass near us, moving pebbles into a mysterious shape that had meaning only to her.

'I like school.'

'Why?'

I shrugged. 'I want to go to university.'

Abel snorted.

'What?'

'University is not that great.'

'How do you know? You have never been.'

'Baba went.'

'And he has a good job, and a nice house.'

'He is getting fat,' said Abel. 'He spends all day at the office looking at pieces of paper. He wears glasses. I do not want to be like him.'

This was blasphemy. Babamukuru was the most successful man I had ever known. That anyone had ever known. He was like a mighty chief from one of the old stories.

'I want to be like your father,' said Abel.

'Like Baba?' I was not sure whether to be proud or shocked. 'Why?'

'Because he is a man,' said Abel. 'He works at a proper man's job.'

'Baba has always told me that a good job means you wear a suit every day,' I said.

Abel kicked his feet and splashed me with brown river water. 'It does not matter,' he said. 'But I do not want to go to university.'

Hazvinei made a noise. I had not realised she was listening.

'You must not say these things, Abel. She will want to copy you.'

'Girls do not go to university,' said Abel. 'It doesn't matter.'

We heard more and more about the *tsotsis* those days, but now the radio voice was calling them 'terrorists', a word I found very hard to pronounce. They lived outside the borders of Rhodesia, the radio told us, but crossed the Zambezi or came over the hills from Mozambique to do terrible things in the darkness. We heard that a white couple had been killed in Hartley, and the boys started to tell each other stories about the dreadful things that the terrorists did. Abel, of course, was the expert. He told me that terrorists made you cut off your own lips and ears and cook them in a stew.

'Then they make you eat them,' he said. 'And you are not allowed to be sick afterwards. You have to swallow them right down.'

'*Nyarara*, Abel,' I said. 'You do not know what you are talking about.'

After that, though, I checked under my bed for terrorists as well as for *tokoloshes* and other evil things. But the evil thing that came had nothing to do with the terrorists at all.

One day, when Abel and I passed through the centre of the village, we saw that there was some commotion. A group of adults had gathered in the dry, swept space in the middle of the village and stood with their arms folded, muttering and looking from side to side.

'What's going on?' I asked.

'How should I know? Come on.'

Abel and I pushed our way through the crowd to stand at the front. There were the usual smells of body odour, Sunlight soap and ash, but another smell floated above all these and caught me at the back of the throat, acrid and dry.

'They are afraid,' said Abel.

I looked at the faces. Abel was right.

'What are you two doing here?' said Simon-from-the-bottle-shop. We were not allowed to call him Simon to his face, because he was an adult and deserved respect, but that was what we called him when alone. He gave me a clap on the head. 'Go home.'

'What is happening?' Abel asked.

'Eh-eh, this is not the place for you. Where are your Amai and Baba?'

'In town,' said Abel.

'Don't be cheeky.'

I looked at the waiting faces. Amai and Baba were not among them. 'Amai is at home,' I said, 'and Baba is working.'

'Then go home and find your Amai.' He gave me a shove. 'I am serious, eh. Go.'

'Yes, VaMakoni.'

'Yes, VaMakoni.'

We dipped our heads like good children and moved away. As soon as we were out of Simon's sight, we exchanged glances.

'Can we stand at the back?'

'Someone will see us. Come.'

Abel led me past the goat fences and through the long, itchy grass to a half-dead acacia tree. He climbed. 'Here.'

So easy for him – one quick movement! It took me longer, but I managed to clamber up beside him. We perched our bottoms on the hard branch and balanced ourselves. Just enough leaves to shelter us; not enough to obscure the view.

'Good, yes?' said Abel.

'Be quiet, I am listening.'

But there was nothing to hear. The crowd was silent. My eyes swam with tears, and I blinked. When I opened them again, there were three figures in the centre of the circle.

We had heard of minor troubles in the village for a few weeks now. Tete Patience, one of Amai's friends, had died from a mysterious illness, and some chickens had gone missing. We had seen the N'anga many times over the past few days, wandering about the village and casting his bones, but Baba had forbidden us to go near him, and we obeyed. At least, I obeyed, and I kept watch over Hazvinei and Abel to make sure that they did too.

'Is that the N'anga?' I whispered to Abel.

'I don't know.'

Animal skins, rough and matted, patterned with black and white and brown. Faces painted red and black under dried and rustling feather headdresses. The shapes underneath were wrong; neither human nor animal, but hunched, twisted, malignant things.

'Are they people?'

'Of course they are people. Don't be stupid.'

But I could tell Abel was afraid too, from the raised hairs on his arms. We shrank down, trying to make ourselves as small as possible.

'Do you think they can see us?'

'No. Be quiet.'

The figures started to jump. As they leapt, I saw human legs underneath the skins. As they leapt higher I saw wizened, shrunken breasts.

'They are old women,' I said.

'Shut up, Tinashe.'

The crowd separated. The women and girls moved to the

front and knelt in a circle. I recognised aunties, and some of the older girls from school. I became aware of a rhythm, a pulse at the back of my skull, and a low, insistent humming that made my teeth rattle. I saw the women's hands coming together in a slow, monotonous clap, and I saw their mouths open, but the sound did not come from them. It came from the ground and shivered up through my feet into a dark-red, secret part of my brain.

The masked women danced. They leaped impossibly high for their old, spindly legs, and noises came from behind their face paint that did not sound human. As I watched, they stopped being dancing figures and became stripes of angry colour, red clawmarks in the dark earth.

I felt myself swaying. Abel caught hold of me, his nails digging into my skin.

'Tinashe!'

I blinked. The colours became dancers again.

'What are those?'

They held long switches with tails at the end. I had not noticed them before. Had they been concealed under the skins?

'They look like zebra tails.'

The rhythm and singing grew louder. I held my hands over my ears and willed it to stop, but Abel leaned forward, intent. It stopped. I realised that I had forgotten to breathe, and took a deep, painful gasp of air. One of the dancers stepped forward. She ran around the circle, low and crouched, holding her switch in front of her and making it shiver and rattle in her hand. The women ringing the circle sat with their heads lowered. A stink of fear rose up to Abel and me in our hiding place.

The dancer continued her circling, but now ululated, a high, vibrating note. The switch moved with its own shuddering life, twitching and jerking in her hands, pulled by an invisible force. It nosed its way forwards, ignoring the chanting and ululation, and came to rest in front of one of the women. She was skinny and tall, with a long face and a cut on her heel covered with a pink plaster. The chanting stopped. The woman raised her eyes to the horsetail switch, and I saw sweat dissolving her face, running into her open mouth.

The woman screamed.

'*Muroyi!*' said a voice from behind the mask. The woman collapsed, arms outstretched. Her skirt spread out in the dirt, and she looked like an old chicken taking a dust-bath. The other women ululated, their voices turning into a shimmering heat haze in the air, an eerie, rising sound like the midnight song of a hyena. Abel stood still, listening. It was my turn to pull at his arm.

'Abel, come on. We have to go home.'

'Listen.'

'I can hear it. It is none of our business.' My palms and the soles of my feet were cold and wet with sweat. Abel seemed to come back to life. He looked at me sidelong and then jumped down from the tree and started to run.

I looked over my shoulder as we ran back up the hill to our house. Above the shouts and the wailing, I could hear a crackling, as if someone were crumpling up paper. I saw an orange glow. And then the smoke, rising from one of the huts.

We ran.

'Do not tell Baba what we saw,' I said to Abel through my gasps, clasping his wrist.

He shrugged me off. 'Why would I?'

'Just don't.' I was finding it hard to breathe. The smoke clogged my lungs.

'Abel. Tinashe.' Amai was standing on the *stoep* when we got home. 'Come inside, quickly.'

'Amainini,' Abel put on his best innocent face, 'what is happening?'

'There is trouble. Come.'

We sat inside and watched the sky redden and boil, the smoke making laughing faces against the clouds, the ululating competing with the evening song of the crickets as the witch's hut was burned. It smelled like hot fat and woodsmoke.

Women have a natural tendency to become witches. Everyone knew that. And the witch-smellers had a duty to sniff such women out.

Chapter Six

I was the one who heard Hazvinei's first words, on the day she turned seven years old. I was building little mud-houses for her in the dirt while she watched, piling the mud into a cone shape and sticking pieces of grass on the top to make a thatched roof. I had become impatient with the game, and laid the grass on haphazardly.

'You are doing it wrong, Tinashe,' said a voice from Hazvinei's mouth.

I stopped and stared at her. She stared back, unblinking.

'Look.' Her small brown hand took a blade of grass and rested it gently on the top of the roof, making sure that it aligned perfectly with the others.

'Hazvinei, you are talking!'

She looked at me as if I were mad. 'Yes.'

'When did you learn to do that?'

She turned her palms upwards. 'I do not know.'

'Can you say my name again?'

'Tinashe.' She was contemptuous. Of course she could talk. I felt embarrassed for the times I had crouched over her, speaking in that high, soft voice that you use for babies. She must have thought I was a fool.

'We should go and see Amai and Baba,' I said, standing up and holding out my hand. I was eager to show them; to bring this prize home. When he heard Hazvinei speak, Baba exclaimed and embraced her, lifting her onto his shoulder and laughing. Amai, however, collapsed into a chair and started to cry.

'What is wrong, Amai?' I tugged at her shoulder. 'It is good news.'

'I am happy,' she said, wiping her eyes with her apron.

Amai walked through the *kopje* with Hazvinei the next morning, stopping to speak to everyone she saw and showing off Hazvinei's new ability. The women exclaimed among themselves and Amai smiled. I could not wait for Abel's next visit, so that he could hear my little sister speak too.

Now that Hazvinei could talk, she ruled our house with even more tyranny than before, and collected friends among the *kopje* kids as honey collects flies. I had plenty of friends, even when Abel was away, but I also enjoyed being by myself with ample time to pick at the scabs on my knees or lie on my belly and watch the silent marching of ants. Now a crowd surrounded us at all times, as did shouts, laughter and even tears, for Hazvinei was not always kind to her friends.

No other girl ran with our gang, but the older boys accepted Hazvinei as soon as she could keep up. When she was very small, the boys took turns carrying her when we went on our expeditions. When she grew, she could out-run any of us. Soon, she could out-swim us, too. She moved like a brown fish in the water, curling her body into happy shapes and ducking her head right under. She swam further out into the river than anyone else, just as she ventured further into the bush than anyone else.

When the next term started, Baba announced that Hazvinei was old enough to join me at the village school.

'It will be nice for you to go to school together,' said Baba. 'Eh, Tinashe?'

'Yes, Baba.'

Hazvinei made a face at me behind Baba's back – eyes crossed, tongue protruding. 'Yes, Baba,' she said when he turned to look at her.

It was unusual for girls to go to school, but Baba did not treat Hazvinei as other girls were treated. She did not have to do all the chores that were customary. He allowed her to sit on his lap after meals, and he bought her presents from the store – ribbons for her hair, pretty pencils with shiny wrappers, Freddo Frogs that she did not share with me. This confused the people on the *kopje*, for whom tradition and custom were everything. '*Kudzidzisa mwana musikana kupedza nguva nepfuma*,' said the women of the village – an old proverb meaning that there was no point in educating a girl-child.

Baba gave Amai money to buy Hazvinei new clothes for school. I had outgrown my old clothes as well, and there was a hole in the bum of my khaki shorts, so Amai took us both on the bus into town to visit the school uniform store. Going into town was a great treat. Hazvinei and I pressed our faces against the bus window, ignoring the chatter and the squawk of caged chickens, and stared at the impossibly high white buildings and the hundreds of people, black and white, who walked the streets. Our whole *kopje* would fit inside one of those buildings. I looked at a smartly dressed black man with a suitcase, who walked with a firm, decisive step, and I knew that I would be like him one day. He was smiling. Almost everyone was smiling, it seemed. The heaviness and the threat of the *tsotsis* that we sometimes felt in the village did not seem to reach into town.

But I was wrong.

'Look.' Hazvinei poked me.

Scrawled words on buildings. Men were busy with buckets and brushes, scrubbing them off. I saw 'ZANU' and '*Pamberi*' and '*Viva Chimurenga*', scribbled in red paint.

'Sit up straight,' said Amai. 'Come away from the window.'

When we arrived at the department store, we did not go to the bright, clean section where uniforms hung straight down from plastic hangers, but to the second-hand section where clothes slumped in cardboard boxes. They smelled of old sweat and Surf powder.

'Here you are, Tinashe.'

Amai brought me a pair of grey shorts, a grey, buttoned shirt and a blue jersey. When I tried them on in front of the mirror, I felt like a king.

'Some of the boys wear long socks and black lace-up shoes,' the shop assistant told Amai.

I looked at the rows of new school shoes, black and shining and smelling of fresh leather. I would have to polish my shoes every week, and take good care of them, I knew, but I would not mind. I would be careful. I would take them off before playing football with the other boys.

'I am sorry, Tinashe,' Amai said. 'We cannot afford those at the moment.'

'Many of the boys wear flip-flops,' said the shop assistant, seeing my embarrassment. 'And they will be cooler in the summer.'

But I did not want to wear my old flip-flops. I looked in the mirror again. I could see the jersey fraying at the seam under the arm, and the grey shorts had a faint, creamy stain at the very front.

Hazvinei sat on a stool, kicking at it with her heels. 'I don't mind not having a uniform,' she said. 'Tinashe can have the shoes instead.'

'Don't be silly, Hazvinei.'

I did not get the shoes. Amai bought some for Hazvinei instead, because she was a girl and her feet were softer.

'The shoes are uncomfortable anyway,' said Hazvinei. 'You are lucky you do not have to wear them.'

When we climbed back onto the bus for the long, sweaty journey home, I voiced a secret thought. 'Why do we not visit Babamukuru, Amai? Since we are in town.'

'No, Tinashe.'

'We could telephone to let him know that we are coming. He would not mind.'

'No, Tinashe.'

'But I want to see Abel!'

'Tinashe!' Amai silenced me. 'Stop this. We are not going to visit Babamukuru.'

'We never visit him,' I said. 'I want to see his house.'

'It is not possible. He has not invited us.'

'Why not? Why has he never invited us?'

Hazvinei stared at us both with wide eyes, her thumb in her mouth.

'Tinashe, we do not speak of these things.'

'But I don't understand!'

Amai smacked me on the arm, hard. 'Be quiet,' she said. 'And do not bother your Baba with this when we get home. Do you hear me?'

Silence. Sniffs.

'Do you hear me?'

'Yes, Amai.'

The glory of the shopping trip and the new clothes was spoiled. We rode home in silence.

Amai did not tell Baba about my questions, and Baba told Hazvinei and me every morning how lucky we were to go to school.

'You two have an easy life, hey?'

I did not feel like I had an easy life. I had to get up every morning, fetch water from the pump, stack the firewood, feed the chickens, wash myself and flatten down my hair, make sure Hazvinei washed herself and flattened down her hair, and then walk to school. On the walk, Hazvinei made me carry her school things. Baba did not make Hazvinei do anything she did not want to do. Amai tsked and shook her head, but did not complain.

Instead, she said '*Ah-ah, inga munongozvizivawo pachivanhu pedu*'
– That is just how things are – a phrase I heard often while I was
growing up. There were certain things girls were meant to do
and certain things boys were meant to do, and Hazvinei did
neither.

She liked to scare me. She had the power to make my heart
beat faster, and to make the little hairs at the back of my neck
stand up so far that I imagined them straightening out, turning
from curly black wires into straight ones, especially when she
told me ghost stories in a whisper as we lay on the grass in the
evenings. I was not sure where she heard them – whether she
had been hanging around the cooking fires to hear the stories of
the old women, whether she made them up, or (as she said)
whether the spirits really had whispered them to her.

She told me about ghosts who walked the roads at night when
everyone was asleep. They looked just like people, she said, but
they had no faces, and their feet were on backwards.

'Backwards?'

'Yes! Shush. Listen.'

She told me that these creatures wandered in search of a face.

'How would you steal a face?'

'They just rip them right off.' Hazvinei lifted herself up on
one elbow and grabbed the skin of my cheeks, giving it a yank.

'Ow! Stop.'

'Shush,' Hazvinei said again. She crept forward on her hands
and knees until she was right by the hedge. 'Listen.'

I crawled over to her. 'What?'

'Listen.'

We sat there in silence, looking through the hedge to the empty
dirt road. And then I heard it. A shuffling, scraping sound. Feet
on sand and gravel.

'It's just someone coming home from the shebeen,' I
whispered.

'Shush.' Hazvinei's eyes shone. I could see them, even in the darkness. Her body tensed, almost quivering. I felt the hairs on the backs of my arms start to rise, slowly, like a porcupine's quills.

'Hazvinei.'

'Be quiet!'

The footsteps grew louder. I swallowed, and realised that my mouth was sticky and difficult to close. My stomach grumbled.

A figure came into view around the corner – a woman, barefoot. Relief was cold water in my veins. I saw the glint of light off Hazvinei's sharp little teeth.

'There,' she said, as if she had just discovered the answer to a thorny problem. I looked back at the woman on the road. She had stopped, and was watching us through the hedge. Her gaze did not feel right. My eyes rebelled, blurred and refused to see.

'Look,' said Hazvinei.

The woman's face was blank – a smooth expanse of skin where there should be eyes, a nose, a mouth.

I heard someone scream, and realised it was me. I heard Hazvinei laughing. I backed away from the hedge, fell, heard my breath rush in and out. Darkness, dew-wet grass, the spiralling stars, then the cosy yellow light of indoors and the comforting flesh of Amai under her apron.

'*Maiwe*! What is the matter?' She held my tear-wet face in both hands. 'Hazvinei!'

Hazvinei came in, still snickering, lit up and fizzing with energy. 'Tinashe thought he saw a ghost,' she said.

Baba laughed. 'A ghost?' He ruffled her hair. 'Have you been telling your stories again, my little lioness?'

Her wicked, triumphant face!

'You are too old now to be scared by ghost stories, Tinashe,' said Baba.

I buried my face in Amai's lap and willed the tears back up, like snails retracing their shining trails. Ghosts were a bad omen, I knew.

Abel arrived the following morning for his next holiday. The last time he had visited, I remembered, there had been a large bruise on his face, blooming at his ear and sending tendrils of purple and blue into his eye socket and up into the roots of his hair.

'Eeeeh, *mukomana*.' Baba had gripped his skull to get a closer look. 'What have you been doing to yourself?'

'I fell.'

Baba stared into his face. 'How did you fall?'

'I do not remember.'

Something flickered across Baba's face. He released Abel. 'See your auntie,' he had said. 'She will have some *muti* for you.'

Abel had become as beloved on the *kopje* as Babamukuru. 'You look just like your father,' people told him whenever he visited, reaching out to touch his hair and grasp his shoulder. Abel was a Babamukuru in miniature and blessed with the same good looks and good fortune. We heard many stories of how adventurous Babamukuru had been as a boy, how reckless and full of energy. How he had been the first among his friends to kiss a girl; how he had killed many snakes; how he had been the best dancer in the *kopje*.

I swelled with pride, but Abel stayed silent.

'Why do you never say anything?' I asked him. 'Why do you never tell them that you are proud of your father too?'

'He is different now,' said Abel.

When Babamukuru and Abel arrived this time, however, Babamukuru seemed in a very good mood, rubbing his hands together and smiling.

'I hear this daughter of yours is speaking now, eh?' he said. 'Where is she? I want to see her.'

'She is out with her mother,' said Baba, shaking his brother's hand. 'They will be back soon. Will you come in and wait, *mukoma*? I am about to listen to the news.'

Babamukuru and Abel came inside and Baba fiddled with the dials of the radio. It had a mind of its own. Hazvinei said that a *tokoloshe* lived inside because sometimes it would work and sometimes it would spit and crackle like a cornered mongoose and refuse to tell us anything at all. Babamukuru sat with us at the table, nursing his enamel cup of tea in his two hands, while the static gave way to a loud whistle and then an English voice that told us about *vakomana*, the rebels, as it always did. *Vakomana*. Boys. A harmless word, unless you knew that it also meant freedom fighters. Abel and I listened as we would listen to a bedtime story, resting our chins on our hands and blinking with sleepy eyes, half-aware and half-dreaming. Babamukuru and Baba, however, leaned forward and became intent. We heard that the Communists were training the rebels, and that some of them had weapons from China. China was so far away that I could not imagine it at all. The guerrillas were moving among the people in rural Rhodesia like fish in water, the radio said, spreading their lies and stirring up trouble. Abel pinched me, hard, under the table and I yelped.

'Quiet, Tinashe.'

When the news finished, Baba switched off the radio. 'It sounds like the rebels are gaining ground,' he said. 'They are becoming more powerful.'

'Do not be ridiculous,' said Babamukuru. We perked up. Babamukuru was the head of the family. If he said that it was ridiculous, it must be ridiculous.

'I beg your pardon, brother?'

'This is not the way to go about it,' Babamukuru said, wiping his mouth as if that were the end of the matter. 'Slinking through the bush and spreading stories. Coming out at night. Attacking farmers.'

'What else can they do?' Baba spoke politely. 'There is no other way.'

'It is not up to men like that to change the way things are,' said Babamukuru. 'It is for men like me. Men who have gone to university. Who have good jobs. Not men hiding in the bush like animals.'

Baba pressed his lips together and said nothing. Babamukuru reached to pat me on the head. 'You will be one of those men, eh, Tinashe? You will be like your Babamukuru and become an educated man. Yes?'

I nodded and he laughed, but there was an edge to the sound. Baba said nothing.

Before the silence could stretch into something darker, Amai and Hazvinei came in from the river, and Amai started to fuss and flap around Babamukuru. To think that the head of the family would arrive while she was out, and have to fend for himself in her kitchen! This would not do. A fresh pot of tea must be made, and the best biscuits must be put out on the table. Babamukuru must stay longer so that Amai could show him the hospitality that was proper. He protested, but no one could resist Amai. Hazvinei stood on one leg in the doorway, chewing at a fingernail and refusing to come in.

Baba beckoned to her. 'Come. Sit.'

She came reluctantly, perching on the edge of her chair and swinging her white-socked legs.

Babamukuru smiled at her. 'I hear that you are talking now, finally, eh?'

Hazvinei glanced at Baba, then at me.

'Answer your Babamukuru,' said Baba. Amai paused in her wiping of cups and boiling of water to watch us. Hazvinei said nothing.

'Hazvinei,' said Baba. 'Answer your Babamukuru. Do not be rude.'

Hazvinei stared at him with wide eyes.

'I am sorry, brother,' said Baba. 'She is shy.'

'That is all right.' Babamukuru seemed to have recovered his good humour. He placed both palms flat on the table and leaned towards his niece, smiling a wide white smile and speaking loudly and slowly, as if she were not right in the head. 'How are you today, Hazvinei? Eh?'

She glared at him. I could see trouble coming. 'I am not stupid,' she said, her voice sharp.

'Hazvinei!' Amai stood frozen.

Baba reached to grab her, but she jumped down from her chair and ran. Abel covered his mouth to hide his grin, and Babamukuru leaned back in his chair and smoothed down his tie with both hands. 'You must teach her some manners, Garikai,' he said.

Baba set his jaw. 'Go and find your sister, Tinashe,' he said. 'And bring her back here right away.'

I ran to find Hazvinei. Abel followed.

It did not take long to find her. She stood in front of the chicken run, her arms wrapped around her chest as if she were cold.

Abel examined her. 'So, are you talking properly now or not?' he said.

'Yes.'

The sound of her voice startled him. He turned to me. 'When did this happen?'

'Not long ago.'

Abel looked her up and down. 'Maybe. Why did you speak that way to my father?'

'I do not like him.'

'Hazvinei!' I was shocked. 'You cannot say these things.'

Hazvinei shrugged.

Abel laughed. 'She is cheeky, this one!' He flicked her cheek with a careless finger, and she smiled.

'You are in big trouble with Baba,' I told her.

She shrugged again. We heard the sound of Babamukuru's car starting.

'See?' I said. 'You made him angry.'

'He did not say goodbye to you,' said Hazvinei to Abel.

'I do not care,' said Abel, and scuffed his toes in the dirt.

Baba made Hazvinei apologise on Babamukuru's next visit, but although she spoke to him politely after that, there was an under-current of something in her voice that made Babamukuru frown. Abel thought this was hilarious, and he and Hazvinei fell about with laughter at jokes I did not understand. They had a secret language, those two, and plodding, dogged Tinashe could not always keep up with it. Sometimes I wished that my sister had stayed silent forever, and I was ashamed of wishing it.

Abel grew faster than me, and taller. By the time Hazvinei was eight and I was eleven, he was only a head shorter than Baba, with a close-shorn, handsome head and those perfect white teeth. He and Hazvinei could both run faster and swim better than I could, but I read all the books that Abel brought me and did not care. While I read, Hazvinei and Abel played rough games together, wrestling in the dirt and shouting and laughing. Neither of them did their chores as they were supposed to, but they did not get into trouble. No one could deny Abel and Hazvinei any pleasure, these two white-toothed, smooth-skinned children with loud laughs and the hearts of two lion cubs.

One day I did not feel like reading and instead lazed with the others in the cooling sun, waiting for Baba to come home.

'How is school going?' I asked Abel.

He shrugged.

'Are you enjoying it?'

'No.'

'Why not?'

'School is not important.' He picked at a scab on his arm.

'Leave him alone, Tinashe,' said Hazvinei, who lay on her stomach watching a trail of ants.

'But you are going to college,' I said.

'Maybe.'

'Babamukuru says so.'

'Tinashe. I do not want to think about school. It is the holidays.'

We sat in silence for a moment, until a voice made us jump.

'*Iwe.*'

We looked around, startled.

'Yes, you.'

A white man stood at the gate. He wore small spectacles, like Babamukuru, and his sunburned scalp shone pinkly through the damp parting of his hair.

Abel and I looked at each other.

'Yes?' said Abel finally.

'Come here.'

Abel stood, and walked to the gate. After a moment, I followed, brushing the red dust from the seat of my pants. Hazvinei stayed where she was, watching the neverending march of the black ants.

'Where is your father? Hey?'

Abel looked at me.

'At work,' I said.

'When will he be home?'

'I don't know, sir,' I added.

'Well, tell him that I am looking for him. Hokay? You can remember that?'

'Yes, sir.'

The white man squinted at me with watery eyes, then turned and walked away. I saw a car parked on the other side of the road; a city car, sleek and menacing in shape, with a red haze of dust on its undercarriage. The white man climbed in, and as he lifted his leg I saw the gleam of highly polished shoes beneath the raised hem of his trousers. It was only then that I realised I had not asked his name.

'He is a new one,' I said. 'I have not seen him before.'

'Are you going to tell Babamudiki?' said Abel.

'Yes. Of course.'

'I think it was a policeman.'

'He was not wearing a uniform.'

'Still. Perhaps a special kind of policeman.'

'Well, then I must tell Baba.'

Abel shook his head. 'I do not like it.'

'That is because you have been listening to too many radio stories about the *vakomana*.'

Abel pushed me. 'Shut up.'

When Baba returned from work, he picked up Hazvinei to embrace her, and nodded at Abel and I.

'*Manheru*, Baba.'

'*Manheru*, Babamudiki.'

He sat and unstrapped his heavy boots that smelled of old milk left in the sun. He clasped one of his bare feet in his hand. It was blistered and bleeding.

'What happened, Baba?'

'It was a long day, Tinashe. A long day of hard work.'

He stretched his arms behind his head. His skin was softened and stretched with labour, glistening with sweat. Abel sat like him, lengthening out his legs in just the same way, watching him closely to catch the way he sighed and blinked his eyes.

'Baba,' I said. 'Someone was here looking for you.'

'Oh yes?'

'A white man.'

He straightened. 'Who?'

'I do not know his name.'

Baba leaned back. 'What did he look like?'

'He was not wearing a uniform.'

'Ah.' Baba was silent for a moment.

'Baba?'

'Yes, Tinashe?'

'What did that man want?'

'He probably wanted to ask me some questions,' said Baba.

'About what?'

'About the freedom fighters,' said Abel. 'Like we heard on the radio.'

Baba flicked his eyes to Abel, and back. 'Yes. There have been rumours,' he said. 'Do not worry, Tinashe. It is nothing.'

'I have heard stories about the freedom fighters,' said Abel. He swelled out his chest. 'They hide in the forest like *tokoloshes* and jump out to fight the soldiers. They can change themselves into animals.'

Baba laughed. 'Where are you hearing these stories?' he said. 'From your Baba?'

'No. He does not like me to talk about them.'

'They are not true,' said Baba. Abel deflated. 'But I can tell you a story that is true. You have heard of Mbuya Nehanda?'

Abel shook his head. I nodded. Abel pinched me. 'You haven't.'

'I have heard of her,' I said. 'I just do not know the whole story.'

Baba stubbed out his cigarette and leaned back against the tree. Abel and I sat with our legs crossed, as men did.

'You want to hear?' said Baba.

Yes, we nodded.

I have heard many versions of Nehanda's story over the years. I do not remember the words that Baba used to tell the story on that day, but I have my own version of it that I have learned from many repetitions by many different people. Others will tell a different story, but this is mine.

Dzepfunde.

The spirit Nehanda was a *mhondoro* — a lion spirit — the most powerful, and one that chooses only chiefs and sisters of chiefs to carry its message. A lion spirit protects a whole region, a whole people — not just one family, as most spirits do. And a *mhondoro* only possesses those who have the heart of a lion to begin with.

The original Nehanda was once called Nyamhika, daughter of Mutota, the first Monomatapa, a king. She had a brother, Matope, from a different mother. To increase his power and to make his line strong and indestructible, Mutota ordered Matope to commit incest with his half-sister in order to produce a son. I do not know how they did this: whether the king let Nyamhika walk under the cool moon to her brother's hut and couple with him in the secret darkness, or whether she performed the ceremony in full sunlight, in the open air, in front of the king himself. I do not know whether she enjoyed it: whether she felt the power that would create an empire forming between them like flame, or whether she submitted as a daughter who must obey her father, whatever that father demands.

After this, Nyamhika became known as Nehanda. She walked with a new pride, a new knowledge, a new bitterness. She was a lioness now, and even her father was afraid of her. But he was grateful also, as his empire spread and his rule extended until he was the greatest and most powerful king that had ever lived. He gave Nehanda a portion of his empire, and she grew in power also; more so than her brother and father did, and more so than they suspected. She did not die, as they died (for even the greatest kings must relinquish their hold on the land and become ancestors one day): instead, she became the Nehanda spirit, giving knowledge, predictions and power that could not be destroyed in battle. For five hundred years, the Nehanda spirit, forged in fire and incest, appeared when she was needed to those who were great leaders themselves.

After those five hundred years, Nehanda was reborn in the body of Nyakasikana, the slim-hipped, dark-as-honey daughter of a king. When the white people first appeared, Nehanda told us to be friendly towards them. Later, though, she told us to fight. The earth was unhappy with the whites, she told us: they had brought locusts and *rinderpest*, and our dead cattle burned in damp, steaming piles, our food going up in smoke. *Mwari* spoke through Nehanda and told us to fight, and not to fear, because the bullets of the white men would be turned to water.

We had forgotten the power of water: how the rains break tree-spines and flatten fields of crops.

The whites captured Nehanda, and sentenced her to death by hanging. Twice they tried to hang her, and twice her neck would not break. It was only when a fellow prisoner told them to remove the tobacco pouch from her belt that the hanging was successful.

'They say that there is a new Nehanda,' Baba told us on that day, 'that her bones have risen again, as she said they would. She will help us in our fight.'

'Our fight?' I had heard about the freedom fighters on the radio, but their fight had no place in our half-asleep, baked-brown village.

Abel's lips parted, but he did not speak. I saw words in his eyes, though, and knew that his quick, sharp-toothed brain was at work on this new story.

'Where is she?' he asked. 'Is she here now?'

'They say that she is in another country,' said Baba. 'Where it is safer. But she will come again.'

'Why?' Abel again.

'People like Nehanda,' said Baba, 'are very important to us. To speak to the spirits is a great gift, and it is given for a reason.'

'Could I speak to the spirits?' said Abel.

Baba laughed. 'If you could, you would know it by now,' he said. 'It is not something you can learn.'

'But I can do other things,' said Abel, too quietly for Baba to hear.

Hazvinei had said nothing during Baba's story, but when I looked at her I saw a strange light in her eyes. Baba brushed himself off and went to wash before dinner.

'Hazvinei?' I said. 'Hazvinei!'

But she did not hear me.

The white men stayed in the *kopje,* and it became normal for me to greet men in uniform as I walked through the village, and to pick up their discarded Coke bottles to take to Simon-at-the-bottle-store. Simon loved having the white men around. He stocked up on bottles of Castle lager and packets of *biltong.*

'They have so much money!' he said. 'They buy so many things. It is good for the village, Tinashe, no matter what people say.' And he wagged his finger. I was not sure if it was good for the village, but it was certainly good for Simon. He bought a shining new bicycle and parked it outside the bottle store to show it off. We *kopje* kids crowded around it, close enough to mist the red paint with our breath, but Simon was ready to shoo us away with a broom if we got too close. The white men laughed at our simple ways, but they did not know the joy of freewheeling down the hill on a new bicycle with fresh tyres and pedals that did not stick. I did not like the fact that they watched us all so closely, but I did like the free sweets and the sudden increase in the number of glass bottles I could exchange for coins.

No one besides Simon and the children liked having so many whites in the village. Cattle began to sicken and die, and people whispered that it was because of the strangers that walked among us like ghosts. Some of the goats broke down their pen and were lost. Bad luck hovered like a cloud of flies in the air. It even touched our family, in our nice brick house with the proper fence and the clean-swept front yard.

Abel called over Hazvinei and I to examine something he had found inside the gate. 'What is that?'

'What?' I looked where he was pointing, and could see nothing. 'There.'

Hazvinei crept forward on her hands and knees. 'I see it.' She traced something with her fingers in the dust.

'What is it?' I could not see. I came closer, craning to see over the bent heads of my sister and cousin. And then I saw what they were seeing: a perfect paw-print in the dust, sharp-edged and clear.

'It is probably one of the dogs,' I said.

'Don't be stupid,' said Abel. 'Do you know any dogs this big?'

Hazvinei fanned out her fingers and placed them over the print. Her whole hand fitted inside with plenty of room to spare.

'It cannot be,' I said. 'It would not come this close to the house.' Because Baba would keep it away, keep us safe, I thought but did not say. 'And there is only one print. Someone may have made it for a joke.'

No one said 'leopard'. We stood in silence, looking down at the paw-print.

'Fine.' Abel scuffed the print out with his foot. 'It is nothing.'

We went to bed early that night. Abel fell asleep at once; I heard his snoring and and occasional grunt. As I lay there, thinking, I felt a weight on the end of the bed. A *tokoloshe*, a mischievous night spirit that sat on your chest and stopped your breath. I sat up, my heart trying to escape through my ribs, and saw that it was Hazvinei.

'Hazvinei, it is the middle of the night.' I kept my voice low, so as not to wake Abel, but my mouth was dry with fear, and it was hard to swallow. Hazvinei's eyes shone white in the darkness.

'What do you want?' I asked her. She shifted her weight, getting comfortable. Abel shifted in his sleep and sighed, but did not wake.

'Why are witches always women?' she whispered.

'What? You woke me up to ask this?' I slumped backwards. 'Can't it wait until morning?'

'I was thinking of Nehanda,' she said.

'In the middle of the night?'

'Nehanda was not a *muroyi*. No one calls her that.'

'Of course she was not.'

'But what is the difference? Why are *varoyi* always women?' said Hazvinei with great patience. 'Why are they never men? We call men N'angas when they do the same things.'

I sighed, resigning myself to being awake a while longer. Abel did not stir.

'That is impossible,' I explained kindly, 'because if they were men then they would not be witches.'

Hazvinei stared at me, flat-eyed. When she spoke again, it was with the slow, babying voice she used to talk to the chickens. 'That is what I am saying. Why? There must be men who are witches too.'

'I don't understand.'

'What is wrong with you, Tinashe? I am asking why the witch-smellers only pick out the women from the crowd to see who is the witch. They do not look for men. Why is that? Why couldn't it be a man poisoning the *mombes* and making them sick?'

'Go to bed, Hazvinei.'

'But why?' she persisted.

'Men are N'angas. They are not *varoyi*.'

'Why?'

'Hazvinei!'

'Why?'

'Because *varoyi* are women,' I said. 'That is just how it is.'

Hazvinei snorted. 'You are a fool,' she said. 'Watch that a

dung-beetle does not crawl in through your ear and steal your brain.'

She melted into the black. I hoped that she was going back to her room, and not to sit and fume outside where the leopards were. But even Hazvinei was not that careless.

Time passes slowly in places like the *kopje*. The hot sun melts and distorts it like *sadza* cooking on the stove, turning it soft and malleable, expanding it almost without your realising it. Every day was much the same: chores and lessons, rumours whispered in our ears, games played in the dust and hours spent swimming in the river. The river was our plaything, we *kopje* children. During the day we trusted it; perhaps a little too much. It rolled onto its back and let us tickle its belly, a friendly brown snake with a soft underside. There were times, though, when the rains turned the brown river to a black mamba that moved too quickly to be safe. More than one baby was lost to the river's long, swallowing throat.

Abel, Hazvinei and I were not swallowed. Not yet.

The river is a living thing, Baba taught me. The long throat of the river swallows water from the sky. When you drink from it, you are not drinking ordinary water (the kind that collects in rain barrels and the evening leaves of plants): you are drinking a story told by a deep voice filled with knowledge of the sky and the earth. You are drinking a god. And, as a god, the river is capricious – you cannot trust it. It can bring illness as easily as refreshment; death as easily as life. And it steals the years from you as you sit quietly at its edge, dangling your toes in the water. You go from baby to boy to man without realising it, in those long, hot days.

Chapter Seven

The year of 1973 was filled with ghosts and the rumours of ghosts. We heard whispers. *'Vaenzi vauya* – the strangers have come.' According to the rumours, instead of living outside the borders of Rhodesia and only coming in again to raid or cause trouble, the rebels walked among us now, infiltrating the villages. Some of the men from neighbouring villages had vanished, they said – just disappeared without warning and without saying goodbye. Their wives and children carried on with chores and lessons as if nothing unusual had happened, answering questions with flat, unseeing stares. The *kopje* remained largely untouched, but the whispers continued.

The white men smiled less and did not give us chewing gum as before. Instead they watched us with colourless eyes and asked us questions when we left the *kopje*. Where are you going? Why? They collared the kids in particular, because it was known that a village child could act as a *mujiba* – an errand boy for the rebels – sneaking out under pretence of play and smuggling information or supplies. When Abel came to stay with us now, he was under strict instructions from Babamukuru to stay within the bounds of the village and to visit the river only when a large group was swimming or washing there.

'The last thing Abel needs is any trouble,' Babamukuru said. 'He is going to take a scholarship exam in four years' time, as I did. I will not allow him to do anything that will affect his future.'

I was old enough to start high school now, but although

Baba allowed me to continue lessons at the village school, he told me I could not go to a proper senior college.

'We cannot afford it, Tinashe,' he said. 'I am sorry.'

Abel attended a good school in town. I had seen his smart blazer and the straw hat he wore.

'What about Babamukuru?' I said.

Baba looked at me without expression. 'What about Babamukuru?'

I knew that I should have stayed silent, but I could not. 'Babamukuru said that I would be an educated man like him. When he visited. He promised that he would take care of my school, Baba. He promised.'

Baba was silent.

'We could ask him for the money,' I said. 'He promised.'

The blow across my ear surprised me. It was merely a slap, but it made my head ring. I staggered backwards, more from surprise than from the weight of it.

'I do not want to hear you talk about this again, Tinashe,' said Baba. 'Is that clear?'

I shook my head, trying to clear it.

'Babamukuru has done many things for our family,' said Baba. 'You must be content with what we have. I will not have you *shupering* and bothering him with all your questions, and I will not have you talking that way. Is that clear?'

'Yes, Baba.'

It was a small thread of sound, but he heard it and seemed satisfied. I did not mention high school again. I read Abel's cast-off books and tried to teach myself the things that he was learning, so I would not fall behind. When he visited a few days after my fight with Baba, he dumped a pile of books in my lap and raced straight to the river with Hazvinei. I was sitting in the dust of the yard with my newsprint exercise book when they returned.

'If you are not careful you will need glasses like Baba,' said Abel. 'Reading all day.'

I threw a pencil at him. He flopped down beside me in the shade, laughing, and Hazvinei stretched out full-length on the tiles of the *stoep* to dry off. We stayed silent, and I concentrated so hard on my reading that I almost did not hear the voice that spoke from our front gate.

'Hello again.' English words.

I turned, and saw the white policeman who visited Baba from time to time. We had not seen him for months now, and I had imagined that Baba was no longer suspected of hiding his knowledge of the rebels.

'I am here to see your Baba,' said the policeman. 'Is he home?'

'I do not know,' I said in English. 'We have just come back from the river.'

I saw us through his eyes — scruffy *kopje* kids with dust in our hair and holes in our clothing.

'What do you want?' said Hazvinei.

The white man smiled, showing yellow teeth.

'It is a good day for swimming,' he said. 'We go down there sometimes as well, when we have finished work.'

I imagined him skinny and pale, dipping a cautious toe in the water.

'Does your father often go out after work?' said the white man. 'Does he go down to the river as well?'

There was a question behind his question, but I did not have time to answer it. Baba was at the door.

'*Vana*. Go and play.'

'But Baba, we have just come home . . .'

'Go.'

He stepped forwards to talk to the white man. Hazvinei and I hovered for a moment.

'What did I tell you?' Baba's voice was sharp. He said something in English, quietly, to the white man, and then to us. 'Now.'

We ran, Hazvinei clutching my hand as if I could protect her from everything bad that there was in the world. As we ran, I wondered if Abel had told Babamukuru, safe in their brick house in town, about the suspicions of the white policemen who still visited Baba to ask him questions. I doubted it.

Sometimes ghosts are not the remembered shadows of the dead, but people who blow into our lives by accident; they are ghosts because we were never meant to meet them. To see them is a dangerous thing, and they bring bad fortune whether they want to or not.

Late that night, my *mboro* woke me with the strong desire for a piss. I did not want to get up, because I remembered the yellow teeth of the policeman and the snake-like hiss of the radio he carried, and I was afraid he would be waiting for me in the leopard-filled darkness outside the comfort of my bedroom. I tried to sleep again, but my dreams were full of snakes and rivers and waterfalls. I got up, careful not to wake Abel. He was a dark shape on the mattress, breathing sour sleeping breaths, and he did not stir.

As I shuffled through the thick darkness, I heard voices from the kitchen. I stopped, my knees stiff and unyielding, and listened. Two voices, yes, but they were not speaking English and they did not have the crisp rasp of the white man's voice.

I opened the door to the kitchen. Two figures sat at the table.

'Tinashe!'

Sleep greased my eyes, and their faces swam and swirled like oil at the bottom of a pan.

'Tinashe, go to bed.'

83

My eyes cleared. I saw Baba, hollow in the electric light, and another man, his bare back curved and ridged with bone. The strange man turned to look at me. His shoulders heaved with every breath; his nostrils flared. He was wet, as if he had run through the rain, but it was not raining outside.

'Tinashe, go back to bed,' said Baba.

'Babamudiki? What is happening?' Abel appeared in the doorway. I had not even heard him approaching.

'What are you doing?' he asked me, and then caught sight of the stranger.

The unknown man curled his wide mouth into a smile. 'Hello, Tinashe,' he said. 'Your father has been telling me about you.'

'*Manheru*,' I said, not sure if it were indeed evening still, or closer to morning. Abel pushed his way through the door to stand next to me.

'I am Abel,' he said.

The curly mouth smiled again.

'This is Chenjerai,' said Baba. 'He is visiting us.'

'Come. Sit,' said Chenjerai.

I looked at Baba. His stillness told me that I was given permission, and I moved to stand at the table. Abel followed.

'Do not wake your sister,' said Baba.

'No, Baba.'

'No, Babamudiki,' said Abel.

'This is not your son?' said Chenjerai.

Baba shook his head. 'My nephew.'

I noticed three things. I noticed a pan of water on the stove. I noticed a sour smell that came from a pair of tweezers sitting on the table. And I noticed a dark, soaked bandage at Chenjerai's shoulder.

'I am sorry to have woken you,' said Chenjerai, who was younger than I had first thought. Eighteen, perhaps, like the boys who hung around the bottle store and kicked cans.

'Where do you live?' I asked him. 'I have not seen you before.'

Baba took a sip of tea, looking at me over the cup's rim. 'It is rude to ask too many questions, Tinashe.'

'I am sorry, Baba.'

'It is all right,' said Chenjerai. 'I live in the bush.'

In the bush. A *mukomana*. A freedom fighter. Beside me, I felt Abel stand up straighter.

Chenjerai saw my excitement, and smiled.

'You are staying nearby?' I said. 'All of you?'

'Tinashe. You know we do not ask these things,' said Baba.

'It is all right,' said Chenjerai again, but he did not answer me.

'Can I have some tea too?' I asked, pushing my luck. I half-rested my bum on one of the kitchen chairs.

'No,' said Baba. 'You need to go back to bed. Chenjerai is going now.'

Chenjerai flicked his eyes to Baba, then back to me.

'I owe you something for waking you, yes?' he said. 'Hold out your hand.'

I held it out, palm up. I could feel Abel's eyes on me.

'Close your eyes.'

I closed them. The electric light made my eyelids red and angry.

'Here.'

Something smooth and cool rolled into my palm; something small and heavy. I opened my eyes. An object of dull grey, rounded, with a misshapen end, like a tiny river stone. I smelled the metallic stink that had filled the kitchen when I first arrived.

'It is a bullet,' said Chenjerai. 'It will bring you good luck, I think. It was good luck for me.'

'In a way,' said Baba.

'I am happy for whatever luck I get,' said Chenjerai, and winked at me. '*Chisarai*.'

I was dismissed. '*Chisarai.*'

Baba opened the door. A sudden wind, night noises, the smell of dry grass and dew. Chenjerai went, smiling, into darkness, and Baba closed the door again.

He looked at us both. We looked at him. 'I did not want to wake you,' he said.

'How did you know that man?' I said. 'What was he doing here? Is it something to do with Nehanda? Is that why the policeman came to see you?'

'*Nyarara.*' Baba hushed me. 'Come.' He held out his hand, cool and strong. I took it, Abel took the other, and we let him lead us back to our bed.

'You will not mention this, *vakomana*,' said Baba. He bent down to look us in the eyes.

'No, Baba.'

'No, Babamudiki.'

'You promise me?'

'Yes, Baba.'

'Yes, Babamudiki.'

'We must all do our part,' he said. 'But we must also keep quiet about it.'

'Yes, Baba.'

'Yes, Babamudiki.'

'Good boys. Now off to bed.'

Even in the close darkness of our room, Abel and I dared not talk about it; but I had forgotten about my *mboro*. A hot, sharp pain in my side reminded me that I had some piss to let out, but I did not want to go back through to the kitchen, as Baba had told me to stay quietly in bed. Instead, I opened the little window and stood on my bed, aiming into the darkness.

'What are you doing?' Abel asked me in a whisper. 'Are you going to follow him?'

'No.'

Even the full moon looked like a distended bladder, yellow and swollen. It was a good job; I only left a few drips on the windowsill.

'Are you sleeping, Tinashe?' came Baba's voice from the next room.

'Yes, Baba,' I said, and jumped back into bed to burrow my nose into the familiar, musty smell of my pillow.

When I awoke the next morning, Abel was staring into my face. I pushed him away. 'What are you doing?'

'Are you awake? Do you remember what happened last night?'

'Yes.' I rubbed the back of my arm across my eyelids and blinked to clear the stars. I remembered a bullet; a bowl; the curved ridge of a spine. 'Yes.'

'Chenjerai,' said Abel. *Beware*.

'What?'

'Chenjerai. His name.'

'Oh.' I felt beneath my pillow, remembering, and pulled out the bullet. It was warm, and I imagined it smelled of the dark, rich scent of Chenjerai's wound.

'Let me see.' Abel held out his hand.

'No. He gave it to me.'

'Give it to me.'

'No.'

A scuffle. The bullet fell to the floor with a clatter.

'What are you boys doing?' came a voice from the kitchen.

'Nothing, Amai!'

Abel lay on top of me, breathing heavily.

'He gave it to me,' I said, and gripped the bullet in my fist. Silence for a moment. Abel glared at me. I held his gaze.

'Fine.' Abel rolled off me. 'But we will go to find him today.'

I snorted. 'How are you planning to do that?'

Abel pressed something to my arm. It burned, and I yelped.

I had forgotten his habit of collecting the hard black seeds that littered our yard – when rubbed hard against the concrete floor, they became hot and stung the skin. Abel always kept one or two in his pocket for moments like these.

'Don't you want to see them?' said Abel. 'The guerrillas. Perhaps they will let us join them.'

'Don't be stupid,' I said. 'We are kids. How could we be useful to them? They will laugh at us. And we will get into trouble.'

'Well, I am going to look for them,' Abel said. 'You can stay here, like a good boy, and read your books.'

I did not see Abel for the rest of the day. He wandered into the patchy scrubland behind our house, and I did not bother to follow. I knew that he would not find anything. A *mukomana* would not be much good at hiding if he could be found by a little boy with seeds in his pocket. Abel came home disappointed and silent, but it did not take long for him to rally the rest of the *kopje* kids to play a game he had invented – one that became the favourite of all the *kopje* kids during those school holidays. This was one game that we did not play in front of the adults. They may have smiled at *Sarura Wako* and *Mahumbwe*, but they would not smile at this one.

We played it away from the village – particularly, away from the whites that drifted through. We divided into *vakomana* and whites. No one wanted to be the whites, which is why we had team leaders who selected us one by one, to keep things fair. If you had been a *mukomana* last time, you had to take your turn at being a white. Abel was the only one who seemed to enjoy being on the white side, because he had a considerable talent for acting out long and painful death throes. His throat-rattles, foaming mouth and rolling eyes were quite wonderful to witness, and we all enjoyed seeing him murdered. Things were no different today.

'I'll be the white policeman,' said Abel.

'I want to be the policeman,' Hazvinei said, bristling. It was an unheard-of challenge.

The boys shifted, uneasy. 'You're a girl.'

'So what?'

'So you can't be a policeman, *benzi*.'

Laughter. Shoulders relaxing. You did not mess with Abel, even if you were pint-sized and pugnacious Hazvinei, with your clever, slanted eyes and sharp little claws.

'You can be one of the freedom fighters,' I said, trying to keep the peace. 'The women fight too.'

Hazvinei snorted.

'I will be a freedom fighter with you,' said Chipo.

'No,' said Abel/Policeman. 'You have to be the burned corpse of a white. Lie over there.'

Chipo lowered herself to the ground with great dignity, choosing a spot where her green dress would not become too disfigured by dust. She always had to play the corpses.

'Hazvinei, you will be an excellent freedom fighter,' I said. 'It is harder than being the policeman.'

'Fine.' She shrugged me off.

The guerrillas hid in the bushes and waited. The whites (walking with their necks stiff and their legs apart, the way white men did) marched past. We leapt at them, shouting and waving our arms, and they fell to the ground with fright, shouting words at random in English. Then came the climax: the same every time. We rushed at Abel/Policeman and hit him with our pretend *badzas*. He shrieked and yelled out to the spirits to save him, rolling his eyes and waving his arms like a mad person. It was hard to hit through our laughter. When Abel/Policeman had enough of this clowning, he clutched at his throat and sank to his knees, making horrible bubbling, gurgling sounds and letting his tongue hang out, as the skinny *kopje* dogs did when it was too hot. When he finally died, we stood silent for a moment before cheering and stamping our feet in the hot dust. Chipo rose from the dead to join us.

'One day I will be a freedom fighter,' I said to Hazvinei.

'Me too.'

'It is too dangerous for you,' I said.

'What do you mean? You said that women can be guerrillas.'

'Yes, but not you. Not in real life.'

'Why not? I am strong.' She nipped a piece of my soft underarm skin between her fingers and twisted.

'*Iwe*! Stop that.'

'I am just as strong as you.'

'That is not the point.'

'Why not?'

'I have to keep you safe,' I said. 'Baba tells me so every day. Do you think I am going to let you go running into the bush with a gun?'

Hazvinei stuck out her lower lip. It was fat and shiny, a *chongololo* of discontentment. 'I am better than both of you,' she said. 'You will see. I will make a better *mukomana* than you or Abel.'

'You cannot be a *mukomana*,' said Abel, who had heard us. 'You are a *musikana*, a girl.'

Hazvinei pushed him. 'I will tell Baba that you play this game.'

'Fine,' said Abel. 'Tell him. I do not care.'

'I will.'

'Go ahead.'

Hazvinei stared at him for a moment, and then turned and ran. I watched her white socks flashing as she sprinted towards the house.

'You have upset her,' I said to Abel.

'She is being a big baby. Who cares if she can be a freedom fighter or not? She is a little girl. I don't know why she is so angry.'

'I have to go with her,' I said.

Abel shrugged. 'Stay here. She will not really tell Babamudiki.'

'But I cannot leave her on her own.' I started towards the house. After a moment, Abel followed.

'Do you think she will really tell?'

'It doesn't matter. We have to talk to her. Come on.'

When we reached the top of the hill we saw something flashing silver in the sun.

'What is that?'

I could not focus on it. 'I don't know.'

Abel ran past me. It took me a moment more of standing and staring to realise that Babamukuru was here, parked outside our house, talking to Baba. And Hazvinei. What was he doing here?

'Abel!'

As always I was the slow elephant, lagging behind my cousin and sister. Babamukuru's face was almost invisible behind his glasses when I caught up to Abel. Hazvinei hung behind Baba, clutching his hand and staring at Abel. Baba's hands were outstretched, palm up, as if he were placating Babamukuru or calming him down.

'Baba . . .' Abel began, but could not finish. Babamukuru caught him such a blow across the side of the head that he fell, clumsily, landing on hands and knees in the dirt. Babamukuru hauled him up by his ear. Baba made a jerky movement, clenching his hands into fists, but did not intervene.

'What is this I hear about you? Hey? What are these games that you are playing?'

Baba stepped forward, conciliatory hands held out again, but Babamukuru ignored him.

'Get in the car.'

'Brother, you were to stay for dinner,' said Baba.

'I am taking this one home.' Babamukuru let his flat gaze trail over me as well. I shrank under it. 'I was going to surprise you,' he said to Abel. 'I was going to take you and Tinashe to the movies in town, at the new Kine. And now look what you have done.'

A chance to go to town and see a film on a big screen — perhaps with Cokes and sweets as well! And a ride in Babamukuru's car. I hated Abel in that moment for inventing the *vakomana* game and taking away my chance to live like a smart town boy instead of a grubby village kid.

'They are just playing,' said Baba.

'And where are they getting these ideas? Hey? I do not let my son listen to this nonsense.'

Baba flicked his eyes to me. A stranger sitting in our kitchen. Blood in a bowl.

'It is the other children, Babamukuru,' I said. 'They invented the game.'

'They should not be playing with such things. It is not a suitable game for my son. For anyone in my family.'

I looked down at my feet.

'I am ashamed of you both,' said Babamukuru, 'playing at being these animals when you know better. Get in the car, Abel.'

As my cousin passed me, I breathed in his scent of shame and sour fear. He climbed into the front seat and fastened his seatbelt with an over-loud click. Babamukuru climbed into the driver's seat and started the engine.

'Goodbye, Garikai,' my uncle said as he started the car. 'I will come another time.'

We watched them go. My face burned as if Babamukuru had hit me as well.

'He did not take Abel's things,' I said. 'He still has books here.'

The car winked in the sun, sharing a secret. Baba took our hands – me on one side, Hazvinei on the other. I saw Hazvinei's quick, dark glance. She did not look sorry.

Chapter Eight

The next school holidays came and went without Abel, and without a letter or phone call from Babamukuru. Baba and Amai did not speak of it. Hazvinei and I went to school as usual – Hazvinei leading her friends into trouble – and I finished in the top of my class again. This was not saying much, however. My teacher did his best with the small number of books he had, but we learned many of the same lessons over and over. I had the books that Abel had left behind, but I fretted that there would be no more, and that I would be no better than any goat-herding village boy who had never bothered to attend lessons at all. Abel would overtake me; he would go away to a good school and forget me; and I would not see him until he drove up in a silver car and a nice suit to visit me and my family in our little brick house that he had paid for.

'Is Babamukuru still angry, Baba?' I asked when over four months had passed with no news.

'I suppose he is,' said Baba.

'Is he angry at me?'

I saw Hazvinei roll her eyes.

'I am sure he is no longer angry with you, Tinashe,' said Baba, laying a hand on my head.

'You see what you have done, Hazvinei?' I said to her in private. 'Now Babamukuru will never let Abel visit again.'

She pushed me away irritably. 'You worry too much. It will be fine.'

'All because you could not keep your mouth shut,' I said. 'I wish you had never learned to speak at all.'

I did not see Chenjerai again. I wondered what had happened to him – whether he had moved on to continue his work, or whether he had been injured again. Or caught. I woke up sometimes in the night, thinking that I had heard the clink of cups in the kitchen or the hum of low voices, but the night was always empty. After Babamukuru's anger, the visit from the freedom fighter did not seem as exciting. It seemed reckless now, and dangerous. I wondered why Baba had taken him into our home while my mother and sister slept and the white policemen patrolled outside. Had he thought about the risk he was taking? Was it the first time he had done such a thing? I thought about the bullet, neatly removed and rattling in its bowl, and the way Chenjerai had spoken to Baba – as if he knew him, or knew of him. I did not think it had been the first time.

Perhaps Baba was not keeping the leopards at bay at all. Perhaps he was inviting them in. And as I remembered Babamukuru's face as he took Abel away, I wondered if he had suspected as much.

Without Abel and Babamukuru, the long days flowed past unchanging and dim as the river water. The only excitement came from the news on the radio, as the troubles in Mozambique and stories of 'protected villages' in Rhodesia occupied everyone's thoughts. I wondered why we needed special villages to protect us from the rebels.

'It is not to protect us from the freedom fighters,' said Baba. 'It is to protect the whites from us.'

I occupied myself with reading all the books that Abel had left behind. When I finished them, I read them again. I wondered if I would ever get another stack of shining new books, if Abel never returned. I wondered if Babamukuru would forget about me.

'Where is your city cousin?' said Little Tendai. 'Did your monkey sister scare him away?'

'He will come back,' I said, but was not sure I believed my own words.

'You are too serious, Tinashe.'

'I am not too serious.'

'You are. You are always reading your school books.'

I kicked at a pebble. 'That is what you are supposed to do with school books.'

Little Tendai shrugged and moved on to a more interesting topic. 'Why do you think all those whites are here, anyway?'

More whites than ever were passing through the *kopje* as rebels poured in over the borders of Mozambique and Zambia and infiltrated the villages. The policemen and soldiers drove in, parked, bought a cold drink from Simon-at-the-bottle-store, watched us with those too-pale eyes, then left. The people of the *kopje* watched the movements of the whites with interest but detachment, as they observed the movements of the termites that built great red-earth cathedrals in the grass. It was best not to wonder exactly what they were doing, Baba said, as their actions were none of our business and they would not hurt us. It was safer, also. I thought of the policeman who had come to talk to Baba. I thought of Chenjerai.

'What do you think they are doing?' I asked Little Tendai.

'Probably looking for *vakomana*,' he said in a dramatic whisper.

'You still think there are *vakomana* nearby?' I suddenly had an urgent need for the toilet, remembering the bullet safe and cold in my pocket.

'I think so,' said Little Tendai, who had no idea. 'They are probably watching us from the bushes right now.'

I knew Little Tendai was teasing me, but I turned around anyway. *Chenjerai*. A word meaning *beware*. I caught a glimmer of movement – a bird probably, or a cane rat darting for cover.

'They might need someone to help them,' said Little Tendai. He gave me a push. 'They will come to me, because I am the strongest.'

A scuffle – friendly and not-so-friendly, all at once. When Little Tendai had me pinned, he smiled at me with all his teeth. 'They kidnap people, you know,' he said. 'They make you join them. Maybe they will come and get you from your bed in the middle of the night . . .'

'Shut up, Tendai!'

I broke free and ran. I had had enough talk of the *vakomana* for one day.

'Perhaps the whites are as crazy as your sister,' Little Tendai shouted. 'Perhaps they are here chasing ghosts.' He made a crazy-ghost face – puffed cheeks, crossed eyes – and ran home, laughing.

The *kopje* kids tried to play the *vakomana* game again, but Hazvinei and I did not take part. They gave up after a while, as well. It was just not the same without Abel.

Baba and I were chopping wood in the garden when I saw the white policeman again – the one who had visited Baba when Abel was last here. He waited at the gate, watching us, and said nothing. When I met his eyes, he smiled at me.

'Baba! Baba.'

'What is it, Tinashe?'

'It is the white man. The one that came to the house that time.'

Baba turned around and saw him. 'It is all right, Tinashe,' he said. 'I have talked to him. It is all right.'

The white man raised a hand in greeting.

'*Mangwanani*, baas,' said Baba.

'*Mangwanani*. Any news?'

'No, baas.'

'We're having a hell of a time finding these boys,' said the white man. 'But we'll get them eventually.'

'Yes, baas.'

'Sorry about before,' said the white policeman. 'You understand. We have to question everybody. Appreciate your cooperation.'

'Anything I can do to help, baas.'

The policeman turned his attention to me. He obviously did not remember me. 'Who's this?'

'My son. Tinashe.'

'Tinashe?' The white man shaped his lips around the words. He gripped my hand unexpectedly – I had never made a handshake before, and did not know what to do. I assumed it was a display of power, so I left my own hand limp and submissive within his.

'Handshake like a wet fish,' said the white man. 'Put some oomph into it. Like this.' He gripped my hand tighter. I heard the little bones in my fingers creaking, and I gave a half-hearted grip back in the hope that it would make him let go. It did.

'You can always judge a man by his handshake,' said the white man. He smiled at me. His eyes were watery in the bright light, and there was moisture on his lips. I found his mouth fascinating. It looked like a wet, red fish hiding in his face.

'Well, cheers.' The man raised a hand in a half-wave. He was done with us, I could see, and anxious to find someone else who would be of more help. Baba winked at me, and smiled as he turned back to his *badza* and the stack of wood.

I had noticed that my sister's breasts had grown, that her smell had become stronger, that she sweated more, and I teased her about those things – but I did not understand where all the sudden male interest in Hazvinei had come from: the teasing, the pulling of her hair, the flipping up of her skirt. She was just

Hazvinei. She did not matter – not in that way – but a few weeks after the white man's visit, Hazvinei pulled me aside.

'Tinashe,' her voice was low and urgent.

'What?'

'Tinashe, come here.'

I came over. I saw she was holding a piece of cloth.

'What's that?'

'Look.' She held it out. It was a pair of her underpants, stained a rusted brown.

'Why are you showing me that? Did you poo your pants?'

'No! It's not poo.'

I looked closer, and sniffed – a rich smell, repellent but also somehow attractive. 'What is it?'

'I don't know. I've found it in my panties every day this week.'

'Is it blood?'

'It looks a bit like blood.' I crouched down next to her, and we both stared at the offending piece of fabric.

'What have you been doing about it?'

'I have been washing them in the river.'

'Oh.'

We sat for a moment.

'Have you talked to Amai?'

'No.'

'Why not?'

'I don't want to.'

'But this could be a . . . woman thing.'

'I don't want to.'

'But why not?' I was exasperated. 'I will bet you that she knows.'

Silence.

'If you don't tell her, I will. You shouldn't be bleeding from your . . . You shouldn't.'

Hazvinei snorted. 'Fine. I'll deal with it on my own.'

Being a woman was a dark and mysterious thing. Boys were straightforward. We had all seen one another's *mboros*, when we were having pissing contests in the swept dust of the yard. Whatever women had underneath their skirts was hidden from us. I had seen Hazvinei in the bath years ago, but I knew that it was not the same any longer. Something different must have grown under there, and it fascinated all of us. The boys in my class took to flipping up girls' skirts in the playground, but all we saw was their knickers. I heard a rumour that Chipo would show her privates for a Coke, but I did not want to ask her in case the rumours were not true.

Hazvinei did talk to Amai, in the end. I knew, because I saw Amai helping her to cut clean cloths into little strips, and I saw them having conversations in low voices. Hazvinei was one of Them now – one of the women.

'I am a *mhandara*,' she said with pride. She walked differently, stood taller.

'What does that mean?'

'It means that I am a woman.'

'You are not a woman.'

'I am!' she slapped me. 'Mai says so. We are going to have a party.'

'A party to celebrate you messing in your pants?'

Another slap on the arm.

'No. But the relatives are coming for a party. Amai told me. And they will see that I am a woman now.'

'Even Babamukuru is coming?' She had impressed me now.

'Yes.' She stuck out her tongue and ran back to the house, pausing only to shout over her shoulder, 'See, Tinashe? You do not know everything after all.'

Amai impressed upon me that I was not to speak of the blood ever, to anyone, as it was taboo, but Little Tendai and I debated the business. Neither of us knew what it meant, really, for Hazvinei to be a *mhandara*; but neither of us wanted to admit it.

'It means that she can get married,' said Tendai.

'She is only twelve years old.'

'I have heard of twelve-year-old girls getting married.'

'Not Hazvinei. Baba would never allow it.'

'Who would want to marry her, anyway? She would bite your *mboro* right off.'

'She does not bite anymore, Tendai.'

'Still.' He shook his hand as if he had burned it. 'She's too much.'

'Too much for you, maybe.'

'No one will pay *ro'ora* for that one. She is not worth even one cow.'

I saw the way Tendai stared at my sister and I knew why he spoke like this.

'Someone will pay a whole herd of cattle for her one day,' I said. 'You wait and see.'

The party was going to be one of our biggest yet, and Babamukuru was coming. Baba had told me so. I begged Amai to cut my hair and to take special care with my smart white shirt so that I looked my very best when my uncle and cousin arrived. When Hazvinei and I saw the silver car winking from the bottom of the hill, we did not know whether to run towards it or run away from it. The other *kopje* kids had no such worries, and ran shrieking to chase the car's dusty wake and wave in the windows. I saw Chipo and Little Tendai down there. Hazvinei called for Baba.

'Baba is at work, Hazvinei.'

She stood on one leg, poised to run.

'Stay here.'

'I want to see Abel.'

'Abel might not even be in the car, Hazvinei.'

'He is.'

'How do you know?'

'I just do.'

The car huffed up the hill. As usual, it wore a skirt of red dust, and the bonnet was splattered with flies. When it halted, Hazvinei ran to the door, but jumped back when Babamukuru stepped out. He wore little round sunglasses clipped to his spectacles, and I could not see his eyes.

'Tinashe. Hazvinei.'

I shook his hand. It felt dry. The passenger door opened with a click and Abel stepped out.

'I am going to talk to your uncle,' Babamukuru said to him. 'You stay here.'

Abel stood next to his suitcase. We looked at him, still paralysed. He was taller, thinner, especially around the face. His hair was cut shorter, barely covering his scalp, and I could see the bald shine of his skin through the whorls of hair. He looked like a man now, with a dark shadow on his upper lip and new strength in his jaw.

'Hello,' I said.

'Hello.' His voice was deeper. In six months, Abel had grown into someone that I did not recognise.

Hazvinei hugged him. This was rare. She did not like to touch or be touched, but she wrapped skinny arms around his back and dug in her nails – half-hug, half-attack.

'So you are staying again,' I said.

'Yes.' He pulled a plastic packet from his pocket. 'I brought sweets.'

The sugar cigarettes we loved. We puffed on them, pretending to be grown-ups, and Abel's suitcase lay forgotten in the dust.

'You have titties, now, Hazvinei,' said Abel, and made a grab for them.

She shrank away. 'No.'

'You do. Like a fat *ambuya*.'

She stuck her tongue out at him.

'Next you will be having babies.'

'Shut up, Abel!'

He laughed and went inside to put his things in the bedroom.

It was a good party. The women brewed sweet *mahewu* from *mielie* meal, and I was allowed to drink some. Amai gave Hazvinei a necklace of bright white beads that she had bought from the store, and they looked like bubbles of river-water against her long, dark neck. Babamukuru talked and laughed with Amai and Baba, his anger seemingly forgotten. As usual, Tete Nyasha had not come and so Babamukuru sat in magisterial state on a stool, surrounded by admiring relatives.

'She looks pretty,' said Abel. He had managed to acquire a whole chicken leg, and was not sharing any with me.

'She looks all right.' I watched Hazvinei laugh.

'She is growing tall,' said Abel. 'Soon she will be taller than you.'

I shoved him – my height was a sore point – and then I looked at the fire, where the men sat. Baba and Babamukuru were talking in low voices, gesturing vigorously.

'What do you think they are talking about?'

'Who knows?' Abel tore off another strip of chicken. 'Politics, probably.'

It was possible. I knew that Babamukuru and Baba did not agree when it came to such things as the *vakomana*. But, from the way Babamukuru kept glancing at us, and at Hazvinei, I was not so sure.

Hazvinei came running to us. 'Abel! Dance with me.'

'I am eating.'

She tugged at his arm. 'You have to dance with me.'

She pulled him to his feet. Abel went, reluctantly, to dance with the others around the fire. Hazvinei was glowing, trium-phant, her feet covered in ash and dirt. I watched them. When Abel returned to his seat, he was breathless and dripping.

'It has been a long time,' I said.

'Yes.'

'Is Babamukuru still angry with you?'

Abel shrugged. 'No. I do not talk about the *vakomana* any more. Babamukuru thinks I am concentrating on school.'

'Are you?'

Abel did not answer me. Instead he stared into the fire for a moment and then said, 'Portuguese rule has ended. In Mozambique.'

'What does that mean?'

'Don't you know anything? Don't you listen to the news?' I pushed him, stung. 'I do. I listen with Baba.'

Abel's teeth flashed in a smile. 'It means that we are next.'

I clutched the bullet in my pocket and felt it smooth and cool against my palm. Excitement rose up in my stomach and I had to run to sluice my head under the water from the pump, so that I would not be sick from nerves. Something was changing and, that night, it felt as if Hazvinei's blood and Abel's deep voice and the news from Mozambique were all part of the same terrible and wonderful thing.

Babamukuru left the next morning, but Abel stayed with us. After the party, Hazvinei's breasts filled out even more; and with them grew the curve of her cheeks and lips, so that even her face changed shape. The aunties took her away from the house to instruct her in different aspects of womanhood. When this happened for the first time, Hazvinei was sleeping in late, and the auntie sent me to fetch her.

'Hazvinei.'

She stirred. Her cheek was creased into lines by the pillow. 'What?'

'Auntie Yevedzo is here to see you.'

She did not seem surprised. She sat up and swung her legs over the edge of the bed. 'Just let me get my shoes.'

'Where are you going?'

She did not answer me, but tied her *dhuku* across her head in silence. Without a head-covering, she looked like a dangerous animal, but as soon as she put on the *dhuku*, she blended in with the other girls. As much as Hazvinei could ever blend in anywhere.

She went to the door, where Auntie Yevedzo was still waiting.

'Yes?' she said. She was so rude. If I had said that, I would have felt the flat of an avenging auntie's hand across my ear. Because Hazvinei said it, Auntie Yevedzo smiled.

'Come.' She beckoned and, to my surprise, Hazvinei followed.

'Hazvinei!' I called after her.

She turned slightly. 'Go back inside, Tinashe.'

'Where are you going?'

She flapped her hand at my words as if they were mosquitoes. 'I won't be long.'

Hazvinei did not tell me what happened in those weekly hours. I tried asking Amai, but all she would say was, 'It is forbidden.' When I asked Baba, he told me not to speak of it at all. I knew that it had something to do with that strange brown blood, with childbirth and with the body parts that Chipo would show for a fizzy drink (the rumours were confirmed), but I had to be content with my ignorance.

When Hazvinei returned from her time with the aunties, she seemed taller somehow, and a strange scent hung about her. She would go straight to the bedroom and lie on the bed, staring at the ceiling until she fell into a sleep so deep that neither Amai's touch nor Baba's voice could raise her.

'Tired out from all her play,' Baba said.

I stood in the doorway of Hazvinei's room and watched her; the gentle rise and fall of her suddenly fuller chest, and the faint smile on her lips. She was a stranger to me now – a mysterious guest in our house whom I did not understand.

Chapter Nine

'Tighter,' said Hazvinei. We sat in the red dust of the yard: Hazvinei with both arms raised above her head; me wrapping one of Amai's old *dhukus* around her chest. We were going down to the river to swim, and she did not want her newly acquired breasts to stick out.

'I can't pull it any tighter.'

'Yes you can.'

'This is as tight as it will go.' I found Hazvinei's breasts both fascinating and repulsive; big mosquito bites with a dark circle in the centre of each. The nipples had little goosebumps around them, like lumpy *sadza*.

'You are like our goat,' I said. 'We will be able to milk you to get milk for our tea.'

'Be quiet, Tinashe.'

'They are horrible,' I said.

'*Mazvita tatenda*. Your thing isn't much better.'

My hand cupped protectively over my *mboro*.

'It looks like a *chongololo*.'

'It does not!'

She stuck out her tongue. 'I have seen it when you are peeing. It wiggles around like a *chongololo*. And it smells.'

'It doesn't smell. How do you know so much about *mboros*, anyway?'

'The *zvidhomo* tell me.' Dwarf spirits – the ones Hazvinei blamed for every missing item in the house. 'They do not have them themselves.'

'Oh really? Then how do they piss?'

'They don't. They don't need to.'

'Everyone needs to piss.'

'Not a *chidhomo*. They collect them from other people. If they come across a *mukomana* wandering in the bush by himself . . . someone like you, Tinashe . . .'

'Yes, you are very funny.'

'Chop chop!' She brought the side of her palm down. 'Like chopping firewood. And they keep it in their pockets.'

'You talk a lot of nonsense, Hazvinei.'

'Don't worry. They only collect big ones. You are safe.'

'Be quiet.'

'Can you go tighter?' Hazvinei stared at her chest.

'No, they are flat. Any tighter and they will never pop out again.'

'Good.' She lowered her arms. 'It is not fair.'

'What?' I got to my feet, brushing the dust off my bottom.

'You don't have to wear a shirt when we go swimming.'

I shrugged. 'That is because I am not a goat with udders.'

Hazvinei kicked me on the shin, hard, and Abel arrived as the fight was starting. He slept in later these days, and spent a long time shaving in the mornings to keep his chin smooth. Secretly, I did not think that he needed to shave quite so often – he did not have that much hair – but he liked to stroke his jaw as the older men did and to tease me about my perfectly smooth face.

'Are you coming to the river?' he said now.

'Yes.' Hazvinei gave me one last bite on the wrist, leaving a jagged bracelet of marks, and ran. She was faster than me, with long, graceful legs, and I knew I could not keep up. She made fun of me when I ran. She called me Rock Rabbit. 'First sign of danger, *pffft*,' she would say, and mimed with her fingers the bounding action of the little rodent as it bounced away.

Abel caught up with her and I trailed behind, feeling the sun hot and angry on the top of my head.

We reached the river. My river. Sleek and vicious as a mongoose. It greeted me with a smile, rolling onto its back and letting the sun catch its smooth pelt. It smelled of dust, of rain, of warmed river stones.

'Eh-eh, Tinashe!' Abel grabbed me by the arm. 'Your sister beat you here.'

I struggled, but he was stronger, and threw me into the brown water. I surfaced, mouth full of bitterness and grit, laughing. There were worse things than being thrown into cool water on a hot day. We had reached that mysterious age when we were not meant to swim together anymore – boys and girls – but we did it when the adults were not around and watching us. This was one of those days. Hazvinei kept the tight cloth tied around her chest.

'Eh-eh, Hazvinei!' Abel shouted, 'You hiding your titties now?'

'Shut up.'

The boys kept teasing her and the loudest one was Abel. He called her all kinds of names, but the one that annoyed her the most was '*mombe*', cow.

'Careful your udders don't squirt milk into the river!' he said.

Hazvinei stuck out her tongue, and dived into the water in one long, fluid movement. I held my nose and ducked beneath the surface into the muddy translucent world below, feeling the relief as the eternal burn of the sun became a dimmer, softer heat. We were careful to swim in the fast-moving parts of the water, to avoid bilharzia and the mosquitoes that skated on the surface. I opened my eyes, just for a second, to get my bearings, and saw Hazvinei. She was cross-legged on the riverbed and her eyes were wide open. I could only keep mine open for a few seconds before the grit and tang of the river water closed them for me. I swallowed a lungful of foul-tasting water and spluttered to the surface.

'Where's Hazvinei?' called one of the older boys. She had not appeared.

'She is fine,' I said. 'She can swim better than any of us.'

I watched the others splashing, the sun turning the churned river into fire. Flies hovered above them, waiting for an inch of skin to emerge from the water. Hazvinei had still not surfaced. Abel was splashing and laughing with the other boys, and did not notice.

I ducked underwater again and struggled to stay down. Deeper, deeper; and then I found her again, still sitting on the bottom, cross-legged, eyes closed. Her mouth moved as if she were talking, and air bubbled out of her lips. When I tugged on her arm she opened her eyes and looked at me with annoyance, but followed me to the surface. I broke through the water gasping and half-sobbing in relief, but she did not even take a deep breath of air.

'What's wrong?' she asked me.

'I thought you had drowned.'

She shrugged me off. 'You worry too much.'

'I do not. I just don't want you to kill yourself. Baba would be angry.'

A snort from Hazvinei.

'What were you doing down there, anyway?'

'I was talking.'

'Talking? Who were you talking to?' I asked. I was afraid, but I smiled so that she would not know I was afraid.

'I was talking to a *njuzu*,' she said.

Amai had told us stories about *njuzu* – spirits with the body of a fish and the head of a beautiful woman. They lived in rivers and pools and pulled down their prey to an underwater prison.

Njuzu knew all kinds of magic, good and bad. They could drown you or teach you great lessons. It was said that the witch doctors learned their wisdom from *njuzus*.

I examined Hazvinei for telltale signs of lying – that little smile that she could not hide.

'They do not exist.'

'Yes, they do.'

'No, they do not, Hazvinei.'

'What are you two doing?' Abel appeared, damp and steaming in the sun. He shook his curly head, spattering Hazvinei with oily water. She pushed him.

'*Iwe*! Get away.'

It took only a few seconds for us to dry. When we first left the river we glistened, slick and wet, but after a few steps the sun had eaten all the water and our skin once more crackled on our bones like paper.

'Don't do that again, Hazvinei,' I said.

She stuck her tongue out at me. 'At least I can hold my breath longer than you. You would have drowned.'

'It is not funny.'

We walked back to the *kopje*. Abel stayed behind with the older boys, but Little Tendai ran to catch up with us, and Hazvinei strode off, leaving us to follow. Little Tendai admired the sway of her slim hips beneath her cotton dress as she walked away.

'Your sister is strange,' he said.

I pushed him. 'No, she is not. You are an idiot.'

He pushed back, and we shoved each other and laughed as we turned the corner into the main road. Simon-from-the-bottle-store leaned out of his door to shout to us. Did we want something? Yes, we did, but we had no empty bottles to exchange for goods. Simon flapped his hand at us. *Voertsek*, then.

'*Maiwe.*' Little Tendai nudged me as we turned on to the school road. 'Whites.'

Three white men – boys, really, only a few years older than we were. They were walking towards the village with quick, firm strides. Clearly they had some business to attend to. Tendai and I looked at one another – it was best, we agreed silently, to stay out of their way.

'*Mangwanani,*' said one of the white boys with a dreadful accent. His hair was cut too short, making his ears look like the wide, dusty wings of a moth.

'*Mangwanani,*' said Little Tendai and I. *Smile, look stupid, be polite but say nothing of importance.* We would be past them soon, and gone. Hazvinei, however, still striding ahead of us, stayed silent.

'Hey,' the boy called after her. 'You. *Mangwanani.*'

Hazvinei turned to stare at him.

He took a step back, still enough of a teenager to feel embarrassed when a pretty girl ignored him. Then he remembered the gun on his back and the cigarettes in his pocket, and rallied. 'What's the matter? You deaf?'

Hazvinei gave a toothy smile, turned, and kept walking. The white boy spat in the ground at his feet, leaving a dark spot in the dust and a bead of saliva trembling on his lower lip.

'You teach your nanny some manners!' he shouted to me.

Smile. Look stupid. Be polite. Those were the rules, and Hazvinei was breaking them. I waited until we were out of sight of the white boys before running to grab Hazvinei by the elbow. 'What is wrong with you?'

She shook me off. 'I don't want to talk to them.'

'You do not have to talk to them. You just have to behave like someone with a brain.'

She stuck out her tongue.

'You are going to get yourself in trouble today,' I said. 'Why are you in such a bad mood?'

'She is strange, I told you,' said Little Tendai.

'Leave me alone.' And she ran, her feet kicking up a cloud of red dust.

'She has been strange all day,' I said. 'All this nonsense about a *njuzu*.'

On the morning of Abel's next visit, I arrived at school to find Farai and Tatenda kicking each other in a circle of chanting boys.

'What is happening?' I asked my friend Moses.

'They are fighting.'

Moses was not very clever.

'Why?'

He shrugged. 'For Hazvinei.' At first I could not see her, but then I spotted the small figure watching with a smile. Although all around her the red dust kicked up by the fight stained clothes and settled in hair and eyes, she was clean and untouched.

'Why are they fighting for Hazvinei?'

'I do not know.'

After seeing the *njuzu* and becoming a woman – or at least, insisting that she had become a woman – Hazvinei had become even bolder than before. She swaggered through the house as if she were a boy. Baba found it amusing; Amai told her off and made her scrub the floors and clean the pots.

'I am grown-up now, Tinashe. You have to respect me.'

I shoved her. 'Be quiet.'

'You have to be nice to me. Otherwise I will tell the *njuzu* about you.'

'Be quiet about this *njuzu*, Hazvinei. People will think you are crazy.'

She stuck out her tongue. 'She tells me things.'

'Who?'

'The *njuzu*.'

'You saw it again?'

'I see her every time I go to the river.'

I shivered her words off my shoulders as a *mombe* shivers off a fly. 'Hazvinei, you must stop talking about this.'

'Why don't you believe me?'

'Because you always say these things. You told me a *chidhomo* ate my peanut butter, when I know it was you.'

'This is different.' Her eyes were bright. 'The *njuzu* told me that I could only see her once I became a *mhandara*. She said they have been waiting for me.'

'Why?'

'The *njuzus* have things to teach me. That is what she said.'

This is one of Hazvinei's stories, I said to myself. I clenched my hands into fists.

'They said that they taught the N'anga too.'

'Hazvinei, go to sleep.'

'I want to talk to him.' She hugged her knees.

'The N'anga?'

'Yes.'

'You must not talk to him. He will think you are crazy.' He will think you are a witch, is what I thought but did not say. I had heard stories about women who ate their own children and wandered naked at night hunting for animals. *Varoyi* – witches. The word was enough to make even Baba shudder. The less Hazvinei said about this, the better.

'I really did see it.'

'Fine.' I rolled over. 'You saw it. Now go to bed.'

I did not hear her go. I leaned my head on my arm and breathed in my skin's sharp scents of river water and soil.

Boys continued to fight for Hazvinei's attention. They pinched and hit one another. They climbed trees in front of her, kicked footballs as far and as hard as they could, swam across the river and stood with their legs apart and their hands on their hips when she was watching. The other girls made tutting noises through their teeth and whispered to one another, but Hazvinei did not care. I told Abel about this as we walked back from the river together in the shade of the evening. Hazvinei, Little Tendai and Chipo were with us as well, trailing behind and kicking at stones.

Abel fell back to pinch Hazvinei's arm. 'What are you doing to these idiots?'

'Leave me alone.'

'You are just a skinny piccannin,' said Abel. 'Why would they fight for you?'

'Shut up, Abel.'

'No, tell me.'

She shrugged. 'There is nothing to tell.' She looked over her shoulder at Little Tendai, who was lagging behind us, watching her walk. Even he seemed to have fallen under her spell these days.

'Nothing to do with the *njuzu*, then?' said Abel.

Hazvinei scowled.

'I was just joking.'

'I want you to stop joking about that,' I said. 'It is not funny. Stop encouraging her.'

A can skidded past us, followed by a gang of boys playing impromptu football. They shouted and pushed each other, fighting for the can, but their eyes were on my sister.

'The *njuzu*?' said Little Tendai, who had overheard.

'Yes.'

Tendai made his crazy-ghost face at me again. 'I told you. There is something wrong with your sister.'

We scuffled in the dirt for a little while, but stopped when Hazvinei spoke.

'The *njuzu* told me to go somewhere,' she said. 'Not that you care.'

'Where?'

'I am not telling.' She strode ahead of us, knowing that we would follow.

'I'm coming,' said Abel.

'All right.'

'I am coming too,' I said, which was not necessary. Everyone knew that where Hazvinei went, I followed. Where Abel went, Little Tendai followed. And Chipo trailed behind all of us. We laughed and talked as we followed my sister. This was a game – it had to be. Hazvinei would lead us in circles and then laugh at us for being so gullible.

Little Tendai's feet made strange footprints in the earth. One foot was bigger than the other, too big for shoes, and Tendai's Amai had made him a little sandal out of the base of one his father's *pata-patas* and a length of string.

'Your foot will keep the *tokoloshes* away,' said Abel, who had somehow become the second-in-charge of this expedition.

A lazy, dry-grass-smelling, heat-heavy evening, with a sleepy whirring and clicking underfoot – crickets, asleep under the earth, who had woken at the vibrations of our footsteps. We collected red mud on our ten still-damp feet, and blackjacks and ticks on our still-damp clothes. Soon the cool water of the river seemed impossibly far away. We had never been cool. We had always been hot and panting, eyes stinging from the salt of sweat. Through the heat haze, Hazvinei looked like a spirit floating above the ground. A spirit in a green and white gingham dress with a white collar. If I stared at her for long enough without blinking, she disappeared in a mess of colours.

'We are back where we started,' said Abel after a while. I woke from my hot, sweaty trance and saw that he was right. We were almost back at the *kopje* – just on the outskirts. We stood on a small rise, among lightning-blackened granite boulders, looking down on our village.

'I'm going back to the river,' said Abel.

'No!' Hazvinei hugged herself, full of her own cleverness. 'Look.'

A hut, separate from the others, with a white-painted stone at the front and a black chicken pecking optimistically at the dust. The witch doctor's hut.

'What are we doing here?' said Chipo.

Hazvinei skipped. 'I am going to go inside.'

Four pairs of eyes stared at her. 'You are crazy,' said Abel, speaking for us all.

'The N'anga will be inside,' said Little Tendai.

'No, he won't.'

'Yes he will. How do you know?'

'The *njuzu* said.'

'Stop talking about the *njuzu*.'

Abel pushed her. 'You are making this up to get us into trouble.'

'No!'

'You wouldn't go inside anyway,' he said. 'You just want to look like you are not scared.'

'I am not scared.'

'Bet you a shilling.'

'Fine.' Hazvinei spat on her hand. Abel shook it. 'I want to see inside. I am going. You can stay here.' Hazvinei lifted her skirt in two hands and stepped down the rocks as carefully as an old goat. We stood watching her. She paused and looked back at us.

'Come!'

'It is too far,' I said. 'We are not allowed to play out here.'

'So?'

'You are just showing off,' I said.

Hazvinei stood with her hand on her hip and one bare foot already outstretched to take the next step. Beautiful; precarious.

'*Usaita semukadzi*,' she said to us. Do not behave like a girl.

Stung, Abel jumped over the rocks to join her, his strong legs having no trouble leaping from one to the other. Little Tendai looked at me, his black eyes completely surrounded by white, and then followed Abel. I looked at Chipo, and she looked at me. I saw her wavering. I started to walk down and, after a moment's hesitation, she followed.

'Why do you think he lives here?' said Abel as we climbed down. 'So close to the rocks?'

We all knew not to climb on the rocks when there was a storm and the lightning licked them with a hot tongue.

'He is the N'anga,' said Little Tendai. 'The lightning would not strike him.'

'So you are the big clever know-everything now?' said Abel.

'He talks to the spirits. The spirits control the lightning. Everyone knows this.'

The shriek of the N'anga's rooster made us jump. It blinked at us with knowing, reptilian eyes.

'Hazvinei, are you sure we should be doing this?'

'Don't you want to see inside?'

Of course we did. We walked softly, softly, to the hut. The rooster glared at us, swivelling its wrinkled neck to watch our movements.

'He will put a curse on us,' said Little Tendai, so quietly that I almost didn't hear him.

The door was shaped like any other hut door – nothing frightening about it. Hazvinei clasped the handle.

'It will be locked,' I said.

It was not locked.

'He will be home,' said Abel.

He was not home.

The door opened into a room like any other room. Except for the shelves. And for what was on the shelves.

'They are dead babies!' said Little Tendai.

Abel clapped him around the ears. 'They are animals.'

Rows of tiny skulls, gleaming toothpaste-white in the gloom.

'Where do you think he gets them?' Abel, fear forgotten, ran his finger along the rows of bones as you run a stick along a fence.

'He finds them?' I ventured. I had an uncomfortable vision of the N'anga throwing live dogs into a pot of boiling water and watching as the flesh and hair melted off their bones. The air smelled of decay.

'There are so many.' Abel stopped. 'And look at these!'

A tinful of teeth. Just an ordinary shoe polish tin, still stinking of black licorice and eucalyptus.

'Are any of them human teeth?' Abel sifted through them, ignoring the chalky, unpleasant sound. He was determined to find a corpse somewhere here, I could tell.

'I have found it,' said Hazvinei. We had forgotten about her in our ghoulish rummagings.

'Found what?'

'His medicine stick.'

The N'anga's medicine stick! The source of his powers, as we thought, and the thing that had caught so many of us around the back of the knees when we got in his way. The stick that pointed out witches and criminals. The stick that talked to the spirits. The stick that had once turned into a snake before the whole *kopje* (or so we had heard from our parents).

'Here.' Hazvinei waved it, struggling a little under its weight.

'Put that down!'

'Why? Are you scared?' She narrowed her eyes and pursed

up her lips in a way that was meant to imitate the N'anga. She shook the stick and made ghostly noises.

'Hazvinei, please stop.'

The gourds on the stick rattled and banged against each other. I smelled that strange, sickly smell again.

'It is just a stick,' said Hazvinei.

'We need to go,' I said. 'We have seen inside. You have won the bet. We need to go home.'

Abel held one of the monkey skulls on his hand, and made its jaw open and shut with a snap. 'Look, Tinashe.'

I looked. And so I did not see what had happened when the scream came from behind me.

'Tendai!'

Hazvinei, standing with the medicine stick in her hand. Little Tendai, on the floor, writhing.

'He is playing,' said Abel. But I knew he was not. I knelt beside him and watched his teeth chatter around his pink tongue.

'Hazvinei, what did you do?'

'I did nothing!' Indignant, drawing herself up to her full height. She crossed her arms against her chest, letting the stick fall. 'I did not do anything.'

Only the creak of the door told me that Abel had left. Running home like a scared lizard darting across the wall! It would have made me laugh if I were not so frightened. Chipo looked at us with wide, black eyes, and then followed Abel. I crouched with my sister on the dusty floor, holding Little Tendai's shuddering shoulders.

'Hazvinei, help me turn him over.'

Tendai's body did not feel like a human body anymore. It was stiff, and jerked as if he had been struck by lightning. His eyes were open, but had rolled back in his head and turned white. He looked like a drunk man.

'What do we do?' said Hazvinei. She stared at Tendai's crazy-man face with more interest than fear.

'We have to take him back to the *kopje*. Pick up that stick. Put it back.'

'What, over the rocks? You are crazy.'

'What else can we do?'

Hazvinei shrugged her slim brown shoulders. 'All right.'

Little Tendai was so heavy in my arms that I wondered if he really had been cursed. Surely no boy could weigh this much? Or perhaps my own arms were weak with fright.

I had a foolish hope that when we left the hut Little Tendai would recover – or, perhaps, that he would stop shaking, smile and say 'Fooled you!' I could feel my laugh bubbling inside me already, waiting for my fear to evaporate in the bright sunlight. But he did not wake up.

When we arrived at the *kopje*, Tendai was not convulsing as wildly.

'Perhaps he is getting better,' said Hazvinei. 'Perhaps we should put him down here and see?'

'No. We should take him home.'

Hazvinei followed us. Soon she was not the only one following us: others spotted us, and saw what we were carrying, and started to exclaim. One of the mangy *kopje* dogs sniffed at Little Tendai's head. I felt the burn of tears behind my eyes, and held them back so strongly that my head began to ache.

'What has happened here?'

'Is that Little Tendai?'

'Where is his father?'

'What happened?'

Simon-from-the-bottle-store came out to see the commotion, as he always did.

'Simon,' I said, 'we were playing, and Tendai fell over and started to shake. I can't find his father.'

Simon loved nothing better than a Situation. 'I will take him to the clinic!' he said. 'You. Go and find the father of Tendai. You, fetch water.'

Other adults scurried to obey.

'Where is your sister?' Simon asked me.

I turned. Hazvinei was no longer behind me. I had not seen her go.

'She has gone home,' I said, hoping it was true.

I ran to our house. It took me ten minutes. The sun hardly moved and my shadow was still a noon-time puddle under my feet.

'Hazvinei!'

Nothing inside but the cool of the shade and the smell of floor polish. A lizard on the wall raised its head to blink at me with flat eyes. I stood outside, feeling the sun's accusing stare on my head. I looked down. And saw the footprints in the dust.

Baba would feed me to the night-time leopards.

I followed the footprints, cursing Hazvinei in my head, feeling my eyeballs grow hot and full with tears and my bladder grow hot and full with nervous urine. They led into the bush. I should have guessed that Hazvinei would go into the bush.

You did not go into the bush by yourself. The youngest child in the *kopje* knew this. When you were older, yes, when you were tall and had knowledge and a weapon, then you could venture into the bush on your own. But Hazvinei was not tall. She was not wise. Snakes; animals with teeth and claws. We all knew about the spirits that whispered to you and led you astray when you wandered too far. They opened up paths for you, paths that looked like they had been made by human feet, and then closed them when you wanted to turn back. They led you on with distant voices and little lights.

'Hazvinei!' My voice was tearful now, shamefully so. A man did not cry.

I found her. She sat – not as a woman should sit, with her

legs flat in front of her, but cross-legged, as a man sits. She
stared in front of her, tears running down her cheeks as if her
eyes were melting in the sun. She did not hear me. I touched
her skin, expecting it to burn, but it was cold.

'I am sorry,' she said in a colourless voice.

'Hazvinei, come.' I pulled at her arm. 'We have to go home.'

She did not look at me. She yielded to my tugging, but
could not stand alone. I lifted her. Her head lolled on my
shoulder.

'I will take you home,' I said.

It took me a long time. She walked heavily, and I had to support
her. When I arrived, Baba was home. He stood on the *stoep* beside
Abel, who had dark petals of worry beneath each eye.

'Chipo is telling everyone,' he managed to whisper to me.
'Everyone will know.'

Baba did not speak. He took Hazvinei from my arms and
carried her to the bed that he and Amai shared. She had stopped
crying, but she was silent and grey.

'Baba. I am sorry.'

He drew the blanket over her — the wool one that itched.

'Baba?'

'Tinashe. What has happened?' Baba did not turn his eyes
from my sister.

'I do not know, Baba.'

Silence.

'I talked to Simon. He said you kids were playing in the
bush and something happened to Tendai.'

'He got sick.'

He held my gaze and sighed. 'We will talk in the morning.'

I swallowed. 'Yes, Baba.'

The only person in the village with his own car was Simon-
from-the-bottle-store, who needed it to pick up crates for the

shop. Baba wrote a note to Babamukuru saying that Hazvinei and I were unwell and that he did not want Abel to become infected, and he asked Simon to pick up Abel that night and drive him into town. Abel and I sat on the *stoep*, waiting for him.

Abel was silent and frowning, looking even more like a grown man in the dim light.

'You ran away,' I said.

'I know. I was frightened.'

'Of the N'anga?'

'Of Hazvinei.'

I touched his shoulder, awkwardly. 'Little Tendai will be all right.'

'We do not even know what is wrong with him.'

'He is just sick.'

'No, he is not,' said Abel. I could not look at him. 'You saw what happened, Tinashe, when she touched the medicine stick.'

'Don't be stupid.'

'She spoke to a *njuzu*.'

'No, she didn't.' I pressed my palms against my cheeks, holding in the words that wanted to spill out.

'She is like Nehanda,' said Abel.

'Abel, stop saying these things. They are not true.'

He stared at me. 'Why are you afraid?'

'I am not.'

We heard the sound of a car engine. Abel stood, hefting his suitcase. 'You know I am right, Tinashe.'

I did not wait to see him leave. I went inside to sit at my sister's bedside and watch her breathe. When the headlights swept through the window and across the wall, she stirred, but did not wake.

Chapter Ten

Women were dangerous. Everyone knew that. It was as much a fact as the wetness of water, or the heat of the sun. I remembered this when I woke the next morning and faced my sister across the breakfast table. Abel's place was empty. I wondered what he was thinking, back in his comfortable house in town and far away from the witch doctor's magic.

'*Marara sei?*' asked Hazvinei, knowing that I had not slept well at all. She too had violet smears of fatigue beneath each eye, but ate her food with a great appetite. I wanted to ask her what had happened at the witch doctor's hut – what she remembered – but I dared not with Amai there.

'Have you heard about Little Tendai?' Amai sliced bricks of white bread and spread them with margarine.

I felt my shoulders grow stiff. He was dead. I knew he was dead. 'No.'

'He is better today,' said Amai. She lifted the lid of the pot to watch the milk and water boiling for our tea. 'It is so strange that he would be taken ill so suddenly.'

My bread was dry on my tongue. 'Yes, it is very strange.'

'It must have been frightening,' said Amai. 'I am not surprised that you were upset. Perhaps you will think twice about wandering into the bush now, eh? Who knows – perhaps Tendai was bitten by a snake.'

Hazvinei ate her bread daintily while I shivered. I was not safe yet. The N'anga would know. He would know what we had done. It was only a matter of time before he cursed us as

the *muroyi* had cursed Little Tendai's twisted foot. I saw the
N'anga's dark-clotted eye rolling up at me from my breakfast,
and I could not eat.

'Are you well, Tinashe?'

'Yes, Amai.'

She rested a hand on my head. I felt dank, nervous sweat
start on my forehead.

'I do not want you getting sick too,' she said. She poured
me a bigger cup of tea than usual, as everyone knew that tea
was good for warding off sickness. I drank it slowly, feeling
the sharpness of the leaves on my tongue, and watching Hazvinei
drink her own with no signs of concern at all.

After breakfast, we went to the river. I said that we wanted
to cool down, but really I wanted to talk to Hazvinei alone.

'Go gently,' said Amai, smoothing Hazvinei's hair. 'The fresh
air is good for you, but you must not tire yourself.'

I waited until we were a safe distance from the house before
I spoke. 'Hazvinei, what happened at the N'anga's hut?'

'What?'

'You know what I am talking about. You had the medicine
stick . . .'

She kicked at a stone. 'Nothing happened.'

'Hazvinei. I know it was you. What did you do?'

'He will be fine.'

'What will the N'anga say? He will know. He will know
that we went to his hut and touched his things. What are we
going to do? What are we going to tell him? What if Little
Tendai does not get better?'

Hazvinei blinked as my questions buzzed around her head
like flies. 'He is getting better,' she said. 'Amai said.'

'Hazvinei!'

'Tinashe! I don't remember what happened. I don't know.'

'How can you not remember?'

'I do not remember anything,' she said. 'I do not know why Tendai is sick.'

'What will the N'anga do?'

'Who cares? He is an old man with a stick and a handful of dirty old bones. Little Tendai will be fine,' said Hazvinei. She dragged a long switch of grass behind her, leaving a narrow, snakelike trail in the dust.

I said nothing more. We did not speak of it again that day – I tried, but Baba and Amai smiled and patted me on the head and told me that everything was fine and Tendai would be well soon. Of course he would be better. Of course Abel would come back. Everything was fine. They seemed to have decided that Tendai's illness was one of those mysteries that would never be solved. He had always been unfortunate, they said. Just look at his twisted foot! We had been playing; Tendai had fallen ill. That was all.

Little Tendai did not come to school anymore – he continued to have fits that left him covered in bruises. He did not play with us, and he no longer followed us down to the river. We saw him sometimes as we walked to school, his nose pressed against the kitchen window. He did not wave, and we did not acknowledge him either.

'He has always been sickly,' said the adults, shaking their heads. The adults nodded to each other, saying that you could catch all sorts of things if you wandered about the bush by yourself in your bare feet. They told the small children about Tendai in order to scare them. 'You see what will happen if you do not listen to me?'

Babamukuru telephoned to check on our fictional illness. Even though Baba told him that we were well again, however, he did not want to let Abel come and visit until he was sure it would be safe.

'You say that other boy is sick? Tatenda?'

'Tendai.'

'Tendai. He is still sick?'

'Yes, but not with the same illness.'

'But they became sick together.'

'It was a coincidence. Nothing more.'

'Still. Abel has exams coming up. He has to be careful.'

I missed Abel. There was no one else I could talk to. I did not see Little Tendai anymore, and Chipo was avoiding me. I could not blame her. When I closed my eyes, I saw the shadow of the medicine stick, a dark vein of fear on the red of my eyelids.

Although our visit to the witch doctor's hut remained a secret, things were still not right in the *kopje*. Once more there were rumours of a leopard outside the village, as children had found pawprints in the dust, and Simon-from-the-bottle-store swore that he had seen a pile of droppings (although they vanished before anyone else could confirm his story). Men were troubled by strange dreams and awoke tired and pale. Women reported that the milk from the cows was sour as soon as it left the teat. The N'anga wandered the village with his rattling gourds and the children shrank from his footsteps. I watched him from a safe distance. When his bad eye looked in my direction I turned away, imagining that he would stop in the middle of the road, point one trembling finger and say, 'You! You are the one who caused all this trouble! You and that *muroyi* sister of yours!'

But he did not see me. And I kept my knowledge to myself.

Worst of all the misfortunes, the rainy season came, but no rain. The *mielie* plants died in the ground, falling with their leaves spread in front of them like yellow hands. The waterhole became a puddle surrounded by earth; the mud around the edges cracked like dry lips, with little swirls of white scum.

We let our chores slide. I went out to the chicken run with

my bucket of feed and scattered a handful on the ground, but the chickens barely moved. They sat in the one small patch of shade, huddled together with dusty feathers. I left that one handful and carried the bucket back to the house. It was heavy and burning hot from the sun.

Hazvinei became even more irritable than usual. There was not enough water for her to have her own tub for washing, and so we had to share.

'I will get all your germs.'

'You have all my germs anyway.'

She pushed me. 'I get it first.'

'But I have to get ready for school!'

Hazvinei ducked her whole head under, which Amai always told us not to do, and looked up at me with mocking eyes through the stream of bubbles that floated up from her nose.

After another week, however, even Hazvinei had run out of energy. Two of our chickens died, and the goat was sick. There just was not enough water to go around. One of the little boys in the *kopje* drank from a stagnant puddle out of desperation, and died of dysentery that bled his insides out of his mouth and his bottom.

Thirst swelled my tongue. The pump was almost dry.

'Only use what you have to,' said Baba.

I tried digging for water. When I reached the part of the ground that was wet, I dug further, but the water retreated from me and hid lower and lower down so that I could never reach it. It was teasing me. In the end I picked up a handful of the mud and put it in my mouth, sucking it to get the moisture. It tasted of salt and metal.

The plants were dry and exhausted. People wilted. When I tried to remember the feeling of water falling on my head, that sharp mineral smell and the craters the raindrops made in the dust, I felt as if I were telling myself a story, repeating something

Amai had told me long ago. Soon, even the sky looked dry and dusty. People stopped saying 'the rains will come soon' and started to say, 'the rains are not coming'.

When the rains do not come, the witch doctor is called.

'We are cursed,' said Hazvinei.

'Don't talk nonsense.' I ate my dinner and tried to ignore her. If we were indeed cursed, I knew why. The N'anga knew what we had done. He was punishing us. He would tell the whole village.

'It is what people are saying,' said Amai. 'They are saying that there is a curse on the *kopje*, and that is why there is no rain. The N'anga is going to talk to the spirits for us.'

'When?' asked Hazvinei. She had stopped eating, waiting for Amai's response.

'Tomorrow,' said Amai.

I felt sick. Hazvinei glowed for the rest of the evening with a sort of strange nervous energy.

'I have never seen the witch doctor talk to the spirits before,' she said. 'I want to see how he does it. How he calls the rain.'

'You are staying here,' said Baba. Amai poured him a second cup of tea.

'Why?' Hazvinei glared at him. 'I want to go and watch.'

'Because I told you so.'

'But why?'

'Hazvinei!'

'But Baba . . .'

Baba put down his tea with a clang. His face was closed. 'Stop arguing with me. I am your father and you must listen to me. You are not going. It is not a safe place for you and Tinashe.'

'But . . .'

'Hazvinei, we are not going to speak any more about this.'

Hazvinei closed her lips tightly. She did not speak to Baba again during dinner, but I knew that the matter was not decided.

I woke with dry crumbs of sleep edging my eyelids and fear in my belly. Today was the day. The sun was high in the sky already, even though it had barely risen, and the dew seemed to smoke and vanish in the hot air. When Amai pushed my morning bowl of cereal in front of me, it looked like the cracked earth outside.

'Tinashe, will you get me some water from the river?' said Amai after breakfast. Baba had already left, and it was just the three of us sitting at the small kitchen table.

'I will go too,' said Hazvinei.

'No.'

'Why not?'

'I need you to help me with some things at home. You must stay here and do your chores, Hazvinei.'

'Why? Where are you going?'

'I am visiting *Sisi* Taradzai.' Amai pushed back her chair and tied her *dhuku* around her head. 'This dry weather is making her sick. Be good while I am out, *vana*.'

'I don't want to do chores,' Hazvinei glowered.

'I will stay with you,' I said. 'And I will go to the bottle store and get us Cokes.'

'That is a good idea.' Amai fished in her pocket for a coin. 'Here. And stay away from the N'anga, remember.'

Hazvinei shrugged, still sulking. 'Fine.'

I stood and took the coin from Amai, happy to have a job to distract me from the day's events. 'I will be back very soon, Hazvinei. Wait for me.'

'I am not going to run away, Tinashe.' She folded her arms.

I ran down to the bottle store. There had been a big party in the shebeen the night before: lots of empty bottles to hand in for coins. I picked them up as I went, and Simon-from-the-bottle-store took them from me, whistling through the gap in his front teeth, and counted out my money.

'What are you going to do with it, eh? Buy beer?' he laughed.

'Could I have two bottles of Coke, please?'

'Two bottles? One for you and one for your girlfriend, yes?' Simon-from-the-bottle-store went to the Coke fridge, which had once been red and was now a dusty pink, and opened it. It smelled of stale ice. A fly that had been knocking its head against the glass was released, and came to buzz around my head instead.

'One for me and one for my sister,' I said.

'Eh-eh, you are keeping that little *chongololo* in your pants, then.' He handed me the misted bottles, which were already starting to sweat.

I used the handle of the fridge door to open my bottle. A fine, sweet spray dampened my hand, and the bottle cap clattered on the floor.

'Take it back to your sister before it gets warm,' said Simon.

I took my time walking home. It was too hot to hurry. I watched the air shimmer and break, turning to water in the heat and making the landscape waver and ripple. The ground shone red and was hot under my feet. There is nothing better than sucking on a cool Coke bottle, slippery with condensation, on a day so hot that your hair is melting to your head. I did not see the white men until I was almost upon them.

'*Iwe*, piccannin!' One of them pushed me. 'Watch where you're going.'

'Sorry, sir.' I stumbled. My Coke, already precarious in my sweaty grip, slipped from my hand and spilled onto the ground like oil. The white men laughed. There were several of them, I saw now, sprawled in the dust and playing cards. No wonder I had not seen them – the browns and greens of their uniforms disappeared into the long grasses, and even their slumped khaki bags looked like dusty boulders. The men smelled of sour milk and unwashed clothes.

What were they doing here? They were waiting for something, I could see, and with this many supplies they could have settled in for a long stay. I was aware of the guilty weight of the bullet that I still carried in my pocket.

'Got a spare?' said one of the men. I realised that I was still holding Hazvinei's bottle of Coke, still sealed and cold.

'Yes, sir.'

'Don't suppose you feel like donating it to the cause?'

They laughed. I stood, clutching the neck of the bottle and feeling my heart thump in the hollow of my throat.

'Leave him alone,' said one of the men, younger than the others.

'What about it, hey?' said the first man.

'He wants your Coke, boy,' said another. I blinked and handed over the bottle. Sorry, Hazvinei, I thought. I will have to find another way to distract you from the witch doctor.

One of the men rested a hand on my shoulder – a friendly hand, but I could feel its strength. He had a gold wedding ring on his finger; hot from the sun, it burned my skin. I wondered where his wife was. In town, probably, in a big house with green lawns and water from the taps, far away from this wind-eaten, fire-scarred red land.

'I hear there are shenanigans today,' he said.

I did not know what shenanigans were, but I could guess. 'Sir?'

'You have not seen anything?'

I kept my eyes very wide and my face very stupid. The white man stared at me.

'You have heard nothing?' he said.

'Sir.' Neither yes nor no.

'Bloody primitive business.'

'Sir.'

He let me go. 'The boy's an idiot,' he said, and 'Run along home.'

I kept walking, looking down at my shoes. The empty Coke bottle winked in the sun. When I kicked it, it made a hollow clonk, then rolled away in an arc. There was still enough of the black liquid in the bottle to leave a little trail of drops that evaporated almost as soon as they hit the dust. I wanted to get away from them. The heat was oppressive now, pressing down on me. The witch doctor, the drought, the laughter of the white men – these things clustered around me and darkened my vision. I could feel bad fortune building like the storm clouds we so desperately wanted. I swerved off my usual path and into the bush, where I would be hidden. I pressed in deeper, wanting to get as far away as possible.

Soon I could no longer hear the white men's voices, but I heard something else: a crisp rasp, like a snake moving through grass. I turned around slowly, hoping not to startle it – or hoping that it was something that I could run from. Instead, I saw a pair of human eyes looking at me. A man, fewer than six feet away from me, leaning up against a tree trunk. A *mukomana*. Chenjerai, was my first thought, but it was not Chenjerai. He was still and silent, and his skin blended into the grey bark behind him.

'*Maiwe!*' I jumped back.

The man slumped. There was a rifle on his lap, and he tried to close boneless, grasping hands on it. A *mukomana*. Who else would be out here in the bush with nothing but a gun?

'Who are you? What are you doing here?' My voice sounded too loud. I heard that rasping sound again, and saw the muscles in the man's throat convulse. His tongue was indecently red inside his slack mouth.

'Who are you?' Was he pretending? Would he pick up his

rifle and blow my brains out, here in the hot, cicada-humming bush?

We stared at each other. I felt my muscles relax. A fly landed on the man's lip, and he did not twitch or brush it away. I moved forward, curious now.

'What is wrong?'

The rasping sound I had heard was his breath. He looked like one of the drunks outside the shebeen, but he also looked sick. If I had to picture a ghost I would have pictured this grey, sagging man with his dead eyes and foam around his mouth.

'What can I do?' I said.

The man's hand twitched.

'I will get help,' I said.

The fly that had been buzzing around his lip landed on his eyeball. He did not blink. I could hear a buzzing in my ears as I backed away. Special Branch Poison. We had all heard about it. The stories said that white men poisoned objects that the *vakomana* used – radios, blue jeans – and it killed whatever it touched. I had half-thought the stories were not true; just made up to frighten children like me. But here was a dying man in the quiet of the bush.

We have very specific beliefs about the dead: their bodies and their bones. I have already told you what happens to us after we die, how the *mweya* and the *nyama* go their separate ways. But what happens to the meat left behind? We like to be buried in a particular way, so that we can begin our afterlife in the traditional way, undisturbed; not poisoned and propped up against trees, left to die in the bush, or to be eaten by animals.

I ran. I left him. I left him there. I ran until I had a stitch in my side and my vision shone white and speckled. I did not notice that I was falling until my chin hit the ground. I vomited a sweet, sticky mass into the dust and stood hunched, my hands on my knees, watching the ants swarm over my vomit. It was nearly all gone when I straightened up.

Hazvinei. I had forgotten Hazvinei. I had forgotten the N'anga and the spirits and the drought. My stomach heaved again, but there was nothing to come up. I ran until the saliva in my mouth was sticky and I had to clasp a hand to my side to hold in my breath.

'Hazvinei!'

No one was home. The house was cool, quiet, filled with the tiny thoughts of spiders. No Hazvinei. I ran again, slipping on the polished *stoep*. I felt my shirt soak and cling to my armpits.

I knew where she would be. I followed the sound of the crowd, and arrived to see the circle of waiting people. I stood on tiptoe, trying to see. I caught a glimpse of a pink gingham dress, the rebellious curve of a cheek.

'*Iwe!*'

'*Pamusoroi, pamusoroi,*' I apologised as I pushed my way through. When I finally reached the front, my ear was even more bruised from all the clips and slaps from angry adults.

'Tinashe?' Hazvinei turned, as if she had been expecting me.

'Hazvinei, what are you doing?'

'I am watching the N'anga.'

'You know Baba said . . .'

'Baba said, Baba said.' She shrugged one shoulder.

'Hazvinei, I will get into trouble. Baba told me . . .'

'He will never know. We'll leave before it's over. It will be fine.'

'The N'anga will know that we went to his hut. The spirits will tell him.'

Hazvinei looked at me with contempt. 'Don't be stupid, Tinashe.'

Was my panic for nothing? I swallowed my frantic breath and stood still. 'Has it started yet?'

'No.'

The N'anga stood in the clearing, licking his lips and sucking his teeth as old men do. The witch-smellers came out now, holding pots full of sweet, thick beer. I had seen the old women brewing this stuff before, stirring and stirring it in great *shambakonzi* pots outside their huts. If a fly was seduced by the sweetness and fell in, so much the better. The brew helped you to communicate with the spirits – or just made everyone drunk, according to Abel.

The N'anga drank first, then the musicians. When they had smacked their lips free of the sticky stuff, the old women let the crowd take it in their hundred hands. Hazvinei managed to grab the pot as it was going past.

'Quick.' She took a swig and passed it to me. I lifted it to my lips, not wanting to look like a coward. I only intended to wet my closed mouth with it, but Hazvinei slid her hand under the base of the pot and tipped it up, so that my mouth filled and I swallowed involuntarily. It was sickly; thick as honey.

'Hazvinei!' But it was I who received a sharp clip on the ear from the adult standing next to me, who pulled the pot out of my hands. Hazvinei grinned.

The men who played the drums and *mbiras* sat in the dust with their instruments, settling them between their knees. The drummers brushed the dust off the tightly drawn goat-skins and touched them softly, as if stroking a cheek, and they began.

It was not music. It was a heartbeat – a dark red pattern. The shuffling and whispers of the crowd died down, and people started to sway and hum. I saw others in the crowd begin to dance with strange, jerky movements, their heads thrown back and their throats exposed, and when I looked down at my feet for a second time, I saw that they were dancing too.

The witch doctor entered the trance state. His eyes rolled

back in his head; he spasmed and shook. His teeth rattled in his skull.

'The spirits are possessing him,' said someone in a whisper.

His spasms stopped, and he closed his eyes. When he opened them, I drew in a breath. They were completely white, with no sign of a pupil.

Hazvinei pinched me.

'Stop that!'

'Then stop looking like a frog waiting for a fly.'

'His eyes are gone!'

'He's just moved them back. Like this.' Hazvinei rolled her eyeballs back in her head, and poked out her tongue.

The dance became a painting and my feet became paint-brushes, stamping and stirring up the red earth, the yellow bush, the blue sky. My own eyes rolled in my head. Something hot and sweet spread from my feet up my legs to my stomach and heart and finally my head, filling me with a kind of terrible joy. I felt as if I could shout and sing, or stab someone to see the spurt of blood, or kiss someone right there in front of my sister and be proud of the singing life in my *mboro* and in my veins. I stopped being Tinashe and became everyone. I only returned to myself when the witch doctor started to speak. I craned my neck to hear what he was saying, but then noticed that Hazvinei still had the whites of her eyes showing.

I nudged her. 'Hazvinei. It is not funny.'

She did not move. Her mouth hung slack and open. I was in no mood for her games.

'Hazvinei.' This time I pinched her, hard, and she fell over. The N'anga stopped talking. The people near us moved back, and I felt the attention of a hundred pairs of eyes.

'Mai! Baba!'

I called for them, but I heard no response. Hazvinei arched her back and took a great, rasping breath. Her throat became long and taut, and the air she drew in through her mouth seemed to whistle as it passed down the narrow passage to her lungs. She looked like she was sucking in something more than air. The veins in her neck stood out, angry and purple.

No one was paying any attention to the N'anga now, and he shrugged off his spirit possession as easily as he shrugged off his feather cloak.

'*Iwe!*' he walked to Hazvinei, his eyebrows drawn together in a frown. 'Stop that, *musikana.*'

He moved to touch her, but jerked his hand back and shook it as if she had burned him. '*Maiwe!*'

Hazvinei fell to the ground and started convulsing. Each convulsion drew her higher, arching her back until she was bent like an angry snake.

Someone screamed. Then the excited babbling started, as everyone pointed and stared.

Hazvinei's convulsions stopped. Silence from the crowd. She sat up.

'She is fine,' I said. 'She fell.'

Hazvinei and I were on our own now, in the centre of a circle of open mouths. I tried to touch her, but her skin burned like metal in the sun.

'Hazvinei. Hazvinei, get up.'

She looked at me with empty eyes, and a string of meaningless sounds came from her mouth. Her teeth were white and pointed, inhuman.

Amai was pushing her way through the crowd behind me. I could hear her voice. '*Pamusoroi, pamusoroi.*' The crowd was so tightly knit and intent that she had to elbow her way through.

Hazvinei's voice – or rather, the voice coming out of Hazvinei – spoke louder and more urgently now, stringing nonsense syllables together into a long, liquid babble. She turned her head this way and that, staring at the crowd with blank eyes. Whenever her gaze fell on someone, that person backed away.

'Mai! Come quickly!'

Hazvinei's legs tucked themselves under her body and raised her. She looked like the wooden toys they sold in the market.

'*Muroyi*,' the whispers ran.

I ran to the crowd and wrestled the pot of sweet beer from the man holding it. I swung it towards Hazvinei. The beer splashed in Hazvinei's face and she fell, clasping her hands to her eyes. As she fell I saw a shadow leave her, something white and malignant that paled her face and darkened her eyes as it departed. She hit the ground. Her knee started to bleed. And then she looked up.

She stared around at all of us, her head dripping with beer. A baby started to cry.

Amai made her way through the crowd at last, and dropped to Hazvinei's side, cradling her in her arms as if she were still a baby. Baba followed, pushing past me, and stood over them both.

'Baba,' I said, but he did not look at me. He picked up Hazvinei's body and held her as he had held her when she was born, letting her long legs dangle. He carried her through the crowd, while Amai and I trotted behind him, avoiding the eyes of our friends and neighbours. I did not look behind me, but in the redness behind my closed eyes I saw the shape of the N'anga, and I knew that he was watching us go.

That night, the rain came. It was angry, drumming its fingers on our tin roof and shouting through the cracks in our doors and windows. I heard it calling to us, tempting us to come outside. When we did not answer, it threw itself against the walls in anger.

Hazvinei slept like a dead person that night, and heard not a thing. In the morning we saw that the rain had turned the ground to red, bloody sludge, and it had flattened our *mielie* plants.

Chapter Eleven

When Hazvinei woke, she was pale and dazed. Amai and Baba did not speak. They helped her to dress as if she were a baby again.

'We are taking her to the N'anga,' said Baba. 'He will tell us what to do.'

'But, Baba . . .'

'You be quiet, Tinashe,' he said. 'If you had looked after your sister as I had told you to, this would not have happened.'

I felt the shameful heat of tears.

We walked to the N'anga's hut. Hazvinei did not speak; instead, she walked with her head down and her mouth closed. I wanted to talk to her, but Baba did not let us have a moment alone.

'Hazvinei!' I whispered. She did not turn her head.

'Hazvinei, do not tell the N'anga . . .'

'What are you saying, Tinashe?' Baba looked at me.

'Nothing, Baba.'

We passed many people on the way to the N'anga's hut, and, as each person was one that we knew, we had to stop and exchange a few words with them for fear of offending.

'Mai!'

'Be patient, Tinashe.'

We reached the outskirts of the village. All the other houses had a tidy, swept yard in front, and the floors gleamed with red polish, but the N'anga's yard was choked with weeds and thorns, and his shack was filthy. There was no reason for him to have an untidy yard; many women in the *kopje* would be happy to sweep it for him. He just preferred it that way. The same black cockerel was pecking at the edges of a rain puddle, and swivelled one yellow eye to look at me. I avoided his gaze, afraid that he would give me away. I would not have been surprised if the cockerel had opened its beak and spoken like a man.

'Baba.'

'It is all right, Tinashe,' he said.

'*Go-go-goi!*' Amai knocked on the door-frame.

A muffled voice from inside.

'He is coming,' said Amai.

I needed the toilet badly.

The witch doctor came out to greet us, standing so close that I could smell his sweaty, raw-onion smell and hear the dull rattle and clink of the bones in his necklace. He was skinny, hung with grass and gourds and necklaces and bracelets. A greenish film covered one eye, and a dark clot floated in the middle of the other. He leaned his old face down to mine and grinned at me. I did not look at him. I felt that he could pluck my knowledge directly from my eyes, like a bird cracking open a snail shell to get at the meat inside.

'That girl. *Pfoo.*' A disapproving outward breath, half a whistle.

'Yes, N'anga.'

'And you want me to look at her?' He spread his wrinkled palms. 'Why?'

'Please, N'anga.'

'Why would I help this one after what she has done? You saw what happened yesterday. You are lucky that the spirits listened to me and brought the rains despite your daughter's behaviour.'

'She has not been well,' said Baba. 'She is not speaking. Like Little Tendai.'

'That one.' The witch doctor clicked his tongue.

'Is he better?' said Amai.

'I have given him *muti*. He will be better.'

'And you will do the same for Hazvinei?'

He shrugged.

'We also want to know her future,' said Baba. 'We are worried about her, after all of this. We want to make sure that she will be safe.'

'It is a girl. What is the use of knowing her future?'

'We have money.' Amai brought out her handkerchief. It made a clinking noise.

'It will need to be more if I am to ask the spirits about a girl,' said the N'anga. 'They will not like it.'

Amai fished in her pocket. Another clink. The N'anga closed his palm.

'Bring her in.'

'Wait outside, Tinashe,' said Baba and followed the N'anga inside. Amai stopped to touch my cheek, then took Hazvinei in too. I stayed in the mud, watching the water-patterns the heat made above the road, and shooing away the flies that landed on my leg.

Amai and Baba stayed in there for a long time. I could hear voices, but they were too muffled for me to understand. Once I heard Hazvinei wail, a high, pure sound, like the cry of a bird.

An auntie passed me. 'What are you doing by the N'anga's hut, Tinashe?' I could see the greed in her smile as she scented gossip. 'I am sure your Amai would not like you to be there.'

'Amai is inside.'

'Eh-eh?' A considering glance at the shack, and at me. 'With Hazvinei?'

'Yes, Auntie.'

'It is terrible, what happened yesterday. Is she sick?'

I stayed silent.

She stared at me for a few minutes, then turned away. 'I hope for good fortune.'

'Thank you, Auntie.'

I watched her big, round bottom waddle down the road.

The shadows changed shape. The round patch of sun on my head moved from one side to the other. My tongue dried out and I wanted water. There was a tap outside the witch doctor's shack, but I did not dare drink from it in case Amai came out.

But would she see me? Surely there would be time for me to have a drink and come back to my spot on the ground. Surely Amai would not be angry. In fact, she would probably be angrier if she came out and saw me dried to a crisp, like an earthworm toasted on the tarmac. 'Why didn't you get yourself a drink, Tinashe?' she would say. 'Why didn't you use your brain?'

I got to my feet with difficulty, feeling the blood itch and tingle as it returned to my legs. The tap was right next to the N'anga's hut, by a window. I would have to stay down and not let my head pop up when I drank, in case Baba saw me. I watched one of my hands climb the tap like a little brown spider. Up, up, and it was there. The metal burned my palm, leaving a thin, transparent layer of skin on the handle. A screech as the tap turned, and then the cool, blessed ribbon of brown water, straight onto my parched teeth and tongue. I drank, and felt my stomach balloon up and out, and my skin go from wrinkly-dry-old-man skin to soft Tinashe skin again. I lay on my back in the sun, feeling fat and satisfied.

'Throw them again,' said a voice in my ear. Baba's voice! I sat up so quickly that I banged my head on the pipe. The voice was inside, however, drifting out to me on a breeze. That breeze must have been looking to cause trouble.

'I have thrown them again. They say the same thing,' said the N'anga.

'You will not tell!'

'I must.'

'N'anga, please . . .' and the sound of Amai's cupped hands clapping. Hazvinei wailed, and Baba raised his voice again. I wished for ear-lids as well as eye-lids, to close out these sounds.

When I reached my spot again I sat cross-legged and listened to my heart boom and slosh in my chest. I could not hear words now, just the angry voices that rose and fell. I wrapped my arms around my head, so that I could not hear, and sat like that even when the sun started to melt my skin into sweat that ran down from my elbows into my ears.

Amai and Hazvinei emerged from the hut.

'Mai!' I stood on shaky legs. She did not look at me.

'Where is Baba?'

'He is inside talking to the N'anga. We must go home and get dinner ready for him, yes, Tinashe?'

'Yes, Amai,' I said. 'What did the N'anga say? About Hazvinei?'

'He said that she is a good girl,' said Amai, 'and that we must look after her.'

'But . . .' I could not say what I had heard.

Amai took my hand. 'Let us go home.'

Baba came back late at night, smelling of salt and beer. Amai had already given Hazvinei and me our dinners, and Hazvinei slept, but I could not. I wanted to see Baba.

'*Manheru*.' Baba looked tired. Amai poured him a cup of tea and we sat in silence. Baba's eyes were red at the edges, and his hand shook when he lifted the enamel cup. I sat still, breathing only shallow gulps of the smoky air, as if I could take up less space that way.

'Is everything all right, Baba?'

'Yes, Tinashe.'

'What did the N'anga say?'

'It is time for bed, Tinashe.'

Still I hovered. 'Did he say anything about me?'

'About you?' Baba looked as if he were going to say no, but changed his mind. 'Yes, Tinashe. He did have something to say to you.'

I swallowed, and felt my *mboro* shrink in my trousers.

'He told me to tell you that you must look after your sister, Tinashe.'

I almost wet myself in relief.

'He said, make sure that Tinashe takes care of Hazvinei. Make sure he watches over her.' Baba put his hand on my shoulder. 'And I want that too, Tinashe. You must take care of your sister.'

'Yes, Baba.'

'You must stay with her always and make sure that she does not get into trouble.'

'Yes, Baba.'

'You promise me?'

'Yes, Baba.'

'Say it.'

'I promise.'

'Good.' He released me. 'And one more thing, Tinashe.'

'Yes, Baba?'

'You are not to go to the N'anga's hut, or talk to him ever again. He is not a good man for you to know. Yes?'

'Yes, Baba.'

'You will remember these things?'

How could I not remember? If I have any sort of talent, it is a talent for remembering. I remember things that everyone else forgets. I suppose, in my own way, I am cursed.

'Good. Good night, Tinashe. Sleep well.'

The N'anga came to visit us in the morning. Baba answered the door. He showed no surprise, as if he had expected this.

'Tinashe, wait outside.'

I sat on the *stoep* and watched a swarm of red ants dissect and carry away a dead bird. Only the feet remained when the N'anga emerged from the house. I shrank back to give him room to pass, but instead he stooped and breathed a foul stink of air into my face.

'Your sister has brought misfortune to your family,' he said, 'As I said she would.'

'What do you mean?' I tried to turn my face away. I felt the heat of his laugh on my cheek.

'Ask your Baba.' And then he was gone.

Chapter Twelve

I did not have to wait long.

Baba and Amai kept Hazvinei indoors, but that did not stop the whispering. Baba barely spoke to me. No one came to our house. No one greeted us when we passed them in the street. Even the aunties crossed the road to avoid us, and Simon-from-the-bottle-store would not pay me for the empty bottles I brought him. The N'anga did not visit us again, but we saw him speaking to groups of people in the *kopje*. They glanced at our house and shook their heads.

I dreamed of old women in red and black masks.

Babamukuru telephoned to see if Hazvinei was better, and if it was safe for Abel to visit. Baba told him that Hazvinei was still unwell. When he had finished talking, Baba left the kitchen without even glancing at me and went straight to Hazvinei's bedroom.

Have you noticed how bad fortune comes to you like an eagle out of the blue sky, grasping you in its claws before you can squeak or run? When you look back, when the danger has passed, you see that there were signs. Flies buzzing above the water. The smell of blocked drains. Amai held her nose when we walked to the store, and we made jokes about it being caused by the old men who stood outside the shebeen.

'It is because of that girl,' the villagers said. 'She interfered with the spirits, and now they are punishing us.'

Cholera came to the *kopje*. It covered us in a swamp of

illness, infested with rumours and lies, and it felt as if the whole village were haunted. Our family slept all in one bed again, for the first time in many years, as if we could keep one another safe by staying close. Baba, Amai, Tinashe and Hazvinei, crammed together in the hot and sweaty room. Our heads were so close together on the pillow that I imagined I could hear everyone's thoughts, and I could not sleep with all the racket. The wind growled and snarled outside. I heard it scratching at the windows and doors. The white men vanished like curling smoke, scared off by the disease.

We stayed inside for a week. Hazvinei and I were not allowed to go to school. Instead, we spent our time fighting and pinching each other indoors.

When the week ended, we thought we had escaped. We thought that all those hours Amai had spent praying on her knees had saved us from the plague. She pleaded with God for hours and hours, her hands clasped so tightly that her brown skin turned white at the joints, as if she believed that the tighter she gripped her hands together, the more effective her prayers would be. Even Baba got down on the floor next to her and prayed, although he kept his eyes open. I knew that keeping your eyes open meant *Mwari* would not hear you. Amai had told me. But I said nothing.

'It is the *njuzu*,' said Hazvinei one night.

'What?'

'The *njuzu*. The one I talked to.'

'Hazvinei, this is no time for your ghost stories.'

She stared at me. 'The *njuzu* told me that this sickness would come. She told me I would fall sick. But she told me that I would recover.'

'Did she say anything about the rest of us?' I asked. I kept a smile on my face so that Hazvinei would think I was joking, that I did not really believe her. But I did.

'No,' said Hazvinei. She turned the smooth curve of her face away from me. 'She did not mention you.'

Hazvinei was the first of us to fall sick. When we woke up one morning, she did not. Towards noon, she voided her bowels and moaned. I knew she was humiliated, which was a comfort – as people got sicker and sicker with the cholera, they became too ill to remember what embarrassment was. Hazvinei still knew. That meant she was not dying – not yet. Amai stripped the sheets from the bed to wash them.

'We need to move her,' she said.

Hazvinei moaned. She had still not opened her eyes. She drew her knees right up to her chest.

'Do not be afraid,' said Amai.

Together we lifted Hazvinei off the bed. She felt light and bony in my arms, like a vervet monkey instead of a human girl. Her ankles and feet were naked and vulnerable. I held her while Amai put the new sheets on the bed, and then we rolled Hazvinei onto it. Her body went rigid, and the air filled with the swampy, sick smell of diarrhoea.

'Go and get some rags,' Amai told me, and I went outside to rip up old cloths, soak them in the bucket and bring them back in.

Amai pulled Hazvinei's nightdress up and wiped her buttocks gently. The diarrhoea was watery, thin and pale, soaking through the cloth as soon as it touched it. It looked like goat's milk, or the water in which Amai rinsed the rice. When Amai had finished, she held Hazvinei as if she were still a baby, rocking her gently through her convulsions, while I brought her rag after rag soaked in cold water.

Hazvinei was no longer just herself, but an object, a totem. The neighbourhood kids crept up to our house to peer in at her through the windows. When I yelled at them, they ran away in terror and excitement. Hazvinei had become one of the ghosts in her own stories; a tale told at night to frighten local children.

The cholera spread quickly, after Hazvinei; or because of Hazvinei, if you listened to the rumours. At first we heard the names of those who had been infected, but soon there was no one on the streets to tell tales and name names.

I sat by Hazvinei's bed, feeling a white worm of guilt writhe in my gut. I felt like dead meat, rotten and seeping, worth nothing. I helped Amai change the sheets and dribble water into Hazvinei's mouth. Baba came in every morning before work – he could not afford to stop working – but he did not speak to me. He bent over Hazvinei, touched her damp forehead, and then left the room. I knew that he thought this was all my fault for letting Hazvinei go to the N'anga's ceremony.

'He is angry, Tinashe,' Amai whispered to me. 'But he loves you. It will be all right.' She handed me another bucket to empty.

I stopped going to school. I spent all my time by Hazvinei's side, memorising her face until I could tell by the smallest bead of sweat whether she needed fresh water or clean sheets. I made sure that Baba saw me sitting there, and on the third day, he relented.

'Good boy, Tinashe,' he said when he saw me emptying Hazvinei's bucket outside.

Because we spent all our time watching Hazvinei's yellow, old-woman face, we did not see Baba getting sick. I do not think that even Baba noticed, until he collapsed. Two of his friends brought him home, pale and crusted with vomit. When Amai saw him, she started to wail. She did not stop until he was on his bed, and then she became a nurse again and comforted and crooned over him while she fetched water and buckets. I felt the spirits closing in around the house. They were the black fur at the edge of my vision; the dank, musty scent that closed my throat and reached fat fingers down my nostrils, stifling my breath; the laughter in the night. I felt them coming, walking on two feet like men, a silent, waiting army surrounding us, waiting to be fed. I could not hold them back. I was not strong enough. Perhaps Hazvinei would have been able to, but she was sick too and could not help me.

I did not let Amai or Baba see the spirits, though. I helped Amai nurse Baba and Hazvinei, and I did the chores. The thin, watery smiles from Baba would keep the leopards at bay for a while at least.

Baba was more worried about Hazvinei than about himself, of course. 'I am a warrior, Tinashe,' he said through cracked lips. 'I will be fine.'

Hazvinei did not even know that Baba was sick. Amai and I ran around all day with water and clean cloths, and she lay with her head to the wall. We could not tell her; there was nothing she could do. After two more days of this, my father looked like an old man. He was shrunken and dry, wrinkled on the bed. He smelled of bad diarrhoea, a smell worse than the manure on the fields or the smell of the Blair toilet at school. The blanket was stained with something that looked like tea – brown and watery.

The day my father died was a bright, fragrant day, the ground damp and steaming. The rains had come in earnest at last, and drenched us every evening.

'Tinashe.' He hooked one of his fingers at me. 'Come.'

Amai watched me as I walked to him. Her eyes were so tired that the whites had become yellows. She looked ugly, and I felt guilty for thinking that she looked ugly when she was so sad and everything was so terrible.

'Baba.' I rested my head on his chest. His breath was a seed rattling in a gourd. I heard the creak and click of his ribs.

'Take care of your sister.' I thought he had said this, but I realised that it was only in my head. Baba had said nothing more, and could not.

'Go now, Tinashe,' said Amai. I looked back at the bed and, as I watched, a fly that had been buzzing around the room landed on Baba's eyeball, right on the milky surface. Baba did not blink, or move.

'Tinashe. Go,' said Amai. I went outside and sat on the *stoep* to watch a line of ants form around a discarded mango pip. After a few moments I heard wailing from inside, and I felt a stream of noise that smelled and tasted like vomit rise up my throat and out of my mouth.

We did not tell Hazvinei. Amai could not, I think. She did not even touch Baba's body after he had died.

Hazvinei raged and fought against the cholera, silently. She hardly moved. She stared at the ceiling with her teeth clenched and went somewhere else in her head.

Amai became an old woman in those few days. She grew thin. Her cheeks lost their shine. She spent most of her time at Hazvinei's bedside, holding a soaked cloth to her forehead or dripping water into her mouth. We had been told to feed the sick water with sugar in it. I seemed to spend all day stirring clumps of our stale, sticky sugar into water. There were always a few crumbs that refused to separate and sank to the bottom. When I wasn't making sugar-water, I was opening all the windows that I could and scrubbing everything, even the walls, to get the smell of sickness out of them – a cloying, green smell, like avocados rotting on the ground. It clung to everything, even to my own hair and skin. I liked to do this. I liked to work. It stopped me from remembering.

Hazvinei stirred. She opened her eyes. She stared up at the ceiling, bleakly, as if she were disappointed to have woken up in such a world. The room seemed shabbier – the patches of mould on the walls that Amai could not get out, even with the strongest bleach, seemed to have spread.

'Hazvinei,' I said.

She rolled her head on the pillow until it faced me.

'Hazvinei,' I said. I felt sad to tell her this news, but I also felt a strange thrill. Bearing bad news makes you very powerful. All you need to do is to force air up through your lungs to your mouth and teeth and shape a few words, and you change the world.

'Baba is dead,' I told her.

No tears. She looked at me for several minutes without words. I did not speak either; just twisted my hands in my lap.

Hazvinei turned her head away from me on the pillow, and I left the room. She slept for another week, and when she was not asleep she was glaring at the ceiling, with her teeth grinding together and her jaw jutting out.

I did not want to believe that Amai was sick too, even when I saw the signs. I could see that her face was waxy, and had gone from the deep shine of a macadamia nut to the colour of the brown scum that floated on the surface of the waterhole. I could see that she was tired, and thinner. But I said nothing. Amai could not be sick. Baba could not be dead. None of this could be real.

It was when I was changing Hazvinei's blankets that I knew. I heard a noise, and stepped outside to find Amai kneeling on the polished step, a puddle of vomit on the ground in front of her.

'Mai!'

'I am fine, Tinashe.' She was too tired to put any enthusiasm into her lie, but she did smile and rest a hand on my shoulder. 'Check on Hazvinei, yes? I'm going to lie down.'

I sat by Hazvinei. She was in one of her strange waking states, with her eyes open and dry.

'Amai is sick,' I said.

She said nothing. She did not even move.

'Say something.'

She rolled her eyes towards me, but her lips did not move.

'Say something!'

Hazvinei stared at me for a moment, and then looked away again. We sat there for hours. I watched my shadow move on the wall, and I pressed a hand against it, as if I could stop time moving. As the sun set, the shadow grew paler, until it was white under my black hand. Outside, the leopards laughed.

Amai grew worse. I brought her fresh water as often as I could, running with the bucket from the bottom of the *kopje* all the way to the top. If the disease were a leopard, I could have wrestled with it, tried to kill it, even if it consumed me too. But all I could do here was carry the water bucket up and down, up and down the *kopje*, and wipe the foreheads of my two family members with a damp cloth to take away the worst of the sweats, and clean up the diarrhoea that soaked into the sheets and into the floor. After a few days I did not even notice the smell.

'I should write to the aunties,' I said. 'We should send someone to get them.'

'No, it will be fine,' said Amai, and smiled.

'How is your father?' she would ask sometimes, when she had forgotten. I did not know whether to tell the truth or lie, so I did not answer, even when she became more insistent. She always remembered on her own, anyway – after a while.

I did not know what to do with Baba's body. It lay on his bed for three days, until it started to smell and flies started buzzing around it like tiny vultures. When the house smelled of rotting food, I knew I had to put Baba somewhere. I went to one of our neighbours.

'Please help me,' I said. 'Baba is dead.'

The man shrank against his doorframe. 'The cholera?'

'Yes, and I do not know what to do with his body.'

'Ask your mother,' said the man, and was about to go back inside when I said, 'She is sick too. And my sister.'

'What has your family done, to be punished this way?' he asked, but I saw the knowledge in his eyes.

'We have done nothing.'

'I cannot help you,' he said.

'Please. I just want to know what to do with my father.'

'I'm sorry,' he said, and closed the door.

It was up to me to grasp Baba under the armpits and feel the slither of his dead skin under my hands as I dragged him off the bed. I could not let my mind look at what I was doing. I felt that if I looked into his face, saw the drying fluid in his nostrils, his congealing eyes, the indecent life of his still-growing hair, I would go mad. I pretended Baba was a chicken meant for the pot, one that I could carry by its scrawny legs without feeling.

I did not know what to do with him – it – once we were outside. There was no one to help me. I dragged the body as far away from the hut as I could, making sure that it was well out of Amai's sight, and carried armful after armful of straw from the chicken run to cover it. I kept going until I could see no skin. I did not tell Amai what I had done.

On the day she died, Amai was imbued with magical strength. She got out of bed and scrubbed me until I shone. She pulled a comb through my tangled pelt of hair, ignoring my yelps and holding me firm until they subsided. She often held me in that death-grip; usually when I had done something wrong and was in for a smack.

She knew she was dying, and she wanted to leave everything clean. She swept the red dust in the yard, leaning on the broom after every few steps, and polished the tiles on the floor. Then it was my turn. She had not scrubbed me clean like this since I was a little boy. Even though I was now taller than her by a head, she could still pin me under her arm and go to work on me. When she finally released me I was more red than black.

She made me put on the suit I wore for church on Sundays. I sat in my uncomfortable suit in the stifling heat; sat by her bed as she struggled for breath. The air was as thick and damp as a lick from a dog's tongue. I felt my own breath move in time with hers. It was a strange night, spent sitting in funeral clothes while the spirits prowled around our house. I could hear a difference in the night sounds: there were the usual distant barking of dogs, cries of night birds and creaks and snaps of small animals in the bushes, but there were also heavier footsteps, and great, slow breaths that circled us and our tiny haven of electric light, waiting for my mother to join them. At about three in the morning, she succumbed to the disease with a mad rattle of breath and a great sighing that spread like ripples in water over the *kopje*.

When she had finally gone, the world was rinsed clean, and the air felt cold and pin-sharp. I carried Amai's body outside, as I had carried Baba's, and covered it with straw from the chicken house in the same way. I lined them up, side by side. There were flies around Baba now. Their senseless buzzing was comforting in a way. The tiny, relentless noise said no, you will never be able to understand. There is death, it said, and then there are the flies and the dust and the hyenas, and there is no reason for it.

I went into my sister's room once again. 'Hazvinei,' I said.

She moved her lips, but no sound came out. She licked them with a dry, white tongue and tried again. 'Tinashe.'

'Amai and Baba are dead,' I said. It was a relief to say it; to not be the only person in the world to know.

Hazvinei turned her face away. I did not see her cry.

I sat in my sweaty Sunday suit, which I had not taken off

since Amai died, watching Hazvinei breathe. When I could bear it no longer, I went outside to sit on the *stoep*.

Little Tendai was sitting in the dirt road, making patterns in the dust with a stick. I could see the knobs of his spine through his dusty skin. I could see the hole in his red shorts, the rubber peeling away from his *takkies*. Only his face was different: swollen and purple, the eyes bulging unnaturally. He had not spoken to us since his fits began, and I knew that he was angry. He had kept our secret, yes, lest he get into trouble as well, but he was angry.

'My parents are dead,' I said to him, feeling the words with my tongue, testing the taste of them, as if they were a new and unfamiliar sweet from the corner shop.

'You will have to go to the Salisbury Children's Home,' said Little Tendai.

'No we won't,' I said. 'We are going to go to Babamukuru, or one of the aunties.'

'They won't want you,' said Little Tendai. 'You're carrying cholera.'

'We are not!'

'Your sister is.'

'She's better.'

'She's carrying cholera. And she's mad.'

'She is not mad.'

'She talks to people who are not there. She brings curses on us.'

'She does not!' I picked up a stone to throw at him, but missed.

'You'll see,' said Little Tendai, wagging his finger at me. 'You are cursed, your family. And it is because of your sister.'

He stood up and walked back to his house, trailing his stick behind him. His mother was sick too, I knew, and I hoped that she would die.

I did not go back to the house straight away. I walked through the bush, towards the N'anga's hut. I knew he did not like our family, and that he would be angry with me, but he was the only person who could explain what had happened, and why. He could help me. He could tell me what to do with Amai and Baba's bodies, those straw-covered shapes in the yard, and he could tell me what to do with Hazvinei.

The buzzing of the flies became louder as I pushed through the harsh yellow grasses. I started to see flies before my eyes, as well. They had followed me from home, from where they hovered over Baba's dead and hardening eyes, and now they danced, little black specks in front of my face. The heat haze seemed to make a throbbing, pulsing noise – high-pitched, like the half-heard, half-felt song of crickets. I burst out of the bush. For a moment I did not know where I was, and then I recognised the black chickens. I had reached the N'anga's hut. His rooster extended a scrawny neck and cocked his head to one side, examining me with a red eye.

'I am just passing,' I said.

The rooster scratched at the dust. I felt like a fool for talking to a bird. Then I saw what the chickens were staring at, and I stopped.

The N'anga lay face-down in the dust. The ground around him was wet – from his bowels? Or was it blood? I looked at it without emotion. Caring for others is a luxury, I had discovered. I had only enough energy for my own family.

I stepped up to his hut cautiously. I half-expected a ghost to loom out of the doorway – after all, if anyone was going to come back and haunt the living, it would be the N'anga. His hut was disappointing, though. It had been neatly swept, and smelled of nothing more mysterious than urine. His bundle of bones and herbs sat in the corner, guarded by his medicine stick. No one had touched it. I carried the bundle and the medicine stick out of the N'anga's house. I did not know if he had family who would come to clear out his belongings, or whether the villagers would pick him apart and carry him off as ants carry off a dead bird. I knew that I should not touch these things; that they were nothing to do with me. And yet I carried them into the bush and lit a fire.

I unwrapped the bundle. It smelled like an old man. There were a few jam jars filled with powders, and some herbs, and a few old, bleached bones. That was all. They smelt mildewed and sad. I unscrewed the tops of the jars and dropped the powders into the fire. I expected the flame to change colour, or some kind of explosion, but there was nothing. I thought of the old man crouching outside his hut, pounding up his potions in his old pestle and mortar, and I felt sorry for him.

I threw the medicine stick in last. The flames licked it, curling their fingers around the smooth ebony, but it would not burn. After watching it for a while, I stamped out the fire and let the stick rest where it was. Someone would find it, or not. It did not matter.

'Hazvinei.'

She lay where I had left her. Nothing had changed. The pale shadows stretched and splayed across the walls.

'I am back,' I said, and my voice echoed in the empty house.

That night I lay awake, waiting to be haunted by the N'anga. I expected some kind of visitation; a *ngozi*, returned from the world of the dead to avenge the destruction of its beloved property. But there was nothing. The world was cool and still, the only noises crickets and the distant laughter of hyenas.

I do not know why I was the only one in my family to escape the cholera. I am not so conceited as to think that I was protected, somehow. I think it was Hazvinei who was protected; kept alive, for whatever purpose. If anything, I believe that I was too small and insignificant for the spirits to notice.

Chapter Thirteen

All our relatives came to the funeral, except for the two that were most important: Babamukūru and Tete Nyasha. They sent flowers from their garden instead – flame lilies, birds-of-paradise and bougainvillea. Our own garden had been given over to vegetables – practical, edible plants – and I could not imagine growing these bright and slippery blooms. Babamukuru sent a note as well, on a card with a bowl of flowers on the front and a message inside: 'Sorry to hear of your loss.' He had signed his name underneath: flourishing and swirly and confident, the signature of a powerful man.

On the back of the card he had written, 'Will come to pick you up next week.' And that was all.

The family whispered about Babamukuru's absence – perhaps he was afraid of the infection, they said, or perhaps he had not been allowed to leave his work. I did not know what to tell them.

Hazvinei and I stayed with the same neighbour who had refused to help me with Baba's body. The village could not leave two orphaned children alone, even if it suspected that those two children were bad luck for the entire *kopje*, and so this man had been told to look after us. Perhaps he also felt guilty – I do not know. I do not remember much about those days. Grief was a sickness worse than the cholera. It ate our days and our nights, leaving only crumbs of memory that I still cannot quite piece together.

'Your uncle is coming to get you,' said our neighbour. He

had telephoned Babamukuru once the risk of infection in the *kopje* was past, and I could see in his face that he was glad to be rid of us, the remnants of that cursed family that had produced the *muroyi*.

On the day that Babamukuru was to arrive, Hazvinei sat with her arms wrapped around her knees and said nothing. I smiled and said a few words to our neighbour, to be polite. When he moved away, I touched Hazvinei on the shoulder and she jerked away from me.

'Hazvinei.'

Nothing. She glared straight ahead.

'It will not be so bad, living with Babamukuru.'

Nothing.

'You will see Abel again.'

A fly landed on her arm, and she did not bother to shake it off. I wondered why my voice kept talking on and on, telling these big lies.

Amai and Baba were in the ground now. I had seen them lowered into the two fresh-dug holes, their faces covered demurely with cloths and their graves coloured with the petals of Babamukuru's flowers. I had watched as the hollow reed was inserted into the crumbling red soil of both graves, and I remembered what Baba had told me.

'They will look after us,' I said to Hazvinei, who stood silent within the curve of my arm. 'Amai and Baba. They are ancestors now.'

Hazvinei said nothing. She was thin and grey from the cholera, her teeth too big for her face, and her breath stank of sweetness. I wanted to stay – to wait for the white worms of soul to crawl from my parents' graves. I wanted to know that they were not entirely gone. But there was no time for this. We were leaving. We were to live with Babamukuru in town.

I remembered how excited I would have been to visit Babamukuru, before all this.

We heard the hoot of a car horn.

'Here he is,' said the neighbour. He sat on the other side of the yard, reluctant to come too close in case he caught our bad luck.

I stood and grasped our bag – an old canvas one that belonged to a friend of Amai's. Our family had never owned a suitcase, because we had never travelled anywhere.

Hazvinei stayed seated.

'Come on,' I said.

She looked up at me, but did not move.

'Fine.' I went and stood by the side of the road. I looked over my shoulder and saw my sister's spindly, unhappy shape, bent over as she stared at her bare feet.

She has caused all this, I heard myself think. This is her fault.

No. It was mine. *Look after your sister, Tinashe.* I had not done a good job.

Babamukuru emerged from his silver car. He wore a grey church suit, suitable for the solemnity of the occasion, dusty on the trouser-legs, and carried a black hat in his hand. We looked past him, trying to see through the glare of the windows, but the car was empty. No Abel.

'*Mangwanani,*' said Babamukuru. He looked us up and down. I studied his face for resemblance to Baba, and I found it in the wide flare of his nostrils and the way his eyebrows grew uneven towards their outer edges.

'*Mangwanani,*' I said. Hazvinei said nothing.

'Well,' he said, 'We are all very sorry about your father and mother.'

Silence. From me, a polite, grieving silence. From Hazvinei, a rude, staring silence.

'I am sorry that we could not come to the funeral,' said Babamukuru. 'It was impossible for me to change my plans.'

We said nothing.

'You are thin,' said Babamukuru. He did not say 'and dirty', but I could see his distaste. Truthfully, we had forgotten to wash in the days following Amai and Baba's funeral. It did not seem important.

'Where is Abel?' said Hazvinei.

Babamukuru did not answer her. 'Your Tete Nyasha is looking forward to seeing you both,' he said instead.

I muttered something that I hoped would satisfy him.

'Come here.' He grasped my shoulder and embraced me. I felt the rough, male scratch of his beard, smelled his aftershave and sweat. I felt a shameful bulge of tears in my throat, and swallowed it, as a *mombe* swallows her ball of grass, saving it for later.

'Hazvinei.' Babamukuru held out his arms to her. She did not move. 'Come.'

I stood safe within the circle of Babamukuru's arm, watching. Hazvinei moved forward, reluctantly, allowing herself to be embraced – and then stepped back.

Babamukuru took off his little rimless glasses and wiped them with a handkerchief from his suit pocket. 'Yes, yes, it is very sad,' he said. 'Now, you must help me load up the car.'

He strode into the house. I followed. Hazvinei stayed where she was, staring at nothing.

Babamukuru whistled through his teeth as he sorted through the kitchen cupboards, stacking pots and plates. 'There are cardboard boxes in the car, Tinashe,' he said, giving me the keys. 'Get some for me.'

The keys were cold and unfamiliar in my hand. I went to the car and put them in the lock. The little knob by the window popped up with a sound like a gunshot, but when I tugged at the door handle, it came off in my hand.

'Ee-ee,' said Hazvinei from behind me, shaking her hand as if she had burned it on a hot stove. 'You're going to be in trouble.'

'Be quiet, Hazvinei.' I tried to put it back.

'What is Babamukuru going to say?'

'Be quiet, I said.' I held the handle and stared at the car, as if I could fix it with sheer willpower.

'What the hell are you doing?' Babamukuru had come up behind me. He snatched the handle from my hand.

'I am sorry, Baba . . .' I began, and stopped when the grief rose up in my stomach. Babamukuru's eggplant cheeks went a deeper purple, and his eyes bulged behind his glasses.

'Sssst.' He blew air out between his front teeth. 'This is not a good start, Tinashe.'

I helped Babamukuru to remove the boxes in silence, then followed him indoors and helped him to pack. Our cutlery and plates, our bedding – that which had not been burned to cleanse it of the cholera. There was also a photograph of all four of us in a plastic frame that Amai had bought from Simon's shop. I did not see my own reflection very often, as we had no mirrors, and I remembered how often I had taken the photograph frame down to look at my face.

'Here, let me keep that,' said Babamukuru. He took the frame from my hand and tucked it into his coat pocket. 'I'll look after it, hey?' He touched my hair. His hand was heavy, with too-long nails that scratched my forehead.

'Yes, Babamukuru.' I watched as he stowed the photograph in the box, piling Baba's clothes on top of it. His work overalls. His smart church clothes that smelled of mothballs. Bile rose in my stomach, and I thrust my hand into my pocket to clutch the bullet that Chenjerai had given me. It sat cool and round in my palm, protecting me from the bad fortune that still hovered in the air of the house like a cloud of *tsetse* flies.

Hazvinei did not help us at all, but sat on the back step, picking at her toes.

'Is that all?' said Babamukuru when we had finished.

'Yes, Babamukuru.'

'You are both free of the infection?'

'Yes, Babamukuru.'

He sighed and took a last look. 'Eh-eh, what has happened here?' he said. 'What has happened here?'

We did not answer, and he did not seem to require an answer.

The car smelled of hot plastic when we climbed into it.

'Boys ride in the front. All set? Put on your seat belts.' Babamukuru showed me how to pull the uncomfortable length of material across my chest. The buckle was almost too hot to touch, and I left a layer of fingerprint on the metal.

'Is there anyone you want to say goodbye to? Your friends?'

I thought of Chipo. Little Tendai. 'No, Babamukuru.'

'Good.' He started the car. 'Let us go.'

The people of the *kopje* watched from their doorways and windows as Babamukuru's car trundled down the dirt road. I could feel their relief. I saw them smile. One or two waved. Simon-from-the-bottle-store did not wave, but watched us, unsmiling, as we passed his shop.

Babamukuru shuddered as the smell of stagnant water and sickness floated to us from the *kopje*. He rolled up the car window. 'Soon we will be out of this place,' he said.

We passed the N'anga's hut. His black chickens still pecked at the dirt outside, and the open door of the hut was a wide mouth opened in a silent laugh.

'Babamukuru, what is that?' A dark stain on the air behind the car, coiling like smoke, following us.

'It is just the exhaust, Tinashe.'

I knew better. We had not left our bad fortune behind. It

followed us, a black, stinking cloud, as we drove away from the *kopje* and onto the plains. The air became heavy and fat with heat, pressing down on my head and stuffing my lungs with cotton wool. Tears rose in my throat, and soon it was hard to breathe.

'Can I open the window again, Babamukuru?' I asked.

'No,' he said.

I could feel Hazvinei behind me, shifting in her seat.

'I told your father,' said Babamukuru. 'I told him that nothing but bad fortune would come to him because of his actions.'

It seemed as if Babamukuru were talking to himself, but then he turned his head and fixed me with a blank gaze from his round, rimless eyes.

'Babamukuru?'

'And now I have two more children.' He smiled. I did not know whether to smile back. 'You will be good children for me, yes? Tinashe? Hazvinei?'

'Yes, Babamukuru.'

Hazvinei said nothing, but Babamukuru seemed satisfied that I had spoken for us both.

'Good,' he said. 'It is different, in town. It is not the easy life you have had in the country. You will have to get used to behaving like well-brought-up children. No more running around in the bush.'

I remembered him telling Abel that life in the country was much harder than the easy life in town, but I said nothing.

We passed over a bridge, and I saw the brown glint of water far below. My beloved river. I knew that it flowed through the city as well, but it would be different there; different as Abel and I were different. Hazvinei would not talk to the *njuzu* again. I would not be barefoot, swimming Tinashe again. And so when sleep rose like water over my head, I welcomed it.

When I woke up, I saw that we had already driven through

the town centre and were passing houses with high, white walls and green lawns outside. Grass as I knew it was yellow or brown, and I was not used to this wet, green lushness.

'It is a nice neighbourhood, where we live,' said Babamukuru. 'It is the best neighbourhood.'

Hazvinei rolled her eyes at me. I refused to look at her.

'Here we are,' said Babamukuru.

We pulled up to an iron gate. Beyond it I could see a low bungalow, bigger than any house I had seen before, edged with bright flowerbeds. So this was where Abel lived. I looked at the white walls, the many windows. I pictured him growing up here, reading his schoolbooks and eating his meals. Abel had lived with us for weeks at a time. Babamukuru had visited us. Even Tete Nyasha had visited us, sometimes; but this was the first time I had seen the famed house with the legendary inside toilet. Perhaps this was why the house looked unfriendly to me, with its blank windows and burglar bars imprisoning the front door.

Babamukuru stopped the car, leaving the engine running. 'Open the gate, Tinashe.'

I moved with care, trying not to disturb my stomach.

'Chop chop.'

I felt rusty metal under my hands, and heard the creak of hinges.

'Open them wide. Wider. You don't want to scratch my car, do you?'

I breathed one last gulp of the fresh air, and then climbed back into the hot car. We rolled and rattled over the gravel. When we came to a stop, Babamukuru helped me to lift out our bag, and Hazvinei looked at me over his bent head to make a face with crossed eyes and tongue sticking out.

'Come along, *vana*. And don't walk on the grass,' said Babamukuru.

The grass was green with fat blades. We passed a tap. Babamukuru stopped, stooped and twisted it on. Snakes of water rose out of the lawn, writhing and nodding their heads in the air. I stepped back.

'What's the matter?' said Babamukuru. 'Have you not seen sprinklers before?'

I shook my head. No.

'These people from the country,' chuckled Babamukuru, shaking his head. He seemed pleased.

'The spirits don't like this place,' Hazvinei whispered to me as we followed. I elbowed her.

'Hazvinei, stop trying to scare me.'

'I'm not.'

'You are.'

'I'm not. It is not right to trap water like this to make one garden green.'

'Be quiet, Hazvinei.' If we were going to have to live here until we were grown up, I did not want Tete Nyasha and Babamukuru seeing Hazvinei's strangeness too soon. Or at all, if I could help it.

'This is your home now,' said Babamukuru. 'It is a very nice house. You will be happy here.'

I thought of the red dust in our yard, the scrawny chickens, the cool red concrete of the *stoep*. 'Yes, Babamukuru.'

I wondered if Hazvinei and I would have our own rooms, separate from Tete and Babamukuru. I would probably share a room with Abel, I knew, but I liked to picture my own quiet, empty space – perhaps with a desk for my studying. I imagined Babamukuru patting my head and giving me pocket money, perhaps letting me play football on the big green lawn. I imagined cold drinks in proper glasses with ice from a shining refrigerator. Hazvinei kicked at the ground, raising a cloud of red dust.

'Hazvinei, don't do that. You will dirty your nice white socks.'

The front door opened, and Tete Nyasha emerged, arms outstretched, fingers groping the air. '*Vana!* You have arrived.'

Hazvinei took a step back, but I was not quick enough. My nose was pressed into a fat arm and the breath was squeezed out of my body.

Tete Nyasha had that look of a mother – round cheeks, round body, a smile, combed hair under her *dhuku*. She even smelled like a mother, of strong soap and floor polish. The hug from her cotton, freshly-ironed body gave me a pain in my stomach, because it was not a hug from Amai.

'We have not seen you in a long time, Tete,' I said politely.

She waved her hand vaguely. 'We have all been very busy. It is very good to see you again, Tinashe. And Hazvinei.'

Hazvinei shrank back from our aunt's embrace. 'What happened to your face, Tete?' she said.

I had not noticed. Trust Hazvinei's sharp eyes to see the dim purple swellings at Tete Nyasha's ear!

Tete touched them with a wavering hand, and smiled. 'It is nothing. You will be good children, hey?' she said.

'Yes, Tete.'

She put a hand on my shoulder, and moved to put one on Hazvinei's as well. Hazvinei twitched her body away, almost imperceptibly – just enough to make Tete Nyasha's hand grasp empty air.

I did not see Abel until I almost walked into him. He stood behind Tete Nyasha, silent.

'Abel!' Hazvinei moved to hug him, but he stepped back. He was very tall now – a good head taller than me.

'Abel, say hello to your cousins,' said Tete Nyasha. 'Tell them you are sorry about your uncle and auntie.'

Abel smelled strongly of sweat: a raw, rough smell with a

spice to it that I did not recognise. He smelled dangerous, like a man. I remembered the kitchen: Chenjerai, the bowl of blood. *Vaenzi vauya,* the phrase went – the strangers are coming. Abel was a stranger to me now, removed by grief and memories that we did not share.

'How are you, Abel?' I said.

'I am well.'

'It has been a long time since we last saw you.'

'Yes,' he said. 'I am sorry to hear about Babamudiki and Amainini.'

They had been second parents to him, I knew, but I could see nothing in his face. Perhaps he did not want to show his emotion in front of Babamukuru.

'Abel will show you where you are sleeping,' said Babamukuru.

Hazvinei had been watching this conversation with narrowed eyes. When we fell silent she pointed to a door in the kitchen.

'Is that the toilet?'

Babamukuru's famed indoor toilet, with its taps full of water and fresh towels daily!

'Yes, Hazvinei. Do you need to go?' Tete opened it for her. Hazvinei went in without saying thank you, and slammed the door.

'Poor girl, her stomach is unsettled after the journey,' said Tete Nyasha.

Hazvinei stayed in the bathroom for two hours. Tete Nyasha tried to coax her out with soft words and promises of food; I banged on the door and told her to stop being stupid. But it was only when Babamukuru unscrewed the doorknob and opened it that she emerged, prickly and indignant as a wet cat. It was a quiet dinner, that first night, as Hazvinei and Babamukuru glowered at their plates and Tete Nyasha and I made polite, stilted conversation. Abel sat in silence, speaking to no one, but his dark eyes flicked from one person to another, Hazvinei in particular. I felt a hollow in my stomach, even though I had just eaten. Abel did not speak to me at all, not even when he showed me the room that we were to share, with its twin beds and tall bookshelf. I wanted to tell him everything that had happened, but he was a mystery to me – as tall and unreadable as the *mukomana* that I had met all those years ago.

Our first night in Babamukuru's house was the longest I had ever spent. It felt as if morning were a rumour, as if the sun had set on the world and would never rise again and Hazvinei and I were the only two people who knew it. I shrank beneath my thin wool blanket and breathed the unfamiliar petroleum scent of the pillow. When I heard my sister's voice, I was thankful.

'Tinashe.'

I could see Hazvinei's shape, a darker black against the night. She moved across the room and climbed onto my bed. Abel did not stir.

'Your feet are cold,' she said, sliding her feet between mine. The dry skin on her heels rasped against my leg hairs.

'It's not so bad.'

'It's a shithole.'

'That's not true. It's a nice house.'

'That's not what I meant.'

We lay there, breathing shallowly.

'Abel hates us.'

'He doesn't hate us.'

'He isn't talking to us.'

'It is just because everything is new. And he must be sad too.'

Hazvinei snorted.

'It is better than going to the orphanage.'

'Not much.'

'Hazvinei! At least we are together.'

I could almost hear her thinking in the darkness.

'Yes,' she said finally. 'I suppose.'

We lay there breathing each other's air, thinking our own thoughts.

When I woke up on that first morning after we had arrived at Babamukuru's house, I was relieved. Babamukuru was in charge of Baba's property now, and in charge of us. I did not feel ready to become the man of the house – shamefully, because I knew I should step up and claim my place – and I was more than happy for Babamukuru to delay my maturing for a few years more.

It was a small and shameful thing to think, a maggot of unworthiness uncoiling in my heart. But only our ancestors are going to hold me accountable for those thoughts. And my ancestors have plenty for which to punish me already.

Chapter Fourteen

Life in town was very different from life on the *kopje*. For a start, we woke when the sun was already in the sky rather than before dawn. Babamukuru left for work at eight o'clock in the big silver car, and Abel walked to school. Tete Nyasha worked in the house or sat in the living room, leafing through magazines. Babamukuru and Abel returned for dinner, which was always meat and potatoes or *sadza* with gravy and bowls of vegetables from which we could help ourselves. After dinner, we bathed in the shining bathroom and slept in crisp, cool sheets. These were simple things, but to Hazvinei and me they seemed like the customs of a foreign tribe.

I had heard Abel's stories, but assumed he was exaggerating when he spoke of the five or six different jars of jam on the breakfast table or the avocado-green refrigerator with its bottles of Coke inside. Coke available whenever you wanted it, for free! I could not believe it. Tete Nyasha told us to help ourselves to the food and drink in the house. Hazvinei was happy to open the refrigerator and eat whatever was inside – and then to leave her mess of crumbs or wrappers sitting out on the kitchen table – but I could not bring myself to eat without asking permission. I did open the doors of the refrigerator and pantry, however, just to look at the wonders inside. I developed an obsession with tinned food – bean salad, pickled onions, asparagus. I liked to look at them, to pick up each tin and turn it over to feel the weight and the slosh of whatever was inside. Tete Nyasha kept a stack of food magazines in the kitchen, with dog-eared corners where she had marked favourite recipes. I could not believe that whole publications were devoted to food – growing it, buying it, preparing it, serving it. There were pages of glossy pictures – meals photographed like beautiful women in fashion magazines. I had never seen such meals before I came here; such colours. I asked Tete Nyasha if I could take some of the magazines to my room to read.

'You do not need to ask, Tinashe,' said Tete Nyasha. 'This is your home now.'

She had bought us drawers full of new clothes as well, still with their smart cardboard labels and store-bought smell. I now owned a pair of white *takkies* just like Abel's, and a striped tie like Babamukuru's that I could wear to church. Hazvinei had a neat pile of cotton dresses, pink and white and blue, and patent-leather Mary Jane shoes with silver buckles, still in their Bata box.

At first I became lost in the corridors and rooms of the new house, but gradually I learned its shape and character. There was the shining kitchen with its blue-speckled plastic counter-tops; the dim dining room with the wood table that gleamed flat and dark as water; three bedrooms, each with a set of flowered curtains and an ornate tissue-box cover on the dressing tables; the green horsehair sofa and chairs of the living room, and its nubbly mustard carpet that felt rough underfoot. Tete Nyasha covered every surface in photograph frames and china set on lace mats, and each chair had its own woven mat as well. Tete Nyasha told me that this was to keep the chair back clean. I dared not rest my head back in case I marked the white lace with the oil from my hair.

I had never seen such a profusion of furniture and shining surfaces – my head felt crowded with it all. The bathroom in particular rendered me speechless; the gold taps and the pale green bathtub in which Hazvinei and I washed every evening seemed too luxurious to be possible. And if I longed for the cold, bitter water of the *kopje* pump and the dim brown sweep of the river, I did not admit it.

The days of the cholera were green, sticky, humid days that smelled of sweet vomit and the algae that floated on the water's surface down at the dying waterhole. The smell clung to me. I sniffed it when I pulled my shirt over my head in the morning. I could not get it out of my nostrils. My hair seemed choked with the stuff. I could not speak, because the cholera coated my tongue.

'What's the matter with you, *mukomana?*' said Babamukuru, giving me light cuffs around the head that were meant to be affectionate. I could hardly hear him through the thick mulch of cholera that plugged my ears.

'Be kind,' Tete Nyasha scolded him. She enfolded me in her arms, damp and cool, and so large that they seemed to surround me entirely. I let my head rest on the fresh cotton of her dress, and the cholera receded a little.

We believe that you must not comment aloud on any new place, as it attracts attention from the spirits. It is better to stay silent than to risk offending them by saying something incorrect; if you do offend them, they will cause you to get irretrievably lost, doomed to wander forever. We even have a word for this: *kuteterika*. Sometimes, in those first weeks in town, I thought that this had happened to me; that I would never learn my way around this big city with all its signs and lines and roads. I did not know if Hazvinei felt this way as well. She did not talk about Baba and Amai; I did not even see her cry. Perhaps she was still recovering from the illness. Perhaps it had sucked her emotions dry, as it had her body. Perhaps, and I think this was the real reason, I just did not understand her.

Abel did not speak to us often. He was not the laughing,

boastful cousin that we had known on the *kopje*, but a polite stranger who greeted us when we awoke and wished us a good night's sleep in the evenings, but said nothing more. He left for school early in the mornings and stayed out late. I soon realised that Abel spent very little time at home now.

'He is popular, this one,' said Babamukuru. 'And he always does his homework. He is a good boy.'

We ate our meals with Abel and asked him to pass the sugar, but he did not laugh and play with us as he had on the *kopje*. I shared his room every night, heard his night-time mutterings and listened to the sounds of his dreams, but I had no idea who he was.

'You do not want us here,' I said to Abel one evening as we got ready for bed.

'That is not true.'

'You do not talk to me anymore.' I sat on the end of my bed, knees drawn up. 'What is wrong? Did I do something?'

'No.'

'Then what?'

'Nothing is wrong.' Abel slid his shirt over his head. He had the beginnings of chest hair, while my chest was smooth and bald.

'I do not believe you.'

His eyes were surrounded by white. 'It is fine that you are here.'

Helpless, I stared at him. We had played together since we were born. He was another sibling to me, almost half of myself. And now I did not know him at all.

'Please, Abel.' A shameful catch in my voice, unbefitting the man I was suddenly supposed to be.

'What really happened, Tinashe?' he said.

'What do you mean?'

'What really happened on the *kopje*?'

My heart beat in my throat. 'You know what happened. The cholera . . .'

He shook his head. 'This all started with the N'anga's hut. You know it.'

I remembered Hazvinei wielding the medicine stick; the red eyes of the cockerel.

'You did not visit again,' I said.

'I know what happened, Tinashe.'

I shook my head. 'It is nothing like that.'

'No? Baba told me about the drought.'

I climbed into bed, drawing the blanket up over the goosepimples on my skin.

'You see?' said Abel. 'You do not want to talk.'

'Good night,' I said.

And I lay in the unfamiliar darkness, listening to the sound of traffic from the road and clenching my teeth together hard so that I would not cry.

So Babamukuru knew about what had happened in the drought. I wondered what else he knew. Had Baba told him about the visit to the N'anga afterwards? I thought I had burned that knowledge along with the powders and potions, but perhaps it still hovered around us. The bad fortune could not be allowed to follow us to town.

Every morning all three of us helped with the chores. Babamukuru could have employed a maid – he was wealthy enough – but he wanted Abel to learn to work for himself. I did not mind. I had performed the daily chores since I was old enough to carry a bucket, and Hazvinei, for once in her life, was made to scrub floors and clean dishes like everyone else. Some small, shameful part of me was glad about this, although there were plenty of times when she was able to cheat me into doing them for her, by claiming tiredness or headache or debilitating grief. Then she would sit back and watch me as I worked, biting on a piece of sugarcane she had torn from the bush.

We learned the mysteries of the indoor toilet. I went in the garden for as long as I could, but after a few days I worked up the courage to use it.

'Don't forget to wash your hands,' said Tete.

The toilet was green and cold, made of porcelain, with a pile of toilet rolls on top, covered with a woollen tea cosy. I took a piss, being careful not to drip, washed my hands and went into the kitchen again.

Dinner was on the table.

'You start your meals,' said Tete Nyasha. 'I'm just going to the powder room.'

We sat down at the table. There were proper napkins, cloth ones, with brass rings around them.

Tete Nyasha came back with a serious face. 'Tinashe.'

I was very confused. I had washed my hands. I had made sure that there were no splashes.

'You must flush the toilet when you have finished,' said Tete. 'It is the silver handle on the side.'

I felt Abel's eyes on me. My cheeks grew hot. 'Sorry, Tete.'

'It is not your fault. Just remember to flush from now on.'

'Okay.'

I could not even take a piss without doing something wrong. I missed the sweet stink of our outdoor toilet at home, where I could count the moths around the bare bulb.

Tete Nyasha had been a stranger to me, but since Abel would not talk to me and Babamukuru was at work all day, I spent a lot of time with her in the kitchen. She was glad of the company, although disappointed that Hazvinei did not want to help her with the baking or join her for gossip and cups of tea.

'Why did you never come to visit us, Tete Nyasha?' I asked.

'Oh, well . . .' she wiped her hands on her apron. The bruises on her ear had faded to a dull shine now, but a new swelling showed at the edge of her jaw. ('I am so clumsy,' she said with that high-pitched laugh that Hazvinei loved to imitate. 'I am always walking into things.')

'I was very busy,' she said now. 'I have told you.'

'But you never came to any of the parties,' I said. 'You would have liked them.'

Tete Nyasha turned to the sink. 'I am very happy to have both of you here, now, Tinashe.'

Tete Nyasha had been pregnant after Abel, we knew. Amai had talked to the aunties about it in a hushed voice at home. Hazvinei had overheard (as she always did) and she had told me (as she usually did). We knew, therefore, that Tete Nyasha had become pregnant twice after Abel was born, but that both babies had died in her stomach.

'The spirits took them,' Amai had said. She did not say that Tete Nyasha had done something wrong, but disapproval hid behind her words.

'It would be easier if she had more bloody children of her own,' said Hazvinci. I told her not to speak that way, but secretly I agreed.

Tete Nyasha always had to be touching us. Even while she was making dinner, she liked us to sit nearby, and she would put out a hand to smooth our hair, or grip our shoulders. Hazvinei shivered off Tete Nyasha's hands as if they were so many flies landing to suck the juice from her skin. Hazvinei was perpetually annoyed those days: knees drawn up tight to her chest, arms crossed, elbows sticking out ready to poke the ribs of anyone who came too close.

'Try to be kind to her,' I said when we were giving the chickens their night-time feed and stacking the firewood.

'Why?' Hazvinei threw the feed at Tete Nyasha's chickens as if she hated them. The chickens, being chickens, did not care, and pecked at it anyway. They were fat and lazy and produced one egg a day between them, if that. On the *kopje* they would have been sentenced to the pot.

'Because she is our auntie.'

Hazvinei snorted.

'Is that not enough reason to be polite?'

'I am being polite.'

'You are not.'

'She is a silly, fat old woman,' said Hazvinei, 'and she smells.'

'She does not smell.'

'She stinks of floor polish.'

'She spends all day on her hands and knees polishing the floor. Of course she smells of floor polish.'

'And she is stupid. Oh, Hazvinei, you're so clever! I don't know how you know the things you know.' She imitated Tete Nyasha's high-pitched, breathy voice. I smiled despite myself.

'Hazvinei, she just wants to look after you.'

Hazvinei spat, a round glob of liquid that made a tiny crater in the red soil. 'That is what I think of Babamukuru, and that is what I think of Tete Nyasha.' She dropped the feed bucket on the ground with a clang that echoed off the walls. 'I want to go back.'

'Hazvinei, stop that. Babamukuru will be angry.'

'I do not care.'

'You like Abel. Do you not want to stay with him?'

'Abel is different now. Tinashe, you are just trying to make everything quiet and peaceful, like you always do.'

'And what is wrong with that?' I asked, but too late, because she had gone inside.

I wanted to be quiet and peaceful. We were safe from the spirits here, I thought. They could not live in this place with its unnaturally green grass and rain that rose like magic from the ground. Hazvinei had not talked about the spirits since we arrived in town. She had not woken me at night, whispered secrets in my ear or tried to show me the shape of something invisible. I hoped that the cholera had taught her a lesson, as it had taught one to me.

One night at dinner, Babamukuru sat back in his chair and wiped his mouth. 'Well, you can't sit at home during the day much longer,' he said. 'It is time for you to go out to work.'

'Work?' I said. It seemed disloyal to think about starting something new when our parents had not been dead three months.

'You are going to start school with Abel, Tinashe,' said Babamukuru.

This was more than I had expected. A shameful bubble of happiness rose in my stomach. Abel's school! Desks and new books and proper examinations and the chance of university after that. A school tie, a blazer and smart leather shoes. I swallowed. 'Really?'

Babamukuru saw my expression and smiled. 'Yes, Tinashe. You have been a good boy, and I know that you work very hard at school. You will be a little behind, but you will soon catch up, I know.'

'Thank you, Babamukuru.' I resisted the urge to clap my hands together, as Amai would have done. He looked like a god to me in that moment, even with his napkin tucked into his collar and his forehead shining with sweat. He turned to Hazvinei now, and said, 'You will stay at home.'

Hazvinei looked up. 'What?' she said.

'Don't be rude, Hazvinei,' said Tete Nyasha. She put a hand over Hazvinei's, but my sister jerked her own hand away from underneath.

'To help your auntie with the chores,' said Babamukuru.

'Fine,' said Hazvinei, and carried on eating.

'It will be good for you,' said Babamukuru. He was staring at her with a strange, intent expression. Hazvinei looked at him, lifted a forkful of mashed potato to her mouth and put it in, still looking. It was very disrespectful for her to hold a man's gaze in such a way.

'It will be good for you,' he repeated, louder.

Abel dropped his fork. It clattered in the silence.

Hazvinei stopped eating and looked at Babamukuru. 'Why?'

'You need to learn what hard work is. I have noticed Tinashe doing your chores.'

'I don't mind,' I said quickly.

'It is not a man's place,' said my uncle.

Hazvinei's eyes were so narrow that they almost looked closed.

'You need to learn a lesson,' said Babamukuru. He held out his water cup. 'Get me a drink.'

Hazvinei stared at him.

'Fill your uncle's cup, Hazvinei,' said Tete Nyasha, an anxious smile on her face. 'You should be glad to do something for him, after he has taken you in and been so kind.'

Abel said nothing, but chewed his food and kept his eyes lowered to his plate.

Hazvinei took the cup. A smile fattened Babamukuru's face. He watched as she stood and walked to the refrigerator. And then he watched as she furrowed her smooth brow as if she were thinking, pursed her lips and spat a white, unladylike gob of saliva into his cup.

Babamukuru pushed back his chair. It fell over. Tete Nyasha scrambled to pick it up, and I went to help her.

'No, Tinashe,' she said, flapping her hands at me. 'Sit down. Sit down. Stay quiet.'

Babamukuru looked at Hazvinei for a long time. Then he looked at Tete Nyasha, who was flapping at his elbow, tugging at his sleeve, asking him to sit down. The purple in his face faded back to brown, and he sat.

'Hazvinei. Go to your room,' he said.

Hazvinei left, walking tall. I felt as though we had escaped something terrible, although I did not know what it was I feared. I did not dare to look at Babamukuru's face, but I glanced at Abel's. He was grinning. I had not seen him smiling so widely since we moved to town.

I was happy that Babamukuru was sending me to Abel's school, and ashamed that I was happy so soon after my parents had died. Abel gave me some pieces of his old uniform to wear until Tete Nyasha had time to buy me new clothes. I did not care; they were better quality, even second-hand, than anything I had worn on the *kopje*, and I could not wait to visit this land of shiny new books where I could sit at a proper desk, instead of on the floor. Tete Nyasha made us each a packed lunch with a coin hidden under the sandwich.

'What is that for?' I asked Abel.

'The tuck shop.'

'What is that?'

He shrugged. 'You can buy sweets there,' he said, 'or Cokes.'

Money for doing nothing at all! And the sandwich had thin slivers of ham inside it, flat and pink as a dog's tongue, and smears of yellow mustard. I could not wait for lunchtime to come so that I could eat it.

'Does Babamukuru take us to school?' I asked. Now that would be something, arriving in his big silver car!

'No,' said Abel, picking up his school suitcase. 'We walk.'

The school was a long, low, white-washed building on stilts, to keep it away from the easily flooded clay soil. Boys who looked just like me, in uniforms just like mine, kicked a football around outside. They all had shining, freshly polished school shoes and socks pulled up to their knees. They looked well-scrubbed and healthy, with fat cheeks and smooth skin. I felt grey and thin next to them.

'This is my cousin.' Abel kept the introductions as brief as possible. I had worried that he would ignore me at school, leave me to my own devices, but he stayed by my side as the boys greeted me. I was glad he stayed there, because it was the first time I had heard a school bell and I would not have known to go inside and sit down at one of the wooden desks.

Once the lessons started, though, I was at home. I recognised the books. I recognised the fresh sawdust smell of new exercise books and the taste of new pens. I put my hand up to answer my first question, and I was so excited to get the answer right that I forgot to be embarrassed at standing up to answer when I should have remained in my seat. My grin had become painful by the time the bell rang again and we were released for lunch.

'You are enjoying this, hey?' said Abel.

'Yes,' I said, as if he could not tell.

'You always liked school,' he said. 'I never understood it.'

But he softened, and when we opened our twin lunchboxes to eat our twin ham sandwiches, he introduced me to his friends. I did not remember all their names, but I was happy to be part of a gang again – even as its smallest and skinniest member. I saw the sideways glances and heard the quieter, whispered words meant only for Abel and not for me, but I thought that this was because I was an awkward country cousin, and I did not mind.

After school, Abel had football practice.

'You must try out for the team as well,' Babamukuru had said. 'You will be good on the field together, yes?' His two boys, making him proud.

'Yes, Babamukuru.'

Abel had packed two sets of his football kit. The shirts had red numbers on the back. When school finished, the boys who were staying for sports practice went to the changing rooms, while the others went to catch the bus or walk home.

'Are we going to change?' I asked. Abel did not move.

'You can,' he said. 'I have something to do.'

I clutched our bag and waited.

'Go on,' he said. 'I will see you at home.'

'Where are you going?'

'And do not tell Baba,' he said as he walked away, leaving me standing on a field full of strangers in clothes that did not fit me properly.

When I returned home from soccer practice, I was hot and angry. I had become lost on my way back from school, remembering the route wrongly from that morning, and the kit Abel had given me was stained and smelled of sweat. Some of the boys showered at school and changed back into their clothes, but I had come to the bathroom to find my school clothes gone – hidden as a joke by some of the boys with whom I had talked earlier. Without Abel there, it was clear that I was a rural nobody who would be treated as such. I found Babamukuru's high wall and iron gate amongst all the other high walls and iron gates on the street, and I opened the front door of his house to find Abel and Hazvinei eating sandwiches together and Tete Nyasha standing at the sink.

'Tinashe!' She folded me in a fat hug, and then sniffed. 'Why are you wearing your sports kit home?'

'I lost my uniform,' I said. I looked over her shoulder at Abel, who was staring at me with no expression.

'You are filthy,' said Hazvinei. She wrinkled her nose. 'And you stink.'

'Abel told me that you stayed later to play with the other boys.' Tete Nyasha wagged her finger. 'I know it is exciting to start at a new school, Tinashe, but you must take care of your clothes, yes?'

Anger was cold and hard as the bullet Chenjerai had given me. I had left the precious bullet under my pillow – now I wished I had it in my hand so that I could throw it at Abel's impassive face.

'I am sorry, Tete Nyasha.'

I resolved to do the best I could in school. Clearly Abel was not to be trusted. No one there was to be trusted. All I had was myself and my schoolwork, and I was determined to make the most of this opportunity. It was all I had.

Chapter Fifteen

It was easier to hear the news in town. Baba's *tokoloshe*-possessed radio was stored along with the rest of his belongings, but Babamukuru had a smart new radio and received the newspaper every day. Over breakfast we listened to the bulletins, and then Babamukuru flicked through the musty-smelling pages, pursing his lips and shaking his head at the reports of terrorist activity. He passed the comic pages to Hazvinei and I to read, but he did not offer anyone else the bulk of the paper. If I wanted to see the headlines I had to fish it out of the kitchen bin. This is how I learned that black majority rule was meant to come in two years' time – that important men had spoken and deliberated, and that this was the result.

'You see, Tinashe,' said Babamukuru, 'this is how important things are decided – by educated men talking. Not by guerrillas killing each other in the bush.'

I wondered what Abel thought of this. He said nothing, but the expression on his face told me that he did not place much value on the voice of Babamukuru's radio.

Even here in town, however, we could not escape the white policemen. There were two who walked our neighbourhood and I had come to know them over the past weeks – to look at, at least, and to shout a greeting. I did not mind them. They kicked a football around with us boys occasionally or gave us chewing gum. Walking home, I saw them standing at the corner of Babamukuru's road, listening to their hand-held radio – a crackling, braying voice telling them about a 'disturbance'. A disturbance on our green, silent street?

I walked faster, but I heard the younger one call to me.

This was the first time he had spoken to me directly, and I wondered how he knew my name. Babamukuru was an important man, I knew, but his skinny country nephew could not be of much interest to men like this.

'Sir.' I stopped.

'*Mangwanani*,' said the policeman in careful, accented Shona.

'*Mangwanani*.'

'*Marara sei?*'

'For God's sake, Stephen,' said the older, fatter, hairier policeman, who had come up behind him. 'We don't have all day.'

The younger man smiled at me, and I smiled back. I liked him. His Shona was not perfect, but it was good: and at least he bothered to try and work his way through the long traditional greetings that made most white men impatient – white men like this other one, whom the people of the neighbourhood called *njiri*, warthog. Njiri always looked hot and red, like a piece of boiled beef fresh from the pot and dripping, and his beard moved up and down when he talked.

'We have to get a bloody move on,' he was saying to the other. 'Can't waste our time jawing with the piccanins.'

VaStephen waved his hand at Njiri, indicating that he should be silent, and turned back to me. 'Tinashe, have you noticed anything strange today?'

I could not escape this, it seemed. They watched us everywhere. 'No, sir.' I looked at the twin wrinkles of VaStephen's cheeks as he smiled, and felt I could ask, 'Why?'

'We've just heard some things.' He was vague. He watched my face and played with the cigarette lighter in his hand, turning it over and over. I did not say anything.

'Well,' he said, 'If you see or hear anything unusual, you'll come and tell me, hey?'

'Yes, sir.'

'Stephen!' Njiri was impatient.

'I'm coming. Run along, Tinashe.'

He adjusted the weight of the rifle on his shoulder, and wandered back through the heat haze to Njiri, who had started tapping his watch. I lifted my hand in farewell, and I tried not to remember the white policeman who had come to see Baba on the day that he told us the story of Nehanda. I missed the *kopje*. I missed my river. But I was grateful to be here.

Despite its size, the house seemed too small for us all as soon as Babamukuru came in for his dinner. I became very aware that Abel, Hazvinei and I were teenagers now. We seemed huge – gangly and clumsy. I saw us through Babamukuru's eyes – leaving sweaty footprints on his polished concrete floor, handprints on his clean white walls, hair in the plughole and, shamefully, drips on the toilet seat. I tried as hard as I could not to take up any space. I hunched over the table when we ate, and tried to be as quiet as possible in the bathroom. I even ate smaller portions and became thinner, as if my body were colluding with me.

Hazvinei, however, became louder. She filled out until the buttons on her dress strained over her breasts and you could see little spoonfuls of skin beneath. She was not fat – she could never be fat – but she became ripe as a mango. She even smelled like a mango, fruity and exotic. How did even her smell take up more space? I felt we were moving further and further away from the Tinashe and Hazvinei I had known on the *kopje*, and thus from Amai and Baba as well. I missed them all. And so I broke my own rules one night, as Hazvinei and I lay on the lawn looking at the stars, and opened up that world that I had made certain to close when we left the *kopje*.

'Hazvinei, tell me about the spirits.'

Hazvinei turned her head to look at me with surprise. 'You told me not to talk about them.'

'Well, I am not telling you that now.'

'You told me never to speak to Abel or Babamukuru or Tete Nyasha . . .'

'It is only us here,' I said. 'Please, Hazvinei.'

We lay in silence for a moment.

'Well,' said Hazvinei, 'there are *mashavi*. They died a long way from home, and they are trying to find their way back.'

'White people?'

'Some of them are white people.'

'What do they look like?'

Hazvinei shifted her head on the grass. I saw the glint of her eyes. 'They are like sour milk,' she said. 'White and yellow. They smell bad. And they look unhappy.'

I sniffed. 'I cannot smell them.'

'That is because you are stupid,' said Hazvinei. This was her answer to everything.

'What else is there?' I said.

'*Zvizungu*. These ones are all white men.' She shrugged. 'They are boring.'

'*Dzepfunde*.'

'Spirits raised from graves,' said Hazvinei, making her voice low and sinister. 'Raised by witches.'

The hairs at the back of my neck prickled. 'What are they like?'

'It depends,' she said. 'Some are like people, but with no faces. Some have no bodies at all. Some have their feet on backwards, and no hands.'

I knew she was trying to scare me, but I shivered. 'And what else? What else is here?'

'*Zvipunha*,' she said, and said nothing more. She did not need to. *Zvipunha* were the most frightening of all – dead infants, haunting their families. To kill a baby was the worst sin of all, unforgivable by the spirits and bringing misfortune not just to you but also to your whole family. This was why Amai whispered about Tete Nyasha and those other women who had lost their babies. My lost brother Simba brushed me with the edge of his moth wings.

I pushed Hazvinei. 'You talk rubbish.'

'Abel did not think it was rubbish.'

Hazvinei told me stories about the spirits every night after that, in secret, as we lay on the damp green grass and breathed in the scent of water. I knew that I should not let her talk – that to speak the names of the spirits was to summon them – but her stories brought back to me the smooth muscles of the river, the cry of the N'anga's black cockerel, and the striped war-paint of the witch-smellers. I did not realise that Abel had been listening until he spoke to me as we lay in bed. At first, when I heard his voice, I thought I was dreaming.

'Tinashe!'

'Abel?' I rolled over until I could see the glint of his eyes in the darkness. 'What is the matter?'

'Nothing. You have to promise not to tell Baba.'

'Promise not to tell him what?'

'What I am going to show you.'

'What?' It felt like the old days, when Abel and I would lie awake and whisper in the dark. 'What are you talking about?'

'I will show you tomorrow.'

'I don't understand.'

'I thought you had changed,' he said. 'You and Hazvinei. But then I heard you talking.'

The leopards scratched at the window. 'What? When?'

'Outside.'

'We were just talking . . .'

'About the spirits – and Nehanda. I heard you.'

'No!'

'Tinashe! There is nothing to be worried about.'

'If Babamukuru knew . . .'

'I have not told Baba.'

'I don't understand, Abel. What are you trying to tell me?'

'Just go to sleep,' said Abel, turning over. 'I will show you tomorrow.'

He left me puzzled and feverish. When his breathing became even and quiet, I was still awake, wondering what Abel was going to show me. The darkness in my belly told me that it would not be anything good – but at least my cousin was talking to me again. I tried to forget that he was only speaking to me because of my sister's ghost stories and strangeness. I did not need the bad fortune to follow us here.

I did not sleep well that night, and I did not raise my hand in any of my classes the next morning. When it came time for football practice after school, neither Abel nor I went to the field. We stood outside the changing rooms looking at each other. I noticed that I was the same height as Abel now – skinnier, but just as tall. We were two men together.

He seemed to realise this as well, because he grinned and held out his hand, beckoning. 'Come.' He led me out of the school.

'Where are we going?'

'You will see.'

Behind the school was a wire fence, sagging in places, separating the cool green smear of cut grass from the bush that grew up the hill behind the white buildings. No one had built on this land because it was too rocky and uneven, and so it was left to grow wild. Babamukuru mentioned it often, shaking his head, as a missed opportunity. They should build something there, he said. It did not look good for the town. Now, Abel led me through the discarded scatter of crisp packets and Coke bottles.

'Careful. There are thorns.'

'Where are we going?' I asked again, and again received no reply.

The wire fence had collapsed in one place, weighed down by weeds. Abel stepped over it, and I followed, my socks snagging on the wire. I stopped to untangle myself.

'Come.'

The weeds and long grass gave way to a dusty slope and loose stones, bushes which were dry and spiky as a bundle of twigs and the flat, grey thorns that covered the ground as profusely as grass. I smelled burning.

'Abel?'

He pushed his way through the bushes with a sound like tearing paper. Behind the bushes was a pile of cigarette butts. Abel sat, carefully, avoiding the ash. 'What are we doing here?' I asked him.

'This is where I come,' he said. 'Every day, after school.'

'Here?'

'Yes.'

'No football?'

'No.'

'This is where you were on that first day?'

'Yes. I am sorry I did not tell you.'

Silence. I looked around. I could not see any attraction in this dry, litter-strewn place. 'Why?'

'I am going to be a freedom fighter,' said Abel.

I swallowed a laugh. I could see from the intensity in Abel's eyes that he would not find it funny. 'What?'

'Remember? I always told you that I would.'

'But we were playing a game,' I said. 'It was just a game.'

He shrugged. 'Maybe to you.'

'What about school?'

'School is useless,' he said. 'It is a joke, to sit there and study when there are more important things to be doing.'

'What do you mean?'

'Do you not listen to the news, Tinashe? Everyone except South Africa is supporting us. The guerrillas have many friends who will shelter them over the border. It is easier for them to come in now.'

'But what do you do?' I asked cautiously. 'What can you do, from here?'

'I can think about the world,' said Abel. 'I can make plans.'

I looked at the pile of cigarette butts. 'Oh.'

'I am going to do more,' he said quickly. 'But for now I am just making plans.'

I nodded. I said nothing.

'I am showing you this because I know that we feel the same way, you and I,' said Abel. 'We saw Chenjerai.'

Did we feel the same? I was not so sure. Walking back afterwards, my head was a fog of thoughts and cigarette smoke. Abel wanted to be a *mukomana*, like the man in the kitchen. He wanted me to be one too. Babamukuru did not know. I felt at once guilty and suddenly grown up. What would Baba have thought? Abel certainly imagined that he would have approved. Perhaps he would have. After all, he did his part for the struggle – I could see that now. But then, look where it had taken him.

As if the direction of my thoughts had conjured him up, I saw Njiri leaning up against his *bakkie* on the side of the road.

'Abel.' I tugged on his arm.

'Shut up, Tinashe.'

'But Abel . . .!'

I felt that the white man would pluck my new knowledge

from my head as a monkey cracks open a fruit to get at the juices inside. Abel, however, was not afraid.

'*Manheru*, baas,' he said.

'*Manheru*.' Njiri was not interested in us. He sucked on his cigarette and stared into the distance.

'*Manheru*,' I said, a beat too late. My feet did not move until Abel grabbed me by the shoulder and manoeuvred me onto the path again.

'You see?' he hissed. 'That is why I did not tell you at first. You have never been able to keep a secret.'

Stung, I shook him off. 'That is not true.'

'It is. And you have to keep this to yourself. You cannot tell anyone. Not even Hazvinei. Yes?'

'Yes, Abel.'

'Good.' He released me, glared and dusted his hands off on his shorts.

I decided that I did not care that he was annoyed. I did not care that he had said I was no good at keeping secrets. My cousin was speaking to me again – including me again – and I was glad.

Every night since we had moved to Babamukuru's house I had dreamed that I sat in the tall grasses of the *kopje*. Grass scratched my skin; an ant climbed over my foot. Then the wind rushed past me and I was lifted right up to the sun, so close that I could feel my skin singeing. I was hoisted onto my father's shoulder. I knew it was my father because I could feel the oil of his skin and the scratch of his blue canvas overalls. I could feel his arms steadying me. But I could never see his face.

When I awoke, I remembered. The knowledge sat on my chest as *tokoloshes* were supposed to do; a malignant spirit, black and hairy, with dead breath and laughing eyes. I had learned that if I closed my eyes very tightly, so that water squeezed out, and clenched my fists as hard as I could, I could make the *tokoloshe* go away. The weight on my chest lifted, but the dream flapped and fluttered in my head like a bright piece of washing pegged to a line, and I could not quite shake it off.

Now, thinking about Abel helped to get rid of my dream. That night, I swelled with the pleasure of having a secret that was just between my cousin and me, separate from Hazvinei. I should have known that there was no way to keep secrets from my sister. I had known her for thirteen years, and she could still read my thoughts and feel my feelings with a touch of her long, clever fingers. In the morning – a Saturday – before I could yawn and stretch, she sat on my bed willing me to be awake. Abel was up and gone already, leaving the two of us to whisper in the early morning light.

'What happened yesterday?'

'What?'

'Tinashe.' She pinched the tender skin of my underarm. I yelped. 'Tell me, then.'

'Or what? You will keep pinching me?'

'Yes.'

'I am not scared.'

When she got her claws into the thick tangle of my hair, however, I changed my mind.

'Abel wants to be a *mukomana*.'

Hazvinei was on fire at once, dancing barefoot on the bed, pinching me, as if that would make the words come more quickly.

'Why? What does he do?'

'Slow down.'

'Why does he want to be a *mukomana*?'

My hand reached inside my pyjama pocket and closed over the bullet. I would not show it to her. But I told her everything else.

'Come on.'

'Where?'

'We are going to find him.'

'Abel?'

'He went out early,' she said. 'I bet he is there. Come.'

'I have just woken up, Hazvinei.'

'Tough *takkies*.'

And she was gone, just like that, knowing that I would get up and flush my sleep-warmed body with cold water from the basin, and follow her. I always followed her.

'Hazvinei. We have chores at home. Babamukuru will be angry.' He will be angry with you, Hazvinei, I meant. And she did not need more reasons for Babamukuru to punish her.

She pushed me. 'Who cares? It is the weekend.'

'Fine. I will take you there. But you cannot tell anyone, all right?'

I led her to the school.

'It is big,' she said, but was not interested in seeing my classroom. She followed me to the place where Abel had taken me the day before.

'See, Hazvinei. There is no one.'

'He must be here.'

'He is not here. Let us go home before Babamukuru sees we are gone.'

'I will find him.' And she disappeared into the bushes.

'Do you know where you're going?'

'I know where he will be.'

'How?'

'*Benzi*.' She liked to call me an idiot many times in a day. 'Come with me.'

I followed her pink gingham bum, indecently cheerful in its colourful bounce. I could see the small, uneven stitch at the hem that revealed Tete's tendency to get distracted while sewing. Red dust powdered my greying *takkies*. Tete would be angry when we got home, pursing her lips and tutting – she could always tell bush dust from regular dust.

'Here.' She stopped

'You're crazy.'

I peered through the bushes, and could see nothing.

'Look.'

The broken sunlight and patches of darkness rearranged themselves, the way a chameleon appears on a branch when you concentrate.

'Told you,' said Hazvinei.

I looked at Abel. Then I looked at the gun he held. He had not seen us. He leaned against a tree trunk, clasping the rifle in both hands and looking down at it. I remembered the poisoned *mukomana* I had seen in the same position before the witch doctor's ceremony, and my belly twisted.

'See?' Hazvinei hugged herself with excitement.

'Be quiet.' Where had he found the gun? Why did he have it? Abel had said nothing about guns. I had thought he was playing at being a *mukomana*, but this was not a toy.

'Hazvinei, we should not be here. Let's go home. And we should tell Babamukuru . . .'

'No!' she pinched me. My fingers felt for the comforting smoothness of the bullet in my pocket, while Hazvinei pushed through the thorns with a sound like paper tearing, and walked towards Abel.

'Hazvinei!' I felt as if my heart had leapt onto my tongue. 'Wait!' I followed, stiffened arms and legs unfolding with painful creaks and cracks.

'Abel!' Hazvinei shouted his name. I felt Abel's movement rather than saw it, in the way a rock rabbit knows when a hawk passes overhead, and my feet started moving before I had commanded them to. I reached Hazvinei and grabbed her pink gingham shoulders just as Abel lifted the gun. She shook me off with an irritated shiver.

Abel kept the gun lifted. And pointed at us. He looked like a stranger.

'I did not ask you to come today,' he said to me.

'I am sorry, I am sorry,' I kept saying, still reaching for my sister's bony shoulders. I did not know this Abel. I did not know what he was capable of. 'We did not mean to disturb you. We were just passing by, we did not mean to . . .'

'We came to see you,' said soon-to-be-murdered Hazvinei.

'Who knows you are here?' said the gun. I could no longer see Abel, just that round hole that spat fire. 'Who followed you? Does Baba know that you came to find me?'

'Where did you get that gun?' Anger made my voice break. 'Why are you pointing it at us?'

Hazvinei and Abel ignored me.

'No one knows.' Hazvinei pushed me forward. 'Tinashe told me about you.'

I felt an urgent need for a toilet. I curled my fingers around the cool bullet in my pocket, and held it out like a talisman. It gleamed dull and grey in my palm. I felt its magic. I felt it even more when Abel lowered the gun, and grinned with all his teeth. 'It is dangerous to sneak up on a man with a gun, yes?'

A man! And he looked like a man in that moment, even with his sparse scrub of a beard and the bobbing bone in his throat.

'Where the hell did you get that gun, Abel?' I said. 'Why do you have it?'

Hazvinei was at his side, quick as a cat. Her long fingers sought out the cool length of the barrel.

'Hazvinei, don't touch that!'

Abel watched her, still with that smile on his mouth. 'I bought it, Tinashe,' he said. 'How else would I get it?'

'Who would sell such a thing to you? How much did it cost? Does Babamukuru know?' I was torn between envy and horror.

'Of course Baba does not know.' He rested it against the tree. 'It is not even loaded. I have to find bullets.'

We were not dead. We were safe. Part of Tinashe lay on the ground with a bullet in his head instead of in his pocket, and a red-soaked shirt. The part that was left followed Abel to the log where he sat.

'How did you find me?' said Abel. 'I am not at the camp. Have you told anyone where I am?'

'No, we have told no one,' I said.

'Except Hazvinei,' he said. 'I told you. You cannot keep secrets.'

'I was the one who found you,' said Hazvinei.

Abel leaned back. 'And how did you do that?'

'It is easy.'

'Like talking to the *njuzu*?'

'Like the *njuzu*.'

'She didn't know,' I said. 'It was luck.'

Hazvinei stuck out her tongue at me.

'You just knew?' said Abel. 'That is a wonderful gift to have, that knowing.'

'I always know things,' said Hazvinei. 'The spirits tell me.'

'She is making it up,' I broke in. 'She is just showing off.' I pinched Hazvinei on the shin, hard. Hazvinei glowered.

'Sit.' Abel sat on the ground. He pulled a bag from its hiding place in the crook of the tree's roots and brought out a chipped enamel pot and a packet of tea. Clearly Abel was better prepared than I had imagined. With the supplies in this bag, he could remain out here for some days. He made a small pile of twigs and leaves and scraped the surrounding earth bare before putting a match to it. He poured water from a flask into the pot, and we watched it writhe and boil.

'Won't Tete Nyasha miss the pot?'

He shrugged. 'I told her a *chidhomo* must have taken it.'

Just what Hazvinei would have said.

'And the tea?'

'I bought it with tuck-shop money. And milk – here.' He reached into the bushes and pulled out a tin box. Teabags, powdered milk, a packet of biscuits.

'You are very organised,' I said. I eyed the rifle propped up against the tree.

'This?' He slid his hand down the smooth length, as if he were soothing it.

'Where did you get it?'

He gave me a sidelong, smiling look. I felt the bulge of the bullet in my pocket and looked down at my milky, swirling cup, imagining that I was sitting in a real guerrilla camp, drinking tea with a real freedom fighter. The image of the poisoned man swam on the surface of the tea for a moment, and I felt a twist of fear in my stomach. I wondered if the tea would taste differently from the tea Tete Nyasha made: whether it would taste of blood, or soot, or sweat.

'*Mazvita tatenda*,' I said before I drank.

'Do you have any sugar?' said Hazvinei. I hissed at her to be quiet, but Abel laughed and passed her a brown bag.

Hazvinei was watching a seething puddle of fire ants on the ground. They had surrounded a dead beetle. As I watched, its meat melted and dissolved, vanishing into a hundred tiny mouths.

'Look.' Hazvinei rested her hand on the ground, among the fire ants. I shuddered.

'Hazvinei! They will bite you.'

Abel, however, said nothing. His eyes were intent as he watched the insects climb up Hazvinei's slender fingers, onto the dusty skin of her arm.

'Hazvinei, please.' I dared not touch her. One bite from a fire ant was agony. When they bit your skin, their jaws closed so tightly that you could not pull them off without leaving their heads attached to your skin. She was wearing her smug, cat-like smile. Showing off.

'See?' she said.

'I see,' said Abel.

The white, squirming bodies made my insides squirm as well, but I could not look away. Soon Hazvinei's hand had become a pale shadow of itself, a pearly glove of ants.

'How do you do that?' asked Abel. He leaned forward, eyes narrowed.

'I don't know,' she said, still watching the ants, her face fat and smooth with contentment. 'I just ask them to come, and they come.'

Hazvinei looked up at me, smiling. She lowered her hand to the ground, and the ants flowed off like honey.

'I told you,' she said to Abel, alight, glowing with energy. 'I told you.'

'You did,' he said, his eyes still on her face. His lips curved in a smile.

'We have to go,' I said. 'Tete Nyasha will be wondering where we are. We need to go home for breakfast.'

'Of course,' said Abel, and stood up. 'Hazvinei, you will come again?'

'Yes,' she said, and jumped backwards.

'Quiet, yes?' Abel put his finger to his pursed lips in an exaggerated shushing motion. 'You don't tell people we're here. You can keep a secret?'

'Yes,' she said. We could keep secrets. Just not from each other. We nodded, two little puppets. Pink gingham Hazvinei and dusty, bullet-fondling me.

'Do not tell Baba, yes?' said Abel.

'But he will find out that you do not go to football practice,'
I said. 'One day?'

'He will not find out.'

'But if he follows you . . . '

'He will not follow me. He trusts me.' Abel looked straight
at Hazvinei as he said this. 'But of course you must tell him if
you are too scared.'

'I am not too scared,' she said, looking into Abel's face. Then
she turned and ran into the bush, dragging me behind her, and
we chased the dissolving shadows all the way back to the house.

Chapter Sixteen

After that, we visited the bush hideout most days after Abel and I had finished school. Hazvinei surprised Tete Nyasha by offering, in her sweetest voice, to run errands for her in the afternoons. When she came home later than expected, she told Tete that she met us at the school gate and walked us home. What a loving family we were! Tete was delighted. She did not keep careful count of the coins she gave Hazvinei for the store either, and so my sister was able to pocket the change.

Hazvinei and I came to know the sloping scrub leading to the camp and the bush where Abel's tin box was stashed. We came to know the long, smooth shape of the gun, although we did not touch it. Abel did not touch it either, except to clean it and to pretend to shoot down birds. I think even Abel was a little afraid of the gun and what it meant.

In some ways it was just like the old days on the *kopje*. The air might smell of petrol fumes rather than cooking fires, and buildings and road might surround our small patch of bush, but as we crouched hot and hidden in the encroaching acacias and long grasses, we could have been back home. Hazinei told Abel the ghost stories that she had told me and he listened with his hands folded under his chin like a child rather than the almost-man he was. They told each other the story of Nehanda over and over. I sat a little distance from them, superstitiously clutching the bullet that Chenjerai had given me to avert the bad fortune that choked my breath. Hazvinei's stories had brought us nothing but disaster, and I did not want to attract the spirits' attention again.

Babamukuru liked to see the three of us spending time together. 'Good boy,' he said to Abel. 'You are taking very good care of your cousins. You are happy, *vana*, yes?'

'Yes, Babamukuru,' we chorused.

'And you are getting good at football now, Tinashe? You will be on the team?'

'Yes, Babamukuru.'

'Good good.' He patted me on the head. I felt the full weight of my guilt under his hand.

The men outside the shebeen knew my sister now, as she passed by them every day to run her errands at the store and visit us at the school gates. They all seemed to agree that she needed a man to teach her a lesson, preferably in his bed. They joked about her, but there was a dark, secret undercurrent to their jokes, a hunger that made them lick their lips and bare their teeth as they talked.

Tete Nyasha took Hazvinei to the shop in town to buy her bras – mysterious concoctions of wire and cotton – but even then her breasts strained against the fabric of her dress. When we walked to the shops, the men who lounged outside the shebeen and wolf-whistled at passing women did not whistle at my sister. Instead, they stared at her with thirsty eyes and stopped their drinking to watch the sulky, passionate swing of her skirt, the way her waist seemed to beg for an arm to slide around it. It was hard for me to see her as an object of desire, my little sister who still bit me when she was angry. I felt the shadow of bad fortune over us again, watching us from the sky, but I hoped that we were safe. I hoped that it could not find us here in Babamukuru's house with its big refrigerator full of food.

And then I heard the new stories. As Hazvinei continued to

ignore the men, not even smiling at them as she passed, they began to whisper. I wish she had smiled, or even called an insult – then they would have laughed and forgotten about her. But their admiration turned to something else, and their gossip reached everyone – even me.

'Hazvinei.' I told her about the men outside the shebeen.

She laughed in my face. 'Do you know why men say this?' she asked me. 'It is because beautiful women are powerful. They want to possess them for their own. But because the men who say this look like a *chidhomo*, they know they will never have these women. And so they say they are witches.'

'They say they have seen you naked at night,' I said. It was difficult to get the words out. 'They say you ride on the back of a hyena.'

'What? I walk at night sometimes.'

I did not know this. 'Are you crazy? Why?'

'When I cannot sleep.'

'How do you get outside?'

'I climb out of the window. It is not hard. And I do not go far.'

'Hazvinei, that is not safe. You do not know what is out there at night-time.'

She shrugged. 'Frogs. Owls.'

'Why? Why do you do it?'

'I am bored, Tinashe. I am here all day.'

'I know, but . . .'

'I would be glad of a *bere* to carry me. I get tired walking.'

'Don't say that, Hazvinei.'

'I am just joking.'

'It does not matter. Do not say such things.'

She was silent for a moment, frowning. Then she said, 'You mean to say those men have been watching me?'

'I suppose so.'

'And you said nothing?'

'Hazvinei . . .' I was afraid, I wanted to say. Of course I want to protect you, but do you realise what these men are saying, Hazvinei? Do you realise what it means?

'Hazvinei, be careful,' is what I actually said. She flicked my arm off her shoulder as if she was flicking off a mosquito. 'Hazvinei . . .'

But she was already running. I followed her, a fearful rock rabbit, running in her shadow.

One man watched Hazvinei more than the others. He was a large, quiet man with a square head and large, square hands. He drank, but he did not seem to get drunk. He did not join in with the lewd remarks of the other men, but listened and said nothing. He watched her at church. He sat in one of the front pews, and he wore a smart black hat, and he watched her.

'Who is that?' I asked Tete Nyasha.

'It is Michael Mapfumo,' she said. 'He owns a furniture shop.'

'Oh-oh.' I had heard of him. He was a good man, people said.

'He is very wealthy,' said Tete Nyasha, 'but he has not forgotten who his friends are.'

'Is he married?'

'No,' said Tete Nyasha. 'He lives alone.'

I imagined him in his rooms above the furniture shop, rubbing polish into his perfectly shined shoes every night on his own. Perhaps cooking himself a pot of *sadza*. Making himself a pot of tea that he would drink alone.

'I do not like him,' said Hazvinei.

'Why not? He is a good man.'

'There is something about him.' She shrugged. 'It does not matter.'

I knew that my sister was bored, and I could not blame her for spending so much time with Abel. To me, it felt like we were playing the *vakomana* game again, just the three of us. But Abel had the scholarship exam to look forward to, and university, when he grew out of these games, and Hazvinei had nothing. I was worried that she would become too attached to Abel and his ideas and ignore the growing reputation that she had among the men of the town. If she were not to go to school, then she must get married – and who would marry someone with those whispers following her?

'There is no point educating her,' said Babamukuru. 'It is good that you care for your sister, Tinashe, but I know what is best for her.'

I had to be satisfied with that – and, truthfully, I was glad to work at my school books without having to worry about Hazvinei. School had become easier as I caught up with the reading and learned to behave as the other boys did. I worked my way to the head of the class, and I started to think that I might have a chance at a scholarship as well. I hugged this secret thought to myself, guarded it as I guarded my lucky bullet, and did not mention it to anyone – not even to Hazvinei.

I did not always go to the camp after school with my cousin and my sister. Sometimes I would leave them to play their games and walk to the store to buy a Coke and sit on the benches outside with my books. I spent some time there, reading and watching the old men who sat outside the shebeen opposite, playing *Tsoro Yematatu* all day – 'Three Rabbits', a game where bottle caps hopped over each other on a hollowed-out wooden board. At the shebeen I felt like a man among men, but sometimes one of the drunks would stagger over and try to start a conversation. On this day, one man in particular stared at me with peculiar intensity. I tried not to notice him, but his stare was so intent and so unblinking that I could feel it like a red ant stinging my temple. When I looked at him, he smiled and waved, as if he had spotted an old friend, pushed back his chair with a great deal of grunting and effort, and walked over to me.

He heaved himself into the chair opposite me, and mopped his forehead with his sleeve. 'Oh-oh! Hot?'

He asked it as a question, and I had to agree. 'Yes.'

We sat in silence for a moment, as he breathed hot, heavy fat-man breaths and sighed loud sighs.

'I recognise you,' I said, trying to be polite. 'Are you a friend of my uncle's?'

The man waved his hand. 'You have seen me here before,' he said. He grinned. He had teeth like clean pips in his fat, purple-black cheeks.

'Let me get you a drink.' He waved at the man inside, who brought us two Chibukus, the thin beer that came in fat plastic tubs with screw-on lids. I hated Chibuku. The fat man, however, up-ended his tub and took a long sloshing, gurgling drink from it. When he had finished, he let out another sigh and smiled at me as if we were conspirators together, plotting a wonderful surprise. 'And do you know what my job is?'

'I do not.' I looked around for rescue. One of Babamukuru's friends caught my eye and lifted a hand as if to wave, but then saw my companion and stopped. He turned away as if he had not seen me.

'I am a witch-smeller,' said the man.

I remembered the witch-smellers from the *kopje*. My stomach turned. 'What?'

'A witch-smeller. You have heard of people like me?'

Smoke rising. The smell of burning.

'Witch-smellers are women. Old women,' I said.

'Not always.' The man laid a heavy hand on my shoulder.

'I did not think you were needed in the city,' I said. I

remembered the old women with red-streaked hair and breasts sagging and wrinkled like old gourds, who pointed their horse-tail switches at the *varoyi* and marked them out. I looked for an escape, but there was no way in which I could leave politely. The man smiled. I did not trust his smooth, fat face and the happy crease of his eyes.

'There has been misfortune,' he said. He swigged his beer, and breathed on me. His breath was sweet, tinged with barley.

I bit my lip hard and tasted blood. 'I do not see what that has to do with me.'

'Eh-eh!' He seemed happy to hear me say this. 'But that is the thing, Tinashe.' He tapped his forefinger against the table. 'That is the very thing. It is your sister that I have come to talk to you about.'

'My sister?'

'Hazvinei, yes? It is a strange name.'

'My father expected a boy,' I said, and the words 'my father' felt like a piece of gristle in my mouth.

'Do you know what the tradition is, Tinashe?' he said.

I buried my mouth in the warming beer. I did not open my lips, but I felt it fizzing against my skin. The scent of the sweet beer filled my nostrils and made me feel sick. It smelled of decay. 'You find witches,' I said, and twitched my shoulders in a half-shrug. 'You will not find any here.'

The witch-smeller rested his hands on the table and touched his fat fingers together. 'Women like your sister,' he said, 'must be married. It is dangerous for such a woman to wander alone. I have spoken to your uncle about this. Her female essence is not guarded, not protected. Not guided in the proper way.' He straightened. 'If she had a husband, things would be different. As it is . . .'

'What is she supposed to have done?' I heard my voice grow sharp, and struggled to control it.

'Men have complained of their seed spilling in the night,' he said. 'Wasted on their blankets when it should go to grow children. Your sister troubles their dreams. She unmans them.'

'That is ridiculous,' I said. 'No one can control dreams.'

'And the bad fortune that has come to us?' he said. 'The accidents? You know that Cephas slipped and cut his head open on this very bar,' he knocked his fist against it, 'last night, as he was talking about your sister?'

I shook my head. I wanted to shake out the sound of his voice that was buzzing in my ear like the whine of a mosquito. 'He was drunk. You cannot believe these things.'

He shrugged. 'Perhaps. But I have heard other things.'

'If they are as stupid as a drunk man slipping and hitting his head . . .'

'I have heard that your sister consorts with spirits,' he said. 'That she talks to them. That she walks alone in the night.'

'She has done no such thing.' I felt a muscle in my leg jump, and my knee hit the table. Lightly, ever so lightly, but the witch-smeller had felt it – I could see on his face that he had felt it.

He tapped his nose. 'I am a witch-smeller, Tinashe,' he said. 'It is my job to know these things.'

'You know nothing,' I said.

'I am saying these things to you for your own good, Tinashe,' he said. 'Do you not want to help your sister? Would you rather not know what people are saying? I am giving you a chance.'

'A chance to do what?'

He stood. 'Do you know what happens when I find a witch?'

I looked at him, and said neither yes nor no.

'You will find out,' he said. 'Everything has been tainted. You. Your aunt and uncle. Your house. Everything.'

I could not look at him.

'Your sister is like a *putzi* fly. She coils under your skin and

she eats you up from the inside, leaving nothing but poison,'
he said. 'I know these things.'

Hazvinei telling Amai it was I who had eaten all the peanut
butter. Hazvinei talking to the *njuzu,* brandishing the N'anga's
medicine stick, bringing drama and complications into my life
at every turn. Hazvinei offering me her school shoes, looking
lost and confused when the spirits of the rain dance left her.
Hazvinei's smile.

I scraped back my chair and I left the witch-smeller sitting
there.

The white policemen lingered in our area, as they had done in
the *kopje* after Chenjerai's visit. This did not deter Abel. He
loved thinking that the police were looking for him as the source
of the rumours of *vakomana*. He greeted them with exaggerated
friendliness, finding excuses to walk past them and smile and
wave. He liked to stand and talk to them, bumming cigarettes
off them when he could.

I did not join them. I felt the white men's eyes on me as I
hung back, and they shamed me.

'Tinashe!' Abel tried to wave me over, to include me, but
I did not come.

'I have to do my homework. I have to study.'

'You worry too much about studying. You will dry up like
an old branch if you work too hard.'

I kicked at stones on my way home and I developed a habit
of clenching my fist around the bullet in my pocket as I walked,
as if it would protect me from the things I feared.

I remembered a time when I had believed that Baba patrolled
the house at night, protecting us from the leopards. There was
no one to protect us now. The leopards were getting in; I could
see their claws in every crack in the walls. I smelled smoke
— the sweet, greasy smoke of burning flesh. I saw the flames

above the *kopje*, saw the shuddering woman in the thin cotton dress. At night, my dreams tormented me with witch-smellers and white policemen and the smell of burning.

'What is wrong with you, Tinashe?' Abel gave me a friendly shove. 'Your face is long.'

'Nothing.'

'Then smile.'

I did not tell him about the witch-smeller. I did not tell anyone – not even Hazvinei. I tried to study, but the black words on the white page made sinister shapes and I could not read them.

And everywhere I went was the witch-smeller. He seemed to arrive everywhere just before I did: standing outside the supermarket, or sitting in the shebeen, or cycling down the road on his too-small bicycle. He grinned at me with his missing-tooth mouth, and waved as if to a very good friend. I did not wave back. How I wished that Hazvinei were a quieter, gentler sort of sister, one who would not trouble me with night-time imaginings!

Abel and I were walking back from the camp when he saw the witch-smeller too, sitting in the middle of a knot of men. The witch-smeller remained silent, but the other men catcalled and shouted. I heard Hazvinei's name clearly, and the word *muroyi*. Abel's face closed down and he walked faster, so that I had to scurry to keep up. We waited until we were a safe distance away before we stopped.

'What the hell is going on, Tinashe?'

He really did not seem to know. Did Abel never speak to any of the men? He did not seem to speak to anyone these days apart from Hazvinei and me, and then it was all about the *vakomana* and stories of war.

'Who do they think they are, speaking about my cousin that way?'

'I am taking care of it, Abel,' I said. 'I am watching her.'

'They have no right to talk about her at all.'

I tried to keep him quiet. 'I do not want Babamukuru to know. They fight enough already. Please, Abel.'

'Tell me who is saying these things. Tell me and I will deal with them.'

'No. Calm down.'

'Tell me their names.'

I turned away from my cousin and his clenched fists. 'I am taking care of it, Abel. I am taking care of my sister.'

He stared at me, flat-eyed. 'You had better take care of her, Tinashe. I am going to be watching you.'

I pressed my mouth into a thin line and said nothing. I did not need Abel to tell me these things. As I watched him walk away, I wondered why he felt so strongly about this. He and Hazvinei spent a great deal of time together and had become close, but he could not have fallen under her strange spell. Such things were not allowed between cousins. The *mhondoro* spirits would not allow it. I put it from my mind, along with the other suspicions that the witch-smeller had sown in me. I would watch Hazvinei. She would be safe. That was all.

Chapter Seventeen

'So. I have made you an appointment at the college.'

Babamukuru had come home fat and fizzing with pride. I was wondering what had puffed him up, and now I knew. I had seen boys from the college before. They wore maroon and gold uniforms; blazers with shiny metal buttons. This was the college that Abel was to attend for his final two years of school – the one that would almost guarantee him a place in a good university. It was also one of the first such schools in the country to accept black pupils.

'You will take an entrance examination.'

'The same exam that Abel is taking?'

'Yes. That one.'

I wet my lips. 'Is it for a scholarship?' Was I supposed to compete against my cousin for the place?

'No. I will pay your school fees.'

'Really, Babamukuru?'

His smile smoothed out his face. 'Yes, Tinashe.'

I did not know what to say.

'You remember that I promised I would take care of your education,' said Babamukuru. 'I have not forgotten. And I have seen how hard you work at school.'

'But what about Abel, Babamukuru?'

'You are both my boys.' He rested his hand on my head. 'I want you both to grow up to be educated men. Yes?'

I did not know what to say. 'Thank you, Babamukuru.'

'You are welcome, Tinashe,' he said. He rested his hand on

my head, as if he were blessing me. 'You are a good boy,' he said. And those four words made me feel so ashamed of deceiving him that I became sick to my stomach and had to sit on the toilet for an hour.

'He is so excited that it has made him ill,' said Babamukuru to Tete Nyasha.

The next day when I left school I did not go to join Abel and Hazvinei at the camp. Instead, I walked for a long time along the streets. Jacarandas popped beneath my feet and left purple bruises on the soles of my shoes. I did not realise the length of time and the distance I had been walking until I stood outside the gates of the college, the fancy school that prepared young men for university, looking at the coat-of-arms on the iron gates and listening to the rough-voiced laughter of the boys who scattered from it like ants from a stepped-on nest.

I stood outside the gates, staring up at them, conscious of my scuffed shoes and too-long shorts flapping around my knees. There was the usual crush of street kids, vendors and ice-cream men outside, but beyond the wrought iron I saw a smooth green smear of lawn and stone buildings, and a black boy in the college uniform. He was taller than me, and lighter in skin – closer to Hazvinei's height and colouring. He had a row of little badges down the collar of his blazer, and they were all different colours with collections of little white letters on each. As I watched, he looked up and smiled at the white boy next to him. I ducked away, as if he might sense my gaze and look up at me. I did not want him to see me, because then he and I would be separate people with separate lives and achieve-ments. I wanted him to be a Tinashe for me, an empty gourd on which I could draw my own face, like the pod dolls that Hazvinei and I made when we were very small.

What did I know? How could I tell from that one quick glance that the black boy was happy at that school, that he had friends and was doing well with his studies? I did not know, of course. But I chose to believe that no one could be happier and luckier than that boy: that no one would be happier and luckier than me when I got in to a white boys' school and got an Education, a proper one that could take me out of this place and into the world.

I told Hazvinei when I got home.

'Why do you want to go there?' she said. 'It is full of whites.'

'It is a good school.'

She shrugged irritably. 'It is just school.'

'It is where Abel is going.'

'Abel is not going to go to school. He has more important things to do.'

'But he is taking the exam.'

'He says he won't take it.'

'He is lying. Babamukuru will make him.'

'No one can make Abel do anything,' she said with pride.

I picked at some dirt under my fingernails. 'I want to go to university and get a proper job, like Babamukuru. You think I should leave school like Abel wants to? Live in the bush?'

She snorted. 'I am going to see Abel,' she said. 'You stay here and study your books.'

I waited for a while, so that she would think it was my own idea to go to the camp. After hearing Hazvinei's reaction, I decided I would not tell Abel about the exam. As it turned out, he had heard already, and did not care.

'It is a big waste of time,' he said. 'I don't know why you are bothering to do it.'

Most weeks, Abel took my homework and copied it. He was meant to be studying for the entrance exam as well, but I did not see him so much as open a book.

'It is your contribution to the struggle,' said Abel. He poked me in the ribs and grinned.

That was fine by me. The solutions to maths problems and the answers to comprehension questions were simple and comforting when compared to the shooting of a gun. Abel had managed to buy bullets now, and had started shooting at tin cans lined up on tree branches.

'Someone will hear us.'

'Stop worrying, Tinashe. No one will hear.'

The sharp snap and echo of the shots sounded very loud to me. I covered my ears whenever Abel took aim.

'It is because he has such big ears, like an elephant's,' said Abel, and pinched one of my earlobes to make me squeal.

Abel did not let Hazvinei handle the guns, but she wanted to. Oh, how she wanted to! Her eyes shone and her fingers twitched as if she could feel the trigger already. Her lips parted as the shots rang out, and she licked her lips to taste the ash and powder.

'It is too dangerous for you,' said Abel with authority. 'Girls are no good at shooting. You will kill somebody.'

'I will not!' Hazvinei was all over him, tugging at his sleeve and jumping so that she could catch his eye. 'Let me try.'

'No.'

I did not try to shoot either. I could have asked. I think Abel would have let me. But I did not want to. He did not comment, but I saw him watching me as I sat with my back against the tree, working on his homework and my own.

'You enjoy this,' he said to me one day.

I shrugged. 'It has to be done.'

'No. You like doing it.' He leaned over my shoulder to see what I was doing. I covered up my neat, rounded handwriting with one hand, suddenly embarrassed. Abel smiled and moved away.

Sometimes, I found it hard to concentrate on school and on the entrance examination after our afternoons in Abel's camp.

I sat at my desk and wrote in my exercise book, but I saw sun-warmed gun barrels, boiled sweets crushed by army boots, bitter tea in chipped mugs. I imagined having a gun of my own. I could feel the long, smooth weight of it against my hip. I fingered the smooth, cool bullet in my pocket and was excited by how small and innocent it was, this little bead of grey. I could not imagine shooting someone. Hazvinei could. She hoisted imaginary guns to her shoulder in our games. 'You are dead,' she announced. And she grinned.

Soon, playing at the camp after school was not enough for Abel. 'We haven't done anything yet,' he said.

'Like what?'

'Like actually helping the freedom fighters. Doing something – for the struggle.'

'We are not ready,' I said, hoping that he would lose interest. Where was he planning to find these freedom fighters, anyway? They were out in the bush or lying low, not strolling the streets looking for teenagers with one gun between them. 'We need to practise more.'

'We are never going to be ready unless we do something,' said Abel.

I enjoyed sitting and talking about our grand plans, cooking on our fire and cleaning the gun. I was content to keep playing this game. I did not want to do anything real. I voiced a thought that I had not shared with Abel before. 'The radio said that majority rule is coming soon,' I said. 'Do we really need to fight any more? Surely the fighting will be finished now?'

Abel sat back on his haunches, contemptuous. 'Are you stupid?'

I got enough of that from Hazvinei.

'You believe the whites when they say these things? Do not be an idiot.'

'But it was on the news.'

'And who do you think writes the news? You think the freedom fighters write the news?'

I was silent.

'We are still needed,' said Abel. 'You will see.'

It was hard to believe in a war, here in town. The guerrillas attacked farms and rural areas and did not come to these wide, dusty streets lined with jacaranda trees. We saw graffiti proclaiming loyalties to one party or another, and we saw the shadow that hovered in the air like petrol fumes, but our lives were largely untouched by that wider world.

I was grateful to be going to school in town. I had heard about the rural schools – mission schools, some of them – that had been attacked by freedom fighters. Many schoolchildren had been abducted and taken across the borders to train as guerrillas themselves. Abel would have loved that, I thought. There were whispers about Nehanda, as well; that she had returned, and that she would lead the freedom fighters to victory this time. The word had its own magic – *nehanda, nehanda* – soft syllables that sounded like a whisper even when spoken aloud. We listened to all of this every morning and evening, and then we came to school and learned complicated mathematical equations as if nothing at all were happening.

I awoke one night to feel a weight on the bed and an insistent pinching of the soft skin at my wrist.

'Hazvinei?'

'You snore like an old *sekuru*,' said Hazvinei. I could see her eyes glinting in the darkness.

'It is night-time. Go back to bed. Do you want to wake up Abel?'

'Abel sleeps like a dead person. He never wakes up.'

'Babamukuru will give you a hiding if he knows you are in our room. Go back to bed.'

She bounced a little on my mattress. I saw the gleam of her

white teeth. 'I think I am like Nehanda. I am going to be a spirit medium. I can help Abel.'

I sat up on my elbow, fully awake now. 'What?'

'You heard me.'

'Hazvinei, you are thirteen years old.'

'So?'

'You are crazy.'

'But I have a gift.' She wriggled on the bed, restless with glee. 'You heard what Baba said about Mbuya Nehanda.'

'Yes, but . . . Hazvinei, you are not Nehanda.'

'No, but I could be like her.'

'We are not of royal blood,' I said. 'Baba is . . . was not a chief.'

'So?' Hazvinei sat upright, righteous, glowing.

'So, you cannot be carrying a *mhondoro* spirit.' I rested my head against the pillow again. 'You must not talk about these things. People will not believe that you are carrying a clan spirit, or even that you are a N'anga. You know what they will say. You know what they call girls like you.'

'Perhaps I am the exception.'

'You are not.'

'How would you know? You know nothing about these things. You do not know what it is like for me.'

'Yes, and I do not want to know.'

'Abel does.' Her eyes narrow, golden. 'We have talked about it.'

'You have?' A worm of jealousy in my breast.

'Abel knows how important I could be.'

'You just want to think you are special so that Abel will like you better,' I said. 'I am sorry, Hazvinei, but it is true. You are just a little girl with too much imagination.'

She opened her mouth to speak, but I was faster.

'If you continue to talk like this, I will tell Babamukuru.'

'You wouldn't.'

'I would.'

'That would mean you would have to stop going to the camp as well. You will no longer be the little *mujiba*.' The errand-boy. A bead of spittle landed on my hand. I wiped it off.

'I do not care,' I said. 'Baba told me to look after you, Hazvinei. You know that. I cannot have you fooling around and getting yourself into trouble.'

Hazvinei held my gaze. 'You would rather stay here? Go to school like a good little boy?'

'School is what will get me a good future. Not fighting. Not the spirits.'

'And what about me, eh, Tinashe?' Hazvinei stood. 'Married to some fat old man. Having a child every year until I break in half. Will you write to me sometimes, from your fancy school?'

'It will not be like that,' I said. But she had gone.

The next day, Hazvinei went alone to the camp, sneaking out before I could notice. I did my homework in the unaccustomed silence, and then followed, walking slowly, kicking at stones. When I arrived at the camp, greeted by Hazvinei's baleful stare, I told Abel about the policemen's questions. VaStephen and Njiri stopped me often to ask if I had heard anything, and I had started to worry.

'Good,' said Abel.

'Good?'

'I want them to hear about us. I want them to know about us.'

'Why?'

'So they can be afraid.'

'Of us?'

'Of course of us. We are *vakomana*. They should be frightened.'

I sat in silence. I did not want to point out that we were still playing the old game we had invented on the *kopje* – that nothing had really changed.

'We all have to start playing our part,' said Abel. 'You said you would bring us supplies, and you have brought us nothing.'

'I do not have any money.'

'What about the money Amai gives you for the tuck shop?'

I had hoarded my coins as much as I could, and we ate what little food we could scrounge – usually fruits that we collected from the ground, fat and bursting with flies. After a while, though, Hazvinei became more enterprising.

We went to the corner shop near the school – the one that was run by a fat Indian man who smelled of onions. A corrugated iron roof shaded a few scrawny chickens and the old men who leaned against the walls. The sweets were in jars on the counter; bright, artificial colours that still attracted us as flowers attract bees, even though we were teenagers now and not scruffy *kopje* kids.

'*Masikati*,' said Hazvinei as we walked in. The Indian man glanced at us, then returned his attention to a fly buzzing inside the ice-cream fridge.

Hazvinei walked along the rows of sweet jars, letting her long fingers trail over them.

'What are you going to do?' I whispered.

'Shush.' She turned and walked back down the row. 'Can we have a bag?' she asked the shopkeeper.

'Let me see the money first.'

Hazvinei proffered her grubby coins, still hot from her fist. He spread it out on the counter.

'Fine.'

We filled a plastic bag with more sweets than we could eat in a week.

'Get some of the Freddo Frogs.'

'I don't like them.'

'I do.'

'They are not for you. They are for Abel.'

When she had finished, Hazvinei gave the bag to the shop-keeper to be weighed. He gave her the bag and her change.

'Now *voertsek*,' he said.

Hazvinei hovered.

'Either buy something else or go home,' said the Indian, and turned his back to shoo out one of the scrawny neighbourhood pigeons that had wandered in hoping for a few grains of meal from one of the overflowing sacks.

Hazvinei watched him go. She saw him stop to exchange a few words with a man who was leaning his bicycle against the wall outside. Her hand flashed out as quick as a black mamba and grabbed three packets of cigarettes.

'What are you doing?'

'Abel likes cigarettes,' she said, and tucked the packets inside her jersey. She spun on her heel and walked out of the door into the sunlight, haloed bright against the open doorway, so that I could see every stray hair on her head and every ball of fluff on her jersey as if they were on fire, and she was gone. I followed.

'Hazvinei!'

The shopkeeper stood with crossed arms, watching us go. 'You not buying anything else, then?' he asked me. I shook my head.

'Bloody piccanins,' he said. 'Don't come in here wasting my time again.'

'No, sir.' I stood on one foot, ready to run, and as soon as he turned away I sprinted after my sister.

Hazvinei carried the sweets and cigarettes in her skirt as we ran down the hill. She did not spill one, even when I pretended to bump into her by accident. Sure-footed and quick, she regained her balance, and it was I who stumbled and tasted dust. When we – breathless and giggling – spilled from the brown bush into the camp, Hazvinei let her booty fall, scattering a rainbow into the brown-and-yellow of the bush. Abel laughed as he scrambled to pick up first the cigarettes, then the chocolate, and Hazvinei grinned at him, glowing with triumph.

'For you,' she said.

'How did you get it all?'

I coated my tongue with Freddo Frog, preparing for a lie, but Hazvinei was too quick. She told the story. 'And I stole the rest.'

Beaming, on fire, shivering with glee. A small, wicked animal.

'She is exaggerating,' I said, but Abel was not listening to me.

He laughed and touched Hazvinei's hair. 'Good girl,' he said. He turned to me. 'Of course, she has done it before.'

'What?'

'She does it often. Where do you think I got those bullets, hey? She has quick fingers, your sister.'

'Where did she steal the bullets from?'

For the first time, Abel seemed to realise that I was not as relaxed and grinning as he was. 'What are you worrying about, Tinashe? She did not steal them from you.' He held out a cigarette. 'Have one.'

'I do not want one.'

What else were these two hiding from me? What else had they been doing without me? I watched them as they blew smoke rings and laughed like the two children they had been, and I left them there to walk the long walk back to Babamukuru's house. I do not think they even noticed that I had gone.

My *sadza* tasted of bile that night. I looked across the table at Hazvinei's smooth, shining face. She still glowed with the success of the day, and I wanted that light to go out. I hated the way that she and Abel smiled at each other, as if they had a special understanding that would never include me. I hated the way that a secret between my cousin and me had become a secret between my cousin and my sister, leaving me on the outside.

'Babamukuru, Hazvinei stole cigarettes.' It was out. Abel flicked his eyes to me, and then down to his plate. He would get me later, when we were alone in our room. I knew it.

'Don't tell stories, Tinashe.'

'I am not telling stories. She still has some in her dress pocket.'

'Tinashe,' said Tete Nyasha. She put her fingers to her lips.

'She has! Look.' I tried to put my hand inside her dress pocket. Hazvinei looked at me, eyes big with betrayal, then grabbed my hand and sank her teeth into it.

'*Iwe*!'

In the commotion that followed, Tete Nyasha got inside Hazvinei's pocket and found a single slim cigarette. Still Hazvinei said nothing.

And then Babamukuru struck Hazvinei with the flat of his hand.

'Babamukuru! Stop!'

He did it again and again, his lips pursed in concentration, his brow only faintly furrowed, as if it were a problem he was trying to solve. Tete Nyasha let out a wail, but although her mouth was expressing surprise and horror, her eyes were not. Abel too. He sat still and said nothing, watching his father hit Hazvinei. I had caused this and I could not stop it.

'Babamukuru! Please!'

I shook off my horror and ran to grasp his arm, but Tete Nyasha stopped me and held me back. 'No, Tinashe.'

Abel sat and did not move. His face had no expression. I caught his eye, hoping to see my own horror reflected there, but I saw nothing.

Once more I struggled to get free, but Babamukuru had finished, and Hazvinei was crouched on the floor. She did not cry. Tete Nyasha rushed to her, and Babamukuru clasped Abel and me by our shoulders and drew us outside. I shrank, fearful of a beating, but he clapped me on the back. He seemed energised, refreshed.

'Now, Tinashe, Abel, I will take you to the shebeen, and you will see what being a real man is like.'

Abel looked at me, but once again I could not read his expression. Babamukuru could not be serious, I thought. But he was.

We left my sister there, crouched on the floor with Tete Nyasha bending over her. We followed Babamukuru as he walked the dimly lit streets with a long, smart stride, the heels on his shining shoes hitting the pavement with a firm clip. At the shebeen, he ordered beers for him and for Abel. Here in the bright lights and noise, the horrors of the evening seemed far away and floating. Hazvinei's dark eyes stared up at me from the puddles of spilled Chibuku on the tiled floor.

I was not allowed to drink, but I felt drunk anyway, as Babamukuru introduced me to friends and laughed so hard that spittle formed at the corners of his mouth. He was a different man, and I did not recognise him. I saw Abel drinking beer and saying nothing, his eyes dark holes in his face. He did not speak to me.

'I warned your Baba,' Babamukuru was saying to me. I saw his mouth opening and shutting like the mouth of a dying fish. 'I warned him about her. She is a devil child, I said when she was born. We knew that such a one would come to the family. A N'anga had told our mother so, long before you were born. Or you, Abel.'

He clapped his son on the back. Abel looked down into his glass and said nothing.

'Babamukuru?' My head rang with the strangeness of the evening.

'She is a *muroyi*,' said Babamukuru. 'The N'anga told him so, but he would not listen. He told Garikai that she would bring a curse upon the whole family, and look how it has happened.' He wagged his finger. 'The N'anga on the *kopje* knew, didn't he? Didn't he? He told your Baba as well. But he would not pay attention.'

'No.' I did not say this out loud, but I heard the word in my head as clearly as if someone had spoken it.

Babamukuru wagged his finger at me. 'I warned him. The N'anga warned him. And now look what has happened, hey?'

Babamukuru rambled, mumbling into his beer, speaking beer-sodden thoughts through the moustache of froth that lined his upper lip, while Abel and I sat in silence and listened.

He told us that women are aliens within the family, always. They have alien blood, different from ours. They are unclean, because of the stubborn way they insist, every month, on leaking blood from their insides. And not the noble, proudly red blood that is shed by warriors and hunters and the beating hearts of prey, but a sluggish, brown blood that is messy and thick as sweet beer.

Alien blood is dangerous, he said. It is unpredictable. It is easily tempted to black magic, and seductive once it has succumbed. It is always on the lookout for magic, always ready to respond to it – and willing. Women have to fight this alien blood all the time, even when powerful spirits bring all their force to bear on them. Because when they do succumb to it, no matter how powerful the demon or spirit who tempted them, it is always their fault. It is the same way as in the Bible. If a woman who has been tempted by a demon then draws a man into sinning – into committing some delicious sin that he enjoys – it is still not the man's fault. It is the woman's. This is just something we know. It is something the women know. If they let themselves be drawn in, then they will have to pay, one way or another.

The more beautiful and intelligent and exceptional the woman, the more likely she is to be a witch. It is just in the nature of things.

He paused and took a final swig. 'There is a saying,' said Babamukuru. '*Guyu kutsvukira kunze mukati muzere masvosve*. From the outside a fig may look delicious, but inside it may be filled with ants.'

We helped Babamukuru home. He leaned his full weight on me, and I struggled up the steps to the *stoep*, to where Tete Nyasha was waiting to take him from me and put him to bed.

'*Mazvita tatenda*, Tinashe,' she said.

'Good night, Tete,' I said. I saw Babamukuru blink, his eyes bleary and malevolent, and I was afraid for her.

'Abel . . .' I tried to stop him before he went indoors.

He shook his head. 'I do not want to talk. Go and see your sister.'

He followed his parents to the kitchen, where the remains of our dinner still sat on the table, and I went to check on Hazvinei. She was asleep. There was something dark on her pillow, and superstitiously I thought it was a spirit whispering in her ear while she slept – but then I saw it was blood. There was a sticky trail on her pillow, and a red dusting of it on the shoulders of her white nightgown. She looked defiant, even in her sleep. I touched her ear, lightly, and her eyes snapped open.

'What?'

'Were you asleep?'

'No.'

'Hazvinei, I am sorry.' I started to weep, to my shame and

embarrassment. 'I am sorry. I did not know. I did not know that he would do this. I am sorry.'

She turned her face away from me.

'I want you to be safe. We could be safe here. We could be safe from all the things that threatened us on the *kopje*, if we could just be careful . . .'

'You call this safe?'

'Babamukuru was just angry. He did not know what he was doing.'

Hazvinei sat up. 'Have you ever noticed Tete Nyasha's bruises, hey? Have you ever wondered why she has cuts on her head?'

'She told me she cuts her own hair and sometimes the scissors slip. And she is clumsy. She walks into things.'

'I knew you were stupid, Tinashe, but I did not know how stupid.'

'I am not stupid!'

She looked at me with old eyes. 'Yes, you are. Why do you think she never visited us on the *kopje*?'

'She was busy, she said. She wanted to come.'

'And why do you think she lost those babies?'

I covered my ears with my hands, to shut out this knowledge. I shook my head. 'No.'

'Why do you think Abel always had bruises and scrapes when he came to stay with us, and Baba never said anything about it? Why do you think Baba and Amai never let us visit Babamukuru's house?'

I rocked back and forth. 'No, Hazvinei. You are wrong.'

She looked at me with pity. 'Why do you think that Abel has a gun and wants to get away from his Baba as soon as he can, hey? Do you still think Babamukuru is a good man?'

I had no answer.

'Go to bed, Tinashe,' she said. 'I do not need you here.'

That night I dreamed of Simba, my phantom brother. I saw

him floating, his little fists and feet clenched together and his eyes screwed shut. I watched him turn and turn in the dim light, waiting for something else to happen. Nothing did. Simba's moth eyes blinked at me from the laughing darkness, and, strangely, I felt at peace.

Chapter Eighteen

Hazvinei was right. I was stupid. Now I saw how Tete Nyasha kept her eyes lowered when serving Babamukuru his dinner, and how she flinched when he coughed or put his drinking glass down on the table too hard. I saw that she had to ask permission to make telephone calls to her family. I saw the way that Abel raised his arms to his face when he argued with his father, warding off a blow, and I wondered that he had the courage to confront his father at all. I saw that neither his nor Tete Nyasha's bruises ever quite went away.

Babamukuru behaved no differently after beating Hazvinei. He carried on as if it were a matter of routine – and for him it was, I saw. He smiled and laughed as usual. He patted me on the head and called me a good boy. He ate his dinner with a big appetite. When I looked at him I could still see the wealthy and magnificent Babamukuru of the *kopje*, the big man with the shining car who was all-powerful and generous as God. It was very difficult to stop seeing that picture – but slowly, slowly it began to fall away. I saw how the men of the town did not speak to Babamukuru unless they had to. I noticed for the first time that no friends visited him; that he drank alone. After church, no one came to shake his hand. I saw that Babamukuru was not the important man here that he had been on the *kopje*; that others knew the truth, as well.

'Why did you not tell me, Abel?' I said to him. 'Or Baba? He could have helped you.'

Abel shrugged.

'I would have helped you,' I said. 'If I had known.'

'And what would you have done?' said Abel. 'The whole *kopje* thinks that Baba is the greatest man in the world. That is why he loves to visit, and leaves Amai at home so no one can see her.'

'Still,' I said. 'You should have said something.'

'It is not so bad,' said Abel. 'It is only when he drinks. And Amai knows to keep out of his way.'

I twisted my hands in my lap. I did not know what to say.

'I will get out of his way,' said Abel. 'As soon as I can, I will be out of here. I am not going to be an old man in a suit that stinks of beer. I am going to live in the bush with the *vakomana* and work with my hands like a real man does. Like your Baba.'

'Baba was not a *mukomana*.'

'But he helped them.'

We sat in silence for a moment.

'Why did you do it?' said Abel. 'Why did you tell on Hazvinei?'

It was my turn to look at the ground. 'I am sorry for that.'

'But why?'

'I was jealous,' I said. 'Of you. And Hazvinei. I wanted her to get into trouble.'

'Well, you got your wish.'

'You know I did not want that.'

Abel stood, shaking his head. 'I knew I should not trust you with my secrets,' he said.

I pressed my fists into my eyes until they were red and sore, but it held back the tears. I deserved it, I knew I deserved it, but I had not known the truth about Babamukuru. I would never have done it if I had known the truth.

Perhaps it was not Hazvinei who drew the bad fortune to us after all. Perhaps it had been me all along.

At the camp the next day, Abel let Hazvinei touch the gun

for the very first time. To make her feel better? Perhaps – but I suspected he might be trying to make me feel worse. She ran her fingers along it, caressing it. It looked like a black snake in her hands.

'It is nice, yes?' said Abel. 'Here, Tinashe.'

He balanced his gun across his two open palms, weighed it, and then held it out to me. I was surprised, but I took it. I liked to feel its smooth weight in my hands, heft it to my shoulder and stare down the barrel. I liked the thrill of knowing that it was loaded. I pointed it at passing birds, lizards, a rock rabbit unwise enough to poke out its head from behind a bush.

'Have you ever killed anything?' Abel asked me.

'Yes,' I said. Insects, a bird or two when I was throwing stones.

He pointed into a tree, where a drab brown bird was sitting. 'Shoot that.'

'What is it?'

'It's a bird.'

'I know, but . . .'

'Shoot the bloody bird. Go on.'

'Why?'

'Because I want to see you do it.'

My heart thudded in my ears. I wished I had never picked up the gun. I wished I had stayed leaning against my tree, doing my homework.

'With your gun?'

Abel spread his arms wide. 'Do you see another gun?'

The metal burned my fingers. The long barrel seemed unfriendly now.

'Go on,' said Abel.

I aimed and shot. Wide. The bird flew off with a flurry of feathers and a smile on its beak. I heard Hazvinei giggle.

'Good job.' Abel cuffed me around the ear. 'Try again.'

'Another bird?'

'No, me. Yes, another bird.'

I picked out one in a tree. A thrush, this time. Bigger. Easier to hit.

'Good. Go on.'

I aimed. I took more care, this time. When I fired, the bird dropped out of the tree so quickly that I thought it might have had a heart attack before my bullet hit it.

'Good. Come on.' Abel walked with me to the tree. The thrush was on the ground, not quite dead, its eyes half-closed, and its little breast heaving. The feathers separated and fluffed out as it inhaled, then flattened when it exhaled. Its feet were curled into claws of pain. 'Look at that,' said Abel. 'You got it in the wing, I think.'

Yes, where the wing became the shoulder. I crouched down. I am so sorry, I wanted to say. I am sorry that I killed you because Abel wanted to prove a point and because I wanted to prove it too.

'You will need to kill it,' said Abel.

'It will die soon anyway.' I looked up at him.

'That is cruel, to leave it in pain. It is better to kill it quickly.'

Is it? It is easy to say when you are not the one dying.

'It is just a bird,' said Abel. 'You think too much.'

He took a step forwards and put the full weight of his foot on the bird's head. It crunched.

'Hazvinei,' he said. 'You try.'

Hazvinei pushed past me and took the gun. I had felt her eagerness behind me as I took aim; I could feel the twitching of fingers that longed to close around a trigger, and her scorn as hot and painful as sunburn when I missed.

'Stand back, Tinashe,' said Abel. He pulled me back to stand beside him. I watched Hazvinei: watched as she took aim, watched as she pulled the trigger, watched as a bird fell from the air. And then I watched as Abel smiled at her, and as she smiled at him, and a shadow passed in front of the sun. Abel and Hazvinei. Hazvinei and Abel. There was no room there for Tinashe any longer, and I could not blame them for that.

They started to go to the camp together without telling me. I sat and read my schoolbooks in the lengthening shadows and did not see them until the sun turned red and I heard their laughter approaching. I was too proud to complain or to ask them to wait. I knew that I deserved this punishment.

I was walking home from school when I saw VaStephen again. He was coming out of a shop with a plastic bag full of food. Groceries. Of course he had to shop for groceries, like everyone else, but for some reason I found it hard to imagine him sitting down and eating as we did. He saw me and waved. In the heat his face was shining and pink.

'*Masikati*, Tinashe!'

'*Masikati*.'

I kept walking, looking down at my shoes and hoping that he would let me go.

'*Iwe!*' VaStephen was coming after me. 'Wait.'

I stopped, but did not turn. 'Yes, VaStephen?'

'Something the matter?'

I could not look in his eyes. Abel was reflected there, still. I could feel it. 'No, VaStephen.'

'Hokay.' He stayed, looking at me.

'Is something wrong, VaStephen?' I wanted to get away. I could feel myself wriggling and fidgeting – ants in my pants, as Amai would have said.

'There have been reports of gunshots,' he says. 'Behind the school. We looked, but could not find anything.'

I stayed silent.

'Have you heard them, Tinashe?'

'No, VaStephen.'

'It is dangerous to play with guns,' he said. 'Someone will get hurt.'

Why did he ask me these things? Why did he talk to me? Was my guilt written all over my face? I clenched my fist around the lucky bullet in my pocket.

'I am sorry, VaStephen. I have to get home.'

'Off you buzz, then.'

I felt guilty for not talking to him. But I did not trust my tongue to form words other than *I have been there. I have heard them.*

An unimpressed Hazvinei stood with arms folded the next day as I reported this conversation.

'It is not safe to go to the camp anymore,' I said. 'It is not safe to shoot the gun.'

'What do you mean?'

'The whites know that something is up. They have heard the shots. They are looking for us.'

'They could not find their own backsides,' said Hazvinei.

'It is not funny, Hazvinei. It is serious.'

She snorted. 'They will not find us. It will be fine. Come on.'

'Now?'

'Yes, now.'

'After everything I have told you?'

'Do not be such a girl, Tinashe.'

I lunged to pinch her, but she skipped out of reach.

'Come on! Or are you too scared?'

'I am not too scared!'

'Then come.'

Once more, I followed her.

'*Masikati.*' Before we had even turned the corner, Njiri loomed out of the grey-green morning light like a ghost. I clutched at Hazvinei's elbow.

'*Masikati.*'

'Going for a walk?' He stood with his legs apart and arms crossed, smiling, but blocking our path.

'Yes, sir.'

'Be careful, hey?' He watched us. Still smiling.

'We are just going to the school,' I said. I pulled at Hazvinei's arm. 'Come, Hazvinei.'

We said polite goodbyes and walked away.

'We cannot visit today,' I said. 'It is too dangerous. They are watching us.'

Hazvinei snorted. 'He does not know anything.'

'Still.'

'It will be fine.' She looked behind us. 'Come on.'

The camp was empty; the ground blank and bare, no trace of cooking fires. A bird shouted at us from the trees. Hazvinei sat under a tree, and waited.

'Hazvinei, we should go. Abel is not here.'

'He will be here soon,' she said.

We waited for a moment.

'Perhaps something has happened.'

'Nothing has happened. You think Abel sits here all day?'

'But Njiri said . . .'

'It is fine, Tinashe. *Gara pasi.*'

I sat beside her. We listened to the high-pitched hum of the insects. I watched a line of ants march over my *takkie*.

'Perhaps we should stop coming,' I said again. 'It's not safe.'

Abel greeted us, throwing down his pack. 'You are here early.'

'The whites,' I said, the words hot and urgent, tea from a boiling pot. 'Njiri. VaStephen. They know that you are nearby. They are looking for you.'

'How do you know?'

'They told me that they heard gunshots. They are looking for people with guns.'

'The whites will not find us,' Abel said. 'They are looking for a big rebel camp, not a few boys playing at soldiers.'

'You are playing?'

'They will think so.'

See? said Hazvinei's raised eyebrows to me. I ignored her.

'So long as we are careful,' said Abel. 'And I know we are careful. Yes?'

Abel's idea of careful was very different from mine. I left school without him one afternoon and found him talking in a low, urgent voice to a skinny man with bad teeth on a street corner. I watched him gesticulate, watched him pull a bundle of notes from his pocket and hand them to the stranger. I watched him take a small packet in return, smile and nod goodbye.

'Abel!'

He turned, startled.

'I looked for you at school.'

'I left early.'

'What are you doing?' The smell of overripe fruit and smoked meat from the street vendors swirled between us. 'You bought something. I saw you.'

We fell into step. Abel did not look at me.

'Is that who you bought the rifle from?' I said. 'Abel? Where did you get the money?'

'It is none of your business.'

'Tell me, Abel.'

He stopped. 'I took it from Baba. All right? Are you happy?'

'What?'

'I took the money from Baba.'

My breath came quickly. 'You are crazy.'

He pushed me. The street vendors and beggars, sensing a drama, nudged each other and catcalled. I shoved him back, and he nearly crashed into a cart of bananas. The woman selling them shouted shrilly, flapping her hands at us as if we were a pair of naughty dogs, and we ran.

'I told you it was none of your business, Tinashe,' panted Abel. 'He is my father, not yours. You stay out of this.'

That night, Hazvinei went to bed early. Abel was out – with his friends, Babamukuru thought – but Tete Nyasha, Babamukuru and I sat together in the kitchen, listening to the radio and reading. The news bulletin came on, and we sat in silence as we always did, hearing that calm white voice tell us that everything would be all right. I could not listen to it calmly, however. I shifted in my seat, scratched my head and banged my feet against the chair legs, thinking of the white policemen.

'Do you have ants in your pants, Tinashe?' said Tete Nyasha. 'Sit still.'

'Yes, Tete. Sorry, Tete.'

'Leave the boy alone,' said Babamukuru. 'He is excited to hear the news.'

Babamukuru loved the news. He sat with his eyes half-closed and a smile on his face. Although he did not approve of the fighting, and tut-tutted when rebel activity was mentioned ('This is not the way to go about things, Tinashe. Remember that'), he liked the lists of statistics in the same way that he liked to write up the family accounts once a month, in neat blue columns of neat blue handwriting. We listened to the stories of raids and skirmishes, of talks in London and America, of weapons from China and Russia. The world expanded when the news was playing. The walls of the avocado-green kitchen fell away and we floated in a larger space. Sometimes I had to rest my head on the fresh-scrubbed table and close my eyes to keep myself from spinning off into the emptiness. I did not want to be carried away by this war, as Abel had been.

Chapter Nineteen

The change was almost too gradual to see, but Hazvinei and Abel continued to drift together and away from me. Soon, several days passed between each of my visits to the camp, and I spent most of my afternoons alone while my cousin and sister went to shoot birds together in the half-light of the bush.

'It is good to see that you are concentrating on your studies,' said Babamukuru, seeing that I spent all my time reading and writing. 'You must not be distracted from the entrance examination.'

Distracted by your sister, I heard him thinking.

'It is a big opportunity for you, Tinashe.'

I knew that Abel was planning a big opportunity of his own. I could see it in his swagger, his bold eyes and his new tendency to talk back to his father. Hazvinei did not tell me what it was, and I did not go with them to the camp to find out. I was waiting to be invited, so that I would not have to go begging, but no invitation came. I sat with my homework in the atmosphere of building excitement, refusing to speak to either of them and listening to Abel's mutterings and sleeping breath with resentment.

I was getting ready for school one morning when Hazvinei came in. I saw that she was getting ready with more care than usual, smoothing Vaseline into her face, paying particular attention to her eyelashes and lips, and tying a fresh *dhuku* over her hair. Abel had left earlier that morning. I watched her smile into the sink as she washed out her cup.

'Where are you going?'

'Nowhere.'

'You must be going somewhere.'

She smiled.

'Hazvinei, tell me. Where are you going?'

'Out.'

'Why won't you tell me?'

'I will see you tonight, Tinashe.'

'I am coming with you.'

'And miss school?' She made an exaggerated surprised face. 'You never miss school.'

'Well, I will miss it today.'

'You do not even know what I am doing.'

'You are going to see Abel. You are going to do whatever it is that the two of you have been planning.'

'I did not say that.'

'It is nothing dangerous?' I said. 'You know that the policemen are watching out for you. And Tete Nyasha will be angry when you are not here to help with the chores.'

'I am just going out,' she said. 'Come with me or not. It is up to you.'

'The walk will do me good.' I stood and made an exaggerated stretch.

Hazvinei smiled at me, her eyes narrowed to slits. 'Fine,' she said.

I followed her. I followed her past the school and the camp, to a part of town I had never visited before. Here there were no lush green verges and manicured storm drains; no high walls and iron gates. The pavement here was cracked like dried skin, and weeds straggled through the veins of dirt that showed beneath the tarmac.

'Hazvinei? Where are we going?'

She smiled.

'Are we going to see Abel?'

She said nothing.

We reached a patch of open ground, littered with paper and cans. There was a white tent in the centre, and from it came the sounds of singing. A church group?

'We are going to church?' I said. 'What is this place?'

But Hazvinei had turned away. I followed her gaze and saw Abel standing at the edge of the road.

'Tinashe!' Abel's smile was big and welcoming. 'It is good to see you. Hazvinei said you would be coming.'

Hazvinei. Of course she did.

'Are you ready?' he asked us.

'Yes,' said Hazvinei.

'I do not know what we are doing here,' I said.

'She has not told you?' Abel picked between his teeth with a fingernail. 'We are doing our part for the revolution.'

He was lit up and cocky with excitement at his first real act as a *mukomana*. I saw that he carried a bag.

'What is that?'

He pointed to the tent. 'They do not support us.' He smiled at Hazvinei — a secret smile. My heart leapt against my ribs.

'Who is "us"? And what is this place?'

'It is a meeting,' said Hazvinei. 'A political meeting. People who do not believe in what the freedom fighters are doing. Abel heard that it was being held here . . . '

'It is good that you are here also,' said Abel. 'Your help will be useful.'

'It sounds like a church group,' I said.

'It is a church group,' said Abel. 'It is a church group opposed to the struggle.'

I could not go home. I could not leave Hazvinei here. She and Abel looked at me – both smiling, both sure of my response.

'What are you going to do?'

'We are going to teach them a lesson,' said Abel.

'Abel . . .' I shook my head.

He laughed. 'Don't worry, Tinashe. I am not going to hurt anyone. But I am going to give them a shock.'

I remembered my dreams of being a guerrilla when I was a little boy. I remembered Abel telling me that my own personal feelings did not matter – that the revolution was more important. That I had a duty. It was a game, I knew, but perhaps it was not a game to him.

'Of course, if you are too scared . . .' Hazvinei began.

'I am not too scared,' I said. 'But this is a stupid idea.'

'It will take five minutes,' said Hazvinei.

'And were you planning to tell me about this, if I hadn't seen you leaving this morning?'

'I wanted to tell you.' Hazvinei's eyes were wide. 'Abel said he did not want to bother you. He knew how hard you were working.'

They looked so alike, those two, as they stood together. Two pairs of bright eyes. Two white smiles. There was no space between them for anyone else.

'All right,' I said. 'I will stay. But you promise that no one will get hurt? What are you going to do?'

'Look.'

We crouched on the ground outside the tent. I could smell my own sweat and the sweat of the others. Abel unzipped his bag and pulled out a bottle stuffed with cotton and with something else that I could not identify.

'What is that?'

'It is a bomb,' said Abel.

'What?' I forgot to whisper.

'It is just a small one,' said Abel. 'It won't do much damage. It will just make a big noise and give them a fright, that is all.'

I looked into two pairs of eager eyes.

'Where did you get this, Abel?'

'I bought it,' he said.

'How? From whom?'

He looked down, fiddling with the bottle.

'From the man who sold you the gun? Where do you meet these people, Abel?'

'It doesn't matter.' He held the open mouth of the bag towards me, and I saw something else inside.

'Cigarettes?'

'*Mbanje.*'

A bomb, and drugs. What had Abel and my sister been doing? Who had they been talking to? I shook my head to rid it of the fug of cholera memories. 'Abel . . .'

He punched me lightly on the shoulder. 'Do not worry. Here, you can look after it. '

I felt Hazvinei's eyes on me as I took the bottle in my hands. I turned it over, smelling its strange scent.

'Have you got it?' Abel asked me.

'Yes.'

Abel finished rummaging in his bag and took the bomb from me again. It was wet with sweat. 'Shit, man, have you been sucking on it?'

'No,' I mumbled.

'I know you haven't, *benzi*.' He clapped me on the shoulder. I flinched away from his hand.

'Tinashe,' his smile dropped off, 'don't be stupid.'

'I won't, Abel.'

'Because if you're stupid, then we all get in trouble. Yes?' He shook me by the shoulder. 'Yes? You chose to come with us.'

'Yes.' *No.*

'Good.'

'Why are we doing this?'

'Does it matter? I say that we have to do this. Do you trust me?'

No.

'Yes,' said Hazvinei.

Planning our *mukomana* exploits back at the camp had felt like deciding the rules of an elaborate childhood game. I had not expected to smell the sweat of the people inside the tent; hear the breaths they took between each line of the songs they sang; see their silhouettes against the tent wall.

'How much longer?' I asked.

'Why? You need to pee?'

'No,' I said, and as soon as I had said it I realised I did need to pee, very badly. I tried not to think about it.

We could hear singing and clapping from inside the tent. One person very close to where we were crouching, on the other side of the cloth, had a professional-sounding voice, like someone on the radio. She rolled the notes in her throat.

Abel smiled at me with all his teeth. And I envied him. To him, this was so simple.

'Are you ready?' he asked us.

I wondered what would happen if the bomb shot my *mboro* off. Would Abel leave me outside, clutching at my bloody trousers? Or would he shove my severed *mboro* right back onto its stump and tell me not to be bloody stupid?

We entered through the tent flap. The singing was louder in here, and it was shady. It was pleasant, standing there in the doorway with the relentless eyes of the sun behind us, unable to watch what we were doing. I felt myself sway on my feet.

Abel led us to the back of the tent. The chairs were plastic and squeaked when we sat down. There was only one other person in the back row – an old white *ambuya* with white hair pulled back with tortoiseshell clips. I imagined her lifting her old, wrinkled arms, the loose skin falling back like the folds of a sleeve, while she tugged and pinned her wiry hair into place. She drew her handbag away from Abel, and shifted her weight slightly. I was suddenly conscious of my eyes, red and itching, and the strong stink of my nervous sweat.

I did not see the moment when Abel lobbed the bottle towards the front of the tent, but I heard the old woman say 'Disgraceful!' as if he had burped or passed wind rather than thrown a bomb. Then there was a bang and we were out the back of the tent, and one of us was laughing, and the air seemed to be full of a roaring sound. I think I heard screams, but I do not remember. There must have been screaming.

I listened to the *whoosh-whoosh* of blood through my ears and the steady drumbeat of my heart. My hearing had gone. All I could hear was a high-pitched whine, as if a mosquito had crawled into my head. I saw people mouthing and dust being kicked up by running feet. We had given them a fright, all right. My head rang. The bomb had been louder than I had expected, but Abel was right – it was a big noise, and that was all.

Hazvinei's face hovered above me. I reached up to touch it. She was smiling.

'Tinashe! Are you all right?'

My hearing cleared as suddenly as it had clogged. It felt like when I had been swimming in the waterhole and had water in my ears, then stood on one leg and managed to knock it out.

'Hazvinei?'

'Yes, it is me.'

I felt stupid and slow.

'Hazvinei?'

'Come on.' She lifted me. I saw that her hair and eyebrows were grey. I wondered if the explosion had knocked me out and I had been asleep for years and years, and everyone in the world had grown old and grey.

'What happened to your hair?' I asked.

She put up her finger and touched her head. Grey ash came

away on her fingertip. 'Come on, Tinashe.' She pulled at my shoulder.

'I can't move.'

'You can.'

I looked down at my legs. They did not seem to belong to me. I expected them to run away without me.

'You can, Tinashe.' Hazvinei pulled at my arm. 'I can't carry you. You have to walk.' She was getting impatient.

I felt like an old man. I pulled myself up. 'Am I bleeding?'

'Of course you are not bleeding. No one is hurt. And now we have to get out of here before people find us.'

'Oh. Good.'

We ran. We ran until our lungs burned and it felt like a hole had opened up in my side and my insides were bleeding out. When we stopped, safely in the bushes, I fell to the ground and clasped a hand to that hole in my side and tried to hold everything in.

'Hey, *shamwari!*' Someone I did not recognise gripped my shoulder with a strong hand, and grinned into my face.

'*Mangwanani,*' I said, and squinted at him.

'What's wrong? We did it!' The stranger passed me a hand-rolled cigarette. I could still see the snail-trail of saliva along the edge of the paper.

'Abel?'

'What, did you blow your brains out in there?'

'No. I don't think so.'

'Good!'

The smoke tasted different – sweeter and richer than a cigarette.

'It is *mbanje,*' said Abel. 'Your first one. A good reward, yes?'

'Where did you get it?'

'I bought it.'

'How?'

'Does it matter?'

It felt a little like I imagined kissing to be – at once soft and fiery, burning your lips as it caressed them. It breathed its sweet-smelling breath into my mouth. My heartbeat slowed.

'Good, hey?' said Abel. He took it from me and closed his eyes as he sucked the smoke between his lips. 'We gave them a good fright,' he said. 'They did not know what hit them.'

'Abel.' I caught my breath. 'You are crazy.'

He laughed, still giddy with his achievement.

'Guns. Bombs. *Mbanje*. You are going to get into serious trouble, Abel.'

'But we are fine,' he said.

We ran back to the camp. Hazvinei and Abel were laughing, clutching their sides, but I was silent. My breath came rattling through my throat, tasting of ash. We passed the school. I should be there, inside my classroom, raising my hand when the teacher asked a question. I should be planning for my time at college. I should not be running after my sister and my cousin again.

Abel rolled me a cigarette, and passed one to Hazvinei as well.

I was ready to use it – to forget, to drift. I wanted to forget them both. I wanted to forget this day. The scholarship exam was close, and as I sucked in the smoke of the *mbanje* I felt that it would save me from everything, and free me from both Hazvinei and Abel for ever.

Hazvinei smoked and then sat in silence, watching us as we talked and laughed in the cooling evening. After a while I thought that she had fallen asleep. We grew quiet, we boys, our heads full of smoke – and we dreamed.

'We should probably go home soon,' I said. 'It is getting on for dinner time. Tete Nyasha will be waiting for us. She thinks we were at school.'

'But first we must wash,' said Abel. We spoke slowly, our tongues made lazy by the *mbanje*.

'What do you think, Hazvinei?'

She did not reply.

Abel noticed, and sat up straight, his fog of *mbanje* dissipating. 'Tinashe, what is happening?'

'Hazvinei!'

She raised her head to look at me. Her eyes were blank, the pupils wider and darker than was natural.

'Hazvinei?'

Hazvinei's eyes rolled back in her head. Her jaw slackened. Her limbs moved and twitched as if she was strung on puppetry wires, and a noise came from her throat that was not a human noise.

Abel drew back. I remembered Hazvinei kneeling on the ground before the N'anga, back on the *kopje*. I remembered her shudder as the spirit left her; the unnatural lightness of her body. I remembered Amai pushing through the crowd to cradle her, as I was pushing through the fug of *mbanje* now. I reached her, lifted her head and clasped it in my two hands, trying to bring her back.

'Hazvinei, wake up.'

Abel knelt beside me, and I saw my own memory reflected in his face. Little Tendai. The medicine stick. Hazvinei's fit.

'*Muroyi*,' came the whisper.

'She is not a *muroyi*!'

'I did not say anything!' said Abel.

'She is not well,' I said. 'It is the *mbanje*. I knew we should not have smoked it.'

'Why would the *mbanje* do this?' said Abel.

'I don't know. Perhaps it is not good for her.' I tried to lift Hazvinei, but she was too heavy. 'Abel, help me. We must take her home.'

Abel held his palms up and shook his head. 'We can't.'

'Abel, she is sick. Help me to carry her.'

'We can't take her home.'

'Why not?' I became angry.

'We have to wash first. Baba will smell the *mbanje* on us. He must not know.'

'Abel, this is Hazvinei.'

'You don't think I know?'

'Then what are we supposed to do?'

He was silent.

'We have to take her home.'

'And what are we supposed to tell Amai about Hazvinei, hey?' said Abel. 'That she had a fit for no reason?'

'Yes.' I cradled her head. 'Take her feet, Abel.'

It was far worse than carrying Tendai through the *kopje*. There, only the birds and rock rabbits had watched us. Here, everyone walking the streets or driving past in their cars could see the two dusty boys hauling the lifeless body of a pretty girl along the pavement. Street vendors shouted and wagged their fingers. Men on bicycles whistled and called to us. Clusters of women laughed or shook their heads and pursed their lips.

'She is sick!' I kept shouting. 'She is sick! We are taking her home!'

There was no one in the yard or on the *stoep* when we approached the house. Perhaps we were lucky this time. Perhaps no one was home. Abel had the same thought, and grinned at me.

'We will have to take her to the bedroom,' I said.

It was difficult to carry her up the steps, but we managed it. In the cool shade of indoors, Hazvinei's face looked peaceful.

'Perhaps she just needs to sleep it off,' said Abel.

We lowered her as gently as we could onto her bed.

'Should we cover her with a blanket?'

'I will take her shoes off first.'

I removed her socks and *takkies*, exposing dusty feet. I did not want to take her clothes off. Tete Nyasha would have to think she was so tired that she fell asleep without undressing. I pulled the faded wool blanket right up to her chin.

'Will she wake up again?' said Abel.

Fear made my voice sharp. 'Of course she will.'

Abel nodded, slowly, without looking at me. 'We should clean ourselves up,' he said. 'And brush our teeth. Or Baba will know.'

I felt the presence in the doorway before I turned around. I saw from Abel's face that he did too.

'Babamukuru,' I said. 'You are home.'

He was early. He never came home early. A wisp of bad fortune coiled like smoke in the corner of the room, and Abel cowered. I felt a sickness in my stomach at seeing Babamukuru as well, but there was nothing we could do now.

'What is wrong with Hazvinei?' he asked me.

'She is not feeling well, Babamukuru,' I said.

Babamukuru stepped over to the bed. He saw Hazvinei's rigid body; the dust and streaks of ash on her face. Why hadn't we thought to wash her face? He saw the unnatural, slow breathing, the clenched fists.

'What is that smell?'

He lowered his face to hers and sniffed.

'Baba . . .' said Abel.

'It is on you as well. What is this?'

'Nothing, Baba!'

'You have been smoking *mbanje!*'

He slammed Abel against the wall with unlikely speed. I stood, frozen. 'Where did you get it?'

Abel did not answer. Babamukuru shook him. 'Answer me.'

'I bought it.'

Babamukuru let him fall. As Abel slumped to the ground, he turned to me.

'And you, Tinashe. You have been smoking this too?'

I nodded, and did not move.

'You are leading your cousin astray now,' said Babamukuru to Abel. Abel did not respond.

Babamukuru hit me. I felt the weight of his hand, and the cool band of his wedding ring against my skin. When he released me, I was gasping and holding back tears.

'Tinashe, leave the room.'

I looked at Abel. He stared at me, but said nothing.

'Leave the room.'

I backed away, reluctant to turn my back on them both. I hovered in the doorway, looking back at the two men and my sleeping sister.

I could hear the thumping and groaning from my room. I could not even be angry, this time, although I wanted to be. His son, his nephew and niece had been smoking a drug and getting up to who knows what when they should have been safe at home. Baba would have beaten me too, I knew it. And I knew that I was more at fault than Abel. Not only had I got myself into trouble; I had also put my sister in danger.

I did not dare to go to the door, but pulled my pillow over my head and waited for it to finish, for Abel to stumble into bed beside me. When he came, he was breathing hard, and I could smell his sweat. I heard the creak of the bedsprings as he climbed into bed.

'Abel?'

No answer.

'Abel? Are you all right?'

'I am fine.'

I thought of Abel. I thought of how Hazvinei followed him and listened to him. I remembered a bowl of blood and the ridged spine of a tall man in the darkness, and I said, 'Do you remember Chenjerai?'

A snort. 'Of course I do.'

I fumbled under my pillow and brought out the lucky charm that I had carried for so many years. 'Do you remember the bullet he gave me?'

'You would not give it to me,' he said.

'Hold out your hand.' I found his hand reaching for me in the darkness and dropped the bullet into his palm, imagining it rolling into the centre and nuzzling at his skin as if it belonged there. 'You can have it now,' I said. 'For luck.'

He closed his fingers around it.

'Take care of my sister, Abel,' I said.

'I will.'

'You must promise.'

'I promise.'

Chapter Twenty

I did not see Abel again that night, but I awoke before dawn the next morning. He was not in his bed, and I knew at once that he had gone. I could tell by the feeling in the house – that special emptiness. He was not sitting at his breakfast, sleeping on the sofa or out on the hard tiles of the *stoep*. He had gone.

I lay still, waiting for Babamukuru to discover what I already knew. I heard Tete Nyasha first – her usual morning humming and clinking of cups and plates, then a wail as she discovered what I later learned was Abel's letter. Babamukuru's quick footsteps as he went through to the kitchen. Raised voices. A thump – perhaps a fist against the wall? The slam of a door, and the rumble of Babamukuru's car engine.

I rolled over and stared at the blank white wall with unseeing eyes.

When he returned from his fruitless search, Babamukuru sat Hazvinei and me down at the dining-room table. We never used the dining room – Tete Nyasha polished the wood to a dark mirror-like shine and it remained empty and perfect all week. We felt like small children, perched on the uncomfortable chairs. Obviously, Babamukuru felt that this occasion needed the added formality.

'Have you read this?' he brandished the letter.

We shook our heads.

'Did you know that Abel had gone?'

More vigorous shaking.

'Do you know where he would go?' He stared at us. We

said nothing. He threw the letter down. 'He says he has joined the freedom fighters.'

Silence.

'Did you know about this?'

I shook my head. I did not dare look at my sister.

'Where has he gone? Do you know where he has gone?'

Babamukuru stared at us for a moment longer, and then walked out. I turned to my sister, to touch her shoulder, to comfort her, but she got to her feet and ran outside.

'Hazvinei! Wait!'

I found her hunched over and gasping in the bushes, throwing up the breakfast that she had just eaten.

'Hazvinei?'

She stared up at me with wild eyes. There were still traces of vomit around her mouth. 'Tinashe.' She started to cry – great, dry sobs that did not sound like crying at all, but like the cough of a lioness in the evening, when she has fed and is announcing to the world that she is here and she is dangerous. There was a threat in Hazvinei's sobs. 'I want to go with Abel.'

'You can't.'

'I must.'

'Why? Why must you? He is gone, Hazvinei. Perhaps it is for the best.'

She shook her head. 'You know I do what the spirits tell me to do.'

'You have never done what anyone tells you to do, Hazvinei.'

'This is different.' The shadows under her eyes were dark violet, and her eyes seemed to be retreating into her skull – more like the eyes of an animal than of a person. She tightened her *dhuku* around her head and got to her feet. 'I feel fine now,' she said. 'We should go back inside.'

We sat together in church that Sunday, Babamukuru, Tete Nyasha, Hazvinei and I. Hazvinei's eyes were swollen and purple with crying; a soft, shadowed colour beautiful in its own way. I saw the curious glances and heard the whispers, but no one approached us. Babamukuru sat tall and grim in his seat, his spectacles winking in the light from the stained glass window and obscuring his eyes. Tete Nyasha fluttered the pages of her hymn book with nervous hands.

Hazvinei did not look at me during the service, although I stole glances at her. I could see the beating of her pulse in the hollow of her neck and the rise and fall of her breathing beneath her lacy church dress. She did not sing the hymns or say the prayers, but she stood, sat and knelt with us at the appropriate times, her face far away.

When the service was over, Babamukuru led us out. The witch-smeller stood against the back wall of the church. He was picking his teeth, and smiling.

'*Mangwanani*,' he said to Babamukuru and Tete Nyasha, who greeted him. He smiled at my sister.

I was the last to leave. I walked past the witch-smeller, avoiding his eye, but he was too fast for me. He left the church by my side, squeezing my shoulder in friendly greeting. 'Have a good day, Tinashe,' he said, and stepped out into the sunshine like a man for whom life is rich and full of blessings.

The whispers of gossip reached long and splayed fingers into our house. I felt them run through my hair, investigating my ears, nostrils, mouth. I felt them creeping to my bed as I lay awake in the dark; drawing back my blanket and crawling beneath my mattress. I knew that Hazvinei felt them too. The rumours clung to us like blackjacks to a cow's hide, just as numerous and just as uncomfortable. Where had Abel gone? What had happened to him? Some of the neighbours had seen him leaving for school bruised and bent over the years, and they had their suspicions. And why were the country cousins still there when the son of the house was not? The preferred theory was that he had joined the *vakomana*. They must be in the area, people speculated. They were coming into town. Perhaps they were recruiting, as they were said to recruit in the villages. Perhaps they walked among us even now – and if the son of a rich man with a comfortable house was not safe, who was?

VaStephen and Njiri walked our street, asking questions; I saw them through the iron gates. They did not look at me, but I saw them glance towards the high walls of the house.

And there were whispers about Hazvinei – of course there were. There were always whispers about Hazvinei. She had bewitched Abel, people said, and driven him away. She had killed him somehow by sapping his manhood. She had brought bad luck to the family.

VaStephen came to visit Babamukuru one evening. He did not have his usual smile for me, and he greeted me in English. 'Get your uncle, please.'

I scurried to obey.

VaStephen's conversation with Babamukuru was long. I stayed outside until it was over. When they came to the door, I stepped back into the shadow of the bushes.

'Good night,' I heard, and 'Thank you.' I watched the white man walk to the gate and settle his hat more firmly on his head.

The policemen might be satisfied, but Babamukuru, Tete Nyasha and I stayed indoors as much as we could to avoid the questions of our neighbours.

'Abel will come back,' said Babamukuru. 'When he is hungry, or needs money. I know it.'

Tete Nyasha twisted her apron in her hands and said nothing.

At dinner times, Babamukuru ate without speaking. When he had finished, he pushed back his chair and went into the bedroom, and we did not see him until morning. He did not look at me. He looked at Hazvinei, though – long looks that she did not return.

'Babamukuru,' I said one night when I could no longer stand the silence. He looked at me. His eyes stung me, making me smart and glow as if I had run through the sharp grass in the yard. Tete Nyasha flicked her eyes to me, to Babamukuru, and then down to her plate. Hazvinei had not moved. Her fingers were listless and uncaring as she squashed the *sadza* into balls and lifted it to a slack mouth. Our family looked drab and dead in the light of the single bulb over the table. I pushed back my chair and left the room, glad to be out.

I remembered when I had believed that Baba patrolled the house at night. There was no one to protect us now. The bad luck was getting in: I could see its claws in every crack in the walls; I could smell the sweet, greasy smoke of burning flesh.

Hazvinei did not protest at her imprisonment. She sat cross-legged in the dust behind our house, tracing patterns with her finger on the ground while the chickens, usually so full of nervous flutterings and squawks, pecked around her as if she were one of them.

'Hazvinei.' I sat beside her. Her skin was as grey and flat as our pewter pots.

She made a circle in the dust, but did not talk to me. When she turned her eyes to me, I saw that they were yellow at the edges. Her frailty and the helpless, nervy tracing of patterns in the dirt made me angry at her. I wanted to shake her until her neck broke, or punch her in the nose and watch the red blood run. I wanted her to become Hazvinei again.

'This is Abel's fault,' I said.

I watched her spit and hiss into life. She pushed me so hard in the chest that I fell backwards into the mess of chicken poo and dirt.

'*Benzi!*' she said.

The blue sky seared my eyes. I blinked, and caught my breath.

'You don't know what you are talking about, Tinashe,' said Hazvinei in a low, urgent voice. 'You don't know anything about Abel.'

'And you do?'

She spat. It evaporated almost before it hit the dust.

'Hazvinei . . .'

She was gone in a whirl of bare, grubby feet and blue cotton. I did not sit up until one of the chickens began to peck at my head, and then I went around the house to the neatly swept front yard.

The noon sun was a wide white circle in the sky. It made everything look like an illustration in a book, flat and highly coloured against a white page. I sat on the kitchen step, freshly polished by Tete Nyasha, and felt its film of red grease slide against my skin. A lizard appeared from a crack in the wall. It was not afraid of me. An inch from my hand, it reared up along its blue-green length and tasted the air with its tongue.

'Tinashe!' Little Tendai, standing in front of our house with his hands on his hips. He was grinning, but kept his distance. I knew that he was not really there – that he was something my mind had created out of the heat and confusion – but I could see every crack on his dusty heels, and every whorl of hair on his head.

'Go away, Tendai.'

'What's wrong with Hazvinei? Why has she not come out?'

'She is sick.'

'Again?'

I tasted vomit on my teeth. I did not know if I were angry or afraid. 'Tendai, go away.'

He laughed. I watched the lizard flatten itself against the hot concrete. Its tail twitched. It swivelled one bead-black eye at me, and started to move towards the crack in the wall. We were friends now, this lizard and I.

'*Muroyi, muroyi.*' His voice was low and taunting.

I put my hand out to touch the lizard. I knew its skin would be soft and cool, and my hands were burning.

'*Muroyi!*'

The lizard shed its tail with a casual flick, leaving a raw and wriggling stump in my hand. I looked up, holding the tail. Tendai was gone.

Hazvinei had not been well since the night Abel left, and she grew worse. She became bloated and thicker about the waist. Her skin hung yellow on her bones. Her ripe beauty became the stink and horror of a decaying fruit.

Tete Nyasha and Babamukuru took her to the clinic. They told me that she screamed and thrashed and had to be held down. I shuddered. I remembered the neighbour who had closed his door to us on the *kopje*. Bad fortune surrounded us like a cloud of flies, buzzing in our ears and landing anywhere it could.

'You just need to eat more,' said Tete Nyasha, and gave Hazvinei extra helpings of *sadza*. She thought that food cured everything.

We did not hear from Abel. Babamukuru's mouth set in a thin line. 'He will come back,' he said.

Tete Nyasha took to her bed early in the evenings, and rose late. Babamukuru spent more time at the shebeen. And Hazvinei grew worse. I begged Tete Nyasha to let her move into the second bed in my room, so that I could watch her while she slept, and it was a sign of her sadness and confusion that she agreed to it. I lay awake for hours in the darkness, listening to my sister breathing and watching the shadows on the wall.

Once again I was to be punished for my anger towards my sister.

'I will pray for her,' said Tete Nyasha. 'And so must you, Tinashe.'

'I will.'

Hazvinei did not think that prayers to the God of churches and priests would have any effect.

'I need to find a N'anga,' she said to me, staring through hollow eyes.

'Where am I supposed to find one here? How am I going to bring one to you without Tete Nyasha finding out?'

Tete Nyasha believed that church was the only place in which to seek supernatural help.

'You must help me.'

Of course I had to. Of course, of course. But some bitter part of me hardened into a stone in my stomach, like the pip in an avocado.

I should have been grateful, in a way, for the lack of distractions. I had all this spare time to study and work, with no one to look over my shoulder and scoff at the diagrams, or remind me that I would never make it as a black boy in a white man's school. It was natural to worry about Hazvinei, yes, but should I not also feel somewhat relieved that Abel was gone and that she was safe indoors? When the day of the examination arrived, I did not feel relieved. I felt afraid. Half of me expected Abel to appear, to take his rightful place. No one mentioned Abel's name, but it hovered in the air like a mosquito looking for blood.

It was all arranged – I would take the bus to the big college while Babamukuru was at work, and he would collect me afterwards. I studied late into the night all that week, stuffing my head with knowledge until it felt like a fat belly filled with too much *sadza*. I felt that, if I moved, it would spill out of my ears.

Hazvinei watched me from her sickbed, her eyes huge and hollow in her face.

When the day arrived, Babamukuru came to wish me luck before he left for work. As he embraced me, he looked over my shoulder, and I knew he was looking for Abel. Perhaps he thought that his son would materialise on this special day, filled with remorse and ready to atone for his sins. But there was only me.

'This is a great opportunity,' said Babamukuru. He rested his hand on my shoulder. It was heavy and uncomfortable.

'This is a great opportunity,' said my teachers.

'This is a great opportunity,' said Tete Nyasha as she gave me an extra helping of porridge for breakfast.

Babamukuru had given me some of his own smart clothes to wear: a shirt with collars and cuffs starched so heavily that they cut into my skin, and a pair of grey trousers that were a little too long for me. Tete Nyasha stitched them up, holding pins in her mouth and crouching down so that she looked like a strange sort of porcupine.

'You can keep these,' said Babamukuru. 'I'm sure you will have need of them again.'

When I looked in the mirror, I expected to see a changed reflection. I expected to see a smart young man, neatly dressed and well-groomed, the kind of person who could go to a good school and then to university. I was disappointed. The shirt was too big for me, and already had little creamy sweat stains under the arms. My neck had made the edge of the starched collar grubby. Despite Tete Nyasha's efforts, you could see that the trousers had been taken up.

A bright morning! A great opportunity! I said these things to myself as I left the house. I remember the sun warm on my head when I stepped outside, and the clean, dusty smell of the air. I picked up my school bag (still holding a rotting lunch that I was meant to take to school the previous week) and the few coins that Tete Nyasha kept in a peanut-butter jar in the kitchen. I got to my feet and ran, ran for the bus that would take me into town, to the school and to the exam. It was good to run, to feel the hot, painful life in my lungs and my legs. I saw faces behind the windows, watching me as I ran, and I felt powerful.

'Wait!' The bus was just leaving. Its exhaust coughed and scared the chickens in crates on the roof. They squawked at me, and the people on the bus grinned. Crazy boy, shouting in the dust!

'You are lucky to catch me,' said the bus driver as I scrambled for my coins. I stumbled down the over-stuffed and moving bus, feeling the metal floor hot underneath my shoes and sat next to a fat woman with a basket of oranges who made sucking, disapproving noises when I sat down.

I looked through the back window and watched the bus plough through the dirt road, sending up two furrows of dust either side as if it were unzipping a dirty brown shirt. I thought of Hazvinei at home, breathing quietly on her bed. I thought of the exam, seeing numbers and letters on the page. I knew my work, I did. I knew I would do well. I was getting out. Away from Hazvinei. Away from Abel. Away from Babamukuru, even. I was free.

When the bus turned the corner, something hollow and dead settled in my chest.

'Sit still,' said the fat woman.

'I am sorry, Amai.'

'What is the matter with you?' She elbowed me with one fat arm, took a banana from her bag, and peeled it. The hot yellow smell filled the bus, overpowering the body odour.

Stop the bus. I had not said it aloud.

'Stop the bus!'

'Sit down.' The fat woman poked me in the ribs.

'Stop!'

The driver whistled through his yellow teeth and told me I was the son of a dirty goat, but he stopped.

'*Mazvita tatenda.*' I pushed my way through the crowd again, getting many slaps and cuffs.

'Holding up the bus.'

'*Benzi!*'

Someone tripped me at the door, and I fell, missed the step, and landed on my hands and knees on the gravel. When I stood, I left two knee-shaped dents on the road.

'Enjoy your walk!' said the bus driver, and laughed.

A fine film of white powder coated me. I held my pencil in my hand, but my other was empty. 'My bag! My bag is on the bus. Throw me my bag!'

The fat woman in the window seat pretended not to hear.

'Please! Please, Amai!'

The bus moved away, taking my bag with it. But that was the least of my worries. This was a part of town I did not know – but then, I supposed, that meant that no one here would know me. Perhaps this was the perfect place.

I approached many people on the street, asking where I could find a N'anga. They looked at me suspiciously – what did this skinny boy want with magic? Finally, though, one showed me to the house of a local N'anga, one who was only too glad to perform tricks for money.

This witch doctor was not like the one on the *kopje*. He wore jeans, and behind his thin frame in the doorway I could see children running on a dirty carpet.

'It will cost you,' said the N'anga when I had explained my mission.

'I have money.' Thank goodness I had kept my coins in my pocket and not in my bag.

'Good.' He packed his bag of medicines and bones. 'Then let us go. Where is your car?'

'I do not have a car. I walked.'

'From where?'

When I told him, he whistled. 'That is going to cost you extra.'

'It is fine.' I was anxious to get this over with. 'Come.'

It was a long walk. When we reached home, finally, I had to bring the N'anga to the house through the sanitary lanes behind the back fence. I waited until I was sure that both Babamukuru and Tete Nyasha were out, then led him to Hazvinei's room, where she lay yellow and sweating on the bed. The N'anga had been talking to me about the many women that he had known – as if I were interested, or wanted to imagine this old, smelly sack of bones with a woman – but he stopped as soon as he saw my sister. He closed his eyes and a shudder ran through him.

'What is the old fool doing?' said Hazvinei.

The N'anga opened his eyes, his jaw still hanging slack. He raised his arm and pointed one bony finger at Hazvinei. 'You have brought this on yourself,' he said.

'No.' Hazvinei shook her head, so violently that beads of fever-sweat from her forehead landed on my hand.

'It is you,' the N'anga repeated.

'N'anga, is there something we can do?' I tried to keep my tone respectful.

The N'anga slid his yellow eyes to me. 'The spirits are angry with her.'

'There must be a way that we can make them happy,' I said. 'There must be a way to make her better.'

'There is not. The bad fortune dies when she dies, and not before.'

'No, old man.' Hazvinei was still. 'You are wrong.'

The N'anga shrugged, and held out his hand. 'The payment.'

I did not want to give it to him. All he had given us was

bad news and worse news. But I owed it to him. I pulled the money from my pocket and watched him close his claws around it. How it hurt!

'I am sorry,' said the N'anga, and got to his feet. He was unsteady, and I caught his elbow.

'Is there nothing you can do?' I asked him. 'Nothing you can give us?'

He sidled his eyes over to me again. 'Here.' He gave me a small, greying bone. 'Take this. Grind it up and put it in her tea. It will help, but it will not cure her.'

I closed my hand on the bone. It felt like a thin finger. '*Mazvita tatenda.*'

The N'anga shrugged. It is no use, his shrug said. But you have paid me, and I do not care.

'You will not tell anyone?' I asked him. 'About my sister?'

'I am an old man. Who would I tell?' He gave a yellow grin, and left.

Chapter Twenty-one

I sat on the *stoep* until Babamukuru came home. Tete Nyasha had phoned him at work and told him the story – I could tell from the sharp clip of his stride. I stood, hands clasped behind my back.

'What is wrong with you?' he said as soon as he saw me. He had brought a present with him, wrapped and ribboned, obviously meant to celebrate my day of triumph. I remembered the presents that he had sent after Abel's first visit to the *kopje*. I remembered how I felt when that shiny new red truck was broken and dirtied.

'You did not go? After everything I have done for you?'

'I am sorry, Babamukuru.'

'Do you even know what it is you have done? There is no way I will be able to set up another exam for you. There is no way. This is not an easy thing to do.'

'I am sorry, Babamukuru.'

I said it over and over, hoping that he would eventually stop shouting and I could get back to Hazvinei. My head rang, and my tongue was dry. I could hear flies buzzing in my head.

'They have only just started to accept black boys into this programme. Do you know that?'

'I know, Babamukuru.'

'And you just do not show up! They will think you are no better than those animals out in the bush with their violent ways. They will think that this meant nothing to you.'

I closed my eyes.

'What is wrong with you? Hey?'

'I am sorry, Babamukuru.'

He clapped me around the side of the head. The flies buzzed louder. 'You have thrown away this opportunity for nothing,' he said. 'Do you know what you have done?'

Of course I knew what I had done.

He wagged a finger at me. He was breathless with anger. 'Your father was just the same. Do you know that, Tinashe? He was just the same.'

Baba. I started to shake.

'I gave him everything, always. Yes, I got the scholarship, because I worked for it, and yes he had to stay home. Yes, yes, we all know that. But when I offered more to him, he did not take it. He preferred to be nothing. Just like you.'

We stared at each other. He raised his hand as if to hit me, but then shook his head and turned away. 'You are as bad as Abel. Are you going to run into the bush, like him? Do you think you can change things with a gun? It is the educated men who change the world, Tinashe.'

He seemed to have tired himself out. He tugged at his tie, loosening it, and did not look at me again. 'Come inside.'

I started to follow him. He stopped, and I almost collided with his broad, angry back.

'And you need not think that I am paying for you to stay in school. Oh no. Not when I see how little you care about it. You are staying home now.'

I was in disgrace for weeks, trapped in the house, slinking around like a whipped dog as Hazvinei became rounder and plumper and filled with healthy light. Babamukuru did not know what to do with us, I could see. Tete Nyasha made us fattening, building-your-strength meals and cups of tea, looking after us as she could not look after Abel, but Babamukuru seemed to have forgotten that we lived with him. We were pale shadows to him.

Strangely, some part of me was at peace now. The spirits had let me exchange my own bad fortune for Hazvinei's. *Baba, I have done what you asked*, I thought – but too soon. I woke one night to find Hazvinei gone from our room. The leopards growled at me, and I went outside.

The back of the house smelled of rotten vegetables and sickly-sweet decaying fruit. I saw Hazvinei's shadow against the wall. She was talking to someone. I heard her voice rise and fall, riding the darkness as a *muroyi* rides on the back of a hyena, and the words she used were strange: neither Shona nor English. I walked towards her, making my footfalls as soft and harmless as I could, and I was about to call to her in a low voice when I saw the shape.

I would not have seen it if I had not glanced upwards. It was blacker than black, a hole in the sky, and I would have taken it for a shadow if I had not seen the sudden cessation of stars where the shape blotted them out. Once I had noticed, I could not stop noticing. I saw the slight movements it made; the breaths that made its sides rise and fall. I saw shadows against the dark, legs like human legs, arms like human arms, and a head that was nothing like the shape of any human head I had seen – and all the time there was the low rhythm of Hazvinei's voice talking to this thing, a soft rise and fall as if she were singing a lullaby to a little baby.

I realised I had not taken a breath and I took one, a great, ragged whistling, loud in the darkness. I felt a sudden, focused attention: an animal awareness. Hazvinei's voice stopped, and something came lumbering towards me, black on black.

'Tinashe, get back inside!'

I tried to turn, but now I could see a face like a vivid mask above my own, striped with colours, a mouth set in a smile at the bottom. Its eyes were holes. Its smile opened. It reminded me of the festival dances back on the *kopje*. The dancers would be normal people, people we knew – the man who ran the corner shop, the man with the chicken neck – and then they would put on the wooden dance-masks and become blank, terrible things. I knew that, this time, there would not be someone familiar and friendly beneath.

Hazvinei shouted something I could not hear over the rushing in my ears. The thing turned its face away, and the terrible pressure was gone. A moment later the night was empty again, with no movement but the pale whirring of moths.

'Hazvinei, what was that?'

She was still. 'Nothing.'

'Hazvinei.' I was still panting, and the 'ha' of her name came out on a ragged breath. My understanding felt sore and stretched.

'It was nothing, Tinashe.'

'I have never seen anything like that before,' I said. 'I have never . . . You were talking to it, Hazvinei.'

'I was asking questions,' she said.

'Questions? About what?' I grabbed her arm. 'About Abel?'

'No.' She was angry, suddenly. 'Let go of me.'

The wall against my back was cool and comforting. 'It is not safe, Hazvinei. What would Babamukuru say, if he knew?' I could not see my sister's face. 'You should come inside,' I said. 'Please.'

I felt her hand cool against my cheek and she drifted past me, a shadow with bare feet.

I kept quiet after that, but I watched her. Something was happening to her – I knew it. The bad fortune must not be allowed to follow us. I had to push it away. I had to keep her safe. Even her happiness and good health made me suspicious. I watched her eat more at dinner, saying she was starving, to cover up her growing belly.

'You must not get too fat, Hazvinei,' said Tete Nyasha, 'or you will never get a husband.'

Hazvinei's weight gain became more and more noticeable. Even her face grew rounder. And gold studs of earrings appeared in her ears.

'What are those?' I asked her.

'What do they look like?'

'Did you get your ears pierced?'

'Yes.'

'Where?'

'At Woolworth's.'

'Why did you do that?'

She touched them, and smiled. Her face was plumped up and buttery.

'Where did you get the money?'

'Where do you think?' Hazvinei poured me a cup of tea from the little enamel pot. A drip formed on the spout and she licked it off luxuriously from her finger, closing her eyes. I watched her closely.

'Who is he?'

'Who is who?' She stirred three sugars into my tea.

'You know who. Who is the man who bought you the earrings?'

'I told you, I bought them for myself.'

Babamukuru noticed the earrings as well. He could not help but notice them. Hazvinei kept turning her head this way and that, holding it proud as a snake's, and touching her long fingernails to the little gold studs.

'Where did you get those?'

'I bought them.'

Babamukuru leaned back in his seat, crossing his arms. Tete Nyasha stirred her tea, the spoon rattling in the cup more than it should.

'With what?'

'With my money.'

'With what money?'

'I have been saving.'

'She has been careful with her money,' said Tete Nyasha, fluttering her hands.

Babamukuru kept his eyes on Hazvinei, who continued to sip her tea. But he grunted and stood up, and did not ask any more questions.

I had my own suspicions.

Babamukuru agreed to let me leave the house, although he did not suggest that I go back to school. He kept Hazvinei indoors, and I saw her small, indignant face pressed against the glass as I left with a list of errands and strict instructions to be back within the hour.

I walked rather than taking the bus. The bus was faster, but when I had time, I preferred to walk through town, smelling the hot tarmac and petrol fumes. I enjoyed the crowds. It was so different from the *kopje*, where every face was familiar; here, one face shifted and melted into another, until I saw eyes, mouths and teeth, and nothing else. The women passed in bright, swaying colour, patterned and fragrant. The men wore grey and brown and blue, and smelled of sweat. I liked to feel the press of unfamiliar bodies against my own, and feel the warmth of new voices in my ear. I walked as if in a trance, too slowly for the businessmen who had somewhere important to be – '*Kurumidza!* What is wrong with you?' – and inhaled the melting tarmac, the petrol fumes and the sweet stink of rubbish in the gutters. Street vendors tried to sell me bananas, bruised mangoes, sugar-cane and green *mielies*. I allowed myself to buy a stick of sugar cane, and ran the gritty, sweet fibres through my teeth, letting the chewed plant matter fall to join the hundreds of others that littered the pavement. Preoccupied with my sugar cane and the colours and faces of the crowd, it took me a moment to realise that someone had grasped my arm with a strong hand. I turned around, expecting red *mbanje* eyes and a dirty knife.

'Tinashe.' The witch-smeller.

I let out a breath. 'You scared me.'

'I did not mean to.'

'I am busy.'

He fell into step beside me.

'What do you want?' I said at last.

He smiled. 'Your sister. She is walking at night again.'

'No. It is not true.'

'I have given you plenty of warning, I think.'

I trudged on.

'It is too late,' he said. 'Your time has run out.'

I stopped. 'Tell me. Tell me what you are going to do.'

'Me? I am going to do nothing.' He spread his empty hands.

'You swear?'

'I do not have to do anything.' He smiled. 'Your sister has done it all to herself. Her curse is coming upon her, and there is nothing that you can do.'

I pushed him, feeling his fat shoulders give way under the pressure of my hands. He stepped backwards, laughing. 'Do not ever speak to me again,' I said. 'Leave us alone. Do you hear?'

I walked until I could no longer feel his eyes on me, and then I ran the rest of the way home. Even though I could no longer see his face, I could feel his smile.

That night in bed, I heard water running outside. I managed to surface from the deep, underwater comfort of sleep and stumble into the moth-studded darkness. It was Hazvinei. She was crouched next to the tap, glistening and silver in the black, as if she were splashed with moonlight.

'Why are you out here?'

Hazvinei tied her *dhuku* over her head. The tip of each wiry hair held a pearl of water, and her scarf was soaked and darkened. 'Washing.'

'At this time of night?' I looked to the stars for guidance. 'It must be past midnight.'

She shrugged, and water shivered off her bare shoulders.

'Where have you been?'

'Nowhere.'

'You are walking at night again? Hazvinei, you know that it is dangerous. You know that the witch-smeller is watching you. I have told you this.'

Silence.

'You have been meeting someone?'

'No one.' She reached her hands up to touch the damp cloth on her head. 'I was hot. I wanted to cool down.'

'You have been out, I know you have.'

'I went for a walk.'

'Did you climb over the gate?'

'Yes.'

'You were meeting someone.'

'I told you I was not.'

She was deceiving me again. I knew it. She knew where Abel was. She was seeing him – or she was seeing someone else. Why did she keep secrets from me? Yes, I had betrayed her once, but only once. On every other day, for all the other years that we had been a family, I had done nothing but look after her.

I watched her the next morning as she ate her breakfast. I saw her smile; saw the way she touched the gold studs in her ears.

I followed her the next time she left the house. I kept my distance. Knowing Hazvinei, she would sense me behind her, and turn. I half-expected her to – but she did not.

A figure stepped out from the bushes. A tall, strong figure, with the same easy, graceful power of movement as a lion. A suitable companion, then, for a little lioness.

Abel. Abel had been nearby all along, hiding. Why? And Hazvinei had not told me.

There was an alert, purposeful look in his eyes. When Hazvinei came out, she glanced at him from the corner of one eye, then started along the road, hips swaying. He watched her go, and waited. I got the feeling that he might even be counting under his breath. After a short interval, he followed.

I followed also.

We made a strange threesome. Hazvinei walked ahead, swaying her hips, never glancing over her shoulder. Abel followed at a distance, kicking at a pebble as if that were the only reason he was walking down the long pavement. And then there was me. I was invisible, I did not exist.

Hazvinei swerved and ducked into the bushes behind the school. Abel followed. I waited a few minutes, so that they would not hear me making my way through the undergrowth, and then went after them.

I could hear voices. A low voice, then a higher-pitched one, and then a laugh. I crouched where I was, and inched my way forwards.

I still don't know what I expected to see – what I wanted to see. The sweat was trickling from my forehead into my eyes, and I dared not reach up a hand to brush it away.

Abel was arched above my sister. She watched him moving inside her with a detached, dispassionate stare. She arched her neck backwards and sighed, bit at the air. Abel pushed himself forward like an eager child. He thought he was in control – he was excited by that thought – but I knew Hazvinei well enough to know that she was completely in charge of what was happening here today.

When Abel finally pushed through the barrier he was straining against, Hazvinei's composure slipped a little. She gasped and pushed her palms out in a small, helpless movement, as if she would push him away. I started forward slightly, involuntarily, to help her, but before I could, she clenched those palms into fists and smiled defiantly into Abel's face. He was the helpless one now, red-faced and flip-flopping like a fish pulled out of the river. Hazvinei unfolded her fists and grasped his buttocks. Her nails dug in, creasing the flesh. Abel looked like he was in pain. His eyes closed.

When he was finished, he pulled himself out. He left a white, shining trail on the red earth, as if his *mboro* were a snail that had been crawling inside her. I felt a shiver. The air filled with a rich, swampy smell.

Hazvinei was still smiling. She folded her legs into herself, neatly.

Abel left. He walked right past me, moving deeper into the thick bush of the hill. I thought for a moment about jumping out from my hiding place and confronting him. I could see it happening in my head: see my fist curl around itself and find a resting place in the smooth skin of his jaw; hear my voice shouting. It did not happen.

Hazvinei watched him go, her lips curled and her eyes half-closed. When he was out of sight, she picked up her dress and wrapped it around herself. I saw her wince. A thin slimy trail wetted the back of her knee.

I knew I should go. I wondered why she had done it. To see what it was like? I had known Hazvinei to do things for less reason. Was it because she really wanted to do it; because she felt the strange stirrings I felt that were relieved quickly and efficiently under the blankets in my bed, or against the wall of the house if I were outside? I knew I would not ask her.

Hazvinei finished cleaning herself, and threw her *dhuku* away. Without it, her head was bare and brave. She looked like a woman as she walked back towards home. I felt sure she would stop, look at me and say, 'Tinashe, I knew you were there.' But she did not see me, and she said nothing.

Why were she and Abel doing this? Did they not know what it meant?

I crouched in the bushes for what must have been an hour after Hazvinei left. I was ashamed that I had stayed there and watched her. I went home. I did not speak to Hazvinei that day. I pushed the whole thing away. I could not push Abel away, though – I saw his face when I slept. And his eyes looked just like the ghost-eyes of my lost brother.

Chapter Twenty-two

The grey-green days of the cholera were back. I woke gasping
and clutching at my throat as it filled with the sweet, stultifying
fluid of sickness, and the air was like soup, too thick and rich
to breathe. Suspended above my bed, the eyes of the N'anga
woke me each morning with their blank stare. I heard the
buzzing of a thousand flies, and the scraping of claws against
the walls.

I tried not to see Hazvinei. Yes, I spoke to her, and helped
her with her chores when she asked, and I even smiled at her
now and then when she smiled at me. But I had also turned
my gaze away, somehow, like a chameleon that swivels his
pointed eyeball in one direction while staring in another. It
was peaceful, living without Hazvinei. I did not have to read
her face, predict her moods; I did not have to watch her strange
ways and disapprove, or collude with her, or try to hide them
from our aunt and uncle.

I got along better with Babamukuru while I was trying to
ignore Hazvinei. He must have sensed that there was space
between us two now, because he was more affectionate with me.

'You see, Tinashe,' and he rubbed my head with his closed
fist, 'being a quiet, polite boy is a good thing. It is better not
to be like your sister, saying everything that comes into her
head without any respect.'

Quiet. Polite. I tried to be.

'What is wrong, Tinashe?' said Hazvinei after a few days of
silence.

Part of me was surprised that she did not know. This was Hazvinei, after all, who had talked to the *njuzu*. Part of me thought that she and Abel had taunted me with this; that they knew I had followed them; that they had put on this show for my benefit.

'Nothing.'

'Something is wrong.' She kicked at my ankles under the table. 'You are upset about missing school?'

'No.' I had almost forgotten about school. 'I told you, I am fine.'

Babamukuru spent longer and longer at the shebeen those days. To forget about Abel? To forget about his niece and nephew? So many disappointments from which to choose. When he came home, he smelled of fresh vomit and stale beer. Tete Nyasha made her voice quieter and quieter in the mornings, so as not to disturb him. We started to take our shoes off when we entered the house so that the noise of our feet on the polished floor did not send him into a rage. Tete Nyasha started to wear her *dhuku* knotted lower over her forehead to hide the bruises.

'We can't stay here,' said Hazvinei. We sat on the *stoep*, whispering. Babamukuru was asleep in the kitchen chair, his jaw spinning a long silver thread of saliva that dampened his collar. The kitchen stank.

'And what do you think we should do?'

It was hard for me to talk to my sister. I forced my suddenly too-large tongue to shape the words – forced my eyes to look into her face. All I could see was that pale streak on the back of her leg.

'We can go to Abel,' she said. She watched my face for my reaction. 'I know where he is.'

'I know you do,' I said.

Hazvinei was silent. I felt her eyes on me. 'How do you know?'

'I saw you.'

'Saw me when?'

'I saw you and Abel. Together.'

A change in the air. Hazvinei shifted her weight; sat with her legs crossed, as a man would. She said nothing. I let the words hang between us, blue and hazy, smelling of woodsmoke and burning flesh.

'Then you know that he is nearby,' she said.

'Yes.' I did not look at her. 'Hazvinei, why did you do it?'

She shrugged.

'Did he make you? Did he hurt you?'

'No!' Leaping to Abel's defence, of course. 'I am sorry I did not tell you.'

'How long?'

'How long what?'

'I made a vague gesture.

'Months.'

'Months? How many months?'

'I don't know exactly.'

'But why, Hazvinei?'

'He is a *mukomana*. Or he is going to be. And I am a spirit medium like Nehanda. He told me so.' Her eyes glittered, feverish. 'It is how it is meant to be.'

I dropped my head into my hands. 'Hazvinei, you do not know what you are doing.'

I felt her anger hot on my skin. 'You are a fool.'

'It is not allowed, Hazvinei. You are cousins. The spirits will not allow it.'

'You are telling me about the spirits?' She almost spat the words. 'You?'

'You know it is true, Hazvinei. You are family. You cannot do this.'

'What about Nyamhika?'

The terrible knowledge felt like fire in my belly. Nyamhika, the king's daughter. The princess who produced a son with her half-brother, and who became possessed by the Nehanda spirit.

'Hazvinei. What have you done?'

The most powerful of all the spirit mediums. Forged in fire and incest.

Hazvinei turned one slim shoulder to me. I could see the curve of her cheek lit by the evening sun. 'You do not understand, Tinashe.'

'I understand that you are crazy.' I swallowed the tears that threatened to overwhelm me. 'Do you know what I did for you, when I didn't go to the examination? Everything I have done has been for you, Hazvinei. Always. Please.'

She shook her head. My sacrifice evaporated like a bead of sweat on her cool, smooth forehead. 'School is a waste of time.'

I closed my eyes and saw the sun red on my eyelids.

'We can go to him.' She moved towards me, her eyes bright with wanting. 'There is nothing else for us here, Tinashe. Babamukuru is not going to pay for you to go back to school. We can go to Abel.'

I scratched at a mosquito bite on my knee until I saw a bead of blood. I did not want to think about school.

'You know that it is the only thing we can do.'

'I will think about it,' I said.

Hazvinei sat back.

'I said, I will think about it.'

'You would rather stay in this stinking house waiting for Babamukuru to throw us out like Abel?'

'He didn't throw Abel out.'

She shrugged, irritated.

'Let me think about it, Hazvinei, please.'

'Fine. But do not think too long, or I will go without you.'

'Not yet, Hazvinei. Not yet. Please, wait.'

I said nothing more until the night that I caught Hazvinei climbing out of her bedroom window. I was taking a piss in the bushes – the indoor toilet made me uncomfortable, even after all these months, and I was beginning to think I would never get used to it – when I saw her pass me by, walking with a firm, deliberate step.

'Hazvinei?'

She froze. Against the moonlight, her silhouette was ringed with silver fire.

'What are you doing?'

'I am going out.'

'You are going to see Abel.'

'No.'

'Tell me!'

'Leave me alone.'

'Then I will tell Tete.'

'No!' She was at my side, her fingernails on my throat. 'Do not say anything, Tinashe, or I promise I will claw your eyes out.'

'Fine.' I was sick of caring for her. 'If you are not back in an hour I am coming to look for you.'

'I will be longer than an hour.'

'Then I will come and look for you.'

She melted into the darkness.

I lay awake, knowing that I should go after her, but feeling so angry that I almost wanted something bad to happen to her, so that she would know what it felt like to be afraid. I told myself that Abel was looking after her now; that I was absolved of responsibility. Then I felt ashamed for wishing bad fortune on my sister, and then I felt anxious about her, and scared. And then angry again. In the end I gave up on sleep, and sat with my arms wrapped around my knees, waiting.

About two hours after she left, Hazvinei reappeared. In the

darkness I could not see her features, and she looked like the faceless ghost we had seen on the *kopje* all those years ago. She was breathing heavily, and smelled strange.

'Where did you go?' I asked.

She did not reply. When I went to her, I saw that she was shivering. It was a hot night. 'Are you all right?'

She said nothing. I led her back through to her bed. She lay like a dead person, and did not move her limbs even when I struggled to get the blankets out from under her so that I could tuck her in. When I had finished, I bent to kiss her on the forehead. Her head was so cold it burned.

'Hazvinei,' I whispered, 'should I get Tete to look after you?'

'No,' she said, the first word she had spoken. Her breath came out in a smoky plume, as if it had been a cold night rather than warm and humming with crickets.

I could not sleep for a long time after that. I was filled with superstitious dread, and every noise was a spirit coming to find me. I do not know if Hazvinei slept, either. I did not feel as though she was asleep. I felt as if we were both staring at the dark, in different places, thinking different things.

Hazvinei went out every night for seven nights. When she came home she was exhausted and pale. I dipped a flannel in cold water and sponged her down. She did not protest. As the cold water moved over her body, her skin stood up in little bumps like the skin of a raw chicken that has been plucked. Her muscles shivered and spasmed under my hands.

'What are you doing?' I asked her every night. And every night she shook her head and said nothing.

I noticed something different each night. On the first, I saw scratches on her arms and legs, as if she had been pushing her way through acacia bushes. I helped her to clean them with strong-smelling violet mercurochrome that I stole from Tete

Nyasha's bathroom cabinet. On the second, I smelled something on her clothes – a sharp, herbal scent.

'What is that smell?'

'Nothing.'

'What is it?'

'I said it is nothing.'

On the third, fourth and fifth nights, I found strange powder on her skin and red earth in her hair. On the sixth night I found a deep, perfectly clean cut on her palm, which I cleaned and bandaged. And on the seventh night, I noticed blood on her clothes. It was a strange, purplish colour, and smelled foreign.

'Is that your blood?'

'No!'

'Whose blood is it?'

She would not tell me. But in the morning I found spots of it on the bushes outside. I followed them. When they stopped, abruptly, at our front gate, I kept walking. I knew where I had to go. This strange instinct led me deep into the bush behind the school, so far that I started to wonder if I should turn back.

I came across something that looked like a cooking fire. A ring of stones had been laid around it in a perfect circle, and the ground around the fire was scuffed and trodden. The air smelled strange – something like charred meat, or ash and woodsmoke – but there was another scent in there, sickly and poisonous. I felt a crunch under my feet, and looked down. A tiny skeletal foot was crushed beneath mine. Some kind of rodent, perhaps. The bones were picked almost clean, but the few rags of flesh wrapped around the bone were soft and wet.

I knew with a great certainty, suddenly, that spirits had been here. Were possibly still here. The air seemed heavy, as if a storm was coming, but the sky was blue and perfectly clear. I smelled water; the slick, green skin of a *njuzu*. I backed away, crushing more tiny bones, but I could not take my eyes off the altar. As I stared, the patch of ash inside the circle grew darker and seemed to spread.

I turned and ran.

After this, I tried not to catch Hazvinei's eye during the day, and I spoke to her as little as possible. I was not ready to talk to her. When I heard her climbing back into her bed at night, I rolled over and made my breathing slow and even, so that she would think I was asleep. She was not fooled. I kept my back turned to her, even when I heard her stumbling. Even when I thought I heard her sniffing, as if she had been crying.

I could not ignore her on the last night, though. She came stumbling into the room and her voice was tangled in her ragged breathing, each word split in half by air rushing in and out of her lungs.

'Tinashe.'

'No.' I pulled the cover over my head, which pulled it off my bare feet. Hazvinei took a big pinch of skin from my foot, and squeezed it in her sharp nails.

'Ow!'

'Be quiet! We don't want to wake everyone.'

'Me? You're the one who crashed in here like a big hippo.'

She put a hand across my mouth. I could taste her sweat, sweet and cold. I stopped trying to talk.

'Here.' Hazvinei turned around and picked something up from the floor. I could not see it clearly in the darkness, but I felt sick.

'What is it?'

'Help me get rid of it.' She held the bundle in her hands. It was wrapped up in an old cloth, and looked like the pieces of meat the butcher folded up in newspaper.

'What is it? I want to see.' I grabbed at the cloth and pulled a corner back. When I saw the tiny brown and bloody mess inside, I recoiled. It was small and shapeless, but I knew what it was.

'Hazvinei!'

'Please, Tinashe.'

'Is it Abel's? Hazvinei? Is this Abel's? What did you do?'

'Help me, Tinashe.' Her voice was low and urgent. She held her hands out to me. When I took the bundle from her, holding it as far away from my body as I could, she clapped her cupped hands together in the traditional gesture of thanks from a woman to a man. As far as I knew, she had never made this gesture before.

I stared at her. 'This is why you were sick. This is why you grew fatter. Why didn't you tell me?'

She shook her head.

'Did you . . .' The full horror of it closed my throat. The altar. The strange smells. The spirits hovering above the ash. She had been leaving every night to do this – not to meet Abel, as I had imagined. 'How did you do it?'

Her eyes were dark and unshining. 'I asked them. I asked them what to do.'

That black shape against the sky; the mask-like face.

'But what are we going to do with it?' My skin seemed to crawl along my body, desperate to get away from the burden in my hands. I felt my fingertips go cold and numb as even the blood moved away from it.

'We must bury it,' she said.

'But where? Someone will see us. Or stray dogs will dig it up.'

'I don't care.'

'But Hazvinei, this is . . .' I could not say it. 'We cannot just leave it to be eaten by animals. We have to give it a proper burial.'

'Where do you suggest we bury it, then?' Her voice was sarcastic.

'Listen!' I was angry and scared, and uncharacteristically brave. 'We will take it to the church. We will bury it in the graveyard. That is the proper thing to do.'

Hazvinei stared at me. 'Fine,' she said.

The church was a small wooden building, painted white. There was a Christian graveyard around it, with tombstones and – most importantly – a fence that would keep out the animals that wandered, even here in the city.

'How am I supposed to dig a hole?'

Hazvinei wrenched at a branch of a tree. After some tugging, it came away in her hands. She glared at me and started walking. 'Use this.'

I followed.

Hazvinei wrapped her cardigan tighter around herself. Her face was desperate and inhuman. I took the branch from her and gave her the bundle in return. She held it far away from her body, her lip curled in disgust.

The night was very still. It felt like it should have been stormy, the sky boiling with clouds and spitting lightning down on us like the wrath of God. But it was a still, clear night – peaceful. Even the moths were flapping lazily, accepting their fiery death with calm resignation when it came, and folding their little furred hands on their breasts when they fell. It was a beautiful night, too quiet for screams or sobs.

I scraped at the ground, bloodying it with the wet, red mud that was just below the surface of the earth. Water welled up between my toes.

'Here.'

I took the bundle from Hazvinei. Her face twisted in disgust, and she almost threw it at me. 'Get rid of it.'

I hesitated. 'Should we say something?'

'Like what? What should we say?'

'Some words.'

'Good riddance, those are some words.'

'That's not what I meant.'

'Just bury the bloody thing, Tinashe.'

I said some words in my heart, just in case, and kept my eyes screwed tight shut so that the words could get to God. Then I laid the bundle in the hole, which suddenly looked pathetically shallow and grubby, a stain of mud in the green grass, and covered it up. The wet earth soaked through the cloth and showed a grisly silhouette. I turned my eyes away.

'Come on, Tinashe.'

When the bundle was covered, it was obvious that something had been buried there. The grass was smooth and green, with occasional dry yellow patches, except for this.

'What do we do now?'

My sister looked at me. 'I want to go to the river.'

'That is a long walk.'

'I do not care.'

We walked close together through the streets. No one looked at us. The town was a different place at night, filled with people intent on their own business, just like us. We stood on the concrete wall, looking down at the black gleam of water beneath us, so sluggish and greasy that it hardly reflected the light of the streetlamps.

'It is the same river that runs through the *kopje*,' I said. 'It is hard to believe.'

'It is not the same river,' said Hazvinei.

'Yes, it is. You know it is.'

She shook her head. 'It is not the same.'

We climbed down until we were level with the water. We could not see the litter and floating debris in the darkness, and it was impossibly peaceful, softened by the night. I wiped my face and tasted blood.

'We will have to go back home,' said Hazvinei.

'Shall we go now?'

'Not yet. I am not ready yet.'

We stayed crouched on the bank. I became aware of myself again. I remembered our days spent swimming in this river; the cooler, cleaner smell it had on the kopje, and its strong tea-like taste. I remembered Hazvinei's stories of the *njuzu*. The sound of the river soothed me. My heartbeat slowed, and the long grass scratched my bare knees and shoulders. After what must have been an hour or more, Hazvinei stood and stretched long brown arms above her head, and sat on the bank, sliding her bare feet into the water. They were a different colour under there, a pale blue-brown.

'Look Tinashe,' she said. 'I am a *njuzu* too.'

The river rolled on its back and played at her feet. Hazvinei ran her hand through the water, and it lit up and danced at her touch. When I put my own hand in, it was just brown, gritty river water, but she brought it to life.

I sat beside her. She felt my shoulder with fingers as light and loving as Amai's. 'Are you hurt?'

'No.'

The axe forgets, but not the tree. The old proverb appeared in my mind. I could not help probing it with my thoughts, as you probe a sore tooth with your tongue.

'It doesn't matter, Hazvinei.'

She ran her hands through the water. The parts that she touched became silky and cool. I felt them against my tired feet. She was trying to comfort me. And then I felt something clutch at my ankles, something unnaturally strong and hot. I yelped, and drew my feet away. They were blistering; burned. The skin on my toes was almost white. Hazvinei stared at me, wide-eyed, but did not jump as I had. She withdrew her feet from the water slowly, painfully. Her toes curled under, and her perfect skin was swollen and shining, as if she had dipped her feet into the cooking fire.

'It is the *njuzu*,' she whispered. Her face was drained of colour – I could see it, even in the moonlight. 'She has turned against me. She is telling me so.'

She raised her eyes to mine, and I saw a strange sight – Hazvinei afraid.

Chapter Twenty-three

Incest. The birth of an unnatural child. The killing of innocents. Hazvinei had committed every possible sin against the *mhondoro*. She thought she was untouchable, but the sluggish swirl of the blood-coloured river told me otherwise. The spirits would not forgive us this time. Babamukuru, Abel, Hazvinei and me: we were caught up in their plans, and bad fortune would soon follow. The witch-smeller was not the only one who would be able to hunt out Hazvinei. Abel was no longer here to protect her, and I had learned that I could not protect her either.

'We have to go,' I said to her.

'I have been telling you that for weeks,' she said. 'We have to go and find Abel.'

'No.' I shook my head, trying to dislodge the claws of the leopards.

'Why not? Where else are we going to go?'

'Abel will not be able to help us. It will be better if it is just you and me . . .'

'And we will do what? Go back to the *kopje*? Dig graves next to Amai and Baba and wait for the jackals? No.'

'Hazvinei.'

'I go to find Abel, or not at all.'

We made our plans as quietly as we could, but Babamukuru followed us from room to room in the dim, closed-up house, listening to our conversations and rarely leaving us alone. Tete Nyasha fluttered about us as usual, but there was an anxious quality to her smiles and the *sadza* she made us tasted of worry and tears.

I knew that something was going to happen. The air had that charged, electric feeling, as if a storm were coming. When Tete Nyasha gave me a hug, there was a crackle of static.

I was right. It happened after dinner, while Babamukuru was picking his teeth clean with a fingernail.

'We might have a surprise for you soon,' said Tete Nyasha to Hazvinei, smiling. She looked at Babamukuru. This must have been a pre-arranged signal, because he got up and left the table, whistling. Hazvinei pushed her food around her plate.

'Tinashe, you coming to the shebeen?' said Babamukuru.

'No, Babamukuru.'

'I think you should come.'

'I am tired.'

Babamukuru glowered. 'Come, Tinashe.'

'I do not feel well. I think I will stay here.'

Hazvinei flicked her cat-eyes over to me, and away. No expression.

Babamukuru shrugged. 'Fine. *Manheru*.'

I sat at the table with my arms crossed, looking at Tete Nyasha and Hazvinei. Tete Nyasha seemed nervous. She started to clear our plates.

'What is the surprise, Tete?' I asked her.

'Do you want to go to your room, Tinashe? I could make you some tea?'

Hazvinei and I moved closer together, almost imperceptibly. I could feel the warmth of Hazvinei's shoulder close to my own, and I felt the way I had when we had been in trouble together as kids. If one of us was going to get a hiding, we both were.

Tete Nyasha gave up, and talked to both of us.

'I have exciting news, Hazvinei,' she said.

Hazvinei said nothing.

'Michael Mapfumo wants to marry you.' Tete Nyasha reached out for Hazvinei's hands, but she crossed her arms. 'We are very lucky. He is a good man. And his *ro'ora* offer is very generous.'

'Michael Mapfumo?' I said. 'The big man from the shebeen?'

'Yes. He is a good man,' said Tete Nyasha again.

'I have never spoken to him,' said Hazvinei.

'You have seen him, though! And he has noticed you for a long time. It could not be better, Hazvinei. Think what a good life you will have.' She laid her hand against Hazvinei's cheek, and smiled. 'How do you think I met your Babamukuru, hey? I liked him, of course, but my parents saw to it that we did things the proper way. The way things should be done.'

Hazvinei sat, enduring Tete Nyasha's caress. I recognised the glint of her half-closed eyes. I saw her hands clench and unclench.

'This is a good thing, Hazvinei,' said Tete Nyasha. 'If you think about it, you will see. Wouldn't you like to have a home of your own? Where you can make your own rules?'

I had to admire Tete Nyasha's tactics. She was shrewder than I had thought. If anything was likely to appeal to Hazvinei, it would be the power to make her own rules.

'You can have children,' said Tete Nyasha. She glowed at the idea. 'You can be a mother.'

'I don't want to be a mother.' Hazvinei's voice was low.

Tete Nyashe took it for bashfulness, I saw. She pinched Hazvinei's cheek. 'You should not be embarrassed to talk about these things! It is good to grow children inside you. It is what a woman is meant to do. Nothing can be better.'

These things should not be discussed in front of a man. Once more, I felt invisible.

'I don't want children,' said Hazvinei, louder this time.

'You will feel differently once you are married,' said Tete Nyasha, still smiling.

'No!' Hazvinei stood. 'I am not marrying that baboon. I am not lying in the same bed as him, I am not touching him, and I am not having his children.'

Tete Nyasha raised her hands to her ears as if to cover them. 'A child is sacred,' she said.

'Hazvinei, sit down.' I tried to catch hold of her, but she shook me off.

'Just because you are a dried-up old woman,' she said. 'Just because you killed your babies.'

'Hazvinei . . .' I stood.

Tete Nyasha seemed to remember that I was there, and clutched at me with blind, searching hands. 'Tinashe, what is she talking about?'

'Nothing, Tete,' I said. 'She is angry. She does not know what she is saying.'

'You killed your babies,' said Hazvinei with cruel emphasis. 'Amai said so.'

Tete Nyasha's face twisted. 'You . . . *hure!*'

Prostitute. It does not take much for a woman to be called a whore. Sometimes all she has to do is show her knees, or talk to a man alone. But for Tete Nyasha to call someone a whore — that showed the earth shifting, the trees changing colour, the skies opening. I saw her reach her hand out, palm open. I did not try to stop her. This was something between women, something mysterious and smelling of that strange inside-body blood that was sticky and dark, and something with which I should not meddle. She struck Hazvinei across the face. Hazvinei's skin leapt up almost at once, dark and swollen, as if the slap had held poison.

'*Musata nyoko,*' said Hazvinei — a terrible insult — and spat. 'You are an unnatural girl! You are evil!'

The last word fell to the ground between them and writhed there. Hazvinei hissed at Tete Nyasha, her teeth bared, and ran from the room.

'Hazvinei!' I started to run after her, but stopped when I saw Tete Nyasha sink to the ground. Her face was wet with tears, like a damp sponge that has been squeezed.

'Tinashe!' She held out her arm for me to help her up.

'I am sorry, Tete Nyasha,' I said, and I ran after Hazvinei.

I found her sitting behind the dustbins.

'I thought you had run away.'

'You would like that.'

'Don't be stupid.'

I sat beside her — far enough away to avoid irritating her. I could feel the hostility rising off her skin like steam.

'We cannot stay here.'

I sighed. 'Please. Let us just wait until morning. Then I promise I will take you to wherever you want to go.'

She looked at me sidelong. 'Do you promise?'

'I promise.'

When we returned to the house, hours later, Babamukuru was home from the shebeen. He was in a good mood, as he always was after a good drinking session. But it was short-lived. Soon he would want to shout and fight. Hazvinei and I knew this, and we stayed silent. Tete Nyasha was deflated, slumped in her chair looking down, up, at me, anywhere but at Hazvinei.

'Hazvinei,' said Babamukuru. 'You are lucky.'

We were silent. I flicked my eyes at Hazvinei, but she was not looking at me.

'Very, very lucky,' he said.

We were all silent. Tete Nyasha's hands fluttered, but she clamped them down onto her knees again.

The silence spread out between us, stretched its legs, wandered around the room. Babamukuru was not going to tell us until one of us asked. My lips and tongue felt sluggish, but I forced them to move into the shape of 'Tete Nyasha has told us the news.'

'Ah.' Babamukuru rubbed his hands together. He was really in an excellent mood. It was very strange to see. 'It is Michael Mapfumo.'

I remembered Michael Mapfumo's cheeks hanging down from either side of his face like a sad pig's.

'Mapfumo.' I said. It was clear I was the designated speaker for me and my sister. Hazvinei was saying nothing.

'Yes. Mapfumo wants to marry Hazvinei.'

'I know, Babamukuru,' I said. 'Tete Nyasha has told us. But he is an old man.'

'He is not old! He is the same age as me.'

I said nothing.

'Yes. It is very good news.' Babamukuru stood up. 'It is very lucky. You are not a complete waste, Hazvinei. You have the chance to be a good woman now. It is very, very lucky.'

Hazvinei raised her head. Her eyes seemed to have sunk into her head. 'Very lucky,' she said, 'to have an old, fat man as a husband.'

Babamukuru paused, not sure if she was being sarcastic or not. Poor man.

She took a long time gathering her saliva. I could see that she was drawing it up from some deep part of her, some place that was full of bile and bitterness. When she spat at his feet it sat on Tete Nyasha's perfectly polished floor, still foaming a little. Tete Nyasha twitched in her chair, wanting to jump up and clean it.

Babamukuru stared at the offending patch of wetness. Hazvinei was nothing if not thorough. It was an impressive spit, worthy of winning the contests I used to have with the *kopje* boys when I was small.

I should have seen it coming. Babamukuru hit her across the face.

'You devil,' he said.

Tete Nyasha grasped his arm. 'Don't, don't hit her. It is not going to make things better.'

But Babamukuru had grabbed an enamel pot from the kitchen.

I jumped up. 'Babamukuru, Hazvinei is sorry.'

'Don't think I haven't heard what people are saying!' Spittle collected at the corners of his mouth. 'I took you in! I have treated you as my own daughter!'

Hazvinei's scorn was palpable.

'I have given you everything. Have you ever been hungry? Have you ever been thirsty?'

I remembered the bruises on Tete Nyasha's face. The bruises on Hazvinei.

'And now we have found you a good man to be your husband, and you say no? You do not understand, Hazvinei,' and he leaned so that his face was close to her own, 'that this is something that has been decided already. We have decided the bride price. You are getting married. And when you have grown out of this defiance you will thank us for what we have done. For me, I am glad to have you out of my house.'

Hazvinei mumbled something, and Babamukuru spun around to Tete Nyasha. He was in a hitting mood, I could see that, and it did not matter who was within reach of his fists.

'What is it?'

'She said,' Tete's voice was barely audible, 'she said that she is not a virgin.'

Babamukuru's eyes were almost all white, his teeth bared.

'Tete Nyasha is confused,' I said. 'It has been a difficult night for everyone. I think we should talk about this in the morning.'

I did not see the pot coming. My vision went black, and I

fell off my chair. For a moment I wanted to laugh. Hit in the head with a cooking pot! It was the kind of thing that happened to cheating husbands.

'You are not a virgin?' Babamukuru was staring at Hazvinei. She had the cornered defiance of a cane rat – all eyes and teeth.

'That's what I said. Mapfumo will not want used goods.' She spoke the words with relish.

'You are lying,' said Babamukuru. 'You are evil, and unnatural, and you are lying.'

Tete Nyasha said nothing. She was exhausted, I could see.

'We shall make sure,' he said. 'Nyasha. You must check.'

'Don't touch her!'

It is traditional for the older women in the family to check the young ones, to make sure they are intact.

'Do it!' Babamukuru wagged his finger in Tete Nyasha's face. 'See if the *fambi* tells the truth.'

'Tunga, I . . .'

'Do it now, or I will do it for you.'

I did not believe he would do it. Tete Nyasha, though, must have believed him, for she started moving towards Hazvinei.

'Get away from me!' Hazvinei stood with her hands in fists at her side. 'I will not let you touch me, old woman.'

'Hazvinei . . .' Tete Nyasha reached out a hand as if to touch her cheek, but Hazvinei slapped it away. 'No!'

'I do not have the time for this,' said Babamukuru. He rolled up his sleeves. 'I will do it. Hold her down.'

Tete Nyasha looked at me.

'I will hold her,' I said, 'If Tete Nyasha performs the examination.'

Babamukuru stared at me. 'Fine.'

Hazvinei turned as if to run out of the room, but I grasped her thin wrists and held her tightly. She kicked, bit and swore at me, slumped and turned to deadweight in my arms, scrabbled her legs on the floor like a cockroach when the light is turned on.

'Hazvinei,' I spoke in her ear. 'If I do not do this, Babamukuru will do it instead of Tete Nyasha. And he will hurt you.'

Hazvinei bared her teeth and snarled like an animal. Her eyes were white all around, and spittle collected at the corners of her mouth.

'You should be grateful that we have found anyone for you at all,' said Babamukuru.

Tete Nyasha looked at me, and then at my sister. Hazvinei had stopped struggling. She lay staring at Tete Nyasha, her eyes wide and unblinking. Tete Nyasha thrust her hand under Hazvinei's skirt. Hazvinei twitched once, convulsively, and swallowed, but did not drop her stare. After a moment, Tete Nyasha got to her feet and went to the sink. She washed her hand while we watched her, and the water ran red.

'She is intact,' Tete Nyasha said to Babamukuru as she cleaned herself.

I felt Hazvinei's pulse quicken under my hands. I kept her pressed down, willing her to be silent.

'Are you sure?' asked Babamukuru.

'Yes,' Tete Nyasha would not stop cleaning her hand. She turned it over and over under the tap water, rubbing at it with the hard, green Lifebuoy soap.

'You are a filthy liar,' said Babamukuru to Hazvinei, conversationally. There was an almost-smile on his face. He hit her across the face once, twice, almost casually, as if he were not thinking about it at all. I released her and we sat together on the cold floor, breathing. A drop of blood from Hazvinei's lip fell onto my hand.

'You will go with Mapfumo,' said Babamukuru. He sat at the table in front of his cooling *sadza*. 'Come. Sit. Eat.'

Tete Nyasha sat beside him. The sound of her chair scraping the concrete was unbearably loud.

'Tinashe, Hazvinei.'

I got up. Hazvinei looked at me for a long time, so long that when she finally took her gaze from me, it felt like a hand had been lifted from my shoulder. She turned and went to her room. All I could hear was Babamukuru breathing heavily, in and out. And then the clink and clang of his knife and fork on his dinner plate as he started to eat. Tete Nyasha and I sat in front of our cooling food. I picked up my fork once or twice, then put it down again. I could not imagine eating. I had forgotten what it felt like to eat.

Tete Nyasha eventually managed to pick up her cutlery and eat her food with some sort of normality. She gulped loudly, though, and drank a lot of water. I could hear the bites of food going down her throat. With that, and Babamukuru's clinking and clanging and loud breathing, the room was unbearably noisy. I watched the gravy separate into brown stuff and clear fat, then congeal.

'Eat,' said Babamukuru, waving his fork at me.

I looked at my plate.

'Eat.'

I picked up my fork again. Perhaps it would be easier if I were allowed to use my fingers, as we used to on the *kopje*, but Tete Nyasha insisted on using a knife and fork.

'I will not tell you again, Tinashe,' he said.

I speared a bit of meat with my fork and brought it to my mouth. I did not think my jaws would work. I put the fork back down.

When it hit the table, Babamukuru stood and came over to where I was sitting. I looked up at him. I could see his pulse in the hollow of his throat. He laid a hand on my shoulder with what felt like tenderness. For a mad moment, I thought

he was going to smile. Then, with a sudden, violent movement, he swept the plate off the table and against the wall.

Poor Tete Nyasha. Her immaculate house.

'Get out, both of you.'

Tete Nyasha and I retreated. Behind us I could hear the
scrape and clink of cutlery as Babamukuru continued to eat.

Chapter Twenty-four

We had to go. Of course we had to go. We left in the early hours of the morning, before Babamukuru and Tete Nyasha awoke, just as Abel had done.

'I want to find the photograph.'

'What photograph?'

'The one of you and me with Amai and Baba. Babamukuru took it from the house when we left.'

'Tinashe. There is no time.'

'It is the only photograph we have.' I looked through drawers as quietly as I could. The house still stank of a dark, secret smell.

'Tinashe . . .'

'Just one more minute.'

I gave up. I did not know where Babamukuru had put the photograph, and I doubted that even he would remember.

'*Kurumidza*, Tinashe.' Hazvinei pushed me through the door and we were outside on the dew-wet grass, hearing the first birds shouting their good-mornings.

'Do you know where Abel is?' I asked her.

'Of course.'

Of course she did. They must have had many secret places together, those two, where they could meet – while innocent Tinashe did his homework and imagined that his sister and cousin hid nothing from him. I followed her out of the front gate and down the road, towards the brown smear of bush that rose behind the houses and the school.

'I went to the camp. He wasn't there.'

'He was hiding.' Hazvinei glanced over her shoulder. 'Come on.'

'Hazvinei,' I stopped her, 'you are bleeding.' There was a dark stain on her navy skirt.

'I know. It is fine.'

'Do you need to get . . .' I was not sure what to say. 'Some cloth?'

'I have cloth. It is not working. It has soaked through already.'

'Is this normal?' I did not know how women were supposed to bleed.

'I am fine. Let's go.'

She moved too fast for me, and was soon out of sight. I slowed to a jog, and let my heart return to its regular rhythm. I knew where she was going. There was no hurry to get there. Bush gave way to clearing, and there was my cousin.

'Abel.'

He looked different: taller, grimmer around the mouth. He stank of cigarettes and sweat. Hazvinei danced around him, triumphant. He did not seem surprised to see us.

Why did he look different? Perhaps it was my eyes that had changed. I no longer saw a hero, my big-city cousin with his knowledge of the world. I saw a dangerous man with a croco-dile smile and quick-moving, clever-fingered hands that I did not trust. I saw his eyes flicker and shiver in his face, always looking, looking and seeing more than you wanted him to see. He saw the shadow in me, and I saw him smile at it. Something dark inside me smiled back, and my stomach twisted.

'Tinashe! Come, sit.' He patted a spot beside him. 'Did you bring me some food today?'

I shook my head.

'Cigarettes?'

I knew he was joking. I shook my head again.

'*Aiee,*' and he cuffed Hazvinei playfully about the head, 'you are too much trouble, you two. You do not visit for days, and then when you come you bring me nothing. Still, I am a generous man, and I will offer you a cup of tea.'

He had his fire, and his pots and tins. I saw blankets, and a zipped canvas bag. He looked like someone who had prepared for a long journey.

Hazvinei took her tea. It was full of sugar, the way she liked it. When Abel held a mug out to me, I did not move.

'Go on, take it. You think I am your Amai? That I will hold it to your mouth for you?'

He thrust it at me. I did not move.

'Fine,' He tipped up the cup, and let the hot tea burn and hiss on the ground. 'What is the matter with you?'

Abel stood, and walked to me. He was a whole head taller now. When he stood so close, my eyes were level with the buttons on his khaki shirt. 'I thought you were coming to join me,' he said. 'Both of you. And now you won't speak to me?'

I said nothing, but I felt my eyes slide away from him.

'What is the matter? Why are you not talking?'

Silence.

'You have a guilty conscience, eh?'

He pushed his face into mine. I smelled *mbanje* on his breath, and I was afraid.

'I am talking to you.' He gripped my shoulder and pushed downwards, so hard that my knees buckled. I tried to push back, not taking my eyes from his, but I folded and crumpled until I was kneeling.

'Abel.' Hazvinei, at his elbow. 'Tinashe is sad about leaving school, that is all.'

Abel stared at me. Then a flicker like a lizard darting over a rock, and his eyes were full of humour again. 'Eh-eh, Tinashe,' he said, patting me on the back as if that had been his intention all along, 'did I not tell you that this school was a waste of time? Yes? And here you are wasting good tea because of it.'

He made me another cup. Although we were only half an hour's walk from Babamukuru's house, the bush swallowed up all the sounds of the town. We could be back at the *kopje*, listening to the slap and wash of the river against its banks. We could be real *vakomana*. I almost managed to convince myself that we would be.

It was a while before Hazvinei moved away from us and I could speak to Abel alone. I did not know what to say to him, but I knew that I had to say something. I love you. I missed you. I will never forgive you for what you have done to my sister. I am afraid of you. All of these things were true. Instead I said, 'Where are we going to go?'

He smiled. 'We are going to find the freedom fighters.'

'Do you know where they are?'

'We will leave the city. If we ask enough people – the right people – we will find them.'

'And how are we planning to leave the city?' I crossed my arms. I felt cold, even though the day was warm. 'Are we going to walk?'

'You think I left with nothing? I took money from Baba's wallet. We will travel by bus.'

I had thought that people would stare. I had thought that people would talk. But, as we pushed our way through the crowds into the sweaty fug of the bus, no one remarked on us at all. Men glanced at Hazvinei, yes, but they said nothing. What had I expected? A thunderclap? A *njuzu* rising from the river to bar our way?

'The first thing to do is get out of the city,' said Abel. 'And then we will start asking questions.'

'Where will we sleep?'

'Outside, to begin with. Until we find them.'

'You really think it will be that easy?'

'With Hazvinei, yes.' He smiled at my sister. 'She knows things. She will lead us to them.'

I was not so sure that I wanted to find the guerrillas. They could be dangerous to us, even if we told them that we wanted to help with the cause. I would keep silent and let Abel talk and, as soon as we were out of the city, I would take Hazvinei and go . . . Where, I did not know. But I would find somewhere where she would be safe. Perhaps I could even persuade Abel to come with us, once this fervour had worn off. Surely he did not expect a camp of rebels to welcome three city kids into their group without any questions or suspicion?

We arrived in the middle of nowhere. I realised how much I had changed since moving to town – the villages looked small and straggling now, and the dust in everyone's clothes and hair made them seem dirty. I had grown used to Tete Nyasha's scented soap and the hot water from the taps.

Abel led us off the road and into the bush, talking constantly. He was alive with excitement, his eyes wide and bright in his face. 'We will find a freedom fighter camp,' he said. 'And we will join them. This is a good spot for us. There are many villages nearby, and there is water. '

He thought it would be so easy. But where else could we go? We could not return to Babamukuru's house. I could not return to school. And there was nothing for us on the *kopje*.

'They will allow you to?'

'Of course they will.' He spoke with confidence. 'And you are coming with me.'

We walked for a long time through the bush, away from town. The heat lowered our heads and weighted our feet. We made a makeshift camp when evening fell, building a fire to keep the animals away and hanging blankets over branches to make a tent. Abel produced the last of his *mbanje*, but neither Hazvinei nor I would have any.

'Your loss,' Abel shrugged, and smoked in the darkness, his eyelids growing heavy and fat.

I awoke knowing that something was wrong, and that Hazvinei was not in the camp. I could smell the oils of wild animals in the air; a rich, musky stink that warned me.

'Abel, have you seen Hazvinei this morning?'

'No.' He was not concerned. He was playing a game with the bullet – tossing it up into the air and catching it, over and over again. It flashed silver in the sun. 'She is around, I am sure.'

'When did you last see her?'

'Last night, just like you. Stop worrying, Tinashe. Hazvinei can take care of herself. She is probably washing, or pissing.'

I left him and wandered around our camp, hoping to see her. When I did not, I moved into the bush, careful not to go too far.

'Tinashe.'

A voice from behind the reeds. I ran, stumbling in the wet soil, and found her. She lay on the river bank, streaked with mud. Her legs were submerged up to her waist.

'Hazvinei, what are you doing?'

She rolled her eyes towards me. She was panting, and her face was blank. I was not even sure if she had heard me.

'Hazvinei!' I skidded down the bank until my *takkies* swelled and filled with water. I grasped her by the shoulders. 'What's wrong?'

She shuddered and made a convulsive, heaving movement. I looked down. From between her legs, tendrils of red were coiling and curling into the muddy water. It was beautiful, like a flame lily opening between her thighs. For a moment I did not realise what I was seeing, and then I saw that it was blood, and I thought that my sister was dying.

'You are still bleeding,' I said. 'Why are you still bleeding?'

'I think something is wrong,' she said.

I did not think that it might be better to leave her still while I fetched help. I did not think to shout out, or try to stem the flow of blood. I picked my sister up as if she were a tiny baby and I cradled her head on my shoulder and I carried her back to the camp as tenderly as I could. 'My little lioness,' I told her. 'No one is as brave as you.'

Abel sat with Hazvinei in the tent. The grass in front of it was stained red from where we had dragged her in and I watched the red droplets turn rust-coloured and then brown, adhering to the grass blades as securely as spilled paint. We would have to be careful that night that animals did not come into the camp, lured by the smell. I waited outside while he looked at her, hoping that by some magic he would be able to cure my sister.

Abel emerged. 'She is still bleeding,' he said. 'Not as much as before. But I cannot stop it.'

'What are we going to do?'

He spread his hands. 'I don't know. We are miles from town now.'

We tried the clinic in the nearest village, but they shook their heads. 'We are sorry, brothers. We cannot help.'

The white men had been in there only the day before, and had dealt out severe punishments to sympathisers.

'Please,' I said. 'We are not *vakomana*.'

I saw them look at our red, nervous eyes, the grass in our hair, the sweat and stains on our clothes. Abel had his wish. We were *vakomana* now, whether we wanted to be or not.

'Even some painkillers. Even some headache tablets. Even a bandage, one bandage.'

They gave us half a packet of Panadol. Nothing more.

'We are sorry, we are sorry,' they kept saying.

We carried her from village to village, and met with the same bad news everywhere we went. Even Abel's charm could not help us.

'We cannot keep moving her,' I said to Abel. 'It is going to make her worse.'

'What do you suggest we do, then? We are miles from town.'

'We could call Babamukuru . . .'

'None of these places have a telephone. And if they did, they would not let us use it. And if they let us use it, Baba would not help us.'

'If we told him that Hazvinei was dying . . .'

'She is not dying. And you do not know him like I do.'

In the morning I went back to the village. This time, I tried the local witch doctor. He came back to the camp with me, and Abel watched in silence as he examined Hazvinei.

'I will not touch her,' said the witch doctor. 'The snake in her womb is eating itself, and that is what is causing the blood.'

Cursed, cursed, cursed. I was sick of hearing it. I was sick of watching people shake their heads and say with mingled sympathy and dark pleasure that there was nothing they could do to help.

'She has done nothing wrong,' I told the N'anga.

'If that is true,' he said, 'then why is this happening to her?'

I had no answers.

I sat by the river that night, by a small fire that I had built. The sounds of the camp were distant, and the shrill buzz of crickets filled my ears like water and drowned my thoughts as I fell asleep. I welcomed this.

I dreamed that Amai fed me soup, spooning it into my mouth as if I were an infant. Her dead face shone with an intricate pattern of light and dark. I opened my mouth as she stretched her hand towards me, and was surprised when my teeth closed on empty air.

'Tinashe?'

I did not want to wake up. I wanted to stay here in this brighter place, where Amai was smiling at me and the sky was full of stars bigger than the moon. I could see huge, indistinct faces looking down at me, their features traced in lines of white light. They smiled through bared teeth. The air smelled of blood and woodsmoke.

'Tinashe.'

Amai turned into the shadows.

'Wake up.'

I did not want to return to my body. I could already feel the pain, numbed and far away. When the voice called to me again, I was imprisoned inside my aching skeleton and bruised skin, a maggot trapped inside a rotting pawpaw. I opened my eyes, which felt swollen and too big for their sockets. Abel, his face carved from wood, a mask of lines spiralling out from his toothy grin. I blinked, and he became a man again.

'You are awake,' he said, without pleasure.

'Yes.'

I struggled on to one elbow and looked around. I did not recognise this place. 'Where are we?'

He shrugged. 'In the bush.'

I remembered. 'Hazvinei?'

Abel's eyes were so dark that the pupil disappeared into the iris. 'She is not well,' he said.

Not well. I remembered the blood. Amai might have known what to do, but Amai was dead. Hazvinei was dying.

'What are we going to do?' I asked him.

Abel stood.

My head felt tight and strange. 'Abel?'

I could not see him. Or Hazvinei. Where was Hazvinei? I sat up and looked around. 'Hazvinei?'

No answer.

'Abel!' I tried to shout, but my throat was dry. 'Hazvinei is alive? She is still alive? She is here?'

Abel knelt beside me again. 'She is here.'

'Where is she?'

He indicated a bundle of blankets. 'She is sleeping.'

'Sleeping?' I could not see any movement; any breathing.

'She is very sick.' He seemed resigned. 'I do not know what is wrong. She might not live for long.'

'How can you say that? She is your cousin!' And more, I thought but did not say.

'There is nothing more that we can do for her.'

'Then you must take her to the hospital!'

Abel did not meet my eyes. Instead, he flicked his gaze to a pile of pots and blankets.

'What are you doing?' I asked him.

'I am packing up.'

I stayed very still. 'Why?'

'I am moving on.'

'Moving where?'

He shrugged.

'How are we going to take Hazvinei?' I asked him.

'I am leaving everything behind, except what I can carry.'

'Then . . .'

'I cannot stay,' said Abel. 'You understand this.'

'But Hazvinei is too sick to travel.'

He moved his eyes away from mine. 'I cannot stay,' he said again. The truth settled between us, a moth landing in the dust.

'You are leaving us?'

'I have to find a camp. I have to join them. Otherwise, what am I doing here? I will come back for you. With help.'

I looked at the still form of my sister. 'You cannot go, Abel. She will die.'

'I will come back. I told you. I will find the *vakomana,* and they will help us.'

I saw that he really, honestly believed what he was saying. There was a light of fanaticism in his eyes; he looked at me, but he did not see me.

'Here.' He dropped something cool into my hand. The bullet. 'It is yours,' he said. 'You should have it.'

I closed my fingers over it.

'Perhaps it will bring you luck again,' he said, and walked away with a strong, optimistic stride. I stood, clutching the bullet and watching him. And then I ran. He did not see me coming. I crashed into his retreating back with such force that he sprawled in the dust, face first. I heard the satisfying crunch of his nose.

'What the hell do you think you're doing?'

He turned around under me, fighting to get up. I was smaller and lighter, but I held him down. His face was distorted by blood and anger. 'Get off me.'

We fought, silent and bitter. We did not fight like men but like boys: scuffling in the dirt; pinching whatever delicate skin we could find; spitting in each other's faces. He bit me on the arm, as Hazvinei used to do. I tugged at the short curls of his hair. When we broke apart, we stared at each other, mouths open and gasping. I waited for Abel to laugh, or to apologise. I waited for him to soften.

I ran at him again. I hit every part of him that I could reach. I scratched at him with my nails and I kicked at his legs. I pushed him to the ground again. If I could not be a brave leopard hunter, I could at least be a little mosquito, buzzing and whining in Abel's ears and hurting whatever tiny patch of his skin I could reach. I could be an annoyance, even if it got me crushed.

To my surprise, I was winning the fight. My blood turned hot. I wanted to beat him until I killed him. I wanted to beat him as Babamukuru had beaten him. I staggered backwards, releasing him, and retched.

Abel got to his feet, coughing and clutching at his side. 'Tinashe.'

I said nothing.

'I have to go,' he said. 'You understand that.'

I felt my fists unclench.

'You understand that, Tinashe.'

'No. I do not understand. I do not understand why you do anything that you do. I do not understand why you would bring us here and then leave us. Why you and my sister . . .' I stopped. 'This is your fault. This is all your fault.'

'It is not my fault that Hazvinei became sick.'

'Yes it is!' I stared at him, panting. 'Do you know why she is bleeding? Why she is sick?'

He shook his head, waiting for me to tell him. I opened my mouth, ready to form the words, and I could not. I stayed silent.

'I have to go.'

And I let him go. What else could I do? I could not force him to stay with us. He should have wanted to.

I did not watch him leave. The bullet was gone, lost in the struggle. I glanced around for it, but it would be impossible to see among the dust and pebbles. It did not matter. It no longer had any significance for me.

We had enough food for a few days, and there was a stream nearby for water. I pulled myself over to where Hazvinei slept. I looked at her dry, drained face and the dark bruises like purple flowers around her eyes.

'It will be all right, Hazvinei,' I said, and covered her with the blanket that Abel had left us. 'He will come back.'

Hazvinei could always tell when I was lying.

For the most part my sister was asleep, her eyelids and lips twitching as she drew in breaths like a man hauling a bucket up from a well, getting a little further every time before dropping it back down. She looked like a much older woman; in fact, she looked like Amai.

She awoke once in the night, for just a few minutes. The cool darkness must have soothed her.

'Tinashe.'

'I am here.'

'I am sorry.'

'What are you sorry for? You do not need to be sorry.'

Ah, the lies we tell to the dying! But lies do not seem important, at the end. Nothing does. Except, perhaps, the memory of two children swimming with a *njuzu* in the slow-moving river.

'Why are you awake?' she asked me. 'It is night-time.'

'I am looking after you.'

She turned her head and licked her dry lips with a grey tongue that was even drier. 'Where is Abel?'

'He is gone.'

She did not seem surprised. 'Am I still bleeding?'

'A little.'

'It was like having my first blood all over again,' she said. 'Except that nothing would stop it. I tried ripping up rags and even stuffing them inside, but nothing worked. I thought that the river would clean me out . . .'

'You are lucky you did not get eaten by a crocodile.'

'I didn't think of that.'

'No.'

'I remember you coming.'

'I am glad that I found you. You should have told someone where you were going.'

She shrugged. 'None of their business.'

'It was mine.'

'Yes.' Her eyes opened properly for the first time. They laughed at me, those slanted eyes. 'Yes. It was yours.'

'Is there nothing you can do, Hazvinei? No one you could . . . ask? For help?'

She snorted. 'Why do you not just say it?'

I did not want to mention the spirits out loud. 'It is bad luck.'

'How could our luck be worse? And no. That is not how it works. Whenever they give me something, they take something in return. And I have nothing left to give them.'

Except your life, I thought, but did not say. And I could see that she was thinking the same thing.

I fell asleep without realising it, beaten down by the day's events. I awoke to see Hazvinei's shining eyes above my own, and pushed myself up on one elbow.

'What is the matter? Are you feeling worse?'

'Mbuya Nehanda is coming.'

'Mbuya Nehanda? The Nehanda spirit?'

'Yes!'

'She is coming here?'

'She is coming here. She is being carried here.'

'Carried?'

'She is too old to walk the distance.'

'But I thought she was Nehanda – the warrior?'

'She is. But Nehanda chose to enter the body of an old woman who cannot fight.' Hazvinei shrugged.

'How do you know?' I looked for a delirious light in her eyes and saw none. She seemed better; energised.

'I just do.'

Of course she did.

'Why is she here?'

'I do not know.' My sister pulled me to my feet as we heard the cracking and snapping of twigs from the bush. 'But she is here now.'

I wondered what magic had cured my sister, but I did not have long to wonder. Four strong men carried Mbuya Nehanda on a litter made of poles and blankets. They settled her down on the dust, arranging blankets around her with care and some fear, and then set about building a fire in our camp. They did not speak to either of us. I thought that perhaps they were dumb – they had that silent, locked-in look about them.

Mbuya Nehanda herself was tiny, frail as the discarded wing of a flying ant, which could blow away at the slightest cough. I had never seen anyone so old. Her face had folded in on itself again and again as it wrinkled, becoming waterless and shrunken. Her skin was blacker than black, certainly blacker than any skin I'd seen before: an ashy grey-black, with no hint of moisture or even flesh beneath, wrapped in a dirty cloth. As I watched, her helpers rubbed a paste into her skin.

'Dung,' Hazvinei whispered.

'Why?'

'To protect her skin from the sun.'

Her skin looked blackened and burned anyway, and the dung paste made it crackle and turn to powder. She wore jewellery – bangles and necklaces that left dents in her dry skin and looked too heavy for her twig-like wrists. As she moved her arms, the bracelets clanged and clinked and the dung powder fell from her joints as if she were dead and crumbling.

They were on their way back to Zambia, her handlers told us, which presented a problem, as the medium could not cross water until the spirit of Nehanda gave her permission. As Nehanda would only give permission after days of prayers requesting it, it could be a long time before Mbuya Nehanda was safely across the Zambian border.

'It is meant to be,' said Hazvinei. 'The spirits meant her to stop here.'

I felt a fear and awe similar to that I had felt when Hazvinei told me stories of spirits in the night. Nehanda stank, yes, of dung and old-woman smell, and her hand on my head was a thin sack full of bones with fingernails that scratched along my scalp, but I felt something pass from her to me all the same.

When Mbuya Nehanda was settled and warmed by the fire, she told her four helpers to sit. She scanned the group with her milky eyes and found Hazvinei.

'I must talk to you,' she said.

Hazvinei came forward.

'Alone.'

Nehanda's bearers looked at each other.

'It is all right,' said Nehanda.

They moved away together, those two women, and the rest of the group stepped back. Mbuya Nehanda and Hazvinei looked strangely alike in the firelight. I do not know what the spirit medium said to my sister, because I fell asleep, lulled by the crackling of the flames and the unexpected warmth. When I awoke, there was no evidence of a fire – and no footprints. Hazvinei lay unmoving.

'Mbuya Nehanda?' I could hear no voices. 'Hazvinei?' She did not stir.

I had dreamed it. I had dreamed all of it. There was no spirit medium here to intervene on my sister's behalf. There was no fire. There was no help to be found.

I have heard people talk about the moment when life leaves a body. I have heard them say that they can see the spirit leave, a pale shadow finally released from its heavy prison, a moth rising towards the moon. I did not see this. I did not see anything. It was only when I said her name and she did not respond, when I touched her forehead and felt it cold and dry and unyielding that I realised. I had expected more from Hazvinei: fireworks arcing across the sky, the howl of the spirits as they called her home. But there was nothing. She looked as she had when she was a little girl, sleeping reluctantly and wishing the day was twice as long, with her sharp little nails hidden inside clenched fists.

Chapter Twenty-five

There my sister lay, her eyes open and unseeing and a bloody mess where her unborn child should have been. I half-expected her to brush up a hand impatiently, sticking out her lower lip, saying 'Bloody flies,' as she used to do. Hazvinei was not Hazvinei without her smouldering, unhappy energy and her quick, irritated movements.

I knelt beside her. I should have done more. It was my job to take care of her, and I had never managed it. I had failed in my task, and I had failed Baba and Hazvinei. I had killed her.

I told her so, but her expression did not change. I shook my head and the thoughts broke up and scattered. I sat down on the grass. It was dry and pricked my skin, but I welcomed the pain.

The body slowly stopped being Hazvinei and became a corpse instead. It glared at me with open eyes, and I kept thinking that I could see her breathe or her eyelids flicker. In the end I turned my back on her to stop these imaginings. But then I thought I could feel her breath in my ear, or her hand on my shoulder. There was no way to escape, so I closed my eyes and let the ghosts touch me and talk to me.

I dug a hole. I had no spade, no proper equipment: I used thick, sturdy branches and chipped away at the dry ground until my makeshift tool broke, then found another. Hazvinei watched me with blank, dusty eyes. Flies gathered.

I do not know how long it took me to dig the grave. I know that I slept on the pile of fresh-turned earth, before waking and continuing my work. I know that the sun had slid from the sky when I rolled my sister's body into the hole I had created. Her skin felt like old rubber. When she dropped into the grave with a wet, solid sound (I closed my ears to it and tried not to hear it), I covered her with earth. It fell on her skin like rain, soft and damp. I did not look. I do not remember falling asleep, but I do remember waking up with a dry, dead taste in my mouth.

And I knew then what I had to do. I found a hollow reed, stripped it from a bush and cut it at both ends, and slid it into the welcoming earth of Hazvinei's grave.

I waited. I waited, sitting on the little mound I had created, letting the sun burn me, welcoming it as I would welcome a punishment from God. I sat still for so long that I forgot what movement felt like. When the thirst or the urge to urinate became unbearable, I wandered to the stream nearby and refreshed myself in whichever way was needed, then came back to sit in exactly the same spot, in exactly the same position. At night I did not light a fire. I slept stretched out on the grave, my head above my sister's head, my feet above her feet. I heard the hyenas whoop. I heard owls and insects and strange rustlings in the bushes and the snapping of twigs, but I did not move. I knew that nothing would dare come near me, not now. I waited for her.

On the third day, she came. I saw her moving through the low scrub, belly close to the ground as if she were stalking me. Perhaps she was. I crawled off the grave, feeling my stiff knees and elbows creak in protest, and settled a few metres away from her, watching.

She stared at me with flat, uncaring yellow eyes that slanted towards her temples. If I had to choose one colour that reminded me of home, it would be that yellow-brown ochre colour of a lion's hide – of dry grass and dry earth and the sun on leaves and twigs. The colour of my sister's skin.

We looked at each other. She walked to the grave, keeping one eye on me. When she reached the hole, she dipped her big, slow head and sniffed at it. Her whiskers stirred the grains of earth beneath her nose.

If I had any doubts, they were gone now.

The lioness held her nose to the hole in the grave for a few moments. When she lifted her head, I nodded to her. This made her flatten her ears and lift one corner of her black lip in a silent snarl. When I got to my feet, she backed away, then turned and loped into the brush. She was invisible almost instantly, blending into the undergrowth.

'*Mazvita latenda*,' I said. 'Thank you.'

I fell into a fever. The sun became the face of a hyena laughing at me from a swirling sky. I do not know how long I lay there. I do not remember the nights. And I do not know how I survived. After a while I gained enough strength to stand up and start walking.

I walked for days. I started to hear the animals talking to me, and it did not seem strange or unlikely. I could hear the high-pitched chorus of ants in the mud at my feet, the anger of the snake whose slumber I had disturbed. The stars flickered in the sky like bulbs about to go out. Colours were brighter, and more changeable. The sky flashed from blue to green to red to yellow, pulsing with each step. It would take more effort to stop my feet than it would to just keep going. My heart drummed in time with the slap of my feet on the ground. I could not remember my life before this walk. After a while, I could not remember my name.

An orange tamarind moon rose, pockmarked and swollen, from the black water filled with the dust of moths' wings and the distant coughs of hippos. A lion cleared his throat, stirring the thick air with a deep rumble. The moon passed behind a hill of balancing rocks, dropped crazily in an impossible tower.

It glowed behind one round rock, a tiny eclipse, before bulging out above and climbing into the vast skyful of tiny winking eyes.

The balancing rocks creaked and groaned and shifted. The night seemed to be full of spirits. Colours flashed across the sky like strange lightning; eyes blinked at me from the bushes. I heard the roaring of wind in the wings of stray birds. I probed the emptiness where my family should be as you explore the cavity of a missing tooth with your tongue. The pain was distant and happening to someone else. I felt as if I was high on *mbanje*, but I had not smoked it in weeks. I could feel the plants growing, hear the high-pitched buzzing of the stars, taste the metallic taste of moonlight.

At the first village I came to, the people hid from me. I must have looked like a madman. I know I looked like a deserter. The village N'anga was the only person who spoke to me. The rest looked through me as if I were a ghost. I was in such a state that I only half-believed I was alive, and I would not have been at all surprised to find out I was a ghost.

'You bring bad luck here,' said the N'anga, shaking his medicine stick at me. The gourds tied to the top rattled and banged together.

'I want some food,' I said. The witch doctor held no fear for me now. My sister was a lioness. I was protected by her and the ghost of my father. I was untouchable. I was all-powerful.

'What spirit do you carry?' he asked me.

I felt myself swaying on my feet. 'I carry no spirit,' I said.

'That is a lie.' He leaned forward and stared into my eyes. I saw my own reflection in them: someone whose irises were ringed with white and red, who had dried spittle at the corners of his mouth. I did not blame them for being afraid of me.

'I do not carry a spirit.'

'I can see it in you.' The man pushed me. 'Leave this place.'

'I need water.'

'Leave this place.'

'Just a drink. From the pump. One drink.'

I could see that he was about to refuse. I let my eyes roll back in my head, as if I were indeed possessed by a spirit. The man backed away.

'One drink.'

The water from the pump tasted like water-weed and earth. It felt like a blessing on my lips, a cool hand laid on my forehead. I let some splash over my head. It evaporated almost immediately, the sun sucking it up almost before it could wet my skin.

I heard shouts, and running footsteps. 'What's going on?' I grabbed the N'anga's arm.

'The whites,' he said. 'They think we are hiding *vakomana* here.'

'*Vakomana?*' Even here, I was not safe from Abel's dreams.

'Freedom fighters.' He broke away and stared at me. 'Go. You have brought trouble upon us. Go.'

I stumbled away on legs that felt shaky and unreliable. I could see men in khaki with sunburned necks harrying the villagers, and I dragged myself across the red, broom-swept ground and into the bush, and started to run. I fell, not once but several times. I heard shouts from behind me. Of course the villagers had sent them after me. Of course, of course. They did not need this kind of trouble. No matter their feelings about the war, they did not want a mad, half-dead terrorist, a stranger, bringing the white men upon them. I held my side as I ran, willing the pain to go away. My feet, which had carried me for days in my hypnotic state, without complaining, were now sore and blistered. My body had given up.

Something tripped me up and I fell, sprawling forwards and

grazing my outstretched hands. I lay still for a moment, surprised at the sound of my breath. Then I looked at the object which had tripped me. The leg of an elephant.

The elephant was dead – had been dead for days – and was partly eaten. Its chest cavity was hollowed out and stinking, but the ribs would protect me from view, as would the few scraps of leathery skin clinging to them, like grubby sheets on a washing line.

I climbed inside. I tried not to breathe, because the stench was so strong. I don't know what I had expected to find inside the elephant – a beating heart? Intestines waving gaily like torn flags? – but I found nothing. A stink, a mess, and shelter that would keep me hidden, that is all. I said a quick prayer of thanks to the spirit of the elephant, and crouched down inside. I could already hear shouts, but I could not hear dogs. If they had brought dogs I was dead already. If they were just men, then I might have a chance. I hoped that their white-man squeamishness would make it impossible to imagine someone hiding inside the carcass of an animal. After a while, I was not sure what was the elephant's blood and what was mine. I felt hysterical laughter rising in my stomach like bile. Perhaps I would live here for the rest of my life, snacking on rotten elephant meat, sleeping with my head gently pillowed on its organs. The laughter felt like hiccups, and I stifled it.

Morning hardened in the sky. I awoke with a dry mouth and the smell of old blood in my nostrils. I felt nothing. No anger, no fear. I left the elephant and walked to the nearest waterhole, where I drank the dank water, not caring if I felt ill, and I did not wash. My bloodied face, looking back at me from the water, seemed fitting.

I walked again. I did not know where I was going. It was only when I felt the heat of fire on my face and heard voices that I realised I was not alone. There were seven of them: white men in uniforms with their sleeves rolled up and their hats off, sitting around a campfire. I had stumbled right into the middle of their group.

'Oi,' said one of them. 'Who are you, boy?'

'*Voertsek*,' said another, but the one who must have been in charge had stepped forward. 'What are you doing here, hey? You with the terrs?'

Perhaps they too thought I was mad. I saw their hands move to their own guns. They were not going to shoot me, I thought; just hit me with the butts of their rifles, and scare me until they heard who I was and what I was doing there. I did not intend to hurt them, but I saw my fist fly out, thick with elephant's blood, and hit their leader in the face. There was blood, spraying out onto his khakis, and I heard a clean, sharp snap, like someone stepping on a twig, which must have been his nose. I remembered the old game we used to play on the *kopje*: whites against freedom fighters. I heard Abel laugh.

'Kerr-ist,' said the man as he stumbled backwards. The others ran towards me. The sky flashed different colours again, and I had that same sense of being able to hear all the animals and plants speaking to me in their different voices. I saw colours, lots of colours. I heard a drumbeat that did not exist. I felt as if I had drunk the ritual beer and was full of ecstasy, dancing and stomping my feet as we did to bring the rains. The white men were in the dance with me, I thought. I could see them twirling and stomping as well, throwing their heads back. Everything had a red tinge. I saw dark drops of some liquid fall onto the grass. Rain, I thought. We had called up the rain. A drop landed on my tongue, salty and metallic, and I laughed. I felt something hard bang into my back; a knee, pushing me to the ground. I opened my eyes and saw the sky, and a large, white face with a beard hanging in it, bigger than the sun. It is the white God, I thought – I have gone to the wrong place.

I wondered if he would punish me, or whether he would take me to the white heaven. Whether I would be allowed in.

The white god was mouthing something. 'Calm yourself down, Sonny Jim.'

I became aware that I was on the ground, on my back. I raised my head slightly and saw a bloodied mess and stained uniforms. A scalp half torn off. By me? My vision cleared and I saw that the scalp was a clump of grass rooted in red earth; that the white men still stood, panting but unwounded. And I saw a movement in the long grasses.

'Bloody fool,' said the white man.

I scrambled to my feet, and I ran. I heard a roar behind me – not the lazy, authority-asserting roar of a lion, but the harsh, hungry roar of his mate. I heard shouting, and screams. I did not stop. I knew they would follow me, those that still could, but my muscles burned hard and bright and my blood ran hot and no one could catch me. I did not feel the thorns and stones under my feet. I did not look back. When I came to the elephant carcass once more, I climbed inside it with relief, as a child climbs into its bed and sleeps without dreaming.

The lioness guarded me all night. I woke to hear snuffling outside, and low noises from deep in the throat. Sometimes a dark shape that observed me with glinting eyes obscured the pale fingernail of moonlight I could see through the arching ribs. Once, I woke to feel a warm, coarse body next to my own, and smelled bloody, inhuman breath. I curled against the rough, matted hide and felt the wild surge of its pulse; I knotted my fingers in the tangle of its hair. I felt its fur wet beneath my face and thought that the lioness was bleeding, as Hazvinei had bled, but when I tasted the wetness with my tongue I knew that it was the salted damp of tears.

Chapter Twenty-six

I wake, and I am alone. My head is clear for the first time in days. I feel clean and newborn. I look around for the lioness, but I can see nothing but the golden stretch of long grasses and scrub and the pinwheeling shapes of birds in the dusty, pale sky.

I sit in the sticky blood and I look at the rows and rows of pawprints in the red earth, circling the elephant carcass. At first I think that only the lion has been here, but then I see that there are two different sets of prints. One circles the place where I slept; the other, the larger set, hovers a small distance away, approaching and retreating, but never coming too close. I rest my palm against one of the larger of the two prints and feel it warm beneath my skin. *Mbada*. Leopard. I was not the one to fight them, after all.

My back is cold where the lion leaned against me in the night. There is a rich, animal smell about me.

'Hazvinei!'

There is no answer. I suppose I do not expect one. But I am grateful for this bright, empty morning, because it means that, at the very least, I am alive. I am even grateful for its emptiness, because it means that I can fill it with something of my own, now that I have no Baba, Babamukuru, Abel or Hazvinei to fill it for me. I have no one to please or to impress. I have no one to care for.

I am not sure whether Hazvinei was my light side or my dark side – the white shadow or the black shadow, the spirit or the flesh. Without her, though, I am wandering this new world with a courage of which the old Tinashe, the fearful Tinashe, would have been proud.

And one day my white shadow will crawl out of my grave and into the unforgiving light, where it will wander for a year as an animal.

And then I will rejoin her.

Acknowledgements

The White Shadow is set during a fictionalised version of Zimbabwe's Second Chimurenga, but many people had to live through the pain and difficulty of the real thing. Many thanks to the friends and family who shared their stories with me.

Thanks also to all the people who made this book possible: my agent, Vivien Green of Sheil Land Associates – as always! – not only for being an amazing agent in all respects, but also for being my mentor and support system throughout the publishing process.

Liz Folcy, Ellie Steel, Fiona Murphy and the wonderful team at Harvill Secker, including the amazing cover artists: I loved the cover of *The Cry of the Go Away Bird*, and *The White Shadow* is no different. It's the kind of cover that writers dream about having.

Particular thanks go to Chiedza Musengezi, who read the manuscript and added an essential and much-appreciated Shona perspective. I am so grateful. Of course, any errors and omissions are entirely my own.

I also owe a huge debt of thanks to my husband, David, for all his support and encouragement – and for the thousands of cups of coffee he has made me.

Andrea Eames was born in 1985. She was brought up in Zimbabwe, where she attended a Jewish school for six years, a Hindu school for one, a Catholic convent school for two and a half, and then the American International School in Harare for two years. Andrea's family moved to New Zealand in 2002. Andrea has worked as a bookseller and editor and now lives in Austin, Texas with her husband. Her first novel, *The Cry of the Go-Away Bird*, was published in 2011.